"So we meet at last, my lord emperor . . ."

Eldrafel's voice fluted, making Andrion's title a jeer.

Andrion lunged, wanting nothing more than to destroy that smug malevolence. Solifrax flared. For an instant Eldrafel's gilt features blanched in the light of the sword.

But the priest did not move aside. He made one languid gesture. Black fire erupted from his fingertips and seared Andrion's hand. The sword was ripped away; leaving an arc of radiance like a comet's tail, it landed with a puff of ash at Eldrafel's feet. Its light winked out. . . .

PRAISE FOR LILLIAN STEWART CARL'S *THE WINTER KING*

"A compelling story. I read it through the night!"
—R.A. MacAvoy

"A remarkable fine and thoroughly engrossing book!"
—Patricia C. Wrede

"Original, imaginative, and believable!"
—Elizabeth A. Scarborough

Ace books by Lillian Stewart Carl

SABAZEL
THE WINTER KING
SHADOW DANCERS

Shadow Dancers

LILLIAN STEWART CARL

ACE BOOKS, NEW YORK

For Lois McMaster Bujold, my oldest friend

This book is an Ace original edition,
and has never been previously published.

SHADOW DANCERS

An Ace Book / published by arrangement with
the author

PRINTING HISTORY
Ace edition / November 1987

ISBN: 0-441-75988-2

Ace Books are published by The Berkley Publishing Group,
200 Madison Avenue, New York, NY 10016.
The name ''ACE'' and the ''A'' logo
are trademarks belonging to Charter Communications, Inc.

PRINTED IN THE UNITED STATES OF AMERICA

10 9 8 7 6 5 4 3 2 1

Chapter One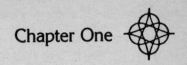

THE SWORD SOLIFRAX flickered in the darkness like the distant lightning of the approaching storm. Andrion gazed narrowly at the blade. It had not shone like this, revealing its latent power, for six peaceful years.

He frowned. He was king of Sardis, Emperor, named Beloved of the Gods, but he had never been able to interpret the omens of the ancient and capricious deities who haunted him. The wind sighed against his face, carrying a tang of something overripe, almost spoiled. Summer waned and a storm gathered in the north. The friends he awaited did not come.

Impatiently Andrion tapped Solifrax across the stone of the parapet, eyeing the spiraling roughness that marred its crystalline blade. He had been only eighteen that night when, enspelled, he had thrown himself against the sword and etched it with the path of his own blood. Now he was twenty-five, and could spare a shake of the head for that distant youth. The desire and the duty that had driven that youth to win sword and Empire made the man who now bore them straighten, set his shoulders, and release a grim smile.

Poets sang that he was born from the mating of sun and moon, melted in the crucible of the gods and poured into the fleshly armor he now wore, an alloy of his father's courage and his mother's integrity. Fine metaphor, he thought, but which of my mothers do they name?

This evening the sun had set early, a blood-red orb consumed by cloud. The night was as dark as a tomb; no stars penetrated the blue-black shroud of the sky, and the waning moon hid its sickly face.

Andrion peered once again from the rooftop garden into the city, dried leaves shifting about his feet. Iksandarun, too, was

1

haunted tonight. The streets were runnels of shadow, the occasional cressets only struggling wraiths of light. Most of them had not been lit. Gods, an emperor should not have to deal with details as petty as the proper lighting of the streets!

Somewhere a brief strain of music sounded, an eerie melody of flute and pipes; then a door slammed, blotting it out. The hoofbeats of unshod steppe ponies pattered along the cobbled avenue. We fought the Khazyari, Andrion told himself with a sigh, when they invaded the Empire; debatable, who was victor and who vanquished, when their prince now rides freely through the streets of Iksandarun. But then, I bought his allegiance with honor and with blood.

There he was. Two dim horse-and-man shapes walked along the avenue toward the palace gates, at one moment garishly defined in torchlight, at the next blots of nothingness in shadow. And behind them . . . Andrion squinted. Indistinct shapes, clotted darkness, crept from alleys to gather like silent storm clouds behind the riders. The streets had been darkened on purpose.

"Harus!" Andrion swore. The name of the god stirred the wind uneasily. He thrust the sword hissing into its snakeskin sheath and sprinted across the garden. In the darkness that pulsed around him he knew what happened to his friends in the street as surely as if he were with them.

Tembujin, Khan of the Crimson Horde, ruler of the imperial province of Khazyaristan, glanced warily from side to side. His tip-tilted eyes glinted like black onyx; the tail of sable hair bound at the back of his head shifted with suspicion.

Thunder rumbled like distant battle, and the wind purred as if mocking the khan and the plaque of the lion he wore on his chest. The young boy he held before him piped, "Father?"

Tembujin soothed him with a touch. "Never mind, Ethan. We are almost there." The great gate of the palace loomed out of the shadows, torches shedding a thick brass light that barely touched the dimness of the avenue. The sentries dozed leaning upon their spears, as motionless as statues.

Andrion sped past the guards who waited in the garden door, calling to them to follow. His oddly supernal vision shivered his mind into facets of dread, anger, calculation—an attack on the khan must be a warning for me—of whom, of what—hurry, hurry!

The huge warrior who rode behind the khan and his son heard the scrabble in an alleyway, the sudden yowl of a cat.

Tembujin set his hand on his long dagger, shrugged his bow farther up his shoulder, clasped the child and urged the pony to leap ahead through the murk into light.

A rush from the darkness. Hands seizing the bridle of the pony. It reared, whinnying in terror as hands dragged Tembujin and Ethan from its back. The khan shouted. His dagger flashed and someone cried out.

The bodyguard attacked. Bodies flew and lay crumpled on the street, but others swarmed forward. Knives flared and fell. The warrior went down beneath them.

In the moment's distraction Tembujin thrust the child behind him, against a wall in the thin light of a sputtering cresset. The boy found himself clutching his father's dagger. Eyes wide, small mouth set, he brandished it before him. In one supple motion Tembujin slipped the bow from his shoulder and set an arrow to it. The assassins shifted uneasily, feinting this way and that. The body of the guard did not stir.

"Cowards," said the khan's lightly accented voice. "Cowards, to sneak in the darkness like rats. Come into the light, I dare you."

The assassins surged around their prey. The string sang, and the foremost went down. The bow was strung again without Tembujin's hand seeming to move.

The wind carried the sounds of battle to the palace. The guards started. One ran inside. One ran forward, counted his opponents, hesitated. Andrion swept by them, playing his clear voice like a herald's trumpet, "Come! Follow me!" The guards steadied in his wake. Others rushed from inside the gates. The avenue filled with a metallic cascade.

A bolt of lightning split the night, cast not from the sky but from the street itself; Solifrax drawn in battle. Tembujin's eyes fired with recognition and relief.

With a cry of outrage Andrion fell upon the assassins. His black cloak snapped behind him like the wings of an avenging god. Solifrax blazed, setting the shadows to dancing. Its threat alone scattered the dark forms in panicked flight.

"Follow them," Andrion snapped. His guards split, some running after the assassins, some forming a cordon around the Emperor and the khan. "Scum! How dare they attack you, Tembujin, here under my very eyes?" The gold diadem on his brow sparked, and his dark hair gleamed with auburn highlights, embers stirred.

The khan still stood poised, bow bent. "This is the third

attack within five days, Andrion. I thought I would be safe here, but your eyes do not see overmuch, do they?"

"You were once an enemy," Andrion replied. "Some have not forgotten."

"Have you forgotten?" The quiet voice was a whiplash of challenge.

Andrion's nostrils flared. "Yes."

Tembujin straightened, letting the bow fall, and bent over his guard. "Rats," he breathed, "to kill him here like this."

"He saved your life and Ethan's. A good man; I am sorry. . . ." Condolences were meaningless to a Khazyari schooled in revenge. Mouth tight, Andrion extended his hand to the child. The boy crept from the wall, trying to saunter bravely, but his cheeks were pale beneath the bronze of his skin. The dagger fell from his hands and clattered upon the cobblestones. Andrion clasped him against his side. "You did well, Ethan."

Ethan, uncertain, said nothing. The glow of the sword was reflected in his dark eyes; he blinked, dazzled. Andrion caressed the child's smooth hair, thinking, Yes, the sword is tantalizing. How well I know.

Tembujin stood with a muffled curse, reclaimed his dagger, saw his son in Andrion's arm and pulled him away.

"He is my sister's child," Andrion said softly. "No matter what you did to her, I would not harm him."

Tembujin opened his mouth. He realized that soldiers clustered around him, their ears gaping even as their faces feigned indifference. He shut his mouth and tossed his head. The black fringe of hair framing his forehead and temples rippled like a banner in the wind. The wind was suddenly cold, but no less rotten.

Several guards returned, dragging two bodies and one wounded man. Andrion inspected their faces but did not know them. They were no doubt simple ruffians hired to do the dirty work by someone too powerful to do it himself. Someone who must be powerful indeed to throw down such a challenge. . . . Andrion's stomach tightened, a soft creature contracting so that only its hard shell is exposed, its mortal belly protected.

The prisoner would have crumpled to the pavement if soldiers had not held him erect. Blood from an arrow in his side was only a dark stain on his garments. Andrion grasped the man's hair, jerking his face up.

"Kill him," said Tembujin.

"Then we shall discover nothing," Andrion returned. He set the blade at the man's throat and asked with perilous calm, "Who paid you to do this treachery?"

The pale light of the sword scoured the man's features of color and definition. His widely dilated eyes were bottomless pits in a face tightened to the bone. "Who?" Andrion commanded.

The man quaked. A sour, sickly odor clung to him, sweat and dirt and something else, something subtly familiar. Solifrax muttered threats against his flesh. His tongue stammered nonsense.

His eyes were as vacant as a dead man's. Nightshade, Andrion realized, and perhaps hashish. The man was drugged, and more. . . . "By the talons of the god!" Andrion spat under his breath, recoiling. The back of his neck tightened, the soft creature inside him cramped cruelly.

"Sorcery," hissed Tembujin, holding the child away. "I have not sensed sorcery since the witch my father's wife died almost seven years ago."

Sorcery, yes; the memory of that odor was seared on Andrion's mind. Who now dared to use such arts, and to what end? He straightened to his full height, half a head taller than any man near him. His rich brown eyes were depth upon depth of light and substance; his face was stern, frost rimming fire. Solifrax hummed in his hand, but he saw only the empty streets, and his own soldiers gazing raptly at him, and shadows discouraged by the light of the sword.

In a few terse words he gave his orders. He spun about. Tembujin and Ethan hurried not behind, but beside him. They strode through the pool of light at the gate and gained the palace.

The corridors streamed like fragments of a fever dream. Lamps were sudden pinwheels against shadows writhing in the corners of Andrion's eyes. If men are shadows dancing at the whim of the gods, he asked himself, and the gods are shadows given substance by man's naming of them, then who truly rules this world?

Is the plot only against Tembujin? Or, as is much more likely, is it a plot against me? And its goal? Not difficult; the lust for power corrupts, and breeds treachery, and the allegiance of the Empire has always gone to the strongest.

Andrion returned the salute of a sentry and thrust Solifrax away. Thunder quivered in the ancient stones of the palace.

Lightning flared, and a dim garden leaped into sudden color, asters as red as blood nodding in a gusty wind. Andrion's black cloak fluttered, encompassing Tembujin. Tembujin thrust it away.

Another sentry, another salute, and the broad wooden doors of the first wife's antechamber slammed. The wide, well-lit room was scattered with tables, chairs, and bright faces turning toward the doorway, expectant and wary both.

Two women sat on either side of a tapestry frame, needles frozen in midair, bits of bright yarn dangling. Tembujin's wife Valeria gulped at her husband's expression, cornflower-blue eyes frightened. "Another attack," she stated under her breath.

"Ursbei is dead," Tembujin returned, flat.

Instinctively Valeria gathered her children, three high-planed bronze faces; Ethan ran across the room and threw himself into her lap, sending a ripple through his siblings. The mound of Valeria's belly concealed Tembujin's fifth child.

Andrion's wife Sumitra looked up. Her fine black brows rose in silent query, but did not try to breach his shell. She set her needle aside and clasped her hands in her lap, waiting with patient dignity. Always waiting.

"Damn you, Tembujin," Andrion said. He released the falcon-winged brooch he wore and threw his cloak down, standing braced in chiton and belt and sword.

Tembujin, sworn at often enough, leaned against a table, crossed his trousered legs, crossed his arms before him and scowled. "Yes, certainly I staged an attack on myself!"

"By Ashtar's golden tresses, man, I believe nothing of the sort! What I do believe is that there are those who think your influence too great. Who resent your having sons . . ." He cast a quick glance toward Sumitra. Her lips thinned, but she did not flinch.

Go ahead, say it. "I offered in the council six days ago to make Ethan my heir; he is my half-sister Sarasvati's son and the grandson of Bellasteros my father, who freed the Empire from the corrupt dynasty that had ruled it. But Ethan is illegitimate, they said. He looks like a Khazyari, they said. He lives with you, they said."

"And I have contaminated him with my barbarian ways?"

Andrion made a sharp, swift gesture, a sword thrust of denial, and looked away from the accusing face.

On the tapestry before him was stitched the face of his

father Marcos Bellasteros, the Sardian conqueror, and the face of his mother Danica, Queen of Sabazel, engaged in some heroic quest. And yet his official mother was Chryse, the gentle sparrow who had been Bellasteros's first wife, who had raised his children by other women after her own daughter Chrysais had married far away.

A proper tangle for the genealogists, he thought. As was Tembujin's family, for Valeria nurtured her husband's two sons by other women as well as her own: Ethan, Sarasvati's son; and Zefric, the son of Dana of man-forbidden Sabazel.

Dana. The name was a razor slicing Andrion's senses. *From birth I have been beguiled by the daughters of Ashtar; my only child is Dana's, a girl, the heir of Sabazel, not the Empire. My wife sits, her hands clasped in her lap, holding nothing. A petty issue. A vital one.*

Who to blame? Tembujin? Sumitra? The gods? Or myself? he asked. And answered, no; anger and hatred are strong liquors that in the end rot what they touch. He inhaled deeply, damping his frustration. And yet his sinews still prickled with the sour odor of sorcery.

Tembujin shook back his tail of hair. "Can you not control your rabble and protect your sworn ally? What must I do to prove fealty?"

Dryly, Andrion replied, "Call me, 'My lord'?"

Tembujin's eye glinted, not without humor.

"Do you mistrust me so easily?" Andrion retorted. "We passed too many tests of loyalty in the war to doubt each other now."

Tembujin looked down at his felt boots, discomfited.

"Did I not defend you," Andrion continued remorselessly, "when some said your half brother died from poison?"

"Kem, my only legal son, would be my heir in any event."

Yes, Andrion thought, we make our children our pawns. Valeria laid her cheek against Kem's head and looked ruefully up at him. Jeweled necklaces clanked on her bodice as the visible signs of Tembujin's power. No, Andrion could not blame her either. He raised Sumitra's hand and kissed its satin warmth, drawing her eyes to his. They were dark, ebony dusted with cinnamon and gold. They were deep, summoning. . . .

A knock at the door. Andrion straightened, stifling another oath. Tembujin lounged against the table, sending petitions and maps scuffling backward, and with elaborate indifference began to toy with a malachite paperweight.

A sentry announced, "The high priest of Harus, my lord."

Well, Andrion thought with a sigh, one cannot know a god by his minions. Fortunately so, for some call me a god. He set his face in affable lines, and when the fat little man bustled in sweeping an acolyte in his train, he nodded with all the courtesy due a priest of the falcon deity.

Bonifacio settled his robes, bowed deeply, bent over backward to look Andrion in the face. "I heard of the attack, my lord, and came as quickly as I could. Surely these evildoers have not injured our beloved emperor?"

"I am not the one who was attacked."

"No, no, of course, my lord, it was your vassal, who lives by your generosity upon our northern moors—"

The paperweight fell with a crash and shattered, sending green splinters skittering across the floor. Bonifacio jumped. Tembujin glanced down, blandly surprised. Andrion cleared his throat. The acolyte stood stiff and silent.

"Surely, my lord, this year you should go to Farsahn, the winter capital," burbled Bonifacio. "Or perhaps, my lord, to Sardis itself. Surely our beloved emperor would be safer in the north, away from imperial plotting."

Tembujin's refusal to use his title was really quite refreshing. "You know of a plot?" Andrion asked.

The priest's plump cheeks reddened with agitation. "No, no, my lord, but it is only to be expected of these devious imperials; it was an imperial chamberlain who betrayed your father, glorious Bellasteros, may he rest in peace, and we can only assume—"

Andrion said briskly, "We can assume nothing. The Empire and Sardis were joined on the day of my birth, and few resented it. Perhaps the assassin was some disaffected follower of the khan's, and the attack had nothing to do with me."

Bonifacio's earnest gaze fell upon Tembujin. "If the khan would allow me to teach him the catechism of Harus of Sardis, I am sure the god would protect him."

"I bow to Harus," said Tembujin, "and to Ashtar, the gods who guard the emperor."

"But, but . . ." Bonifacio squirmed. "Ashtar is a woman's god, named by Bellasteros only out of courtesy to his vassal Danica."

Andrion's jaw tightened. Vassal indeed; Harus rested on Ashtar's arm, consort of the sacred mother. But very few Sardians had ever crossed the borders of Sabazel.

His glance fell upon the acolyte. An odd face, with the pointed chin and large liquid eyes of a fox. The man, sensing the emperor's gaze upon him, stepped back into shadow.

Bonifacio gargled faintly and bounced up and down, trying to earn a response from the emperor. Andrion condescended to look down at him again, and cursed himself for his condescension. Unworthy of a king, to treat a man as a fool even when he was.

"Journey," insisted Bonifacio. "I shall begin to make the arrangements, my lord, if you would permit such a humble servant—"

"Yes," said Andrion. "Begin our move north."

"And if the emperor's respected lady"—Bonifacio turned with a low fluttering bow to Sumitra—"may her virtue be rewarded, would be too wearied by such a journey, she would be well cared for here."

Pompous ass, Andrion thought. He spun about, found himself facing the table, unrolled a map. His hand crimped the papyrus. Only yesterday Bonifacio had urged him to abjure Sumitra as a barren wife. As soon as I am alone, Andrion thought, you will parade every pretty girl in Farsahn and Sardis before me, noblemen's daughters offered like cattle at market. I will notice them, yes, how could I not be stirred by sparkling eyes and round breasts and smooth flanks? But if I have learned nothing else from the implacable beauty of Dana, of Ashtar herself, I have learned the demands and limits of love, and the compromises of the flesh.

Andrion glanced in silent apology at Sumitra. She was unruffled, a serene surface over unplumbed depths of sorrow. Of guilt. By all the gods, Andrion thought, I shall not let Bonifacio or anyone make her feel guilty. The map rolled up with a snap.

With a few tentative drops rain began to fall outside. A damp breeze stirred the draperies with a cool clean scent, and the odor of rot faded. Good. Bonifacio would have to walk back to the temple compound in the rain. Perhaps that would cool his rhetoric. "I shall send for you tomorrow," Andrion told the priest, "and we shall discuss the matter then."

"Yes, my lord." The priest bobbed up and down like a

feeding duck. "Indeed, my lord, as I was telling Rowan here—"

Andrion gently but firmly ushered Bonifacio and Rowan out, shut the door behind them and stood with his back against the panels.

Tembujin grimaced as if he had a bad taste in his mouth. Valeria rolled her eyes. Sumitra exhaled between pursed lips. The older children, released from good manners, swirled out of their mother's arms and scattered across the marble floor playing some spontaneous game with the shards of malachite. The youngest, a girl, toddled into her father's arms, and when he lifted her, tangled her tiny hands in his long hair.

"Could he be plotting against you?" asked the khan, patiently suffering the child's attentions. "Against us?"

"You saw his subtlety toward Sumitra," Andrion replied. "The man could not plot his way out of a market basket. No, I fear . . ."

For the first time Sumitra spoke. "What do you fear, my lord?"

In her quiet, resonant voice the honorific was a caress. Andrion's face softened in response. "It was not carelessness, my lady, that staged the attack on my doorstep. An attempt to sever me from my ally, perhaps; a signal to me, probably; a challenge, certainly. I think that, strange as it seems, Bonifacio is right. We must journey north for the winter."

"Run away?" asked Tembujin caustically.

"Of course not." The diadem sparked. "To see if the attacks follow us."

"Ah, I see. These last few days may be only the tip of the spear."

Sumitra turned to Valeria. "Would you care to come with us, instead of wintering in Khazyaristan this year?"

How could anyone refuse a request made with those lush lips? Valeria, with a sideways glance at her husband, said, "I am a child of Sardis, not of the steppes, and I would prefer to bear this babe in my father Patros's house."

"I daresay my nuryans can watch the flocks," Tembujin said with a shrug of assent. His eye gleamed briefly in a private, somewhat reluctant, but perfectly honest message.

So then, Andrion thought, needing to say nothing, you will not apologize for your doubts, but you will reaffirm your allegiance. Good. I would rather have allegiance than apology. When the khan and his family took their leave and went to their own quarters in the palace, his hand remained warm from Tembujin's strong clasp.

He shut the door and turned to his wife with a grimace; one of the hazards of ruling was a lack of privacy. Sumitra's face was hidden as she picked up her sharp, shining needle and turned it in her hand like a warrior considering his—or her—blade.

Again Andrion's thought shivered; he saw other female hands, light, strong bones and taut flesh, raising sword and shield and bow. Danica his mother. Ilanit her daughter. Dana Ilanit's daughter, his own . . . He bent and picked up a shard of the malachite paperweight. Dana's eyes were as green, and often as brittle.

The damp wind had something in it of asphodel, the lily of love and death, and the anemone, the wind flower. Suddenly, with a yearning so strong it dizzied him, Andrion wanted Sabazel. Sardis was forty day's journey to the north and east; a detour of only a few more days would bring him to Sabazel's embrace in time for the autumn equinox and the fall rites. The water in Ashtar's bronze basin, the shining star-shield on his half-sister Ilanit's arm—surely they held omens for him. He was the only living son of Sabazel, and yet he had not made offering for two mortal years. No wonder the gods tested him again, this time with uncertainty.

Sumitra's needle stabbed the fabric. Andrion started, collected himself, and went to her side. Her long, graceful fingers were wrapped with gold thread. Beneath them an image of Solifrax gleamed in Bellasteros's hand and an image of the shield stone in Danica's. The real sword hummed faintly against Andrion's thigh. The sword of power, given by the gods to he who deserved it, the heroes Daimion, Bellasteros, Andrion.

He touched his necklace, a gold crescent moon with a gold star at its tip, the symbol of sword and shield united in more than temporal power. Who am I, Andrion said to himself, to fear shadows?

Sumitra said, "Surely your councilors would not dare to plot against you. Against Tembujin perhaps, against me, certainly . . ."

Andrion set his fingertip on her lips, stopping her. Always she accepted the indignities of living. He never had to explain, never had to justify, never had to apologize for court-

ing her love after marriage, not before. For coming to her
virgin bed when his body, his heart, his soul had already been
taken—but never kept—by another.

"Is it sorcery you sense?" she said against his flesh.

"Yes."

She laid down the thread, stood, touched his necklace. Her
eyes stirred with decision, doubt surpassed by hope. "Go to
Sabazel, Andrion. Pray to the goddess who protects us for
guidance. And for children."

"Sumi," he sighed, almost shamed by the generosity of
her perception. "Sumi, my lady wife."

Her head, with its sleek sable hair smoothed back in two
wings, came only to his shoulder. Her skin was shining
mahogany, gilded by the lamplight. The tiny ruby in the side
of her nose glinted. Andrion's nostrils filled with the elusive
scent of jasmine. It charred the senses as surely as asphodel
and anemone.

In her eyes was the serenity of deep water, only the surface
rippled by wind. He saw himself there as she saw him: a lean
and well-proportioned body, stiffly guarding against any hint
of weakness; a square jaw, clean-shaven, revealing a tenacity
that might in the less tolerant be called stubbornness; an
incised mouth which would be tender if it were not tight with
the necessity of command. A mouth that had never known
caprice.

Sumitra smiled, accepting him, it seemed, as much for his
contradictions as in spite of them. "Rest, my lord; let me
play for you."

Andrion let her go, but his hands seemed empty without
her between them. "Rest?"

She picked up her zamtak and sat, testing the seventeen
strings with one sweep of her fingertips. The answering trill
repeated the murmuring swish of the rain.

"Rest?" He shook his head. The table was loaded with
papers, stacked by his scribes in tidy piles which only emphasized their quantity. Plans to rebuild lands that had lain
devastated for centuries under the tyranny of the old Empire.
Plans for the nomadic Khazyari to begin a semipermanent
settlement. Petitions, accounts, orders. Letters from councilors and village heads, from Proconsul Nikander in Farsahn
and Governor-General Patros in Sardis; at those names he
smiled.

Then he saw the reports of bandits infesting the wilderness

along the Royal Road to the north, of pirates harassing the sea lanes from Sardis's port of Pirestia out to Rhodope and even to distant Minras. His smile curdled into a frown.

And there was a letter from Minras itself, from his sister Chrysais, announcing the death of her husband King Gath. The news had taken almost three months to arrive. Anything could have happened in three months. He set the letter aside with a sigh. How could he respond, except with banal courtesies; he could not remember ever having met Chrysais, the child of his father's youth. If Sabazel was at the rim of this world, Minras was surely another world entirely.

The music stirred the shadows. Each note was a drop of water, rain upon parched Iksandarun after a summer's drought; rain falling upon Cylandra, Sabazel's guardian mountain, streaming into the bronze basin on its flank.

Andrion drifted upon the music into Sumitra's glistening eyes. She was too proud to offer what might be refused; she was too honest to conceal her consuming need. Her hand stilled the strings, but the music of the rain continued.

Andrion removed the diadem, unbuckled Solifrax, laid the weight of both among the papers. If neither could quell the dread slithering through his mind, he could at least defer dread and power alike until the morrow.

He took his wife's hand, kissed her lips as soft and sweet and moist as apricots, and led her toward the bedchamber. The rainsong smoothed but did not quite mend the frayed edges of his soul.

Chapter Two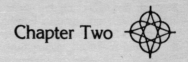

THE WATER IN the great bronze basin rippled with a luminescence like distant lightning, seething the darkness of the mountain hollow. Dana knelt at the basin's rim and pondered the message within. Her fine, precise features were burnished by the light, filled by it; she was a jeweled icon, not fully mortal.

The wind, bearing a faint odor of rotten fruit, stirred her long blond hair. The Sight stirred her mind, and her thoughts wavered with bright images and dark.

She saw blinding sunlight and a sky washed of color. She saw the sea, the deep blue of Ashtar's eyes, slapping upon a steep rocky shore. She saw a smoking mountain, an arena ringed with dark and watchful faces, a sprawling palace. Her throat clogged with acrid dust.

A bull bellowed in her ear, and a voice—Andrion's voice—shouted in rage and terror. She flinched.

Solifrax, brighter than the sun, suddenly extinguished, and the star-shield . . . what? Sumitra, Andrion's wife, lay across the shield as if broken upon it. A fiery chariot bore down upon her, upon Andrion, upon Dana herself. . . . The image was gone. The light in the basin flickered and went out. The wind streamed from the peak of ice-crowned Cylandra.

For a moment Dana sat, blinking stupidly at the night, trying to fill her sudden emptiness with the senses of her own being. We are but shadows dancing for the gods, she told herself, and the gods are the shadows of our own hearts. So where, then, is certainty?

The skein of her Sight was too tangled to interpret. She knew only that some evil befell god-touched Andrion, King of Sardis, Emperor, the only living acknowledged son of

Sabazel. But then, sons were of little account here. She must believe that; Andrion was a wound never quite healed.

Some evil befell Sabazel. With ice in her soul Dana stood, her shoulders coiled, aching with tension. The night was uncannily dark, the sky hidden under a pall of cloud, no moon, no stars for guidance. The soft night sounds of the city were muffled as if by a great hand. The wind—the wind grew in strength, moaning, rushing through the city. Dana's hair whipped around her face and she clawed through it. What was wrong?

She ran down the steps, through her mother Ilanit's garden, through the city to the temple. A city of the dead, it seemed, the frightened faces of its inhabitants only powerless wraiths.

Not powerless, never powerless, Dana insisted to herself.

The pool in the atrium of Ashtar's temple swirled slowly. A mist rose above it, forming indecipherable images. The wind purled through the opening in the roof, and doves cooed uneasily. The wind was tainted. Not for the first time that night the hair on Dana's nape prickled.

Andrion's sister Sarasvati ran from a side room, gasping, "Sorcery! I have not sensed sorcery since the Khazyari witch died!" Her basket of healing herbs and bandages fell unheeded from her hands.

The wind grew stronger. The doves broke into squawking, panicked flight and were tumbled away. The mosaic at the bottom of the pool shifted and jumbled itself into meaningless patterns. Or perhaps Dana simply could not read its message.

Scowling with frustration, she followed Sarasvati from the temple into the street. There they collided with the thin, angular form of the queen's weapons master. Lyris's teeth were set in a snarl of anger and terror mixed. "Evil," she cried, flourishing her javelin. "Evil, such as I have not felt since I was a girl!" She sprang forward, shouting, "Sabazel!"

A howling gale screamed down the slopes of the mountain, ringing from some profound depth of ice and sky. The stone blocks of the city shivered. Flowering vines were shredded and their pitiful mangled petals whirled across the lidded sky.

Lyris, Dana, and Sarasvati stumbled down the street, fighting through knots of women clutching their daughters. The darkness thickened, a black mist blotting the city.

There. The Horn Gate loomed before them. The sentries clung desperately to their posts atop the walls. The wind shrilled. One guard wailed and fell and was dashed against the ground. With a tremendous clangor the gate flew open.

A woman-sized shadow, black against blackness, sprinted down the avenue as if borne on the wings of the wind itself. It carried upon its back a large, shrouded disk. Lyris leaped forward, singing the victory paean; her voice cracked in the force of the gale, but still she sang.

Dana, too, lunged toward the shadow creature. Some cold force, fear made tangible, emanated from it; stunned, she fell sprawling into the street. A whirlwind of fine ash overtook her, blinding her, choking her. She coughed rackingly but could not clear her throat.

Lyris barred the creature's path, her javelin flaring with a faint, watery light. Black fire shot from the shadow's hand and encompassed the weapons master, masticated her, spit her out and left her gasping upon the scarred cobbles. The javelin clattered down and was still.

The dark figure sped through the gates and disappeared into the depths of the night. Slowly, wearily, the gates drew themselves shut. The surviving sentry slid down the rock and crouched trembling against a stone pier. Dana managed a deep breath, steadying her wits and strength, and staggered up. Sarasvati crawled to Lyris's side and lifted her head into her lap.

The sky roiled. The light of a waning gibbous moon and a sparse handful of stars winked through shredding cloud and then hid again, as if fearful of what they might illuminate. In the fitful light Lyris's face was stark white, a blade honed clean of any stain. Her flesh was cold and hard as ice. "Give me my weapon," she wheezed. "I would defend . . . Sabazel. . . ."

Ilanit, Queen of Sabazel, appeared from the murk. She knelt next to Lyris, her face as tight and sere as a bloom nipped by frost. She lifted the javelin, set it in Lyris's hand, closed her fingers about its shaft. "You are Sabazel's greatest defender," she said hoarsely.

Lyris was dead. The moon fought free of cloud, pouring its radiance upon her. Her blank, staring eyes filled with light. They seemed to see beyond the city, beyond the small, mountain-girt country beset by shadow, to a greater reality and a greater peace.

Dana closed Lyris's eyes, preserving that moment's vision.

The moon was eaten by driving cloud. The wind died, abandoning the sky.

"In the name of the goddess!" choked Sarasvati. "What has happened?"

Do not answer, Dana silently begged Ilanit. Please, do not answer.

Her mother clambered as slowly to her feet as if she wore a full suit of armor. She stood, hands dangling empty at her sides. Her hair hung pale and lank about her face, and Dana could not see her eyes. But she could hear the quavering words, "The star-shield is gone."

Shards of ice turned in Dana's heart, and she heard her own voice cry out in desperate denial.

The tireless hooves of the great war stallion Ventalidar bore Andrion across the borders of Sabazel. He outdistanced his escort, straining toward the distant lavender peak that was Cylandra. It firmed and darkened. Tumbled rock at its base became the buildings of a small city.

Ashtar's womb, Andrion told himself. Sanctuary and rest and guidance in the arms of the mother. But my mortal mother is no longer there.

He had accepted that. That was not what was wrong. The sky was hazy, indistinct, the sun only a glowing blotch emitting the thinnest of light. The wine-bright air of autumn was vinegar. A chill wind jangled through the black plume in Andrion's helmet and plucked at his black cloak like a palsied hand. Solifrax rested mutely at his side.

Flocks bleated in fields of dry stubble, and their small shepherdesses glanced at the passing horseman with incurious, oddly aged eyes. Here, too, was drought. The music of Sumitra's zamtak did not echo here. Her moist lips had bid Andrion farewell, giving him for the greater good into the arms of another. But the other, it seemed, had troubles of her own.

Andrion halted Ventalidar before the Horn Gate and dismounted. The horse pawed at the ground, snuffling, as uneasy as Andrion himself. The gates groaned open and Dana emerged, a pale, drawn Dana, with lines like check reins engraved in her face. The stiffness with which she braced herself, arms akimbo, and forced a smile, froze Andrion's viscera. If her heart leaped at the ending of their two years' separation, he could see it only in the tic at the corner of her mouth, revealing . . . No, her face was pinched too tightly to reveal anything. He ached to embrace her, but until she accepted his embrace he might just as well strike her down.

"What is it?" Andrion demanded. "What has gone amiss?"

"If you had not come, I would have summoned you," was her only reply, and she turned to greet his escort. Her quick eye—thank the goddess that at least had not faded—sought one particular face among the mounted men. Not finding it, she said, "You would not keep Tembujin away if he had chosen to come."

"Could not," Andrion amended. "He is escorting our wives to Sardis." Was she resigned to the Khazyari's absence, or relieved at not having to succor him too? He looked down at his greaves. They were dull, having lost their bright polish on the long and dusty journey here.

"Does he no longer crave Ashtar's embrace?"

"He chooses another craving, that for family and rank. But I . . ."

Her glistening green eyes avoided his questioning look, as though he were some strange male animal to whom revealing anything would be revealing too much. "Come," she said. "Ilanit and Sarasvati are waiting for you."

Andrion's mouth was dry. He tried to swallow, but his throat was packed with dust.

The other men gathering for the rites were taken in hand by Sabazian warriors and conducted to the temple square. Andrion and Dana trudged up the narrow streets, past branches of browned lilac and chickens crouching dispiritedly in the dust. When she asked in sterile courtesy about Iksandarun, he answered frankly; at such news the corner of her mouth twitched even faster, but her expression, as bleak as a city razed by war, did not change.

In the queen's garden—once Danica's, now Ilanit's—the limbs of the sycamore trees were prematurely bare and wizened. Anemones and marigolds were only crumbling stalks. It was not the clean nakedness of winter, awaiting the joyous robing of spring; a malaise hung over Sabazel, out of season, out of time itself, as if the tiny country were only a faint image in a scratched and stained mirror.

Andrion followed Dana into the queen's house. He removed his helmet, tucking it under his arm; the diadem on his hair seemed suddenly garish. Perhaps it was discourteous to wear the symbol of a great realm into such a small one. But the diadem had been here before and had long ceased to be a threat. From faded frescoes on the walls faces turned to Andrion, Daimion and Mari remote and impassive, Bellasteros and Danica relentlessly expectant. The unmistakable reek of sorcery hung heavy in the small room.

Gods, Andrion prayed, Harus, Ashtar, whoever you are, do not drive me backward into nightmare. Bellasteros had once lain here enspelled, and now it was Ilanit who turned a thin and wasted face to her half brother. But she was the child of Danica's youth, barely past forty—unfair, he wanted to cry, unfair! He said nothing.

The queen tried to rise from her chair. The effort drained her already pale face and left it a damp green. Sarasvati eased her back down. The hazy afternoon daylight was too weak to penetrate here; an oil lamp guttered in the draft from the open door and cast writhing shadows across the wooden stand that had once held the star-shield. . . .

Andrion's head spun, or else the world spun dizzyingly about him. The shield that had always chimed to his touch, that had glowed beside the sword whether the sword was in his hand or his father's, that had shed its light over his birth—the shield was gone.

His flesh shriveled in chill horror. "What happened?" he asked. His own voice grated his ears.

"It was stolen almost a month ago," answered Ilanit with a bone-deep weariness. "We opened our gates to a woman from Farsahn . . ."

"Or so she said," interjected Dana darkly. "She had a strange accent."

". . . who escaped a forced marriage. She wore an armband embossed with a winged bull; I sensed power in it, but fool that I am, did not dream that power would be turned against us."

"There was a storm," said Sarasvati. "A dark shape ran away with the shield. Later, after counting we realized it had been Rue."

"Rue," repeated Andrion dully.

"She killed Lyris," Dana said.

Sarasvati added, "With a blast of black fire. Sorcery indeed."

Lyris, who had always dared Andrion to prove himself. No, she had not been waiting at the gate, rattling her javelin at the arriving men. Ilanit leaned back and closed her eyes; Lyris had been her pair. Hastily Andrion sought something comforting to say. But there could be no comfort. "She will be missed," he mumbled lamely.

"We searched the countryside," Dana went on, her clear voice shooting each word like an arrow. "We could not find Rue or the shield. We sent messages to Nikander in Farsahn, but no one there had ever heard of her."

"And yet she knew Sardis and the Empire," said Sarasvati. "She once remarked on Ilanit's queenly aspect, that it reminded her of Chryse."

"Chryse?" Andrion replied. "An odd remark indeed. Chryse was as warm as a summer's day, sweet and gentle. But not queenly."

"And she died in Iksandarun seven years ago." Sarasvati sank her teeth deep into her lower lip, remembering the day of the Khazyari victory all too well.

"I would have pursued her myself," hissed Dana, "to Sardis and beyond, but I was needed here, and my Sight bade me wait for you."

Ashtar's humor remained unchanged, it seemed, taking perverse pleasure in requiring her daughters once again to wait upon a man. Andrion set his hand on the hilt of Solifrax and averted his eyes from the women's accusing gazes; the sword's answering tingle was not unlike the chime of the shield its consort. He tightened his teeth so that his jaw ached, his thought groping with vicious thrusts through the miasma that hung about him as much as about the land of Sabazel. Sorcery here, and in Iksandarun as well. His call to Sabazel was only part of a larger pattern. And his role? To show his mettle, at the least.

He bent over Ilanit's blond head—by all the gods, her hair was less gold than silver now—and kissed her clammy brow. She tried to smile, and managed a quirk of her crusted lips. He touched the necklace at his throat. "You and I were born in the light of the shield, Ilanit. Surely it is not shameful to ask me to help."

"Even though you alone were born in the light of the sword, we would ask no other." She did not avoid his searching look but met his eyes; she refused to despair, he saw, even as she could not quite hope. Andrion would have wept at seeing her backed into such a corner, but his eyes were as achingly dry as his mouth.

Muttering some courtesy, he turned and stalked from the room, from the uncompromising faces of the three women, and strode through the garden so fast that the hem of his cloak snapped like a whip. He paused at the steps that led to the basin and on up the mountainside to the holy of holies, the sacred cavern. He did not set foot on the stair. The mountain seemed suddenly menacing, as if the drought had dried its foundations and the great granite boulders were ready to tumble down, crushing man and woman and pestilence alike. No, there would be no omen, no water in the basin, no murmuring stream in the cavern he had once dared. In that distant world he had known his enemy. Now he did not.

"Andrion."

He started. Sarasvati stood beside him. His face cracked suddenly into a smile and he embraced her. Her hair, bright with the sheen of copper, tickled his chin; her eyes were deep lapis lazuli, the color of late evening. The color this evening should have been, held in the purity of Ashtar's thought. But the sky was muted, the setting sun veiled, and Ashtar's thought was as mysterious as a faded palimpsest. If a full moon rose in the east, only a rust-red tint like dried blood smeared the horizon to herald its coming.

"When will you return to Iksandarun?" he asked.

She drew away, only a little, and looked at him quizzically.

"You are the only child of Bellasteros to have imperial as well as Sardian blood. I want to honor you with your proper rank." And bribe my restive councilors with your imperial mother's name? he demanded of himself.

Sarasvati said gently, "I am comfortable here, among women."

"Well, yes, of course. . . ." Andrion indulged in an unfair blow. "Your son Ethan is well."

Her eye glinted and she parried, "So is your daughter Astra." She pointed.

A child, her hair as red as Sarasvati's or the highlights in Andrion's own, entered the garden from the street. She strode as purposefully as he had, small mouth tight, eyes hooded. But he knew those eyes, the deep blue-green of the sea.

"My daughter," he said, "the heir to Sabazel."

The child raised a tiny wicker shield and a stick and began sparring with an invisible enemy. In the midst of one dancing movement she stopped dead, realizing a man watched her. A man stood with his hands on Sarasvati. Warily she saluted. But her eyes, her manner, reserved her thought to herself.

"The world of men," said Sarasvati, "is so much larger

than Sabazel's. I was once a king's daughter, a king's sister, and once I was a slave. Here I am a healer, and that is the only rank I want."

Andrion's cloak billowed in a brief, tentative breeze. The bare branches of the trees chimed discordantly. He would like to believe Sarasvati foolish, but it was his urging that seemed foolish, and selfish as well. Men's games had their own rules, and the Sabazians only played when necessary, though they always played well.

The door of the house opened and Dana appeared. The lines of care in her face eased at the sight of the child playing so earnestly among the dead leaves, a solitary testimony to life and hope. "Astra," she called, "your grandmother would like you to sing to her."

"The lay of Daimion and Mari?" Astra asked, with a sideways glint at the intrusive male presence. "The true one, that gives Sabazel its own?"

"Yes," said Dana. "Yes, indeed." The child vanished inside. Dana turned to Sarasvati and Andrion.

"She does not know that I am her father," said Andrion quietly.

"The daughters of Sabazel have no fathers," Dana returned.

"You do," said Andrion. "As do I."

"But you are not a daughter," Sarasvati reminded him. And, to Dana, "I shall give the queen a strengthening draught. Andrion has encouraged her—even though he is only a man." With a teasing smile she pressed his hand and freed herself from his arm.

Thank you, Andrion thought to her, for that humor that was once our father's. And he wondered suddenly if Bellasteros's oldest child, Chrysais of Minras, had also inherited that temper like a two-edged blade.

Dana took his hand and led him away from the garden. The sun set, the city darkened from featureless day into featureless night, and the moon remained a dim bloodstain upon a suffocating sky.

Andrion stood in the temple courtyard while Dana, in her mother's place, announced the rules of the rites. Someday she would herself be queen, but her stern face as she spoke belied any ambition for the role. He accepted a sparse garland of asphodel from her hand, and set one about her neck in return. Now, at last, she looked at him, surrendering one watchtower of the fortress that was her soul. But still a wariness lurked deep in her eyes, the interior walls yet to be breached.

He turned away from the games, no longer needing to prove himself. Kerith, Dana's pair, was waiting at the door of their house. "So you come at last. I must reach the square in time to choose someone at least more prestigious than an emperor." With a mocking if friendly wave to Andrion, she was gone. He had to smile at her impertinence, and at her discretion; on more than one occasion she and Dana had shared his attentions.

Inside, a baby wailed. Andrion set down his helmet and fanned the embers in the brazier into flame. Red flame, not black. He shivered, from the cool of the evening, he told himself, not from uncertainty.

Dana lifted the infant from its cradle and swiftly changed its wrappings. It screamed, its eyes disappearing into red, raging flesh.

Kerith's child, no doubt. Sabazians paired themselves so that each babe would have two parents. Andrion laid the diadem carefully down and unclasped his cloak. He unbuckled the sheath of Solifrax and propped it against the wall. For a moment he felt as helpless as the child, bereft of the symbols of his kingship. Yet they were only symbols, and if his kingship did not spring from his heart, then he was no king.

Dana sat down, opened her shirt, and set the child to her breast.

Gods, Andrion wanted to shout, everyone has babies! He swallowed and asked coolly, "A boy?"

"He is all of three months old now, and will soon be leaving Sabazel for Sardis. Patros's new wife Kleothera will take him." She stroked the baby's wispy hair and touched the little hands that kneaded her flesh in an ecstasy of fulfillment, daring to love him for the short time he would be hers.

No, Andrion told himself, I shall not resent Dana or the baby or any of the men who might have fathered him under Ashtar's eye. That wound was scabbed long ago.

Raising a brow, she said, "You do not ask if he is your son."

"I can count, Dana." No, the wound was fresh. The coals in the brazier snapped and sighed softly; barely louder, Andrion asked, "Would you tell me if you bore my son?"

"No. You know the law, that the sons we bear are traded for girls. Sabazians have no fathers."

"You do."

"I am . . . fortunate," she admitted grudgingly. "I am also illegitimate, conceived outside the borders of Sabazel, outside the seasons of the rites, when my young and foolish mother lay with Patros during the campaign to Iksandarun."

"Young and foolish," repeated Andrion. "As you were when you lay with me in the sacred cavern."

She did not reply. She looked up, eyes wide, offering Andrion at last a glimpse within. In denying the evils of the outside world, he saw, she denied it all; she would defend her redoubt of custom and law, protecting herself, her people, her land, even though that redoubt separated her from him. He had to come second, always second, for if she sacrificed her laws for him, she would not be Dana.

He spun about, irritated, telling himself he could not afford irritation. He tore a piece from the loaf on the table, poured a cup of thin pink wine. The bread was stale, the wine sour. He set the cup down with a crash.

"We are man-forbidden," Dana said, not patiently but wearily, as if the words had worn an aching groove in her thought. "We are thusly man-cursed."

"But men and men's laws keep Sabazel secure."

"Do they? Or is it a most subtle threat? Creeping contentment, and the solace of a man's arms; the naming of fathers and sons. And soon the borders of Sabazel are breached by peace, and devastated more lastingly than by any armed force."

He had no answer. He watched the red flames in the brazier and their reflection in Dana's face. Her cheekbones were sharper than he remembered, her jaw tighter. Translucent shadow spiraled about her, about himself, filling the room. Maybe the demands of love were indeed foolish.

Dana's lashes curtained her eyes. No, Andrion realized, she was not complacent in her certainty. She was not certain at all. Her troubled soul tried to smooth itself with certainty. It was Sumitra's calm and certain soul that could barely be ruffled by trouble.

Sumitra, daughter of Rajah Jamshid of the valley of the Mohan, bred to be a ruler's wife. Dana, daughter of the queens of Sabazel, bred to be . . . free? In this man-ruled world freedom was the more expensive choice.

Dana detached the baby, wiped his little milk-smudged mouth, prodded a surprisingly loud burp from him, and laid him in his cradle. She lingered, patting his back while he drifted into satiated sleep.

Her shirt still gaped open. Her breasts were round and ripe with milk, reminding Andrion of Sumitra's opulent body. And yet Dana was almost as tall as he, was as lean and well-knit.

He inhaled deeply, trying not to quell the rush of quicksilver through his veins, but to read it. Was it desire for Dana or for Sumi? Gods, what a complex tapestry he found himself weaving. Or had it already been woven, by god and man, snaring him in its knotted threads?

Dana smiled at the baby. Turning, she included Andrion in the smile, her duty apparently served. "Is Sumitra as gentle and patient as she was when we met in Iksandarun—was it three years ago now?"

"Her temper is somewhat abraded by the duties expected of her, I fear."

"To make babies?"

"And are you not expected to make babies in Ashtar's rites?"

Her smile hardened. "You were conceived in the rites. As was Bellasteros."

"His mother died for it at the hand of her husband, Gerlac of Sardis." The flesh crawled on the back of his neck. He opened his arms—you have made your point, come now, I need you . . . Dana, shuddering with the same chill, abandoned reluctance and came. Gratifying, how their bodies warmed against each other.

"And the rumors of Bellasteros's birth haunted him always," she said. "He was king of Sardis. You are king of Sardis. You must be perceived as Gerlac's blood, burden as that name is."

Andrion set his hand on her face and kissed her. Her firm, narrow lips opened; her mouth was as tart and fresh as an orange. Her touch sanctified, as the touch of the goddess purified. . . . "You mean we are not to contest our separate worlds this night?" he whispered against her smooth cheek.

"On certain nights I am permitted to indulge my own foolishness," she replied, so quietly he hardly heard her. But she was smiling again, teasing him and herself both.

Yes, she dared to love him. He grinned, and his body made

it evident that he was not really tired. Confused, wrenched with pain, but not tired. He spread her shirt. He slipped his hands into the waistband of her trousers and pulled them away, his palms stroking her muscled thighs.

She laid him down on the bed and loosened his belt. For just a moment her eyes focused beyond him, beyond the shadows that sifted the dim light in the room. Strange images moved in her viridescent gaze. He could never seize them, never free her from their possession; he would simply have to love her for bearing their burden.

"The bull and the lotus, the shield and the sword. Chariots—Sardis has chariots." She blinked rapidly. "I can see no more, Andrion."

"I do not ask you to see anything."

"I must. The goddess sets kings and queens upon the gameboard, until, tiring of them, she devours them all. . . ."

He hushed her with a caress. She bent over him. Her hair fell about him, a shining curtain closing out the darkness. He set his lips against the warmth of her breast, and her breath fanned him with a long shivering sigh of delight. He drank, and for a few blessed hours his thirst was quenched.

Chapter Three

THE SUNLIGHT WAS diffused as if through gauze into a featureless glare. The moon was a pale crescent hovering uncertainly above the eastern horizon. The sea was dark indigo blue, reflecting no light. Viscous waves probed ceaselessly at the beach, their murmur damped by the humid air. Far offshore a solitary ship stood in toward the land. On its sail was the weathered outline of a winged bull.

Sumitra glanced up at the paradoxically unclouded but shadowed sky. The noon air was warm and still, but the sea emanated a chill breath. She removed the veil which she wore in deference to Sardian custom. "The moon is waxing again," she said to Valeria beside her. "Andrion is returning."

Valeria waddled across the sand in the peculiar gait of the pregnant. She was not so preoccupied with her footing, though, that she could not glance quizzically at Sumitra. Sumi's voice contained an unusual timbre, not an edge but an extra depth. Her dark eyes gazed across the sea with serene patience, as if she were a goddess watching the slow rising of land from water, the slow inundation by water of land. Her full lips smiled secretively.

Valeria, too, removed her veil, and the women giggled conspiratorially. The children gamboled about their skirts, the older the child the farther its venture from protection. Ethan went so far as to climb a clump of soggy driftwood, great cedar logs from the coast near Farsahn. Shouting insults, "Rats, come out and fight!" he began to pelt his brothers with bits of bark. Shrieking with glee, Zefric and Kem joined forces and attacked, flinging curls of sea wrack like limp javelins. Ethan leaped to the far side of the logs and sprinted into the mouth of a sandy ravine. The other boys followed. The little girl glanced up at her mother, toward her siblings, and daringly toddled after.

27

"Centurion," Valeria pleaded, laughing, to the tall soldier who followed close behind. "Miklos, if you please. . . ."

Miklos grinned. "I have children of my own, my lady." He offered a salute, called an order to the four other men of the escort and hurried after the children. Their happy shouts and the plop-plop of their steps echoed along the beach and then faded. White sea birds spun upward, squawking indignantly, before swooping low over the water. A falcon circled far above, hardly deigning to notice the earth.

"We shall have little boots full of sand," Valeria said, "and pouches filled with rocks and shells and strange scuttling creatures."

Sumitra's eye surrendered the image of the children. She grew introspective, listening to some silent message only she could hear.

The soldiers broke formation and began scuffling playfully around the pony cart that had carried the party here. A serving woman stood aloof, staring out to sea. The ship was closer in; a tiny round-bottomed merchant tub, not a naval galley with banks of oars like a huge swimming centipede. The port of Sardis, Pirestia, was a translucent silk-screened print some distance down the coast, more illusion than real. The great city itself was out of sight beyond the coastal dunes and marshes of the delta of the Sar.

"Smell that sea air!" exclaimed Valeria. "As glorious as all the exotic perfumes of the Mohan."

"Salt and rotten fish," Sumitra returned. A brief tremor of doubt crossed face. By way of apology she added, "You grew up in Sardis, by this sea. I did not."

Valeria appraised that tremor. "Sumitra," she crooned, "would you by any chance have something to tell me?"

Sumitra smiled and then blushed.

"Sumitra!"

"Yes, yes. But you must tell no one, because I really should tell Andrion first. . . ."

Valeria laughed, chimes trilling into the turgid air and stirring it. "Say no more. I understand, and I thank you for your confidence. Do you know for sure?"

"My last flow was almost three moons ago," Sumitra whispered. "And my stomach has been uneasy since we left Iksandarun. Andrion, it seems, did not have to go to Sabazel to pray for children. Yet even had I been sure, I would not have stopped him." She faltered, her serenity ruffled.

"Sabazel," sighed Valeria. "Bellasteros, my father Patros, Tembujin, and Andrion himself are all beguiled by the daughters of Ashtar. My mother, Harus rest her soul, dashed herself to death upon her resentment."

"I have met the Sabazians." Sumitra raised her chin, serenity restored. "I choose to believe that the borders of Sabazel encompass us all, and Ashtar offers her grace to those who would accept it."

Valeria responded with a grateful smile, then beckoned to the escorting soldiers; they regained their gravity and with many bows delivered two sturdy stools and the zamtak. They sat down some distance away and began a dice game. The serving woman leaned eagerly toward the sea, balancing on her toes.

Sumitra sat and stroked the strings of her instrument. They keened high and shrill. With a slight frown she stroked them again. Still they did not ring quite true. A sudden gusty breeze jangled along the shore.

"I wonder where that ship comes from," Valeria mused, perching tentatively on a stool. "A winged bull, is it not?"

"Rhodope, perhaps," said Sumitra. She tightened a peg on the neck of the zamtak. The string hummed to her touch. A hum of latent power, not unlike the murmur of Solifrax or of the star-shield of Sabazel.

"That ship captain comes close to the land. The main channel is farther out, by the beacon. Look, Rue seems concerned."

Sumitra followed Valeria's gaze. The ship was actually riding the breakers now. Her fingers plucked the strings of the zamtak and it spilled music into the muted sunlight, the slow susurration of waves against the shore and the harsh call of a sea bird.

The ship's hull hissed into shallow water. The sail flapped thunderously and sailors leaped to furl it. A ramp shot from the near gunwale. Seven dark, robed men poured down it, splashed through the water, ran crunching up the wet sand. The serving woman sped as if the hounds of hell were behind her and clambered onto the ship.

The escorting soldiers leaped up. Sumitra's hand stilled the strings with discordant clang. Valeria gasped.

Long knives glinted with a sickly phosphorescence that was a reflection of neither sun nor moon. The soldiers were quickly overwhelmed. Valeria tried to rise, could not, was swept to the ground and kicked aside like a piece of jetsam.

Sumitra spun first one way, then the other. Her gown wrapped her ankles and she fell. Four men seized her. Her right hand encountered the stool, grasped it, and struck out with it, shattering one man's bearded jaw. The other men tore the makeshift weapon from her and bore her away. She clutched the zamtak and shrieked in terror and rage.

A man in a lustrous purple cloak and cowl stood at the bow of the ship. His eyes, a clear, almost colorless gray, flickered with distant lightning as Sumitra's struggling form was heaved like a sack of meal over the gunwale and hustled below with a protesting clash of strings. Then the light was gone and his gray eyes were as expressionless as mirrors. He shouted peremptorily; the brigands left the bodies of the soldiers sprawled on the mottled sand and rushed back to the ship.

The woman Rue knelt at the commander's feet, head bowed, dark hair tumbling loose from its bindings. Her cloak billowed open; an armband embossed with a winged bull glinted. She swept away her veil to reveal the pointed chin and the large, liquid eyes of a fox. "My lord," she cried, "my lord, have I done well?"

He shrugged, accustomed to being obeyed, and turned toward the beach. She stared at his back, elation dashed.

The ramp was pulled in. Waves lifted the ship. The sail rolled down and bellied booming in the wind. The wings of the bull flapped.

Valeria struggled to pick herself up. Her sand-stained face turned, a pale oval, toward the receding ship. The gaze of those gray eyes struck her like driving sleet, and she doubled over in pain.

The falcon coasted impassively past the feeble moon.

The escort of imperial warriors and Sabazians, each ranked in its own company, plodded under a still, hazy sky that tarnished the golds and russets of autumn. An ox cart carrying Sarasvati and Dana's baby churned silently through dust like the ashes of a burned city. A ghostly moon waned during the night, held aloft by a thin, feeble wind.

Dana rode beside Andrion, her Khazyari bow set firmly on her shoulder, her eyes cold green shards in the shadow of her helmet, her mouth set in bitter resentment. Andrion knew his own face was lined with similarly resentful and impatient puzzlement. He had found little solace in Sabazel. Its flesh,

too, crawled with sorcery, and its winds summoned him to
. . . what? Even ventalidar's harness jangled discordantly.

At Farsahn they were joined by the proconsul and an
additional escort. Dour Nikander was the perfect companion,
asking politely after affairs in Sabazel and Iksandarun, shaking his head in concern, saying nothing more.

To Andrion the company seemed a tiny fly struggling
through amber, through bits of debris that were villages,
farms, military camps. Slowly, painfully, the great sea plain
opened before them and the southern mountains slipped away
over the horizon.

Peasants winnowed sparse baskets of grain beside the road;
the chaff spun wearily into the air and became dust devils
clotting land and sky alike. The workers watched their emperor pass with hurt, bewildered eyes. Here, too, was malaise. But I am well, Andrion insisted to himself as he shouted
encouraging words to his people. When the king is well, so
are you. But then, that is an old superstition, and if followed
far enough leads to the kinds of rite pictured on the ancient
cavern in Cylandra's flank, the summer king slain for the
winter king. . . . I am well. Am I not? He touched Solifrax
and it rang hollowly.

At last, at last, the moon thickened in the pallid afternoon
sky; Sardis and action were only a day away.

Another dust devil appeared, far down the road toward the
east, glinting cold gray in the lowering sun. Andrion squinted
at it; he could not tense any further than he already had. It
was no dust devil at all, but a company of horsemen dressed
in the black-and-gold livery of Sardis. Even as he told himself
he had nothing to dread, his spine chilled.

He turned away from the guardpost where soldiers and
Sabazians set up camp and stepped into the center of the road.
A gust of wind snapped his black cloak behind him; his
helmetless head glinted auburn and gold.

The horsemen were a clump of darkness with many moving
legs. They were separate men. They saw their emperor standing alone, waiting for them, and with many whinnyings and
plungings they pulled up. The lead rider clambered down,
threw himself into the dust at Andrion's feet, offered a rolled
parchment.

Andrion ripped open the scroll, sending Patros's seals flying.
Words marched firm and black across the page: *The lady
Sumitra is gone.*

The world blurred. Trees, fields, buildings faded to indistinct blots; the many watching faces were ghostly wavering shadows. Gone? Andrion repeated. Patros would say Sumitra was dead, if that were the case. But gone?

Andrion crushed the parchment in his fist and cast it to the ground. The messengers quailed. Automatically he made a reassuring gesture, and his voice thanked them and ordered food and water for their refreshment.

But it was he who thirsted. One face steadied before his eyes. "Dana," he said, "Sumitra is gone."

A muffled gasp hummed through the group. Or perhaps it was the wind that gasped, a sudden icy blast slapping his cheeks, waking him. He saw Dana's pinched face groping for balance, needing to ride with him, needing to stay with the wailing bundle Sarasvati held protectively, needing not to care about him and his wife at all—the baby must be fed, duty must be fed, love must be consumed by the practicalities of ruling—ah, Andrion, as rulers we cannot wonder what this means for us, and yet I wonder indeed. . . .

He saw Nikander holding Ventalidar's reins; behind him two soldiers were already mounted. He opened his mouth and found nothing in it, no moisture, no words. He closed his mouth, stifled his soul, took the reins and mounted. He turned Ventalidar east, towards Sardis, and with an oath urged the stallion into headlong flight.

The three horses' hoofbeats were the pounding of his own heart. Sumitra, my shield—who, where, how? Why, by all the gods, why?

The day failed and died behind the riders, bloody sunset streaming over the arch of the sky until it lapped at the corner of Andrion's eyes. Then the red glow was gone. A night seemingly shadowed by smoke and ash consumed the world. Still the hoofbeats rang upon the Royal Road, upon the bridges and aqueducts that Bellasteros had built to make the world smaller but no less terrible.

His thoughts gibbered like bats streaming from a ruin at dusk. Sumitra, gone? Accident or enemy action? Who would dare? What could they gain? Not Tembujin, by Harus's beak, I have learned to trust Tembujin; but if not Tembujin, who? The father of some nubile nobelwoman? For I have no heir, no heir, no heir—the diadem lies uneasy on my brow—the Empire is threatened, my rule is threatened. Gods, for an enemy I could could face and fight!

Ventalidar ran ahead of the other horses. Andrion rode
alone through the gloom, sweating in a fever of recrimina-
tion—if I had not gone to Sabazel, if I had not lingered with
Dana and Sarasvati upon the road, if I had stayed to face my
troubles in Iksandarun, if, if . . .

A glow lightened the horizon; he was surely delirious.
Camp fires, watch fires of the army of Sardis before Iksandarun,
the gold of the shield and the sword raised as one. The sun
was rising. Ventalidar stumbled as the road wound down into
the wide valley of the Sar and then, heartened, pounded on.
Irrigation canals reflected strands of torpid light. The city of
Sardis was a black silhouette against gray dawn, the great
ziggurat of Harus stairsteps into heaven. Andrion looked
back, once. His escort had fallen completely out of sight. A
waxing quarter moon watched him, a faint stain of silver on a
murky sky. Damn the sardonic humor of the gods, will they
not leave me in peace? Or is it my own parched humor that so
cracks the surface of this life?

The gatekeepers hailed the solitary rider. Then, seeing the
great black horse and the black cloak, seeing the pale, even
features and glimmering diadem of the emperor, they fell
back with cries of welcome. Farmers carrying their produce,
fishermen hauling their catch to market, leaped to the sides of
the streets as Ventalidar swept by. And the wind blasted
again, drawn by horse and rider, a cold, clean, uncompromising wind driving away the hazy reek and revealing an achingly pure sapphire sky, Ashtar's eyes opened at last.

Ventalidar stood wheezing in the forecourt of the palace.
"Old friend," Andrion said to him, stroking his lathered
skin, "I am sorry. But no mortal horse could have run so far,
so fast; surely you are indeed god-given." He left Ventalidar
in the care of a groom and staggered up the granite steps, his
limbs cold and stiff, into glaring bronze light. This is the
house where my father grew up and walked in defiance of
Gerlac; Bellasteros, hero of Sardis, had no Sardian blood.

Patros stood at the head of the staircase. His firm hands
caught Andrion's upward stumble. His face swam before
Andrion's eyes; snow-white hair and precise features stripped
by joy and sorrow of any self-consciousness, of any weakness. "In the name of the god!" Andrion croaked. He tried to
swallow and coughed up dust.

"Come, my lord." Patros laid a strong arm tight around
his emperor's shoulders and led him into a bedchamber. The

room was fresh with the scent of lavender, stirred affection-
ately by the cool morning breeze. A woman lay upon the bed,
her dark hair spread across the pillow, cornflower-blue eyes
still soft with illusory dream. A man sat beside her, his black
tail of hair coiling like a serpent over his shoulder.

"He is here," Patros said.

Tembujin rose slowly, as if trying to discern whether this
ashen-faced apparition was really Andrion.

Andrion's stark pallor extended even to the stubble shading
his cheeks. His eyes were coals burning holes in the parchment of his face. He swayed, caught himself, allowed Patros
to seat him in a chair and press a goblet of wine to his lips.
The wine was almost as sour as that he had drunk in Sabazel,
but it cleared his daze. "Where is Sumitra?" he asked.

"Kidnapped," said Tembujin. "Taken away on a ship
whose sail was painted with a winged bull."

"Pirates? Have they demanded ransom? I shall ransom
her!" Andrion's hand closed upon the hilt of Solifrax and it
murmured vengeance.

"They were no pirates," said Patros. "They did not take
Valeria's jewelry. And there has been no message."

Valeria told the tale by rote. "Our serving women were
ill," she concluded, "having eaten tainted food, it seemed,
so we had only the one, a new girl named Rue. It was she, I
fear, who told the brigands where we would be, and when;
she went willingly to them. The commander looked at me
with the strangest eyes. . . ." She shivered. "I lay upon the
beach until Miklos returned with the children, and brought
us safely back to Sardis."

Miklos, thought Andrion, grasping at something, anything.
"Good man. Always been a good man." He released the sword,
flexed his hand, looked curiously at his palms stained with sweat
and leather. That hand had touched Sumitra and Dana as well.

"Not all the children," scowled Tembujin.

Valeria sighed, a breath drawn from the same icy depth as
the wind. "I lost the baby I carried. Born too early to live."

"Lost?" Tembujin hissed. "The child was murdered."

I was born too early, Andrion thought. My parents demanded my life from the gods, for I was to be winter king to
my father's summer king. The skein of his mind tangled,
spinning threads of irrelevancy, even while something snagged
him, something Valeria had said, something Tembujin had
said. He frowned.

"My lord," said Valeria. "Andrion, Sumitra believed herself to be pregnant."

The skein knotted, strangling him. He saw his own face
contort, saw his own body leap from the chair and stand
quivering, reeling from the force of the blow. Who, then,
shall be my heir, when summer comes again? Why, gods,
why? Patros took his arm and he shook it away. Strike
quickly, at anyone, at anything. "Tembujin, did you know
she was pregnant?"

The black eyes crusted with caution. "No. If I had, I
would have wished you and her and the child well."

"Seeing no more chance for your son to rule? No more
chance for you to rule through your sons? No more chance for
you to crow over me?"

"What do you imply?" Tembujin crouched like a lion.

"Andrion," said Patros soothingly.

He did not want to be soothed. His jaw was so tight it
writhed in pain. In another moment his heart would writhe
and he would be unmanned, here before them all. "Someone
plots against me, against Sabazel, someone, perhaps, who
seeks vengeance against those who defeated his people. Who
defeated him."

"Go on, say it," spat Tembujin.

"Sabazel?" Patros asked quietly, but the intensity of his
voice sliced through the others.

Andrion turned, mouth open, and whatever scathing words
he had meant for Tembujin subsided into ash. Gods! he
shouted to himself, have you woven each individual agony
into some intricate, indecipherable pattern greater than its
parts? "The woman Rue, bearing the sign of the winged bull,
stole the star-shield. Ilanit is ill, Sabazel is ill, Sumitra is
gone!"

He could not look at Patros's stricken face, at Tembujin's
and Valeria's shocked eyes; the walls billowed around him,
surged forward like the waves of the sea, threatened to smother
him. Gasping for breath, he spun about and plunged from the
room.

The corridor was cool and dim, dawn still struggling with
the smoky shadows of the night. Bonifacio, attended by a tidy
line of acolytes, stood exchanging courtesies with Patros's
wife Kleothera. At the sudden entrance of the emperor, Bonifacio
halted in mid-phrase, turned his back upon her, bowed deeply.
The other priests bowed even more deeply. I wager, Andrion

thought with renewed irrelevance, that he has chosen no one stronger than himself. Except perhaps that acolyte Rowan who was with him in Iksandarun—yes, there he is, such large eyes—what the hell difference do the man's name or face or strength make?

Patros and Tembujin rushed into the corridor. Their eyes targeted Andrion. Everyone's eyes targeted Andrion. He was pierced through and through as if by black Khazyari arrows.

Bonifacio's vacuous face bobbed before him. "My lord, my condolences upon the loss of your wife. The eyes of Harus will surely guard her in the afterlife. We, his lowly servants, can only continue in this life."

Blithering idiot, Andrion told himself with one last thread of sanity.

Bonifacio continued with properly solemn mien, "The lady Sumitra would doubtless have wanted her lord to take another wife. I have a list of several noblewomen who would be suitable." He produced a piece of paper from his capacious sleeve and thrust it into Andrion's face.

Sanity snapped, and the frayed ends lashed into frenzy. Andrion plucked the list from Bonifacio's fingers, tore it to shreds, dashed the bits to the floor. His hands closed on the priest's feather-trimmed robe. Bonifacio's toes scrabbled for the floor and his jowls flapped in fear as his face approached the rich brown eyes of the emperor and was singed in their fiery depths, leaving him naked of pretense and pride.

"Why are you so sure Sumitra is dead?" Andrion snarled. "Convenient, is it not, that she was carried away in my absence?"

Bonifacio gabbled. Kleothera's veil creased her rosy cheeks as she grinned at the priest's discomfiture. The acolytes huddled around Rowan like sheep around a shepherd.

Andrion threw Bonifacio into their midst. Solifrax blazed, and the morning shadows fled before its radiance. "By the pinfeathers of the god, priest, you shall not come to me again until you come crawling at the hem of my wife's cloak! It is my choice whom I wed, and when and where!"

Tembujin and Patros exchanged a wry glance; Sumitra had not been Andrion's choice, not at first, but it would take a braver man than Bonifacio to remind him of that now.

Bonifacio sprawled, sobbing his fealty. And Andrion realized, as though dashing cold water into his own face, that he was terrorizing the man before his subordinates, that he had lost his temper—Harus, was his temper that of a king or was it not?

Andrion stood as stony as one of his own statues while Bonifacio and his minions scuttled away, colliding in the doorway in their haste to be gone. Their footsteps faded. The wind purred about the palace. Solifrax was dull and heavy in his hand. Tears seared tracks through the dirt on his face, as hot as droplets of lifeblood, revealing the mortal flesh beneath.

"Do you really think Bonifacio is responsible?" Patros asked.

"No more than I think Tembujin is," groaned Andrion. Courtesy, as vital in ruling as doubt; he sheathed his sword and opened his palm to the khan, accepting a slight bow in return. But Tembujin's eyes were still guarded. Yes, of course, in my uncertainty I wound my own right arm. . . .

The tiny rounded form of Kleothera appeared at Andrion's elbow. "Now," she said briskly, "you must rest. I shall let no one else annoy you." She conducted Andrion into a nearby chamber, efficiently divested him of his armor and put him to bed, standing on no ceremony with an emperor a generation younger than she.

She had been the widow of a Sardian officer, not an aristocrat, but the nobility of her spirit matched Patros's own. As Patros gravely accepted sword and diadem, his eyes were drawn to his wife; a happy marriage was still a novelty to him. Marriage, Andrion's mind wailed. Wife.

Kleothera offered him a cup. His hands shook, sloshing the white liquid, and she steadied it for him. "Valerian, almond milk, and anemone," she said, "to help you sleep."

Anemone, yes, he thought. And asphodel, the flower of love and death, the flower of Sabazel. The light of the sword and shield gnawed by darkness. . . . His thought unraveled. Kleothera stroked his brow, and he fell headlong into dream-haunted sleep.

Chapter Four

THE SHIP HOVERED for a moment on the crest of the wave, and then with an odd sideways slither, wallowed into the trough.

In the tiny cabin Sumitra could not tell whether it was night or day. It could have been only a few hours since she had been taken, or it could have been months. Ropes whined amid an occasional rush of feet overhead; boards creaked in agony, as if at any moment the ship would disintegrate and cast her into the pulsing roar of the sea.

Her head, too, pulsed. The stink of tainted bilge water and the reek of the guttering oil lamp hung about her, and her stomach wriggled like some slimy creature found under an overturned rock. In spite of herself she groaned.

Rue hurriedly wiped Sumitra's gelid forehead. The cloth was moistened with saltwater, and it, too, stank. "The first months of pregnancy are indeed difficult," she essayed.

Sumitra fixed the serving woman with a baleful glare. "So you know of that, too. Inspecting my body linen, I suppose."

Rue turned and wrung the rag in a basin, concealing her face.

"I am ill because I have never been on such a small ship before," Sumitra insisted. The tiny flame of the lamp leaped and danced. The cabin was as small as a tomb, the narrow bed the frame of a coffin. Andrion would have to bend double even to enter the door. Andrion. . . . Certainly they had taken her to strike at him. Unless—unless he had chosen this method of putting her aside. But he would not have his own soldiers killed, he would not have her so terrified. If he no longer wanted her, he would simply tell her, as was his right. . . . His face flickered before her, pared of its wry humor, sharp with rage; no, Andrion would never stoop to such a scheme.

The ship wallowed again. Her eyes crossed. The vision

faded. "Why betray me, Rue?" she croaked. "Why betray your emperor?"

"He is not my emperor. I serve another, greater ruler."

Sumitra frowned. Before she could speak, the door opened and a man ducked inside. Even in the dimness, with such uncertain senses, Sumitra could see the opulent Rexian purple cloak he wore. A merchant prince, then, or perhaps a prince of the blood. No mere pirate.

And his face was no brigand's. Its planes were sculpted in creamy marble rather than human flesh, its angles smoothed and polished. His golden hair was bound with a fillet and his golden beard was neatly trimmed; his eyes were as pale and clear as a silver mirror. Something moved there, concealed by the tints of gold and purple, like a shadow in the depths of a crystal ball.

He nodded brusquely. Rue scuttled away, permitted only one yearning glance at his beauty.

So he was the ruler she served. Sumitra tried to straighten her hair and her garments, and succeeded only in sitting up. The ship heaved. She grabbed for the bed rail. The man did not stir. "Who are you?" she asked.

"Eldrafel," he replied, admitting to no particular rank. His long, delicate fingers touched the ruby in her nose. She stiffened, but his hand fell back to his side. "You are Sumitra, first wife of the emperor Andrion Bellasteros." It was a statement, not a question.

She was not quite sure she liked the way those names sounded in his odd, singsong accent. When he spoke again, the words flowed past her before she could quite hear them; his voice was not deep but vibrant, with the low eddies and undertones of a reed flute. ". . . jaw is shattered. He might live, maimed; probably he will die. You defended yourself well."

Oh. The man she had struck with the stool. Nausea swept her again. But Eldrafel's probing gray eyes were not angry; they were self-possessed, with callousness, perhaps, or with a sardonic pleasure at her spirit.

She felt naked before his cool scrutiny, her every thought offered like delicacies on a banquet platter; her head spun and her stomach congealed into a lump of lead. She turned away, and he was gone.

Sumitra gasped for air as if he had taken her breath away

with him. Decisively, she stood. The ship wallowed, and she staggered against the far wall, one step away. There was her zamtak, tossed against a row of amphorae, a couple of the strings loosened and curling disconsolately.

Sumitra took the wet rag and cleaned it of sand. She perched on the edge of the bunk, tightening and then tuning the strings. The plinks and trills were familiar and therefore soothing; slowly the harshness of her expression softened and her nausea ebbed. A tear glistened in her eye and she brushed it away. "What good would it do to weep?" she asked herself aloud.

As if in reply she heard, below the cacophany of the laboring ship, a faint sound of chimes. It was so much like the chime of Solifrax that she started up. Then, with a grimace and a shake of her head, she turned again to the zamtak. The strings hummed under her touch. Music filled the room, a plaintive ballad making whorls in semidarkness.

Again the chimes. Sumitra laid her hand across the strings, but the music hung in the air, summoning light out of darkness. There was a shapeless canvas-wrapped bundle thrown carelessly behind the amphorae. A clear pale light seemed to be shining tentatively through the cloth.

Sumitra stared at it a moment, doubting her senses. But the light was unmistakable; not the crystalline light of Solifrax, but something similar, an otherworldly purity and beauty.

She lay down the zamtak. Slowly, her hands beginning to tremble, she pulled the bundle out and tugged at its bindings. A large disk, metal, but not as heavy as bronze. The rough canvas parted. Beneath was the smooth and glowing surface of a shield.

"No," Sumitra said under her breath. "It cannot be, not here."

In the center of the shield was emblazoned a many-pointed star. It pulsed gently, singing a song almost beyond conscious perception. And yet Sumitra heard. "Yes. It is the shield of Sabazel. By the third eye of Vaiswanara . . ." She smiled at herself. "No. By the blue eyes, by the golden tresses of Ashtar, how did you come here?"

The shield quieted. Sumitra sat a long time, stroking the warm metal surface, brushing it clean of dust, oblivious to the smells and sounds around her. The star tingled under her hands as if kissing them, and when the oil lamp flickered wildly and went out she did not notice.

"So," she said at last. "You, too, have been kidnapped. I must keep you safe, for those who search for you will surely join those who search for me. Although you are essential to Sabazel, and I am not at all essential to the Empire, heir or no heir . . ." Her lips tightened. She whispered, "Ashtar, if Andrion is your child, then so, surely, is this child I carry; keep it safe, I pray, for its father's arms, for will those arms not open to me again?"

The shield flickered with a faint, faraway luminescence and then faded. Sumitra nodded, her prayer answered. Smiling, humming her ballad, she carefully wrapped the shield again and set it beside the bunk, next to her zamtak. She lay down and composed herself for sleep, her hands folded upon her belly. Her great dark eyes stared up into the murk and through it, finding serenity upon the other side.

Andrion stood on a palace balcony overlooking the Sar, rubbing his chin reflectively. The serving girl who had shaved him had been so excited at touching the handsome young monarch, her hands had shaken. But she had not done too much damage. Her fluttering bosom had really been quite lovely; he realized only now that he had noticed it.

The evening sky was scrubbed clean, shining cobalt shading to gold in the west, where the evening star hung suspended. Andrion's thought twisted like wool thread around its spindle, raveling in the spinner's hands, knotting and breaking and twisting again.

He leaned over the parapet to watch Bonifacio and his acolytes—a row of goslings behind a goose—march through a crowd of waiting people to the end of a long pier. No wonder Bonifacio had been up and about so early this morning; it was the Day of Divine Retribution. The priest had no doubt spent the intervening hours catechizing the populace with their year's misdeeds. He made an expansive gesture toward the emperor, a thousand faces turned hopefully up, and Andrion waved; let the ceremony begin!

Children, Tembujin's and others, frolicked down the balcony, their sweet voices innocent of desire or death. A tentative wind wafted Bonifacio's drone upward. With a snort Andrion turned away, doubting if such a passive ceremony could heal the malaise haunting him, haunting his world. Solifrax chimed gently and he touched it, asking it, your will or mine?

He was caught by the domestic tableau in the governor-general's study, figures as vivid as if cast from the shimmering evening light. Valeria and Kleothera sat cooing over Dana's baby. Dana made some pleasantry for her father Patros, who returned it with discreet affection. Tembujin offered noncommittal commonplaces that ran like water from Sarasvati's cool, polite, not entirely humorless, rejoinders. If her eye strayed every now and then to Ethan, if Dana could not keep herself from glancing at Zefric, Tembujin diplomatically did not notice.

Then the tableau cracked, the voices faded. Sumitra was not there. The world was colorless without the bright yarns of her tapestry; it was out of tune without the music of her voice and her zamtak.

The faces in the study, too, turned to Andrion. They chose hope beyond despair; who could blame them? They would flay him alive with their hope. He hid his expression by leaning over to tickle the baby. No consolation; the child gazed up at him with the even green eyes of his mother. Sumitra's child would no doubt have brown eyes. . . .

"We shall name the baby Declan," said Patros. "Kleothera's own niece shall be his nurse."

"I am pleased," Andrion said, clearing his throat.

"We shall send in exchange a baby girl rescued from a garbage pile." Kleothera clucked scornfully. "How could anyone cast out a babe simply because it is female? I had thought such customs forgotten."

"It was Bellasteros who banned such practice," said Andrion, crossing the room to join Patros at his desk. "He always cringed to remember how Chryse's father exposed the younger of her two daughters, embarrassed that Chryse could not bear the Prince of Sardis an heir. That stiff old general lies uneasy in his grave, I wager, because Bellasteros's heir was born at last . . ." Kleothera nodded encouragingly; she was too intelligent not to have discerned the truth. ". . . to the Queen of Sabazel," he finished.

Dana, leaning on the back of Patros's chair, glanced sharply up. She ascertained that Andrion was attempting a black joke, and offered him a slightly off-center smile before looking back down at the parchment her father held. On it was a drawing of a winged bull.

"Ah," Andrion said. Old problem or new, it was still a question of succession.

"Sarasvati," said Patros, "did this from her memory of Rue's armband and from Valeria's description of the ship's sail. I sent a copy to the harbor with Nikander; you may remember, my lord, that his brother Niarkos is an admiral. And . . ."

Patros paused, making sure of his facts. Andrion nudged gently, "And?"

"Sailor's rumors say that the harbor of Minras is guarded by statues of winged bulls. It is their god, Taurmenios."

"Ah," said Andrion. Of course, the dark legends of Taurmenios gathered like smoke on the borders of old tales. Minras, and his half-sister Chrysais, a stranger to him. He turned to Sarasvati. "When Rue said that Ilanit's queenly aspect reminded her of Chryse . . ."

She nodded, following his thought. "She did not say 'Chryse,' did she? She said 'Chrysais.' "

"Chrysais was the sister of that exposed child." Andrion shook himself. These irrelevancies were becoming annoying. If indeed they were irrelevancies. One stitch at a time.

He paced up and down, thinking aloud. Patros's crisp voice, Dana's and Tembujin's quick wits, pulled each strand of thought to its end. The attacks on Tembujin, the theft of the shield, the kidnapping of Sumitra—was it paranoia or insight to see it all as a plot to bring him north and send him rushing heedlessly beyond the borders of the Empire, to turn his eye away from plots here or to draw him to Minras or both. . . . If someone wanted to seize the Empire, he had picked a damnably subtle way of going about it. "Does the power of Gath of Minras reach even to Iksandarun?" Andrion exclaimed.

"King Gath is dead, my lord," Patros reminded him. "He and Chrysais had a son, I think, but he would not be old enough to rule."

"Why torment Sabazel?" Dana asked. "Very few know just how firmly you are bound to it." Patros's face tightened; she did not have to say her mother's name to remind him of her or of dead Lyris.

"We must not leap to conclusions," Andrion stated in his best council-chamber voice, even as he asked himself if he did not already leap. "Someone with a very long arm plays games with me. With us all. It may be someone merely hiding behind Minras—someone here, perhaps, who wants me gone. It may be that the gods themselves use us once again for sport.''

The faces watched him, Patros trusting, Dana resigned, Tembujin almost challenging. "I shall send someone to Minras," announced Andrion. "Miklos and a small company, I think, to scout the lay of the land. A legion to Rhodope, to wait. Nikander will go south to Iksandarun, to govern while I wait here."

Tembujin leaned on the other side of the desk. "I shall go to Minras. My lord."

"My lord?" Andrion repeated skeptically.

"I would prove my loyalty to you. I would avenge my child—and my guard Ursbei."

"Damn it, man, you need prove nothing to me."

The tip-tilted black eyes said otherwise. Andrion spun away from them; *to prove that he does not plot against me, he shoulders my burden and goes away. Suitable payment for my doubting him, leaving me relieved and dirtied by my relief.*

Patros stirred in the currents that swept past him, his eye fixed warily on his elder daughter. *And if I ever doubt Patros,* thought Andrion, *I would be dirty indeed; if his loyalty ever wavered, the night would be too dark to survive. . . .*

"I shall go to Minras," said Dana, addressing not Andrion's face but the wall beyond his shoulder. "Without the shield, my daughter has no land to inherit."

My daughter. But not my heir. Succession, and rule, and I . . . Andrion took a deep breath, but it could not penetrate the knot in his chest. The draperies fluttered in the wind.

Night had crept silently across Sardis. The room was dim, lit only by the soft light of the lamp on Patros's desk. Declan began to wail. Dana took him from Kleothera's arms and opened her shirt. *Here he would be cared for, here she could leave him; here she could leave Andrion to follow the letter of her everlasting law. . . .* A tear ran from beneath her lashes and fell upon the baby's tiny form like a kiss of farewell. It might have been a drop of molten lead on Andrion's heart.

Tembujin bent solicitously over Valeria. His eye touched Dana and passed on, but not before Andrion read their expression; he knew well that reluctant thirst. His mouth tasted the savor of milk and oranges even as his nostrils filled with the scent of jasmine.

The children were shouting. Abruptly, he turned and followed them outside. The stars were bright hard points of steel against the velvet drape of the sky. The moon was cut as cleanly in half as if by the blade of Solifrax. The wind was bracingly cold, ringing toward the sea, and the sword rang in response against his thigh.

Myriad pinpricks of light flared along the riverbank. One by one they seemed to leap down into the dark and quiet stream. Candles in tiny glass cups, red, green, gold, blue, rode on wooden rafts and cleverly folded paper boats down the river to the sea, bearing away with them the year's regrets. A contented sigh rose from the gathered Sardians, and Andrion allowed himself a rueful smile.

Once it had been customary to slaughter a bull or a ram and cast it into the river; as the current swept it away, it carried with it the transgressions of the year before. It was Chryse who had begun today's gentler custom. Perhaps there was a place, Andrion thought, in the midst of the sea, where all those cast-off guilts lay gathered in soggy piles, no longer able to wound.

The lights flowed toward the sea. His thought strained toward the sea. His smile tightened into a grimace. How can I leave my fate and the fate of those I love, how can I leave the fate of the land itself in the hands of others? Even if those other hands belong to the gods themselves. But is it my pride that speaks, or something more practical, a small internal bookkeeper calculating his columns of credits and debts?

The candles dwindled down the glossy sheet of the Sar. Andrion leaned over the balcony after them. And suddenly the necklace of the moon and star lifted from his throat and tugged at him, as insistent as if it would drag him over the railing into the water and draw him, lit bright with his own uncertainty and decision, over the horizon to his fate.

Surprised, he laughed. When had he ever been favored with a sign when he needed one? But then, when had he ever waited for a sign before making a decision? No, he would not grow old and stale, forfeiting that daring that had won him an Empire. If he could not untangle this intricate plot that knotted around him, then he would cut it open.

And surely, surely, murmured the bookkeeper in his mind, the tug of the necklace meant that the Empire would be safe.

"I, too, shall go to Minras," he stated, to the lights, to the necklace, to that part of him squatted in sulky caution over its ledger scroll. ''The water in the sea is salt, but it is there that my thirst will be slaked.''

The necklace fell noiselessly back against his throat. The candles vanished. Their dancing colors were reflected in the stars above and in the star that trembled against his pulse, and never quite disappeared.

Chapter Five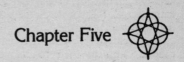

DANA GRASPED THE railing as the deck seemed to fall away from her feet. She thanked Ashtar that the journey was almost over; Minras was a glistening cloud on the horizon. I have probably become so accustomed to this awkward sea scuttle, she thought glumly, I will now be unable to walk on land.

Tembujin and Andrion gazed ahead, black hair and black cloak rippling. The string of the bow on Dana's shoulder sang in the wind; Tembujin's bow, unstrung, lay at his feet. And yet the wind was growing gusty, about to fail. The flesh pricked on the back of Dana's neck, and impatiently she shrugged the qualm away. Not yet, I cannot do anything yet. I must get there first.

Beside her Niarkos averred, "This has been a remarkably fast passage. Not that I ever came here before, my lord, but I believe that twenty days to Minras from Sardis is most unusual. A strong, fair wind made all the difference. She has flown like a crane."

Ah, yes, Dana thought. A ship was "she," for no discernible reason.

"Thanks be to, er—Harus," said Andrion, with a sage nod. The corner of his mouth crimped. Guiltily, Dana hoped, at denying Ashtar, guardian of the wind, her due. She glanced up at the taut sail, at the noon sky like polished silver, and back down at the water foaming past the great blue eyes painted upon the bow of the ship. Blue eyes; sailors were no fools.

"Odd," Tembujin said from her other side. "The—what did you call them, Admiral, dolphins?—are no longer riding the bow wave."

"Perhaps they do not want to come so close to land,"

Niarkos returned, with such heavy-handed nonchalance that both Dana and Andrion glanced sharply at him.

If Nikander was a great turtle, deliberate and laconic, his brother Niarkos was a sturdy sea lion, given to odd bellowings and pawings. He was upset that the dolphins had left; that much was clear.

Niarkos withdrew, leaving Andrion and Dana confronted with each other. Andrion, Dana thought—something about Andrion, some image gnawing the edge of her thought like a hungry rat. The breeze faltered, the air grew sultrier. Andrion wiped a brow shining with more than heat sweat. He had been reticent during the voyage, lighting with only an occasional flash of humor, fearing, apparently, that if he revealed anything of his worries he would reveal too much of his weakness. To me, Dana shouted in silent indignation at him, you are afraid of revealing yourself to me?

But she had to admit that neither had she been in an expansive mood. She had been feverish and snappish as her milk dried up, as she groped for images of the lost shield. Wherever the shield was, there, too, was Sumitra; she was sure of that. But her Sight was uncontrollable, and the vision that snapped sharp little teeth at her now came unbidden and unexpected.

Andrion's clear brow shone in the sunlight. She demanded, "Where did you leave the imperial diadem?"

His eyes widened in surprise. "I gave it to Patros to put on Harus's high altar, as Tembujin left his lion plaque with one of his nuryans. You were there, you saw."

"Yes, but . . ." She scowled; now that she wanted the image it pirouetted mockingly away. "I do not think it is there," she muttered lamely.

Tembujin made a quick dismissive gesture, impatient as always with manifestations of an otherworld he did not touch and therefore did not understand. No wonder he had spent most of the voyage playing interminable games of draughts with Niarkos and his officers as Andrion and Dana stalked about daring each other, daring anyone, to try and penetrate the carapaces they wore.

But now Andrion stared at Dana, believing her words without question, analyzing what could be done. And, of course, nothing could be done. His clenched fist hit the wooden railing; his other fist held the hilt of Solifrax so tightly his knuckles glinted white.

I should not have spoken, Dana berated herself. That warning was a javelin in his back. I should not have spoken.

Suddenly the sail flapped, spilling the wind, and with a heave that sent the three of them lurching together, the ship wallowed dead in the water. Niarkos shouted incomprehensible orders. The hovering gaggle of soldiers was overrun by stampeding sailors. If Miklos had been there instead of on Rhodope with the waiting legion, he would have told the soldiers in no uncertain terms to stay clear; Andrion, suddenly recalling how few retainers he had here, growled a reprimand.

The sail was quickly furled. Oars were produced, and under the walkway upon which Andrion, Dana, and Tembujin stood, the rowers took their places. A drum began to beat cadence, reverberating from the smooth dome of the sky. The wind whimpered.

Dana searched the eastern horizon; there, just breaking the surface of the sea, was a frail quarter moon. They had sailed away from Sardis under a full moon, across waves that had danced, light-spangled, in the wind. She had feared that perhaps they left the moon behind, but no, it had waned, disappeared, come again just as it did in Sabazel.

The name of Sabazel tightened her stomach and drew her shoulders up. If she had left Sabazel behind, so had she left Sardis and its chariots. Chariots had never seemed threatening before, but during the journey her vision had returned again and again; a fiery chariot, sketched in white heat, rushing down upon her.

Minras solidified from cloud into land, seeming more line than substance through its veil of bright haze. Its coast was tattered by boulders like cast-off teeth; its spine was a high serrated ridge, anchored on the far end by the faintest suggestion of stubby peak, on the near by a conical mountain from which a thread of gray smoke curled upward to stain the colorless sky.

"That," said Andrion.

"Yes," Dana sighed. "Yes, I have seen that mountain. I had thought it only a fancy. How can a mountain burn?"

Tembujin grimaced and shook his head.

The mouth of the harbor was a cleft between a promontory and a small island; yes, it was bracketed by two points of light that could well be gilded statues. Beyond it was a city—Orocastria, Niarkos had named it. Dana squinted into the sun's glare. Blocks of gray stone clambered up the steep slope from the harbor; green trees and vines, silvery now in winter, did little to soften the harsh contours of the island and its mountains. In places stony outcrops like razors sliced through city and field, as if reminding human interlopers that the rock had been there first, and suffered occupation with ill grace. And yet from this distance Orocastria seemed a prosperous and peaceful city, the harbor filled with boats and many insectlike figures toiling upon the docks.

Andrion's cloak shuddered in one last wheezing zephyr and lay still. His brown eyes, their flame carefully banked, seemed to Dana to scan the island as though his will alone could summon Sumitra from wherever she was hidden. Touching, Dana thought, how he went after her, how deeply he must care for her. Perhaps it was her submissiveness that appealed to him, or that she was not only a symbol of his reign but of his future realm. . . . Dana spat her musings into the sea as unworthy of them all.

"Gods!" exclaimed Niarkos at Dana's elbow. The statues beside the harbor were quite close now; huge striding golden bulls, wings unfurled, nostrils flaring at the scent of prey, sleekly sinewed shoulders and haunches the embodiment of haughty power. The tip of each curving horn was as sharp as a spear.

But they did not prod Niarkos into exclamation. Across the harbor mouth moved a galley, a behemoth with three banks of oars instead of one. The prow was a long, cruel battering ram. "I have heard rumors of such ships," Niarkos breathed. "I have heard that Minras rules the farther sea; perhaps it does. Look, the city has no walls. With ships like that it needs no walls."

"Would Minras perhaps like to rule the nearer sea?" Andrion asked under his breath.

The trireme vanished behind a statue. Nothing else moved except the slow, glassy waves and the smoke spiraling from the crest of the mountain. The city was silent behind the hazy glare. The drum beat cadence for the oars, and the oars splashed in unison, and the sea beat against the shore, rolling louder and louder.

"If we had been invited," exclaimed Niarkos, "they would have sent a pilot out to lead us in. The tide is changing, but . . ."

But? Dana asked herself, caught by more than Niarkos's apprehension. The mountain puffed out a graceful cloud of dust, accompanied by a low, distant rumble. Maybe it was the gods' smithy. A land wind shrieked past, carrying the stench of decomposing bodies and brimstone. Even as Dana gagged, another, more elusive, odor settled heavily on the back of her tongue. Sorcery.

Andrion tensed, if possible, even tighter. Tembujin's eyes narrowed, needing no supernal sensitivity to know that something was amiss.

The sea was oddly slick, humping into a great swell as if some giant sea creature swam just beneath the surface. The galley slipped up one side of the monster wave and then fell down the other, seeming barely to touch the water, oars flailing.

"Shore current," spat Niarkos, leaping into action.

The drum beat faster. Officers shouted. The rowers steadied and redoubled their efforts, but to no avail. Under the condescending eyes of the alien god, the ship was swept like one of Sardis's candles past the harbor mouth and down the coast toward the roots of the mountain. Buttress upon buttress of dark, scoriated rock loomed forbiddingly close, teasing, withdrawing, approaching again. The sea hurled itself against the jagged shore and burst into spray.

Dana clenched her teeth in a paroxysm of frustration; this is journey's end! This is our goal! We must come safely to shore!

Andrion's broad shoulder was against hers. His face wrestled with opposing expressions, now set indignantly, now wavering with fear. On her other side Tembujin muttered some profane litany in his own guttural tongue.

The water beneath the ship was glassy. For a moment Dana thought she would see right through the blue-green depths to the sea floor, littered with shards of rock and wood and bone that rolled ceaselessly to and fro. Blue-green depths like Astra's eyes. Astra, with her sweet red hair, her legacy stolen—if I do not win back the shield, I shall never embrace my daughter again!

Suddenly the sea seemed to tilt sideways. The ship lurched ponderously, lurched again, and like a scrap of flotsam began to spin. The deck heeled so steeply that Dana, Andrion, and Tembujin clutched desperately at the rail. With cries of fear

soldiers and seaman slipped and scrabbled down the slope of
the deck. Spray filled the air like thousands of tiny sharp
arrows.

"Whirlpool!" shouted Niarkos, clinging to a line at the
base of the mast. The drumbeats stopped abruptly. The rever-
beration of the sea continued the cadence, wave after wave
striking and shivering the planks of the ship. The sea piled into
a wall, mounting to giddy heights before Dana's unblinking,
salt-scummed, eyes. Spires of stone leaped from the swirling
water, clotted with foam like the teeth of a rabid dog. The tall
carved sternpost spun slowly, slowly about and shattered into
splinters against the rocks. A howl of despair rose from the
crew, but their voices were snatched away and devoured by
the roar of the sea.

Ashtar, Dana wailed silently, kill me if you must, but do
not taunt me with helplessness!

The mast snapped like a stick. The rail vanished from
Dana's hands. The men beside her disappeared. The deck fell
away, leaving her suspended for a moment in air and water
mingled into some new element. Then she fell, sliding on
droplets glinting with every color of the rainbow, into some
infinite depth.

Water warm as blood engulfed her, crushing her into a
hollow silence. Her bow was wrenched from her arm. She
fought, clawing with powerful strokes toward the surface—
but where was the surface? Her eyes were filled with a dark
green blur, all shadow, no reality. Her lungs labored, burning. Ashtar! her mind screamed, not now, not here, so far
from home and naked. . . .

Whorls of light spun before her. Her chest was bursting.
She broke the surface, spat, gasped, and was sucked back
under. Then kill me, Ashtar, even as I go about your bidding,
kill me! As if by a huge hand, she was plucked up and cast
onto a hot, abrasive surface.

Her eyes were filled with water and a glare of light. Her
mouth puckered with salt. Her ears rang with a hammering
drumbeat; it was the pounding of her own heart. Waves
sucked at her body and she heaved herself away from them.
Black rocks tore through her shirt and trousers into her flesh.

Andrion, Tembujin, Niarkos. She was alone. She couldn't
tell whether it was saltwater or blood in her mouth. Must get
up. She tried to rise. The land heaved as the water had, and

she fell back onto the rocks, clutching at them, dizzy. Must get up.

She inhaled, exhaled, inhaled. A miasma of rotten flesh filled her nose and she choked. A blurry shape moved in front of her. She squinted.

Andrion knelt just where the water met the land, braced on his arms, chest heaving. His cloak was gone and his wet chiton clung to his body, outlining every straining muscle. Thank the gods, then, Dana thought, for one favor. She pulled her sodden hair away from her face.

Niarkos wallowed in the surf, staggering, falling, crawling. He still held the line. No, what he was pulling behind him was Tembujin's long tail of hair. The Khazyari's body rolled with the waves, limp.

No, oh no! Dana gained her feet and stood swaying, defying the world to throw her down. Niarkos collapsed. Tembujin lay sprawled in the shallows, disappearing under a foamy wave, surfacing again.

The sea lion roused himself. He dragged Tembujin farther out of the water, dumped him among the rocks, and unceremoniously kneaded his chest and back. Tembujin sputtered, choked, retched, and croaked, "A horse, give me a horse, Khalingu take ships and sails and sea." He coughed rackingly.

Several other bedraggled figures crawled from the surf. Dark shapes, planks and men, rolled in the waves farther out. The gentle sea swell gave not the slightest hint of the whirlpool waiting to snare the unwary. Cursing would not help, Dana told herself. The gods disposed of men like pawns on a gameboard, damning or redeeming with cruel impartiality. She turned, walked one wary step at a time toward Andrion, and fell down beside him.

He was not dazed; his eyes were distressingly lucid. "Thank the gods you are alive, Dana," he wheezed, between lips drawn as tight as bowstrings.

She saw then that the clasp on his belt that had held the sheath of Solifrax was torn open. His sword, his father's sword, had been swallowed by the sea. His hands clenched and opened and clenched again, and at last his fingers grasped the necklace jouncing in the pulse at his throat.

She spoke without thinking. "So. Now you know how I feel."

"I have always known how you feel," he snapped.

"How could you?"

Tembujin threw himself down, yelped as a rock ground into some tender spot and said, "God's talons! Do not start quarreling now."

"We are not quarreling," Dana and Andrion chimed in unison.

Niarkos lumbered up and down the beach. He collected the living men, counted casualties, hurled an occasional epithet at the waves that tossed smashed bits of ship and crew onto the beach as carelessly as a kitchen maid throwing away garbage.

Tembujin roused himself and tallied the survivors, reporting acidly that Andrion's company had been reduced to an ignominious force of two soldiers and five sailors, armed only with the daggers still belted to Tembujin's waist and Dana's thigh. "Without a ship," Andrion concluded, "we cannot send to Rhodope if the Minrans prove hostile. And Miklos's orders were to wait a month before coming after us. The game begins in earnest now."

"The game has never ended," Dana returned.

With an abrupt scramble, Andrion stood and braced himself, hands on hips. He offered Dana a nod and a smile, strained at the edges, incongruous between the angry jut of his chin and the embers glowing in his eyes, but a smile nonetheless.

Dana recognized his attitude; it had been hers outside the Horn Gate of Sabazel. He wanted no commiseration over the loss of the sword, as she had wanted none over the loss of the shield. If he could smile, so could she, and she did. If only the wind would carry away the terrible stench that clogged her nose and throat, but here, in the lee of the mountain, no wind blew.

Niarkos stood to attention, sparing himself nothing, to accept his reprimand. Shameful, not only to lose one's ship but to strand one's emperor in the losing. "I am responsible, my lord."

"You could have changed nothing," Andrion reassured him. "You did what you could." The admiral nodded, stoic in the face of devastation, ready to shoulder the next task.

Andrion strode from man to man, making sure that those injured upon the rocks were properly bandaged. With a few terse, tight gestures and phrases he organized them into some semblance of order. Just as they turned toward the city, a solitary man appeared around a pier of rocks ahead. At the sight of the bedraggled company he turned and ran. "All right then," said Andrion. "The dice are cast." Moments later several guards wearing pleated kilts and leather caps burst from the stones waving long, leaf-bladed spears.

Dana quelled her body's jerk backward and the itch on her feet that urged her to run. Run where? she asked herself. This place is far from home. Too far.

"Ah, a welcoming party at last," Tembujin said brightly, and deflected Dana's glare with a toss of his lank hair.

The soldiers were not as large as average Sardian legionaries, but their spears were quite businesslike. Their leader was a dark, hawk-nosed individual identified by the emblem of a winged bull upon his cap. He jostled with Niarkos, asserting his control in a thick but not incomprehensible version of the common tongue, and was surprised when the burly admiral deferred to a much younger man. This youth was a head taller than he; he scowled with annoyance.

Andrion's scowl was barely contained by his own stubborn dignity. With a sarcastically gracious wave of his hand he allowed the guard to lead. As the glowering man marched them off, Andrion set a pace slow enough to irritate him, fast enough that he had no grounds for complaint.

The company trudged past the pier and were engulfed in a miasma of death. Choking, Dana asked herself, do these people leave their dead to rot upon the beach? But it was no charnel house. Low buildings were spaced around a series of vats, and huge hills of dried, empty shells lined the path. Workmen looked curiously up, intrigued by the tall, trousered woman and the high-planed features of the Khazyari. To a man their arms and hands were dyed Rexian purple. Purple, she thought; was she remembering some vague image or foreseeing it?

"So," exclaimed Niarkos. "Here is the home of the famous dye. I never knew it was made from rotten shellfish."

"Beauty from death," Andrion added. "Somehow I am not surprised."

"And has the wind carried this reek all the way to Iksandarun?" demanded Tembujin.

"That would not surprise me either."

The soldiers led them around a buttress of tortured rock, and blessedly, a light, fitful breeze greeted them, sweeping away the stench. With good reason, Dana told herself, were the dye works downwind of the city.

They scrambled up a road edged with aromatic cypresses which whispered secretively among themselves, passing from odd translucent shadow to odd hazy light and back. Then, around another corner, the path became a flagstoned street and the city opened before them.

The avenue was lined with tall gray houses, each sprouting myriad tiny pillars along its facade. Windows and doors and alleys gazed expressionlessly at the passing company. Her sandals crunched on the pavement, and Dana saw that the houses were gray because every surface was dusted with ash. From the smoking mountain, perhaps? And stranger still, more than one building had been thrust askew, as though the island were a great beast that had shaken itself. Tidy piles of brick and pillars awaited repair. But the street was empty, market stalls abandoned, carts left riderless.

Then voices, rising and falling in some liturgical response, echoed down a puff of wind. The bellowing of bulls was suddenly loud among the walls, as if the animals themselves were about to come bursting around the corner, tossing pass-ersby on the sharp tips of their horns.

Bulls bellowing. Dana blanched and her steps faltered. Andrion set his hand firmly in the hollow of her back and bore her along.

The bellows ceased. Music, played on a reed flute, danced along the breeze. And it was Andrion whose head went up, whose cheeks blanched. "Tembujin," he said tightly, "does that melody not sound familiar?"

The Khazyari's eyes narrowed into black slits. "Indeed. In Iksandarun, just as Ethan and Ursbei and I entered the city gate, moments before we were attacked. To signal, I daresay, that the sacrificial animals approached."

"Even Sardis no long sacrifices human beings," replied Andrion. "Not on the altar, at least." The guard made some signal as if to tell them to stop talking, but his gesture withered, scorched by the flicker in Andrion's eyes.

They emerged onto a viaduct. To one side, toward the smooth, glinting water of the harbor, an arena was carved into the hillside. Here was the population of Orocastria, tier upon tier of olive faces looking eagerly toward something on the floor of the arena, something concealed behind a huge garlanded slab of rock. No wonder the streets were empty.

Dana faltered again, her visions becoming too real, too fast. "Of course you saw this place," Andrion whispered in her ear. "Have we ever doubted that? Just remember that not all your visions are true ones."

I should not need him to tell me that, she reminded herself scornfully. She strode on, shoulders square and stiff.

At the end of the viaduct was an edifice that could only be a palace. It commanded the crest of the hill into which the arena was carved; several balconies and terraces overlooked the arena itself. A jumble of windows, pillared corridors, and floor levels layered like some exotic sweetmeat clung around massive pillars of stone. The red, yellow, and blue paint of ornate frescoes shone bravely through their patina of dust and ash.

The company passed under a gateway crowned by great, curving horns. Another Horn Gate, Dana reflected; the horns of a bull, not of a crescent moon. She wondered if here in Minras lingered some memory of the old beliefs that predated even Sabazel, the beliefs predicated on the savage animal powers. Some of those beliefs had expressed themselves in repellent rites; how could one of those ancient queens commit herself to her king and then sacrifice him, turning her vows inside out? But then, she would have thought her commitment was to a greater purpose. . . .

Dana caught one last glimpse of the sea—an alien element, but her only route home. The interior of the palace was damp and chill. The hallway turned, turned again, passed several shadowed frescoes of sea creatures and ships. It burst into a garden, plunged into dimness, ran through a large room or two and then, against a rough stone wall, stuttered off into three separate passages. The guard took the center way. Dana felt smothered, closed in a sarcophagus that no matter how elaborate still reeked of death.

Suddenly they were in a large, airy room that at first appeared to have no ceiling. Squinting upward, Dana saw balconies piled one upon another, their railings thickets of pillars that scrambled as high as the painted roof beams. Each story must have had windows, for the room was quite light, and yet it, too, was hazy, an oddly familiar scent lying heavy on the still air. A throne room, then, or a temple, or both.

How galling, thought Dana, for the emperor, the khan, the heir to Sabazel, to arrive bruised and disheveled, herded like pitiful supplicants before the ruler of Minras. Whoever that

was. Instinctively she drew herself up, as did Andrion and
Tembujin as they strode across the dizzyingly complex patterns of the tiled floor. The leading guard made impatient
shooing motions at them, but they swept by him and approached the center of the room where they stood in a frieze
of defiant caution.

Here was a stone basin, set about with four pillars. Another
set of carved horns stood on one rim, reflected in the water
within. Dana was reminded again of Sabazel, of Ashtar's
basin and pool. She craned forward, wondering if this water,
too, bore a message.

A reflection of the horns, and of her own face peering in,
and of a chair encompassed with carved wings. Then the
water swirled, and her head swirled with it, her thought
caught and yanked away by a snaky tendril of alarm.

Dana saw Andrion's eye glinting almost as brightly as
Tembujin's. Then she saw the woman whose sudden appearance from behind the throne had so ensnared their attention.
She came forward, leaned over the water, and stirred it with
the tip of a beringed finger round and round into a whirlpool.
She looked up, firing a calculating glance from beneath dark,
even brows. Her eyes were shifting depths of blue and violet.
Drowned eyes, Dana thought. The mysterious fullness of the
sea, the command of wind and wave . . . No! her mind
howled indignantly. No one has that power save Ashtar!

The woman laughed. A gesture dismissed the guards, who
hustled Niarkos and the others away. The stentorian voice of
the admiral, keeping his men orderly, was swallowed by the
maze of corridors.

The woman rose, glided back to the throne and sat upon it,
arranged flounced skirts around her, and leaned back with her
arms comfortably splayed upon the wings. "Greeting," she
said. "I am Chrysais, Queen of Minras." Her voice was
honey seeping from a repleted hive, lightly accented.

As though drawn by a thread, Andrion, Tembujin, and
Dana stepped closer. Not one pair of eyes blinked. Incense
billowed from hidden censers.

Chrysais's gleaming chestnut hair was coiled in intricate
waves and tendrils, clasped by golden clips. Her eyes were
outlined in kohl, her cheeks rouged, her lips painted the color
of crushed berries; her face was an unblemished mask, worn
thin at the corners of the mouth and eyes by an underlying

intensity. The open bodice of her gold and purple dress displayed full, round breasts. They, too, were rouged. She laughed again, low and throaty, glorying in her power.

Dana wrenched herself away, feeling the same gut-searing lust as the men, permitting none of it. The woman is no better than a whore, she thought, outraged, to flaunt her charms so brazenly.

And she thought that if Chrysais did sell herself, it would be for more than a few coins. Much more. The way she had stirred the water in the basin, gloating . . . Suddenly Dana recognized the heady aroma of lethenderum, a drug that could weaken the reserve and induce visions.

Andrion cleared his throat. "Greetings," he said. His voice approached its usual timbre and seized upon it. "Does the Queen of Minras usually receive castaways?"

"No," Chrysais purred. "But then, you only appear to be castaways."

"Khalingu," muttered Tembujin, recovering himself with a deep exhalation, "I could have sworn we were shipwrecked."

Dangling amethyst earrings swayed as she smiled. Amethyst and faience necklaces sparkled upon her breast. "Tembujin, Khan of Khazyaristan. Dana of Sabazel. And you," she said to Andrion, "who claim to be the son of Marcos Bellasteros, King of Sardis, Emperor."

"Claim?" repeated Andrion, squeezing the word between his teeth.

"Some secrets are not kept as well as you so fondly believe. It is well known, for example, that Sabazians take many lovers and marry none."

Dana bridled; Danica could have saved herself and Sabazel much pain if she had pretended Andrion was another man's son. At least Chrysais made a direct lunge, not the feint Dana would have expected of one so . . . feminine.

Chrysais acknowledged with only a pleased twitch of her mouth the Sabazian who squirmed like a stranded fish before her.

Andrion's hand closed on empty air at his side, groping for the hilt that was not there, but his words were so firm they seemed to clear the cloying smoke. "Can you look at me and deny that I am Bellasteros's son?"

Chrysais leaned forward. Her arms pressed her breasts together, forcing a muffled growl from Tembujin's throat, and her tongue passed slowly between her lips. Her blue gaze peeled away Andrion's even features, the lambent darkness of his eyes, the lean lines of his body, and evaluated the tension between pride and doubt that strengthened the very core of his being. "No," she said, perhaps gratified, perhaps disappointed. "No, I cannot deny that you are his son."

She had only been testing him. Dana seethed. Her mind simmered. In its steam she wondered if Chrysais had also been testing herself, trying the strength of a blood tie. Blood rites, she thought suddenly. Damned lethenderum.

Tembujin found something very interesting in a corner of an upper balcony, always appreciative of Andrion discomfited, not about to comment on such discomfiture before a stranger.

Andrion smiled, thin as a blade, ordering Chrysais to speak.

"And to what do I owe the honor of this visit?" the woman asked.

Briefly Andrion told the story of Rue, Sumitra, and the shield, but stopped short of mentioning that Solifrax, too, was gone. He did not ask for help.

"Someone hides behind the god of Minras, it seems," replied Chrysais, her lashes veiling her eyes in an expression that was probably intended to be complacent, but was not. "Such impertinence. I shall help you find what was lost, if I can."

You can, Dana wanted to scream. She confined herself to a truculent grumble. You rule here. I see much of Bellasteros in you, too, and little of gentle Chryse.

Chrysais eyed Dana. Her nostrils flared either with amusement or with a bad smell, or both. She stood, summoned courtiers with a clap of her hands, and delivered a series of orders dealing with food, lodging, clothing. She turned in dismissal. Hastily Andrion, trying to prolong the interview, said, "My sympathies on the death of your husband—sister." Dana noticed his emphasis. Good. He was not too smitten with her, ah, charms.

Chrysais's back was to them. Very slightly her spine stiffened. "Thank you," she said, and she was gone.

Servants waited, bowing and scraping. Tembujin shook himself and asked from the side of his mouth, "Are we guests or prisoners?"

"It is hard to tell, is it not?" Dana snapped. She was flooded with relief at Chrysais's departure; she was resentful at being relieved.

But Andrion was staring into the mirrored surface of the basin of water. "She knows too much. The swirling water, now, and lethenderum . . ." Suddenly he chuckled, relieved in turn, almost admitting bewilderment. "Come. Let us make sure Niarkos and the men are cared for, and then lay what plans we can." His voice cut off the sentence like an executioner's sword decapitates a victim.

They followed the servants back into the labyrinth. The air was as dank and still as if they wound deeper and deeper into the entrails of a giant beast.

Chapter Six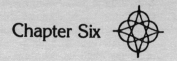

ANDRION HOPED HE sounded calm and confident. But he doubted
that he was fooling anyone. His head seemed to float several
handsbreadths above his shoulders and his loins tingled; the
effects of lethenderum and Chrysais, no doubt. And he had
expected another meek sparrow like Chryse.

Chrysais was altogether too much like Bellasteros. Or like
their father had been when young, veneered by arrogant
bravura. And yet Chrysais, at twelve years older than Andrion,
was no longer a youth. She had had ample time to learn new
skills; her swirling of the water in the basin was suggestive,
horribly suggestive. . . . His thought fractured and spun away
tauntingly.

The servants led them into blessedly free air, to a terrace
overlooking the arena. The evening sun melded sky and sea
into one seamless cloth of gold. The quarter moon hung
disdainfully high overhead. The arena was now a bowl of
twilight, but still the faces watched, enthralled.

Andrion paused by a colonnade. Here on the terrace it was
pleasantly warm, but a chill breath wafted upward from the
arena. Upon it rode not only the husky music of reed flute
and pipes, but tantalizingly, a scent of roasting meat. No
wonder he was light-headed, Andrion told himself; he was
hungry. Tembujin smacked his lips, and Dana essayed a wary
inhalation.

A mound of bone and flesh, one of the bellowing bulls no
doubt, lay on the huge garlanded stone. Next to it were
several smaller mounds. Calves? Andrion wondered. The
altar was surrounded by flaming cressets; in their light one
solitary human figure moved, the focus of hundreds of eyes.

Andrion squinted through the sun sheen into dimness, where
the small torches were preternaturally bright. The figure that

danced around them, weaving light and shadow into an intricate pattern, was so lithe and slender that at first he thought it was a woman. But Dana's sudden exhalation, almost a moan, signaled him to think again.

Yes, the angle of the limbs, the forcefulness of the gestures, were masculine. He was, on this island of dark faces, blond. His hair was held by a thin golden fillet, his beard was neatly trimmed. He wore only a belt, a codpiece, and an assortment of jeweled necklaces and bracelets which winked like laughing eyes as he spun, leaped, doubled back, and spun again. The fires around him flared. His body was gilded in their light, too perfect to be human, a living work of art.

The sun set, and darkness devoured Minras. The flute coiled about a minor key, climbed, slipped downward in a smooth glide. The man danced. Tembujin watched mesmerized. Andrion could have sworn the ground beneath his feet moved.

This was too much. He locked his knees against the wobble, groped for the hilt of Solifrax, and cursed himself for once again succumbing to that habit. So that, Andrion thought with a sideways glance at Dana, is what it feels like to be moved by one's own sex.

She turned abruptly away, her lower lip caught by her teeth; nauseated, he realized, not by the odor of roasting meat but by the other scents flirting with the wind, blood and a hint of masculine musk. He raised his hand toward her and then dropped it, warned by the glint of her slitted green eyes.

The servants were hovering. Andrion targeted the nearest. "Is that dancer the high priest?"

"Yes. King Eldrafel."

"King?" Andrion repeated incredulously. "Wait a moment—"

Tembujin's elbow jabbed his ribs. "Look, look there."

With an annoyed snort Andrion looked. On the terrace below, a woman stood clutching at a railing much as Andrion himself had clutched at the railing of Niarkos's ship. She swayed in the rhythm of the dance, almost swooning. Her ecstatic features were harshly illuminated by a torch.

"I do believe," said Tembujin, his voice spewing venom, "that that is our wives' treacherous serving woman, Rue."

"Rue!" Dana strained over their own railing. "Yes, yes it is!"

Aware eyes were upon her, the woman looked up. Something about the shape of the chin, and the curious liquid eyes; she reminded Andrion of someone, and the resemblance was vital. . . . He grimaced in frustration. Perhaps he had seen her without knowing her, in Sardis or in Iksandarun, but that thought was queasily unconvincing.

Dana hissed and lunged forward, as if she would leap over the railing then and there. Andrion's hand closed on a handful of shirt and hair. "We are not in a position to act. Wait. We know now she is here."

"You sound more like Nikander every day," Dana growled, but she desisted.

At that moment someone burst out onto the lower terrace. It was Chrysais, her flounced skirts swirling, her elaborate coiffure trembling. Her sultry voice was edged now, and her words floated fitfully upward in counterpoint to the music. ". . . told you to go . . . must be cared for . . . dithering around here . . ." She shoved Rue away, toward the interior of the palace.

The woman staggered against a pillar and turned a sullen face upon the queen. "Go!" shouted Chrysais, stamping her foot. Rue fled.

Chrysais's entourage, an assortment of plainly dressed women, stood together like a flock of frightened sheep. As Bonifacio's acolytes had huddled, Andrion thought for no apparent reason.

The music stopped. Eldrafel was gone. The cressets guttered, as if his presence alone had been their fuel. Several robed figures moved toward the sacrificial meat, and the populace began to file from their seats. The servant at Andrion's back shifted his feet and cleared his throat.

"All right then," Andrion told him, "all right."

He and Tembujin and Dana were led to a suite of rooms. Andrion inquired after Niarkos and the others, was told they had been cared for, and then dismissed the servants. Tembujin and Dana stalked silently away, each craving the privacy to curse or weep or throw crockery against the wall, or perhaps all three at once. Andrion found that image quite tempting.

But when he was alone he simply stood, bowed under tormenting thought. Sumitra must be close at hand, but how and when could he find her? He did not even have the cryptic light of Solifrax to guide him. The sword was gone; his body had been flensed of its power. The diadem that he had abandoned was in danger, the Empire he had neglected was— Wait.

I have never been without power, he told himself. I shall not be so now, even in this bizarre world sensed with the viscera, not the mind. I shall untangle this snarled skein, with or without the sword, and I shall come again to Sardis and the diadem.

Impatiently he broke through the introspection that lurked in the darker corners of his mind like mist gathered above a marsh, and found himself in a luxuriously appointed chamber.

The walls were painted with rosettes, waving fronds, and octopi that seemed to swim in the wavering light of an oil lamp. An alcove held a large bathtub, steaming with scented water; not lethenderum, Andrion established with a wary sniff, but something heavier. Plugged terra-cotta pipes emerged from the wall at the head of the tub, providing water from roof cisterns which was then heated by a charcoal fire beneath. Very tidy, he thought.

A contraption set into a wall turned out to be a built-in chamber pot, flushed by another pipe into a system of guttering. Quite clever. Something like that could be installed in the palaces in Sardis and Iksandarun. . . . Andrion almost laughed out loud at being distracted by such homely details.

He discarded his torn chiton, stained leather belt, and sandals, and clad in only the necklace, eased himself into the warm water. A bronze razor and mirror lay on a stool nearby. His kingship stemmed from his heart, but a decent outward appearance never hurt.

Sumitra, he mused. Chrysais. Rue. Eldrafel, the priest-king. He was too old to be the son Patros had thought Gath and Chrysais had had. But she styled herself queen, not consort or regent, and spoke with the assurance of a reigning monarch.

His hand slipped. A drop of blood ran down his chin and swirled across the water like a tiny serpent. The lamplight in the main room flickered as someone entered, and judging by a clatter and an odor of bread, laid down a tray of food. Footsteps, and the door clicked shut.

Chrysais stood beside him. In spite of himself he started violently. Like a vision, nightmarish or otherwise he had yet to decide, she kept reappearing. He laid down the razor and mirror and considered incoherently if the sponge floating beside him was large enough to conceal anything.

But Chrysais's cool blue eyes had already swept him up and down, appraising his body like a mollusk torn from its shell for her dinner. She touched his necklace.

One side of her mouth shivered, pleased. She seated herself upon the stool and leaned forward. A slow, deep breath emphasized the magnificence of her bosom. "So, little brother! You have grown up!"

"Most of us do, eventually." Andrion commanded his only too mortal flesh to remain quiescent—she is your sister, for Harus's sake!—and continued, "To what do I owe the honor of this visit?"

"I thought a private interview would be in order." The rest of her mouth smiled. Andrion saw that she wore a sardonyx amulet, a figure of some kind, not a bull, just peeking from the valley between her breasts. Surrounded by warm ivory skin and the scent of . . . that was it—the lush scent of lotus.

He managed to keep his eyes from crossing. He propped his feet on the far rim of the tub and clasped his hands casually on his chest. He noted that the ceiling, too, was painted. "Tell me . . ."

"No, you tell me."

His brows tightened at her peremptory tone.

"What of Sardis? Do they still throw their daughters onto rubbish heaps?"

So she did remember her ill-fated younger sister. "Such practice has been banned for years, but it happens upon occasion."

"Do they still hide their women behind veils and sell them like cattle at auction?"

"I would not use quite those terms. . . ." Yes, you would. Andrion slipped down until his chin touched the water. You can learn more by listening, he informed himself.

Her voice poured over him. "I was but thirteen when I was sold to Gath. Sold to further Bellasteros's ambitions, to gain him a toehold in the Great Sea. He could not know the Empire would have to be won back from barbarian invaders, and it would be his son who would cast his eye farther afield."

Yes, certainly; he made quite a conqueror, naked and alone. "I believe Bellasteros's councilors urged him to send you to Gath. But it was your choice in the end, was it not?"

"Children," Chrysais said, "can be beguiled by rank and riches, especially when urged by their elders. My dear mother just had to make of me a ruler's wife."

"To some that is a great honor."

"Pah. Meek little sparrow that she was, no spirit, no courage."

Nettled, Andrion said, "If you so scorned her kind of spirit and courage, if you did not want to marry, you could have asked the protection of Sabazel."

"Sabazel!" Her eyes flashed, hard and bright as sapphire.

Ah, he thought, that struck home.

"Women hiding in a hole, preening themselves with their pitiful strength. Danica sold herself to Bellasteros for a morsel of power, just as surely as he sold me to Gath. But only men have real power, Andrion. You know that."

Not necessarily, he told himself, but he said nothing.

"Gath was not a large man," she said, the honey in her voice turned rancid, "but was a brute nonetheless. I was just a child, unbelievably innocent. He split me open like a melon and left me crying while he went to drink with his cronies. So much for the honor of a ruler's wife."

Andrion winced. No wonder she chose to name herself queen.

"I bore him a son, as he demanded. And it was I who gained him the farther sea." Her face clouded, but the shadow was gone as soon as Andrion noticed it. Probably a trick of the light. "Much good that having a son did him. On Minras the succession goes to the king's sister's son, not his own son."

"Ah," said Andrion. "Then Eldrafel—"

Chrysais seized his arm where it lay on the rim of the tub. Her grip was so tight it wrung the dampness from his skin. "How do you know that name?"

So she knows much of me, Andrion told himself, but intends for me to know nothing of her. "We saw him dancing in the arena. The servant told us his name."

"Talkative slaves find themselves—" She sat back and closed her eyes, contemplating an appropriate punishment.

Slave? "I asked him," asserted Andrion. And freed of the sapphire beacons, he hazarded, "You made Gath's nephew Eldrafel your new husband?"

"You are quick," she muttered.

Andrion grinned. "Not as quick as you to remarry, it seems."

Oddly, she did not bridle, but chuckled under her breath, moist as two willow branches rubbing together.

"I beg your pardon," said Dana loudly from the doorway. "I did not realize you were entertaining a visitor, Andrion."

Chrysais concealed her surprise very well. She shook back her hair, stood, smoothed her skirts. The blue eyes met the green ones and in a brief sharp skirmish struggled for dominance. Both women abandoned the battle at the same moment, nothing concluded.

Chrysais kissed Andrion's forehead, letting her nipples brush his shoulder. "Welcome, brother, to Minras." She turned a frosted smile upon Dana. Dana bared her teeth in an expression nothing like a smile, and did not relent until Chrysais was gone.

Andrion accepted a goblet of wine from Dana's hand and gulped it eagerly. It was so sweet it intensified the lingering taste of rot in his mouth. Perhaps Chrysais's lips tasted like that. With a shudder of both lust and revulsion he washed the stains of red paint from his skin and heaved himself out of the water.

"You have been soaking so long you look like a potted fig," Dana said. "Come, Tembujin has found the food, and I fear he will leave little for us."

Andrion wished he could smooth the furrows from her face. But he was drained of will and strength; his thoughts reeled like Eldrafel dancing, dark to light, light to dark. Silently he wrapped himself in a loose robe and followed her from the room.

Chrysais walking alone through the palace galleries was like any five other women walking in procession. Servants bowed, hooded priests raised their hands in respect, guards saluted. She ignored them all, the mask of her face iced with thought, her eyes splinters of corundum.

She brushed past two guards into a sumptuous bedchamber. Several servants tended to a supine Eldrafel, scraping his back, trimming his nails, combing his hair. They looked up at Chrysais's precipitate entrance, petrified in mid-gesture. All except Eldrafel himself, who lay, eyes closed, naked limbs draped not softly over the pillows but coiled like wires.

Chrysais snarled, and the servants scattered. Eldrafel did not move. "Well?" he prompted, voice muffled.

"The Khazyari is exotic meat, but powerless, I feel. Andrion is a proper little prig, and that Sabazian basilisk with him."

The crisp gray eyes opened, considered Chrysais's knotted fists, closed again. "I should not underestimate Andrion's intelligence."

"No. Neither shall I underestimate his power."

The eyes opened again. Eldrafel propped his chin on his hands. "Power? He knows something of sorcery?"

"He wears a necklace, a crescent moon with a star at its tip, that murmurs very faintly." She paced across the tile floor to where a chest squatted beyond the light ring of the hanging lamp. From it she removed a cloth-wrapped bundle. "I cannot understand," she muttered, resuming an argument abandoned without conclusion, "why it took you so much longer to sail from Sardis. They have arrived right on your heels. I thought we would have more time."

"Winds," Eldrafel said. "Foul for us, fair for them. I expected such." He stretched. If he had been a cat, he would have exercised his claws.

"Winds are winds," spat Chrysais.

"Are they?" He sat up. "Bring it here."

She brought the bundle to the bed and laid it down. She laid herself down, draping herself over Eldrafel's back, her arms like vines twining about his torso. He did not notice, intent upon the object he held.

The wrappings fell away. The shield of Sabazel covered his knees. His fingertips traced a slow spiral around the emblazoned star, stirring the metal like clay to be shaped to his will. But the shield lay dull and cold, its rim seeming to shrink from the male body leaning over it.

"See," said Chrysais, her cheek against Eldrafel's shoulder, "it is as I told you, reluctant to reveal its power."

His polished nails, like opals, drummed upon the metal. It emitted a remote tinny jangle. "Yet it bears great power," he mused. And he laughed. "It reserves its strength, does it not? It does not like me. It does not like you."

Chrysais's lower lip thrust itself out. "I see nothing amusing. I have gone to a great deal of trouble to gain this artifact, and it will not perform!"

"Now, now," Eldrafel whispered. He tweaked one of her curls and pulled the sardonyx figure from her bosom. It was a tiny statue of himself. In its place he left an open-mouthed kiss. Chrysais's eyelids fluttered, an addict savoring her favorite drug, and she tightened her grasp upon him.

He slipped through her fingers, left the bed and reached into a giant vase, one of two guarding a small stairway mounting into the darkest corner of the room. From it he pulled another bundle. "Look," he announced. "See what Captain Jemail found among the sea wrack upon the shore! He actually had enough wit to bring it to me." Eldrafel plucked the cloth away. It was Solifrax, the snakeskin sheath shining in tiny ripples of light as though it had never tasted saltwater.

With a squeal of excitement Chrysais leaped up. "I knew he brought it with him. He kept reaching for its hilt at his belt. But I did not think it wise to ask."

"No, not wise at all. Not yet." Eldrafel drew the sword. The crystalline blade gleamed with reflected lamplight. He considered it a moment and queried softly of himself, "Why this roughness on the steel, I wonder, like a drop of acid leaving an etched trail?"

Chrysais approached. He pirouetted, avoiding her outstretched hands. He grinned, flourished the sword, and playfully menaced her, tickling her throat and lifting her skirts with the blade.

Her breast heaved. "Let me see it. Let me touch it. The blood of Bellasteros flows in my veins, and it will wake to me!"

Eldrafel tossed Solifrax onto the bed.

She snatched it up. It gleamed with reflected light, not its own. Its metal was cold, ice cold, and her hot breath fogged it but did not warm it. It seemed to turn in her hands, its keen edge biting her fingertips. With a curse she dropped the blade and sat, a huddle of flounces and jewels and rage, sucking her injured fingers.

Eldrafel snickered. "It tastes your blood and finds it tainted." He dressed, picked up the sword, sheathed it. He laid it against the shield, listening closely, probing them both with his hands, eyes narrowed. Nothing. With a shrug he wrapped them together in the cloth and turned toward the door.

"Where are you going?" wailed Chrysais. "We have been so long separated, my love!"

Eldrafel glanced at her over his shoulder, not quite focusing on her. "Only a moment, dearest. I want to leave these with someone who can perhaps stir them to life, and our service."

"The little brown dove?" Chrysais sneered.

His eyes focused. "He followed her—despite his better judgment, I daresay. He must be besotted with his own wife." And that, too, amused him. "She was most distressed when I took the shield from her this morning. She will be even more distressed to find that it now has a companion." His mirrored gaze at last touched his wife's flushed face, drawing the blood from her cheeks. "Surely you can amuse yourself until I return."

"Indeed," she said with a sigh. "I believe so."

The door shut behind Eldrafel. Chrysais rose, straightened her garments, lifted several skeins of yarn from a basket on a nearby table. The threads lay smooth on her palm, black and gold, purple and red. With her fingertip she twisted and tangled them. Her lips parted with the assurance of power, and her eyes lit with a slow, hot flame. She started up the stairway, toward a door concealed in onyx shadow.

The strands of yarn moved by themselves, coiling up her arms like hunting cobras.

One wing of the palace clambered up to and then stopped dead at a mighty buttress of rock. In some remote time passages had been cut into the living stone, leading to tiny chambers with even tinier windows which overlooked the city and the harbor.

In the largest of the rough-hewn rooms Sumitra stared at the tray of food. She had tried to eat, for the sake of the child, at least, but the poppy-seed cakes and goat cheese stuck in her throat, gritty as the ashes that drifted in the window and covered everything with a fine pall.

She left the oil lamp on the table and peered once again out the window. The night was dark. Only a few lights glinted in the city, and the sea was invisible, just a suggestion of shimmering movement in the corner of the eye. A dim moon and even dimmer stars barely broke the expanse of a sky that hung heavy over the island, a black drape threatening to fall and smother all life upon it.

Sumitra shook away her qualm. She should be grateful; they had come at last to land, two—no three—nights ago now. Barely able to walk, she had been guided by Eldrafel's surprisingly strong arms to an ox cart and carried away like the bundle of trade goods she evidently was. She did not even know the name of this land, but she had her suspicions. Rhodope, perhaps, although that was an ally of Sardis; perhaps distant Minras itself.

If so, Andrion's sister Chrysais was here, and might help. Or might not. Sumi had seen enough palace intrigue in her girlhood to be wary of relatives.

She had seen . . . Her mind crawled, haunted by the image of a Sardian galley approaching the harbor mouth. She had watched from the narrow balcony outside her cell, her hands clasped in hope, and then in terror as the ship was taken aback and spun away down the coast, to disappear so quickly around the jagged base of the mountain that she wondered if she had hallucinated it.

No, she had seen a ship. Logically, it had carried only an embassy—she was but a wife, after all, not an important asset of the Empire. . . .

The bar across the door behind her slid back. She turned. Eldrafel stood in the opening, bearing an irregularly shaped bundle, smiling.

During their long journey—a month on that cursed ship— she had grown to hate his smile. It was so attractive that one tended not to notice it touched his lips only and was never reflected in his eyes. His eyes indulged in a different humor entirely, taunting her with innocuous questions but demanding nothing. She would have felt less uneasy if he had demanded something.

Stiffly, she asked, "Did you bring it back?"

"You have appointed yourself guardian of the shield belonging to your husband's mistress? How touching."

Sumitra felt her cheeks grow hot. Uncanny, how the man could find a scab and pick at it. Even if he were not quite correct; it was Ilanit's shield, not Dana's, not yet. And Dana was hardly Andrion's—well, she was his lover, but only at certain times. He had known Dana all his life. . . . Sumi could only hope that in the dimness Eldrafel would not notice her blush. But he did, and his smile broadened. He threw down the bundle and left. Why did he return the shield? Because it would not shine for him?

Better to hate him than be frightened by him, Sumitra concluded. She bent to retrieve the package and started back. The shield, yes, and something else. Her hands, suddenly cold, fumbled at the wrappings.

She crouched over Solifrax. Trembling, she drew it and stroked the blade marred by Andrion's blood as if it were Andrion's living flesh. He had come after her. He had been on that ship. No one else would have his sword, no one could have taken it from him, except by . . .

Her mind veered. She pursued the thought, horrible as it was, and forced herself to contemplate it. She saw Andrion drowned, saw him transfixed by leaf-bladed spears, saw him slaughtered like a sacrificed bullock at Eldrafel's feet.

Tears welled in her eyes and dropped onto Solifrax. The blade hissed, turning each droplet into a multicolored cloud. Was it trying to reassure her? Andrion had come after her, drawn by a proud anger at the theft of his woman, drawn by love. . . . She sniffed, wiped her eyes, and stroked the sword again. It sighed contentedly under her hand, not unlike Andrion himself. Sparks floated from its tip and danced across the surface of the shield. The many-pointed star twinkled. Sword and shield together chimed, not in unison, but in a chord, faint but resonant.

Sumitra hastily sheathed the sword and covered the shield. She glanced toward the door. Its blank face stared back at her.

She laid the weapons carefully down, fitting the concave side of the sword against the rim of the shield. It was a perfect fit. That was a bit discomforting, in and of itself, but she tightened her lips, raised her chin and said quietly to them both, "Well, I would serve Ilanit and Dana and little Astra rather than Eldrafel any day. That I cannot doubt."

And neither would she doubt that Andrion was still alive and close at hand, and would in time come to her. Alone, or with an army, or with only Tembujin—and yes, Dana would come for her shield.

Sumitra seated herself with the zamtak and began to sing one of Andrion's favorite airs, a simple melody garlanded with all the pleasant clichés of the language of love. "Green

grew the willows along the sea strand/ Bright shone the sun as
we lay hand in hand . . .''

As she played she thought the shield and the sword hummed
along; when she stopped, they stopped. Even though she was
not quite sure what she was hearing, she continued to sing.

A tentative breeze curled in the window, lifted the melliflu-
ous sounds of the zamtak and voice and bore them away into
the night.

Eldrafel stood outside the door, pressed against it as if
pressed against the body of a woman, sensing what passed
inside with more than just his ears. His eyes smiled.

Chapter Seven

IN A STARLESS, moonless night Dana walked the streets of
Sardis. And yet it was not Sardis at all, but an insubstantial
ghost city, all shade, no color. Wraiths plucked at her garments. The wind, foul with irex and sorcery, whined feebly at
her back.

The great ziggurat of Harus was a stack of stone as tortured
as that looming over Orocastria, heaped above the forecourt
of Ashtar's temple. But the temple was not there; an empty
courtyard scattered with the bloodred blooms of amaranth lay
open to the expressionless sky.

Amaranth. Love lies bleeding. Dana shuddered and turned
away. There, at her feet, lay a pile of feathers. A falcon,
pierced with a spear, its wings splayed and broken, its talons
clutching at nothing. "Harus," she hissed. "I no longer wish
you harm."

A light glinted atop the ziggurat. Another answered, winking beyond the runnel of darkness that was the street. The
sound of wheels echoed down the wind. The distant flickering
shapes of fiery chariots appeared in the avenue, speeding
toward the temple compound. Spectral drivers lashed spectral
horses, reins rattling in their bony fingers. Hoof and wheel
crushed the thronging phantoms beneath them.

Dana's heart beat against her breastbone. She leaped onto
the great stones that had once been Harus's ziggurat and
scrambled upward. The two rivers of Sardis glided beneath
her, dark and slick; the sky was height upon height of black
cloud. The light atop the mound shone on, hard and bright.

Gasping and then spitting out the foul taste in her mouth,
she heaved herself over the topmost stone and sprawled beside the high altar. The rock was garlanded with dried and
brittle flowers. In their midst was the imperial diadem, glowing bravely with a clear light. Where that light fell the

garlands were whole, wreaths of dewy fresh jasmine and asphodel.

The chariots rumbled straight up the sides of the ruined ziggurat. With a cry Dana threw herself forward and grasped at the diadem.

Her hand touched it. It flared, encompassing her in its gleam. She was in Patros's study. The governor-general bent over his desk, pen scratching purposefully. Beside him Kleothera sat sewing a bit of embroidery depicting the sea lapping a jagged island, smoke coiling from a conical mountain. Beside her was a cradle. Little Declan giggled, chasing his toes, green eyes sparkling.

A howling gust of wind threw the cradle down. Dana lunged for the child, but he was gone, engulfed by shadow. The diadem slipped from her fingers and rolled away, bounced down the side of the mound, disappeared. Storm clouds churned the sky. The chariots hurtled over the rim of stone and came straight at Dana, implacable.

With a hoarse scream of horror and denial she fell, skimming over the rough rocks without touching them, into the amethyst and blue depths of the sea. Fish cavorted around her, octopi wrapped her arms with muscular tentacles. A hollow drumming in her head became a voice, a male voice. "Dana! Wake up!"

Male hands held her and she quailed. There were the sea creatures swimming across the wall and ceiling of the room, suspended in the peculiar hazy light of Minras. The voice insisted, "It is but a dream!"

"Is it?" she replied. "Is it?" But whether it were nightmare or waking vision did not matter. She trembled, her skin marble cold. "Andrion, I know my father's name. I know my sons. I know you. And I dream of Sardis, not of Sabazel."

The face looking at her was Tembujin's. One side of his mouth tucked itself tight. "Andrion has gone scouting. Will I do?"

She wrenched her thought into control. She sighed, "You have always done very nicely."

The air in the room stirred with the elusive odor of rot. No wonder the Minrans scented their rooms, their water, themselves, with rare and exotic fragrances. But Tembujin, even as he chafed in a Minran kilt, bore his familiar aroma of woodsmoke and grass. Dana allowed herself a moment to rest against his sleek shoulder. Only a moment, just long enough to catch her breath and let the ice water in her veins become blood again.

"You would have preferred another name for our son Zefric?" Tembujin hazarded.

Her face cracked, sloughing off the horror, revealing a crooked smile. "He is your child," she said, "not mine. That is not what I meant."

"I know that is not what you meant," Tembujin returned softly. He did not need to add, Will my recognizing your meaning change it?

With a quick, dry caress Dana put his arms aside and rose.

The hawk-nosed guard who had escorted them from the beach stood beside the door, not before it, in an ambiguous position. Andrion shrugged the short Rexian purple cloak over his shoulder and settled the linen kilt about his hips. At least his own belt, although water-stained, was presentable, and his necklace gleamed at his throat. He stepped out, pretending he was not off-balance without the weight of Solifrax at his thigh.

The guard clattered to alertness, his spear stabbing toward the sky, his disgruntled gaze roaming everywhere but to Andrion.

This would never do. Why, the man was no older than Andrion himself. "What is your name?" Andrion asked him.

The man stared, accustomed to being treated as another frescoed wall.

"Your name, soldier."

"Jemail. Sir."

"I am addressed as 'my lord.' " Andrion folded his hands behind his back and rocked on his heels, the benign disciplinarian. "And what is your rank?"

"Captain. My lord."

"And your orders?"

The man boggled. Andrion drew himself up to his full height, drew out his most deliberate voice. "Your orders, Captain Jemail."

"To—to watch your movements and those of your companions, and to report them back to—" Jemail stopped short.

Andrion leaned toward him and whispered conspiritorially, "King Eldrafel? Queen Chrysais?"

The man looked slightly ill.

"Never fear, Jemail, I will do nothing that you cannot safely report. Carry on."

"Yes, my lord." The color returned to Jemail's swarthy face and he saluted smartly. Andrion wandered away across a terrace garden, his features as bland as possible. Not for nothing had he spent many hours of his childhood sitting before Bellasteros, inspecting the legions.

But unfortunately not a Sardian legion was in sight. No sword, no shield, no Sumitra. A legion would not help. Wits, man, Andrion ordered himself, use your wits!

In the haze the city before him was only a suggestion sketched in light and shadow, the harbor turgid pea green, the huge statues of Taurmenios brass, not gold. Three triremes lay at anchor like giant water beetles. Whether this was the terrace from which he had watched Eldrafel dancing the night before he could not tell. This place was an hallucination.

He could have sworn on Solifrax itself that the night wind had teased him with the evocative music of Sumi's voice and zamtak. "Bright shone the sun as we lay hand in hand/ I gave him my song/ Yes, I gave him my song/ It shall be with him wherever he goes."

Indeed, Andrion thought. But no wind stirred this morning. A shallow pool, the water as taut as a membrane, reflected a pewter sky. Flowering water plants barely creased the surface. Lotus, Andrion realized. Blue lotus. His neck prickled. The bull and the lotus, Dana had said. Her vision had been quite correct. And yesterday she had sensed something amiss with the diadem.

Restlessly he turned and paced back across the flagstones, ignoring Jemail's fixed gaze. Bees droned about a row of tall plants whose wide green leaves nodded despite the stillness of the air. The stillness before a storm. He touched a glossy black berry and it fell into his hand.

"Do not eat that!" said a voice just behind him.

Andrion turned. "I do not intend to. It is nightshade, is it not?"

A fresh-faced boy watched him. "Yes, it is. Poison."

"In a large enough dose," returned Andrion. He threw the berry away.

"Are you my uncle Andrion, the emperor?" the child asked, peering upward from a thicket of chestnut hair. Evidently an emperor should not be standing around by himself, but should have an entourage of pennons and elephants, at the least.

"I am," Andrion replied, "if you are the son of Chrysais and Gath."

"My name is Gard," the boy announced. "Yes, I am the
queen's son. And Gath's, too, but I do not remember him."

Andrion started to offer some sympathy when he realized
what Gard had said. "You do not remember him?"

"He died when I was just a baby," the boy patiently
explained, as if to a backward student. "Before the time
appointed for his death ritual."

Andrion did not like the sound of that; it reminded him too
much of the legends of ancient Sardis and Sabazel both, the
hero-king Daimion sacrificed by the hero-queen Mari. . . .
The child had probably been frightened by some old tale.

He sat on a nearby bench and motioned Gard to sit beside
him. The boy plunked himself down and swung his sandaled
feet to and fro above the flagstones. The motion was the only
movement of the sultry air.

Andrion wanted to ask how Gath died but thought better of
it; he asked instead the compulsory question, "How old are
you?"

"I am almost nine."

No wonder Chrysais had laughed when Andrion accused
her of remarrying in haste. But if Gath had been dead for . . .
eight years, why had she just now sent the news to Iksandarun?
He shook his head, feeling the skeins of this plot tangle
around him once again.

"That," Gard said, gesturing grandly toward the mountain
frowning down upon Orocastria, "is Zind Taurmeni, the gate
of Taurmenios. Sometimes you can hear the sacred bull bellowing in its depths." Andrion nodded. Encouraged, Gard
chattered on. "And that mountain there—oh, you cannot see
it in the mist this morning—will it rain, do you think?—that
is Tenebrio, the ancient shrine. Just beyond is the port of
Akrotiri, where Lord Eldrafel was born."

Andrion glanced over his shoulder; Gard was right, the
gauzy sky seemed to have absorbed the flattened shape of the
other mountain. Ancient shrine, he repeated to himself. Akrotiri.
Eldrafel.

"And the harbor, of course, and the Colossi of the God.
That little island on the far side of the harbor, guarding it
from the sea, is Al Sitar."

The left-hand gap between island and mainland was overseen by the winged bulls. But the right-hand gap, as much as
Andrion could see of it behind the mist gathering over the
harbor, seemed to be open.

Gard followed his eye. "That is a marsh, too shallow for ships. Tall grass and mud and birds. I used to hunt there, when I was little." The feet stopped swinging. The air was stifling.

"You no longer hunt there?"

"I am the heir to Minras," the boy said. He did not sound entirely happy with that role.

"Ah . . ." How to say this? "Your mother told me yesterday that the heir to the throne is always the king's sister's son. Which is why Eldrafel is king now." The "not you" seemed to Andrion to hang in the air.

The boy shrugged resignedly. "But Lord Eldrafel has no sister, no nephew. My mother married him so that he would choose me to be his heir."

Andrion could not believe Chrysais had married the elegant priest simply to assure Gard's rank. And Gard, judging by the studied, almost resentful "Lord Eldrafel," was not overwhelmed either with gratitude or with affection for the cousin who was also his stepfather. It was sobering how much children noticed, even while distorting it by inexperience. What must Ethan or Zefric have made of some of the arguments they had overheard?

Ethan, Andrion repeated. My councilors would not accept my half-sister Sarasvati's son because he is part Khazyari. Would they accept this appealing child, son of the woman they believe to be my full sister, the prince of a respectable if remote kingdom?

A tangled plot indeed, if that were Chrysais's game. And it left too much unexplained. Quite casually Andrion asked, "Eldrafel has no family?"

"None at all." The boy seemed to feel that this was not an undesirable situation. "Gath's sister Proserfina died having him, and no one knows—" He stopped suddenly, lips clamped, realizing that he knew too much.

"No one knows who Eldrafel's father is?" Andrion prompted gently.

Gard nodded, his beet-red face hidden by his hair, and whispered, "Actually, the king was fathered by Taurmenios himself, in the sacred precinct on Mount Tenebrio."

"Yes, yes, of course." Andrion leaned closer to the child, whispering in turn, "My father was the son of the god Harus."

"Really?" Gard's wide eyes were a clear gray, glistening, guileless.

"The gods move subtly," Andrion assured him. And chuckled to himself, subtly indeed. Bellasteros had been fathered by some probably redheaded passerby in Sabazel. Convenient, to explain a mysterious birth by claiming divine intervention. Especially when plotting to seize power.

The boy eyed Andrion's shining necklace. The horizon contracted. Strange curling vapors hung over Zind Taurmeni; the island of Al Sitar was only a looming shape. A sea hawk soared above the city and with one raucous cry spun away into nothingness. The clouds began to curdle into lumps and billows, and the pale sunlight ebbed, leaving the terrace in blue shadow. Andrion wiped his forehead. The moist heat was unbearable, and his lungs labored. Leaping up and screaming would not help.

"Has the mountain always smoked like that?" he asked.

Gard considered. "Always. All my life. It is the breath of the god as he labors, forging land from the sea."

Tembujin emerged from the palace, exchanged stares with Jemail, and inspected the limber branch of a willow tree. Not the quality of the horn and sinew bow he had lost, he seemed to say to himself, but any bow would be better than none.

The Minran kilt and cloak he wore were not purple but brown, with his own dagger nestled at his waist. As he saw Andrion and Gard and turned toward them, his tail of hair curled on his shoulder. Gard gasped, "Is that a demon?"

"Who? Tembujin?" Andrion had to laugh. "I have thought he was." And quickly, "No, no, he was born on the far steppes, you see."

"Mm," said Gard, not quite sure. But still he stood politely and waited to be introduced.

"Tembujin, Khan of Khazyaristan. Gard, ah—Prince of Minras."

Tembujin bowed. Having children of his own, he knew well how they need to be taken seriously.

"Where is Dana?" Andrion asked.

"Browbeating a serving woman into remaking the dress she was left to wear," answered Tembujin with a fond if impatient grimace. "I told her that if I could wear a skirt, she could too. But then, you know Dana."

Oh yes, Andrion thought, I know Dana like a soldier knows when he is transfixed by a spear.

Gard, composed again, asked brightly, "Why would a woman not want to wear a dress?"

"A long story," Tembujin told him. "Very long."

Thunder rumbled in the distance. The stones of the palace shuddered. Chrysais swept out of another doorway, tendrils of hair clinging damply to her forehead, her paint and powder glistening. "Gard!" she called.

The boy jumped.

"Gard! You should have been at your lessons by now!"

Gard scowled, and muttered under his breath, "I am old enough to have a male tutor."

Chrysais's eye lingered on her son, and her caress was so unaffectedly affectionate that Andrion blinked, disoriented. But already she had handed the boy over to the hatchet-faced woman following her. "Run along now," she crooned. "Run along." She turned to the men with a heavy-lashed smile, as taut and lubricious as the weather.

Gard peeked out from behind his governess's skirts and made a face, a leering mask which was only a slight exaggeration of his mother's expression.

"I hope he has not been boring you with his little tales," Chrysais said to Andrion and Tembujin. "He is very imaginative."

"Not at all," Andrion returned blandly.

Chrysais shot an evil look at Jemail. The guard was entranced by the clouds coagulating above the palace. He had been too far away to hear anything, even in the heavy stillness before the storm.

It was so still, Andrion realized, that what he had subliminally assumed to be the droning of the bees was really a nascent riot in the city; the sounds of shouts, muffled crashes, running feet, came faintly to his ear. Chrysais's smile broadened. "You would like to see your men?"

She knows something I do not, Andrion told himself. "Yes. Yes, indeed."

"Come then." She spun about, flounces rippling.

If he were a god, he would try striking them all with lightning, just to make something happen. As it was, he might as well check on Niarkos and the others, and take another look at the city. Andrion inhaled, but the breath did not ease his tension. Chrysais looked back over her shoulder, waiting.

Andrion said to Tembujin, from the corner of his mouth, "You and Dana see if you can stir things up a bit. That is one of your talents, after all."

"Gladly," said Tembujin, with a deep breath of his own.

Andrion caught up with Chrysais. She would have had to hasten to keep up with his stride, but, of course, he did not know where they were going, and so followed in an awkward half pace.

Tembujin flicked the branch of the willow as he went back inside and tried a brief, courteous nod at Jemail. The guard saluted.

Sumitra leaned upon the parapet of her narrow balcony, watching the clouds. Odd how they swirled, clashed, and parted even when the wind was still. They had already lowered enough to blot out the harbor and the skinny little island between it and the sea, and now the city itself was being engulfed by a wave of blue shadow. Thunder rolled around the blotted arch of the sky.

Just as Sumitra turned to go in, she caught a movement in the corner of her eye. She leaned against the parapet, trying to see around the harsh buttress of rock that defined her prison. Down a staircase leading from one chaotic pile of architecture to another walked a man and a woman.

Sumi crushed herself against the stone. It was cold, sapping the warmth from her body, but still she strained outward. Yes, the man was Andrion. The purple cloak and linen kilt were strange, but the lean body, the regal and yet cautious manner, was unmistakable.

One glimpse and he was gone. But his image remained vivid in her mind; he was really here. And the woman with whom he walked? Richly dressed. Immodestly dressed. She slumped back, panting. There was air all around her and none to breathe. If only the storm would break.

The door of the cell opened and Rue entered. Sumitra feigned innocent pleasure in the view. "A beautiful city," she said. "What is it named?"

Rue evaluated her question. The woman was like a fox, both shy and sly. The woman, Sumi realized, reminded her of someone glimpsed for just a moment, cloaked in shadow. . . . No matter.

Sumitra came inside, pulling the clips from the heavy coil of hair on the back of her head. "Comb my hair, if you please." She seated herself on the pillowed chair and shook her hair free. The sleek black waves cascaded down her back. Rue picked up a comb and tentatively passed it through one lock.

Sorry now that she had not cultivated the woman's confidence on board ship, Sumitra leaned into the touch. But she had been sick so much of the time. Thank Vaiswanara that that part of her pregnancy had passed with the end of the voyage. As for Rue—no time like the present. "What is the name of the city?" Sumi asked again.

Reluctantly, like a miser opening a coffer, Rue replied, "Orocastria."

"Ah." The capital of Minras, Sumitra added to herself. Not for nothing had she helped Andrion with letters and maps and accounts. Then the woman he was walking with might be Chrysais. Did she know of Sumitra's kidnapping?

"How long have you served Eldrafel?" Sumi inquired. She picked up a bronze mirror and inspected the jewel in her nose. At least she was provided with every luxury here. That sprawling structure outside her window must indeed be the palace she had thought it to be.

"My family was born to serve the shrine of Tenebrio. Lord Eldrafel was generous enough to take us with him when he came here."

"Are you free or slave?" Sumitra asked quietly.

Rue snagged the comb, jerking her hair, and Sumi winced. "It is good to serve the king. I get food, clothing, a clean room. I merit commendation."

So a slave seeks to reassure herself. Although Sumitra could not imagine Eldrafel commending the gods themselves, she could see him ordering Rue to be reticent. The woman was in thrall to him in more than one way.

Decisively, Sumitra detached the tiny ruby stud from her nostril. "Here," she said. "This is for you, for serving me so well."

Rue's hand lifted and fell. "My thanks, lady. But I cannot."

"Now, now, why should you not have a small gift?"

"Well . . ." Rue took the jewel and held it as if it were a burning brand. Despite the gloom of the approaching storm, it winked crimson. Her dark eyes reflected its light. "I have not done overmuch for you," she murmured.

Sumitra shrugged gracefully. "Well, there is one thing. . . ."

Rue's fist closed about the ruby. "Yes?"

"Can you carry a message for me?" Sumi asked quietly, her voice falling around the serving woman like a smooth satin drape. "To your mistress Chrysais, that I would like to

speak with her.'' That was a wild shot; Rue had named
Eldrafel king, but what did that make the widowed Chrysais?

Rue stared, her eyes so huge they seemed likely to spill
from their sockets and run in black streaks down her face.
Chrysais's name was quite familiar to her. And it was one
Sumitra should not have known.

Sumi made a soothing gesture. ''Just tell her that I would
like to speak with her. A simple enough task.'' From their
bundle beneath the table, by Sumitra's knee, the sword and
the shield chimed.

''I—I—I do not know. . . .'' With a sharp, shrewd glance
Rue laid down the comb, but not the ruby, and slipped out.
Sumi listened; yes, the locking bar was driven home. Reflec-
tively she picked up the comb and began to stroke her own
hair. Perhaps the ruby had gone for nothing. Perhaps not.
Time would tell.

Thunder rumbled in the stones of her cell. The shield and
the sword rang, their notes spiraling upward, higher and higher,
until they passed the limit of hearing. But still they rang.

When Tembujin entered Dana offered him a wan smile,
trying vainly to loosen her pinched, pale lips. He stopped
dead. ''What is it now?''

''A note of music. The shield, keening like the wind in my
heart.''

''There is no wind today,'' Tembujin said.

''The wind always blows in my mind,'' responded Dana.
With a decisive toss of her head, long golden hair dancing,
she turned away from the window where she stood. The
keening was not so much unpleasant as urgent, stretching to
the breaking point the tension already humming in the air.
''We must stir things up a bit. We must act.''

''That is what Andrion asked. He went with Chrysais down
into the city to see about Niarkos. Something is amiss there, I
think.''

''Everything is amiss,'' Dana said darkly. She beckoned
Tembujin to the window and pointed at the crazy quilt of
roofs, pillars, terraces, and stairs crumpled against the forbidding stone piers. ''A little while ago Chrysais came out of
that door there. Behind the colonnade, see?''

Tembujin saw.

''Look. On the roof of that room is a tower, the only tower
in any of that mess. Strange place.'' She frowned, analyzing

her thought. The tower was askew, but how she could tell whether anything was out of plumb in the chaotic construction of the palace she did not know. Perhaps it was askew only to some innate sense of propriety and personal balance. "Do you see the light in the windows?"

Tembujin's narrow eyes narrowed still farther. "Odd windows, like holes ripped in fabric rather than built of bricks and mortar. But a light?"

"Then I do sense it rather than see it," she sighed. "Blue light, ice blue, like dawn on Cylandra's frosty cap. Floating in threads past the windows." The color of Ashtar's eyes, here in this unhealthy place. She cringed. "Let us go see what it is."

"Anything is better than sitting here waiting for the storm to break. Let us stir the pot, as Chrysais did."

So he, too, had caught that inference. But Chrysais had only been teasing them. Please, gods, surely she had only been teasing them. A woman like that should have no power except over susceptible men. . . . Setting her jaw, Dana leaned through the window into the murky light of day. The tiles of a roof lay at about her own height beneath. Ah, a morsel of freedom. She swung one leg up onto the sill.

Tembujin plucked at her sleeve, grinning. "You look like a windstorm in a weaver's shop."

She had to laugh; irrelevant, but true. The serving woman, rolling her eyes and muttering indignantly, had cut the skirt of the dress in half and sewed it into baggy trousers. Then, trimming away the flounces, she had used the material to fill in the bodice. The resulting garment was sexless and clumsy but serviceable. Dana indicated the dagger strapped to her thigh. "I wanted this where I could reach it."

"Yes, yes, of course," Tembujin replied.

"I might need it to shorten a certain tongue," she responded sweetly as she slipped over the windowsill. She dangled from her hands and dropped onto the roof below. Tembujin followed, his sandaled feet landing with a clatter his ruined felt boots would not have made. He snarled at footwear and tiles both and then surveyed the expanse of the roof. His eyes lighted as if he saw the reach of the northern plains open before him.

With many playful jostlings and muttered insults they crept across that roof, around the edge of a terrace, over another roof, and found themselves opposite the targeted door. "Pin-

feathers,'' muttered Dana in Tembujin's ear as they peered
between columns. "It is guarded.''

"Of course it is guarded. Rulers always have their doors
guarded.'' His tail of hair flounced indignantly.

"Not in Sabazel,'' she retorted with an exaggerated sneer.
She scurried bent-kneed around the corner and contemplated a
terra-cotta gutter pipe.

"Not in Sabazel,'' Tembujin mimicked, high-pitched. He
boosted Dana, with a surreptitious tickle, up the pipe and
onto a broad ledge carved with the everlasting sea creatures.
She stepped on a dolphin, a sea urchin, and a crab of some
kind, and shoved questioningly at a set of shutters. They
opened without a creak. Grinning, she popped through.

The room was very large. Even in broad daylight it would
probably be dim; under this darkling sky it was almost impenetrable. Dana blinked. Slowly she began to pick out rich
furnishings, a huge canopied bed, storage chests, pillows, and
chairs.

Her shoulders tensed; the hair on the back of her neck
stirred. Her exhilaration vanished like a candle snuffed. She
inhaled, mouth open—perfumes, lotus and sandalwood perhaps. And another scent, faint but rank, permeating the
sweetness.

Tembujin swung in beside her and barely avoided colliding
with a hanging lamp. His eye fell on a gold box spilling
jewels across a tabletop inlaid with ivory; amethyst and turquoise winked duskily. "Ah, may I do some shopping? Valeria
would look lovely in turquoise.''

"No,'' Dana snapped, whether at the mention of his wife—
whose jewelry was a sign of her husband's power, not her
own—or because of the sudden chill, she had no wish to
analyze. But Tembujin subsided instantly, even he sensing
the odor of sorcery.

Two gigantic vases stood guarding a rising stairway. It
must lead to the tower. Dana picked her way across the floor
tiles. Their complex patterns seemed to shift and swirl beneath her feet, and her head spun. But that insistent keening
in her mind spurred her on. If the shield was there, she would
find it.

The door was not bolted. The latch was so cold her flesh
clung to it; she jerked her hand away. Pushing on the wooden
door itself, Dana and Tembujin stepped shoulder to shoulder
inside the tower room.

A blast of blue-white light greeted them. Not lightning; it came from inside the room, as if the chamber were the heart of a cool quicksilver star. Dana felt a force pushing her back, like the blackness that had knocked her down the night the shield was stolen. But this was blindingly bright.

Floor, ceiling, walls were obliterated. She staggered, and the high note in her mind shrieked. Tembujin's strong hands clasped her waist and steadied her. "It is already fading," he said. "Stand still."

Giddy, she forced herself to shelter behind his body as he stood square, squinting against the light; he seemed to feel no threatening force. And the light did fade. A large black rectangle swelled up, inhaled the brilliance, and became a huge tapestry held upright on a wooden frame.

Dana's dazzled eyes could not quite focus on the cloth; it shimmered darkly, flowing away from her gaze. Shaking herself, testing her footing, she turned to the rest of the now dim and hazy room.

She saw a small shrine holding a winged bull of greenish-black nephrite. Beside it stood a sardonyx male figure, arms looped proprietarily around the massive neck. Brass incense burners, their flames tiny remnants of the consuming light, emitted a wavering mist. The wooden floor was littered with baskets piled high with yarn, colors blending one into another like still-fluid dyes.

Tembujin was inspecting the tapestry. "Does it not try to escape you?" Dana asked.

"What?"

She elbowed him aside and stared fixedly at it, willing it to display itself for her. It was not a stretched piece of linen like Sumitra's embroidered tapestry. It was loosely woven netting, starched into a stiff grid, many, but not all of its gaps filled with stitches in a multiplicity of shadings. Sumitra's efforts, skilled as they were, seemed like twine and rags compared with this.

Because, Dana told herself, this was sorcerous. The incense burners with their heady odor of lethenderum could not mask that distinctive reek. And there were no other lamps, no source for the bright light.

Images were scattered seemingly at random across the netting. Dana recognized Iksandarun, Sardis, Sabazel. Her fists clenched, she recognized the shield. There was the galley spinning helplessly in the whirlpool, there was Solifrax lying among the rabid rocks. There were knives, ropes, a draped altar, a bull brandishing its horns—and pigs rooting in purple muck. Purple Dana understood, but pigs?

The stitched faces of the various human figures were quite familiar—Bonifacio, Ilanit, Niarkos—their expressions frozen like hares suddenly caught in a trap. The fabric seemed to hum, on a note approaching but too shrill to harmonize with the keening of the shield.

"I do not like this," Dana said between her teeth. "The images are too accurate and too vague; they remind me of old stories better left forgotten. And the cloth itself—it sings."

"Sings?" Tembujin coughed and tried to brush away the clinging tendrils of smoke. "What concerns me are the spaces left in the pattern. It is not complete."

Dana drew her dagger and poked tentatively at the edge of the tapestry. A spear of black fire darted out like a serpent's tongue and knocked the weapon clattering across the floor.

Lightning flashed outside, filling the irregular windows with a white light, which while startling, was less bright than the blue flare inside the room. Thunder reverberated down the sky, through the bricks and tile of the palace, and shuddered in the living stone of Minras itself. The tapestry flapped. The floor heaved. The yarn sword and shield, cities and sea, swam before Dana's eyes, the stitches curling and snugging themselves tighter into their assigned images. The fabric swelled larger and larger, as if to devour the room, the shrine, the mortal creatures standing before it.

Dana's courage was sucked from her body and her every fiber thrilled with terror. Tembujin swore, his breath ragged. As one they spun toward the open door.

Eldrafel leaned against the doorpost, framed in lightning and shadow, toying with Dana's dagger. He flipped it. It sailed in a smooth arc through the air and landed upright in the floor, quivering, a finger's width from her foot. Smiling, he purred, "I beg your pardon. I do not believe we have been properly introduced."

Chapter Eight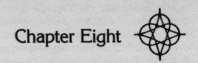

ALL THE WAY from the palace into the town Andrion could hardly sit still. Not only did he feel sure he was waiting for an axe to fall, he hated palanquins, hated being toted about like a helpless infant. And in this one he was gagged by Chrysais's lotus perfume, like her manner so rich and overblown as to verge on decadent.

The palanquin stopped. He shook off Chrysais's overly familiar hand—that, oddly, now wore a bandage—and dove through the curtains into air that was by contrast fresh. "By all the gods!" he exclaimed, staring aghast at the scene before him.

There were his soldiers and sailors engaged in a free-for-all with what must have been the dregs of Orocastrian society. The courtyard of the disreputable inn seethed with engorged faces and flailing limbs; a trail of broken pottery led inside. Niarkos stood in the doorway, a cup dangling from his brawny hand like a flower from the limp fingers of a courtesan, his mouth hanging open, his eyes glazed. The scrabbling Sardians were similarly bleary. Andrion grimaced; they were not even giving a particularly good account of themselves. Were they drunk?

Chrysais anticipated Andrion's question. "We lodged them in a decent hostel. They must have come here wanting cheap beer or cheaper women."

Andrion shot her an exasperated glare. She had the grace not to grin until his back was almost, but not quite, turned. A sailor landed in a bloody bundle at his feet, almost knocking him into the churned and filthy straw, the scummed puddles staining the courtyard.

Harus! Andrion swore to himself. These were all good men, handpicked for trustworthiness, acting like swine! Why?

90

The shouts had attracted quite a crowd, dark eager faces peering out of pillared galleries and around corners, pointing at the Sardians and laughing. Andrion bent and picked up the man at his feet, reprimands bubbling on his lips. The sailor shoved him aside and plunged back into the fray.

Clamping his jaw tight, quelling the desire to pretend the squabblers had no relation to him, Andrion summoned Niarkos. And summoned him again, gesturing with brusque irritation before the man responded. Pulling himself out of some deep morass, the admiral stumbled through the tumult, stood slant-shouldered before Andrion, gazed at his feet with furrowed brow and slack lips and said, "Ah . . ."

Andrion's irritation froze, his reprimands popped and dissipated. Niarkos could not even speak, let alone recognize his emperor. Mere drunkenness could not explain that.

Chrysais leaned from the silk hangings of the palanquin and trilled, "I must return to the palace. Here, these guards shall stay to escort you. And you might need this." She threw him a small purse, the coins inside jangling wildly. Andrion caught it with one hand. Burly slaves hoisted the palanquin. Chrysais blew Andrion a kiss before the curtains concealed her damp, glowing face and supercilious smile.

The soldiers designated to wait stood clumped together, leaning upon their spears, watching Andrion and his men as if they were the most entertaining troupe to play Orocastria for months. Several men who were undoubtedly the local constabulary strolled into sight and without undue haste began to separate the combatants. From their sneering asides, from the quick shoves and kicks they allotted to the Sardians, Andrion knew that the strangers had already been convicted of causing the disturbance.

He ground his teeth. His grasp could easily have melted the coins he held. As he glowered at the miscreants who were his men, he noticed, mingled with the odors of garbage and animals and filth, another smell, faint but unmistakable. Sorcery, of course; he was not surprised. Minras so reeked of sorcery that he actually grew accustomed to it.

He was, he thought, saturated with it, like sweat beading on every tiny hair and shivering with awareness. . . . His necklace stung his throat. It was all he could do to keep from crying out. A buzzing like a swarm of bees stirred his mind and then clarified into a high, sustained chime. A double chime, rather, a chord, the combined singing of sword and shield.

Every fiber in Andrion's body fired with recognition. For a moment he was conscious only of the notes of music, evocative, compelling, urgent. They were close by, then, waiting for him.

With an effort he awoke. Someone was looking at him. Looking at him more closely, that is, than everyone else. It was the tavern owner, judging by the grease and ale smearing his great round belly; his crumpled kilt barely clung to his loins beneath its protuberance. The man's grimy face was set in a fawning smile.

With a crack of his spine Andrion unfurled his full height. He handed the man several coins and pointedly waited for change. He just as pointedly did not apologize for the now dispirited group of Sardians.

The tavern owner returned a few coins and bowed, not so much to the purple cloak as to the bearing of its wearer.

With a curt nod of thanks, Andrion looked around. His men were being led away. He collared the leading constable, demanding to know where they were going. "Drunk and disorderly," the man said. "The penalty is thirty days' servitude." He began to sneer, but Andrion's incendiary glare cauterized his expression and left it a dyspeptic grimace.

An emperor's orders would count for nothing here, Andrion told himself. Save your breath. Writhing inside, he shouldered his embarrassment and his rage and followed the constables and their prisoners down the street. Did the catcalls of the Minrans die away as he passed, or were they simply filtered through the maddening hum in his mind? It did not matter.

His escort of soldiers grudgingly tagged along behind; they had expected him, it seemed, to abandon his men and return to the palace, especially when he discovered that the sentence was to be carried out in the miasma of the dye works. But even if these were not his men, shambling with dazed, bloodshot eyes like beaten animals, like pigs, he was still responsible for them.

The softness of the purse clutched in his hand barely concealed the hardness of the metal it contained; Chrysais's body, Andrion thought, would feel like that. And he thought how odd it was that the day could be so close and humid yet not really hot, but chill. The leaden sky was a black avalanche poised to fall upon the island and inundate it. The air trembled with a frenzied expectancy, as if something rushed irrevocably to its conclusion. The necklace thrilled against his skin.

Chrysais swept into Sumitra's cell, crooning, "Oh, my dear sister!"

That was fast, Sumitra thought. She forced her eyes away from Chrysais's bosom to her face and laid down the pomegranate on which she had been nibbling. Nothing really tasted good here. The tension in the air, not to mention its accompanying reek, was stifling.

"My dear," Chrysais continued. "I just discovered you were here. Poor powerless women that we are, our men never tell us anything."

Do they not? Sumitra submitted gingerly to an effusive embrace, hoping none of Chrysais's paint and powder would rub off on her.

With an elaborate sigh Chrysais settled herself on Sumi's narrow bed. "Married to men that others choose for us. What can we do but what we are told? I do hope, Sumitra, you were not discomfited by your journey here."

"Not at all," Sumi said, at last given a chance to speak. She sat back down. At her knee the canvas bundle remained mute.

"You see," confided Chrysais, "my new husband has ambitions. It was he who brought you here, as part of a much greater plan."

"Eldrafel," Sumi stated. She could not help but wonder what it was like to sleep with something that beautiful and that cold.

Chrysais's bandaged fingers toyed with a small sardonyx figurine hung about her neck. "As a dutiful wife I must do his bidding, of course, but how I hate to see my dear brother Andrion bereft of his helpmeet."

"Mm," said Sumitra. Get to the point, part of her mind said. Another part of her mind was fascinated, like a bird charmed by a snake.

Chrysais flirted with the point, her sweet voice dropping into a cajoling, soothing timbre. "You could free yourself, Sumitra. You could be on the next ship back to Sardis. Eldrafel asks only a small task in return." She shrugged, embarrassed at participating in schemes much too elevated for her pretty little head.

"Ransom?" asked Sumi. She brushed her long sable hair away from her face.

Immediately Chrysais was on her feet, reaching for the comb. "Here, let me help you." She began awkwardly coiling the thick waves.

"No, please, not to bother, Rue was fixing it but I sent her to bring you to me."

Chrysais's hands tightened, yanking Sumi's hair, and she gasped. "You sent her—" Chrysais said, and then caught herself. "Ah, yes, so I should help you now, should I not?"

Between her teeth Sumi muttered some assent. She ordered herself to watch her tongue. Obviously Rue had delivered no message.

"My husband the king," Chrysais went on, "wants to see the magic of the legendary sword Solifrax and the famed shield of Sabazel. He, being a magician of some note, wants to make similar weapons for himself. If you will show him their power, he will send you back with them. Very simple."

Not at all. The man was a sorceror, practicing evil, not the beneficient magic of the gods; Sumitra would bet on that. Bracing herself, she asked, "Why do you not ask Andrion to show you the power in the sword?"

Again the jerk on her hair. But Chrysais, she had to admit, recovered very quickly. "Would you not like, my dear, to free him too?"

Good, Sumitra said to herself, let us forget pretense. She glanced in the mirror and grimaced at the rags and tags Chrysais had made of her hair. "Of course I would like to free him. But the sword is his, not mine. The shield does not belong to either of us. I can do nothing with them."

Chrysais threw down the comb, dragged the bundle from under the table, and stripped the wrappings. The weapons were silent in her hands. Sumi was almost amused to see the expression on the other woman's face, the mask of feminine inanity worn thin, revealing the strength of will and the greed beneath. Whose scheme was it, hers or Eldrafel's? Did she, too, practice sorcery?

"Eldrafel knows that they speak to you." Chrysais's sweetness grew tart, resentful that she had to resort to something so coarse as a threat. "He might well destroy these pretty baubles if you will not reveal their secrets. Where would Andrion be then? Where Sabazel?''

The name of that small country was a hiss in her voice. Sumitra shivered, and despite herself reached protectively to the shield. Its surface swirled beneath her fingertips, and the sword chimed. Sumi started back, for a brief moment irritated at their betrayal. But they must have a reason for revealing themselves.

Chrysais smiled, with her eyes as well as with her crimson mouth. ''Good. Shall I leave you to work with them?''

Sumitra folded her hands in her lap, so tightly her knuckles glinted white. She compressed her lips, refusing to speak.

''Think on it,'' purred Chrysais. ''You are much too intelligent not to appreciate your situation. And that of your child.''

Still Sumitra did not speak. With an aggravated sigh Chrysais stalked out and slammed the door behind her, leaving Sumi to embroider her threats with any number of horrifying embellishments. And yet there had to be a plan in it, the gods had to have a plan.

Sumitra drew the sword and considered it. It rang, and flared so brightly that her shadow went lunging up the far wall of the room.

The serving-woman Rue moved silently, strewing fragrant chamomile on the floor, lighting lamps that struggled feebly against the leaden daylight, bringing a large brass tray and setting it next to the bed.

Eldrafel lounged among the pillows, the pleats of his purple kilt arranged on his thighs. A band around his arm shone tauntingly, the wings of an embossed bull rippling with power. ''Would you like spiced honey wine? Elder wine? A brew of roasted beans that we call kahveh?''

Tembujin sat curved like a bow in his chair, arms and legs crossed negligently, eyes black suspicious beads. Dana sat bolt upright, her hands clasped on her knees, jaw thrust forward. Her emerald gaze followed Rue about the room with such harsh accusation that at last the woman looked up and cringed. But her bearing, that of a child stubbornly sure she has done no wrong, did not corrode.

Eldrafel's brows tilted upward, interested. He beckoned Rue to sit beside him and serve from the tray. For himself he chose the pale elder wine. With a quick shared glance, Tembujin and Dana took the same.

Eldrafel drank, watching Dana over his golden cup. He, too, was golden—hair, beard, body—except for the odd silver eyes. Something moved in those eyes, some remote shadow, a nuance of purpose. His lashes heavy, he let his lips linger on the rim of the cup. Dana's viscera melted. She crossed her knees and knotted her ankles. No, she said fiercely to herself and to him, I feel nothing. Except dirty.

Tembujin frowned at this play. "An interesting tapestry," he said, somewhat too loudly.

"My wife has clever hands," returned Eldrafel.

Dana ignored his lascivious double meaning. "Her spies are good ones, then, to represent places and people with such accuracy."

"Yes," Eldrafel said.

"Bonifacio, for example," Dana went doggedly on. "Why should anyone care to picture Bonifacio?"

Eldrafel's mouth quivered, amused. Turning away from Dana's features, as uncompromising as the slopes of Cylandra, he ran a languorous fingertip down Rue's cheek. She inhaled with a sob, and the color drained from her already pale face so that she seemed an alabaster figurine. Beneath the modest cotton gown she wore her body shuddered.

Dana gagged on the uneasy brew of Eldrafel's sensuality and her own fury. She looked away. On the far side of the room, almost hidden in shadow, was a huge chest. The open lid revealed several small jars and bags, sprinkled with dried brownish green. A collection of herbs, no doubt, like the arnica or hyssop that Sarasvati carried to heal the ailments of daily life. But Dana had trouble seeing Chrysais as a healer.

She gulped her wine, but did not taste it. A frontal assault on Eldrafel, verbal or otherwise, would gain nothing. He could afford to tell them exactly what he wanted them to know; the soldiers outside the door were his. But the tapestry was damning enough.

Tembujin shifted, rather flushed. Dana's eyes were drawn ineluctably back to the bed. Eldrafel was casually tonguing Rue's ear, his body sleek with the knowledge that it was being watched and appreciated by his audience. He had the broad shoulders, narrow hips, and straight limbs of a man, sculpted with a woman's perfection of symmetry and poise. But not a line of his body was soft, not a movement tentative.

While he would not descend to anything so crude as outright lewdness, his fastidious delicacy as he played with Rue did hint at the force he could use if necessary.

Dana surprised herself with a tremor of pity for the woman, a puppet in the hands of such a creature.

Rue's body was so stiff it seemed Eldrafel's next touch would shatter it to dust; her face was shaded more with despair than with pleasure. Which became stark terror when the door burst open and Chrysais stormed in.

Tembujin sat up straight and uncrossed his eyes, glancing shamefacedly at Dana to see if she'd noticed his bewitchment with the androgynous figure of Eldrafel. Dana grasped at rational thought, cooling the heat in her belly. Bewitchment, yes, she told herself. The man is a sorceror, so powerful and so subtle that he does not even smell of it. And he does not care if we know it.

"I beg your pardon," said Chrysais, with a sharp, venomous glance from Dana and Tembujin to the stairway. "I did not realize you were entertaining visitors, my husband." Then her eye fell like a mace upon Rue and widened in angry affront. She tossed something she had been holding, a tiny plait of black hair, perhaps, onto a nearby table.

Eldrafel rolled back among the pillows, his sublime composure unperturbed. It remained unperturbed when Chrysais seized Rue's dress and sent her sprawling onto the floor. Something small and glinting red rolled from the slave's gown into the chamomile.

It had to be Sumitra's ruby stud; Dana and Tembujin stiffened in simultaneous recognition. But Chrysais fell upon the gem before they could move. "Where did you get this?" she demanded of Rue.

Rue crouched, hands raised. One dark eye, its sly luster dulled, rolled toward Dana and Tembujin. "Her," the woman exclaimed sullenly. "She who was brought here. She gave it to me for my service."

"It was in her nose," Eldrafel said to the ceiling. "A custom of the Mohan. So she gave it away freely. I did not think it more than ornament."

Arrogant bastard! Dana squirmed. He does not even pretend Sumitra is not here!

"She gave it to you?" Chrysais demanded. "What did you give her in return? Information about our guests?"

Rue withered. "No, my lady, no . . ."

"By the dark horns of Taurmenios, I shall have loyalty from my servants, or no servants at all!" Chrysais seized Rue by the hair, thrust the ruby back into the slave's dress, and pulled her toward the door. There she delivered both Rue and some unintelligible instructions to the waiting guard.

Chrysais returned rubbing her hands, perhaps less in satisfaction than to clean them, and with a haughty glance at the visitors threw herself down beside her husband.

Asserting her ownership, Dana thought. Eldrafel's elegant facade cracked in a hairline fracture of annoyance. But his voice was as silky as ever. "Since you are our guests here, allow me to offer you initiation into the rites of Taurmenois Tenebrae."

"No, thank you," Dana said. The room was suffocating. She had to escape. She stood, her legs as flexible as willow wands. The room spun slightly, the lamps becoming pennons of light, the shadows congealing into gouts of darkness.

"I attend quite enough rites already," said Tembujin. He rose, testing his footing as if the floor buckled. He cast a wary glance at Eldrafel and Chrysais, but neither made any move to stop him. Indeed, Eldrafel nodded toward the door and said, with a private smile not echoed in the misty purple and silver depths of his eyes, "You can find your way back to your quarters, can you not, since you found your way here?"

Dana's tongue was thick and clumsy. She muttered some sarcastic courtesy and strode for the door with as much dignity as she could muster. Tembujin's tail of hair swished in disdain.

Chrysais leaned against Eldrafel, her fingers grasping at his chest like the suckers of a squid. He touched her with the same self-possessed delicacy he had used to tease Rue, and Tembujin and Dana with her. Chrysais's great moist eyes seemed to flood to the pull of Eldrafel's amusement, washing away the gaudy mask of her face and leaving nothing there, no features, no expression. With thumb and forefinger he slipped her bodice from her shoulders.

Dana and Tembujin fled, slamming the door behind them.

The afternoon was even dimmer than it had been, the sky like the inside of an iron caldron. Dana was still warm and dizzy, from the effects of Eldrafel's blandishments, no doubt. The air strummed itself, as feverish as foreplay prolonged until the climax was unbearably intense.

Tembujin wiped his brow. "I thought we were in trouble there."

"We are. We have been all along."

"But we sprang the trap too soon; the pattern in that god-cursed tapestry is not completed. He had to release us."

"To show his contempt," Dana spat. "Why should he fear us? I have never sensed such power, or such confidence."

Tembujin kicked at the flagstones. "If only we knew what their game is. It would have been so much easier to kill us on the beach . . ."

". . . but they did not. Now they play with us, cats tormenting mice before that last fatal bite."

"We must force the issue," said Tembujin. Despite the firmness in his words, his voice was slurred.

Dana frowned. "Indeed. We shall know what the trap is when its jaws close around us."

A wrong turn brought them to a garden concealed in an angle of the passageway. Various plants were mere sketches in grays and brackish greens in the dense shadow of a great yew tree. With a cry of delight, "Bows!" Tembujin sprang toward the tree and began testing its more limber branches.

"Yew," Dana mused. "Poisonous."

The fronds of the tree sighed as they brushed the ground, too heavy to reach toward the sky. The other plants, some tall, some small, whispered as an errant raindrop stirred them. The tiny pearlescent berries of lethenderum nodded, and waxen blush-white flowers bloomed just at Dana's hand. She bent to pick one. "Black hellebore," she said to herself, and to Tembujin, "Look, more poison. And hallucinogens."

"How does a warrior know such herb lore?" he queried. With his dagger he carved a limb from the tree.

"The queens of Sabazel have not always had to be warriors. I had hoped days of peace came again, so when Sarasavati came to study the healing arts, I did too." She walked slowly from plant to plant, avoiding even the lightest touch of their leaves upon her garments. "Deadly nightshade, hemp, wolfsbane, hemlock, poppy," she muttered in evil litany. "And . . ." Quickly she bent and collected several small woody seedlings. "Antithora, thank the goddess. Bryony. And—ouch! —nettles." She hardly felt the sting; her fingers were strangely numb.

As Tembujin came to join her, carrying two slender yew

branches, he stumbled over a mossy stone. "Quite an appropriate garden for a sorcerer and his wife," he muttered.

The poisonous plants seemed refreshingly honest, after that sorcerer and his wife. "Come," said Dana. "We must make tea of these antidotes."

Tembujin stared at her, slow to react. "We drank the same wine he did!"

"Someone can dose themselves until they become immune to certain poisons. I would expect such from Eldrafel." Yes, she was quite definitely dizzy, and so hot that the moist air lathered her like a horse.

"But if he has nothing to fear from us . . ." Tembujin turned a corner, misjudged the distance, and caromed off the wall. "Perhaps he does. Encouraging, that he does not want us . . . alert." His voice died in his throat. The yew limbs fell from his fingers and he scrabbled after them.

They swam slowly through dim, suffocating corridors where frescoes made mocking gestures and pillars pirouetted absurdly. They stumbled past the lotus pool. Jemail was not at the door; two new guards were. "Andrion?" Dana cried as they entered, but he was not there.

The dye works did not stink as badly today; Andrion's nostrils were as dazed as the Sardians' eyes. Quickly he determined who the foreman was and gave him the purse, buying his men extra food and a clean place to sleep. The purple cloak and smoldering face earned a more respectful response than the coins.

As the soldiers and sailors were set to work stirring vats and opening shells, they collided clumsily with each other, their smudged faces as expressionless as the animals they had become. Niarkos himself meekly lifted a sledge of discarded shells and trundled them down to the beach. He showed no sign he had ever before seen a beach.

Lightning ripped the sky and thunder boomed. I shall free you, Andrion vowed, and tore himself away. So he had been separated from almost everyone now; only Tembujin and Dana—friends, not followers—remained. His necklace was surely charring his skin; his ears rang; his heart strained, pounding against his ribs. His escort was knocking about in some foolish scuffling match. He barked orders at them, and they set off in smart formation several steps behind him.

No disheartenment, he ordered himself. Disgust, at the

ugliness of the game he was forced to play. Anger, and resolution.

The cypresses murmured. Vapors swallowed the harbor and licked at the city. The far buttress of the palace shifted before Andrion's gaze like a cloud; were those windows cut into the rock, or peering eyes?

He found himself beside the arena. He saw only the tracks of bulls upon the sand, rusty stains on the altar, unfaded blooms of amaranth left like offerings on the railings. And from nowhere, taking him completely unaware, realization pounced. Rue's face was that of Rowan, Bonifacio's chief acolyte. The strong one.

The thought was a blow to the pit of his stomach. He stopped dead in the street, gasping, and his escort piled up behind him. Forcing air into his lungs, forcing his feet to move, he trudged on. Thunder reverberated in the ground, welled in a heavy wave around him, consumed the song of the sword and shield. His brow tingled, as though the diadem had been ripped from it.

Andrion thought grimly, Rowan and Rue must be brother and sister. The gods only knew what trouble Rowan was stirring in Sardis; Bonifacio would not notice an armed rebellion unless it dirtied his robes. The rule of the Empire was indeed at stake, and he had come rushing here on a foolish quest. Not surprising, but stupid, very stupid, unworthy of an emperor to abandon his realm for . . . Sumitra. Sumitra and his child.

No. His quest was far from foolish, his journey far from stupid. Surely the tug of his necklace on that balcony in Sardis has assured him of that. Surely, surely . . . I now know without doubt, he told himself sternly, that the threat to me, to my family, to my land, begins here. So here is the place to thwart it.

He could only trust that Patros's keen wits would recognize the threat in Sardis. He could only pray. His lips quirked into an acid smile; the gods moved subtly indeed, like footpads bludgeoning the skulls of unwary travelers.

His spine as stiff as the blade of Solifrax, Andrion strode under the horned gate and into the palace. This turn and that, reversing the way he had come. The escort, panting slightly, was still behind him. "My thanks," he said to them. "You may leave me now." With salutes they left.

At last it began to rain, the mist about the palace thickening, swishing down upon the columns and frescoes, roughening the surface of the lotus pool. Thunder grumbled in the distance. Still the air hummed with expectancy.

Jemail was gone. Two other guards bracketed the door, impassive as ceramic figures. Maybe Dana and Tembujin had circumvented them all, and waited with information. We must force the issue, Andrion told himself as he opened the door. We have no other choice. And if all this—mockery—is meant to make us force the issue, well, we shall know what the trap is when the jaws close around us.

Andrion saluted the guards, who, startled, saluted back. He stepped inside and was greeted only by a shadowed and ominous silence.

Chapter Nine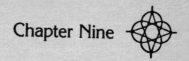

SUMITRA EMERGED FROM her reverie. From the window of her cell she saw land, water, and sky diffused by gauzy rain into mere implications. A chill damp breeze stroked the back of her neck, and her shoulders tensed. Rain was not the conclusion for which the breathless atmosphere of Minras waited.

Solifrax gleamed on her lap, its crystalline blade shining so brightly that the small room was filled by light, shadowless. Odd, Sumitra thought, Rue had not brought food or a lamp, and yet it must be almost evening. Was Chrysais going to let her repent of her stubbornness in dark, hungry solitude?

She asked herself, If the sword and the shield speak to me, does that mean I can speak to them? And yet who am I to call the magic of the gods and demand its use?

Solifrax sighed. "All right then," Sumi said to it. "You can challenge me, the gods can challenge me, only so often. If the issue must be forced, then I shall force it indeed."

The sword murmured sweet nothings against her hands. The warmth of her resolve filled her like strong wine. "If you are Andrion's," she said to the sword, "then so am I. I am the mother of his heir. I shall not fear shadows."

Sumitra laid the sword next to the shield, fitting them tightly together. Solifrax chimed gently and the shield rang in response, the embossed star rippling with light. Their familiarity no longer disturbed her; it was right, somehow, that they should be consorts.

After that initial note of music the weapons quieted, waiting. The silent evening itself waited.

A gleam caught the corner of her eye and Sumitra glanced again out the window. Was the sun at last going to appear, now, almost too late, as evening crept inexorably across the sea toward Minras? The strands of rain were stretched as fine as the silk thread with which she had stitched pictures of the shield and sword, glinting not only silver and gold, but every color of the rainbow.

She let down her hair and combed it. She picked up the zamtak. Her fingers stroked the strings, tentatively at first; then, as they hummed with a power not at all unlike the humming power of the sword and the shield, quite deliberately. She did not play a ballad or a jig, but improvised train after train of rising notes, wordless and elemental, drawn not from her mind but from her soul. Andrion, come, come to me. . . .

Each group of notes did not die away but hung suspended; each new note built upon the ones before, until the air vibrated with melody. The wind freshened, sieving the rain into ethereal threads of color and light. The sword flared, and the shield shone in its embrace, emitting a harmony that grew louder and richer until the ancient stones of the palace reverberated with it, summoned from an age-long stupor.

Sumitra compressed her lips, and unaware of the drop of perspiration that trickled down her cheek, ignoring the brief qualm of nausea her intensity cost her, played on.

Andrion stepped warily into the darkened room, his hand groping toward the hilt that was not at his side. The room was pervaded with a pungent and yet fresh scent, not sorcery, not lotus. Had the rain at last cleansed this unhealthy place?

No. A small pot sat upon a table beside a lamp, matted with what looked like an unappetizing mess of stewed herbs. Two empty cups sat nearby, next to a water jug. Andrion sniffed; yes, the pleasing aroma was wafting from the pot. What had Dana been brewing? Where, for that matter, was Dana, and Tembujin with her?

All Andrion could hear was the rain drifting in sheets across the roof. A chill breeze crept in the windows and tightened his nape. He looked in one room leading off the main chamber, and another, and another. There, two dim shapes lay mounded upon the bed.

It seemed as if black flames licked out from the corners of the room, held at bay only by the sweet smell of the herbs. But when Andrion turned to look directly at the fire, it was gone. He shook his head to clear it of such fancies and approached the bed with a puzzled frown.

The two upturned faces were smooth and peaceful, Dana's

blond hair mingled with Tembujin's black upon the same pillow. So that is what it is like when they make love, Andrion thought, and quickly shrugged that fancy away too. As if Dana would engage in illicit activity.

The two fully-clothed bodies were sprawled like wrung-out rags, felled by exhaustion. Andrion touched Dana's throat. Yes, she was breathing deeply and evenly. He hated to wake her; the tight lines beside her mouth, the worried furrow in her brow, had relaxed, and her lips were actually curved in a slight smile. But it was quite apparent that something had happened.

Surrendering to impulse, he sat upon the edge of the bed, leaned down, and kissed those parted lips. Some hint of sweetness still clung to them, and some hint of bile and bitter weeds as well. His frown deepened.

Dana's lashes fluttered and opened. Her green eyes rolled independently for a moment, and then squinting with effort, focused. "Ah," she croaked. "Would you take advantage of me, Andrion?"

"Of course," he said. "But not as whoever drugged you would have. Is that not what happened?"

Groaning, she stretched. Her limbs did not seem to function as efficiently as she could have wished; to Andrion's regret her face furrowed again. Much as his own was furrowed, with resentful puzzlement.

Tembujin twitched and swore some muffled oath in his own language. With a glance at him, Dana said, "We found evidence of Chrysais's sorcery. But Eldrafel caught us. He is—he is so infuriatingly smug! No reprimand, no questions, only a cup of elder wine." She grimaced. "We saw the herb garden later. The wine was tainted."

"Dana," rasped Tembujin, "countered with herbs of her own. Most unpleasant effects, I must say."

"That was the bryony. An emetic," she added to Andrion. "Then antithora and nettle as antidotes."

Andrion grimaced in sympathy. "He poisoned you?"

"Oddly enough, no. I think we were given a small dose of valerian and opium, enough to make us sleep like babes until tomorrow." She added grimly, "Eldrafel drank the same wine, but I venture to say was not affected. He must be accustomed to such infernal brews."

Andrion did not like that. But then, there was very little here that he did like. The innocence of the child Gard was an anomaly, the neglected loose stitch in an overwrought tapestry. "It is most encouraging," he said, "that despite Eldrafel's smugness he wished to put a stop to your curiosity. He and Chrysais have something to hide."

"Indeed," Dana said dryly, and went on to tell of the tapestry and its many images. "I do not think it can be destroyed by conventional means. I do not know if its destruction would break the enchantments it pictures."

"Ah," said Andrion, enlightened. He told the tale of his own discoveries and concluded, "No wonder I have been thinking of tapestries. And I heard Solifrax singing in my necklace. Am I touched by a tendril of your Sight, Dana?"

"I am so sorry," she returned, quite serious.

"Why?" asked Tembujin. "Convenient, is it not, to have an extra sense?"

"It is not a courier service," Dana said scathingly.

Tembujin raised his hand, warding her glare. "All right, all right. I do not understand your Sight, I could not see the blue light in the tower, but that does not make me weak!"

"It makes you a valuable companion," said Andrion.

Dana added, "The one die in this game that cannot be loaded."

"I would rather not play this game at all," Tembujin retorted. Then, in afterthought, "But I have been enspelled— when Sarasvati cut my hair and gave it to my stepmother the witch."

"That spell was directed at you," said Dana.

"And produced the most gratifying results," Andrion added with a quick vulpine grin.

Tembujin growled a cordially explicit insult.

"I think you cannot sense," Dana went on, ignoring the exchange, "how shall I put it"—nonspecific sorceries."

Andrion's thought veered in another direction. "The tapestry bore images of pigs, and I found Niarkos and his men acting like pigs; it bore images of Ilanit and Bonifacio . . ." The idea spun from his grasp.

And into Dana's. "Unsettling, that Chrysais does not seem to need a specific, like a lock of hair, to work her sorceries. Or perhaps I should say Eldrafel needs none. I believe him to be the more powerful of the two; more control." She added between her teeth, "Of course, stealing the shield would of itself weaken Ilanit. And Sabazel."

Andrion asked himself for the hundredth time, What reassurance can I offer in the face of such malignant strength? If only I could learn the rules of this game. He laid his hand on Dana's arm; yes, flesh still warmed flesh, cleanly and without pretense. And more. His ears, he realized, were buzzing faintly, as if bees swarmed just beyond the boundary of his senses. Dana nodded and shrugged resignedly.

"But why Bonifacio?" asked Tembujin. He stood and rescued what looked like a small sapling from the floor, pulled out his dagger and began shaving the bark from it. "What is the point of enspelling a goose like Bonifacio?"

"Because he has the keeping of the imperial diadem," Andrion snarled. He told them of his realization about Rowan's identity. "The loss of the diadem would affect my land as the loss of the shield affects Sabazel."

Tembujin's knife scraped stubbornly. "Khalingu's teeth! I saw both Rowan and Rue but did not catch the resemblance. All you northerners look alike."

Dana turned and tweaked his tail of hair. "Khalingu indeed! We have not told Andrion that Rue has Sumitra's ruby!"

"Ah?" Andrion exhaled. A torrent of hot blood rushed and roiled just behind his ears.

"Eldrafel," Tembujin said, fending Dana off and relieving her of several long black hairs, "did not even try to pretend the ruby was not Sumitra's. She is here, Andrion, just as surely as Solifrax and the shield."

For a moment he was giddy with her nearness. No wonder he heard her song—how she filled him! And how light was Dana's scrutiny; remote, polite. . . . He cleared his throat. "Good. Then we shall be able to retrieve them all at once." He bolted to his feet as decisively as if he had some kind of plan. The faint murmuring in his mind intensified, becoming a sublime harmony. His necklace tickled his throat.

Tembujin pulled several of Dana's hairs from her head and began plaiting the blond with the black. "Perhaps you two seers will sneer at me for asking such, but why is it that Chrysais and Eldrafel can have the sword and yet Andrion is not enspelled?"

"As we said of the shield and the diadem," returned Dana, rubbing her scalp, "Solifrax does not belong to Andrion. Its beneficent magic is a gift of the gods, a legacy he has earned to supplement his own power, but it is not his own."

"Perhaps," Andrion said, waiving the problem of whose

power supplemented whom's, "it is simply not to their purpose to enspell us now. Any more than we are already enspelled." As though in reproof, his necklace sank sharp teeth into his flesh; he gasped aloud and fumbled at it, but it was cool to his hand.

"They call us," Dana said. "Now."

Tembujin, blissfully deaf, tied the plaited hair to either end of the yew branch, bending it into a facsimile of a small Khazyari bow. He plucked it. "Primitive," he stated, "but if I can find some arrows . . ." The bowstring sang, adding a quick grace note to the music swelling about them.

"Come," said Andrion. "We are summoned."

Tembujin looked at him quizzically. "All right. Fine."

Andrion stepped between the guards at the door with a graceful bow; as they saluted, Tembujin and Dana quickly cracked their heads together. Just as quickly the unconscious soldiers were concealed in the room.

The evening sunlight was like molten bronze. The sun burned just on the horizon, pouring its glory with an almost audible clangor against the blue-black clouds still thronging the east. Sea birds spiraled like pen strokes across a dark but clear sky. The city, the harbor, the statues of Taurmenios were as bright and crisp as gold-leafed miniatures. Sumitra had such a picture, Andrion thought, of her father's palace in the Mohan. Orocastria seemed just as remote, and the quarter moon was so far away as to be merely an idea.

The mountain of Zind Taurmeni blended into the even more massive peaks of storm clouds, but distant Mount Tenebrio was now clearly defined. Its flattened crown dented the arch of the indigo sky. Andrion pointed it out to Dana and Tembujin, adding, "Gard says an ancient shrine is there, and beyond, another port, Akrotiri." Another port, he thought, and barely heard Dana mutter, "The rites of Taurmenios Tenebrae. His shrine, is it?"

The cool, clean wind shimmered with music and impatience. Definitely the zamtak, Andrion told himself, igniting the voices of the sword and shield. He had no doubt that Sumitra was resourceful enough to learn such a skill. He glanced up at the far buttresslike wing of the palace. It was still oddly undefined.

"It shifts as you look at it, hiding," Dana said.

"No," said Tembujin. "It is a slab of rock with windows—narrow windows, like a cell."

Andrion clapped him upon the shoulder, almost cheerful.
"A spell is upon it then. Something is hidden there. Come."

Rolling his eyes, Tembujin settled his bow upon his shoulder and started toward a corridor that looked as if it might lead toward their goal.

"By the way," Andrion asked Dana in diffident aside, "what were you dreaming, to smile so peacefully in your sleep?"

Her mouth softened in a brief unguarded smile. "Of you, and Sabazel, and the full moon."

"Ah," he replied lamely, but she had already settled her dagger in its sheath and strode after Tembujin.

The palace was as silent as if abandoned. Andrion glanced down into the arena. Although his eyes were dazzled by sunlight diffused through cloud and damp, he could see figures crawling along the shaded galleries, gathering for yet another ceremony; they huddled in darkness untouched by the rich light streaming above them. God-ridden people, he thought. Like beasts of burden, moving stolidly from task to task, from rite to rite, believing, no doubt, that their rites are what turn the natural cycles of the world. How innocent. How arrogant.

The three plunged into the corridor. Within moments they were lost. And yet the music was like a guiding thread, now fading, now swelling, and warily they moved on.

This, Andrion thought, is the oldest part of the building. Bulwarks of stone thrust aside the gay paints, the graceful colonnades of the facade. A tangle of squat tunnels ran down into a darkness hardly disturbed, let alone dispelled, by guttering torches. Here was eternal twilight disdainful of the gold and enamel filigree of the outer palace. A distant drip of water played counterpoint to the echo of their footsteps.

Some of the black openings they passed were storerooms, redolent of grain, wine, and oil, with lintels well worn by centuries of feet. Other doorways had not been passed for ages, the dust undisturbed. Andrion's curious glance showed small alcoves, one-time shrines, perhaps, holding votive offerings barely discernible beneath crusted dirt and cobwebs. Tiny leering gargoyles, not bulls. The air was dank, stained with some ancient evil, and his flesh prickled. God-ridden indeed, by deities much darker than his own.

The music thrilled on. They followed into a huge underground area, probably natural cavern, its ceiling upheld by irregular rows of rough-hewn pillars. Giant vases, some cracked and empty, others filled with oil, were ranged among them. An eddying miasma was evidence that some of the slaves whose duties brought them here were ignorant of the clever indoor plumbing available to their masters upstairs.

The music faded for a moment. Through it Andrion heard a shuffle and a moan. No, Sumitra could not be here, in this dark and dirty place. He leaped toward the sound.

Two figures huddled under a dying torch. One man, one woman, crouching as though the approaching footsteps were those of pursuing tormentors.

Andrion recognized them both, and scowled. Jemail was bent forward in a pained arc, his naked back laced with oozing red stripes. When he recognized his erstwhile prisoners he looked quickly away, resentment stiffening his body. Rue did not move. Her hand that had been mopping ineffectually at Jemail's back remained frozen in midair. Her huge dark eyes were stricken, dull with pain and despair, revealing nothing of the woman beneath. Blood smeared her face, and for a crazed moment Andrion thought she had been feasting on Jemail's wounds.

But no. He bent closer, not wanting to help these people, knowing he was honor bound to help any sufferer. And he saw the red glint in Rue's nose, like a drop of crimson blood reflecting the flickering light; the hollow of her nostril had been pierced by the ruby stud, in savage imitation of Sumitra.

"Who did this to you?" Andrion demanded.

With a sigh of reluctant sympathy Dana tore one last flounce from her garment and began peering into the surrounding storage vases. Tembujin scrabbled through what seemed to be a pile of wooden poles. The water dripped in maddening cadence.

"Who?" As if he had to ask.

"Queen Chrysais ordered me whipped," snapped Jemail to a moldy patch on the wall, "for letting your companions disturb her private chamber."

The man's cap was missing; presumably he had been demoted as well. Andrion sighed. Unfair, yes, but soldiers were usually treated less with fairness than with expediency. He was to be an example to the others, no doubt. Andrion hoped that the guards from whom they had escaped moments before would not suffer any worse fate than Jemail had. As if hundreds had not died at my behest seven years ago, he reminded himself harshly.

Dana appeared at his side, her cloth reeking with sour wine. "Vinegar, to cleanse the wounds," she said from the side of her mouth. Rue flinched at her touch, her pale skin becoming almost green; with a grim, self-mocking smile, Dana persevered, not gently but quite thoroughly.

"I suppose," Rue hissed to Andrion, "you will want the jewel back."

"Did you steal it?" he returned.

"No. She gave it to me, for my service."

Dana vented a short, sceptical laugh, and turned her attentions to Jemail. He, at least, glanced at her with grudging appreciation.

Tembujin bent beside Andrion, several dusty arrows tucked into his belt. "All sorts of useful things down here," he said to Andrion, "besides being a good place to lick one's wounds and hide until a storm blows over." And to Rue, "What kind of service? Sumitra would not reward you for betraying her. And my wife."

Rue seemed almost to have forgotten Valeria's existence. She gulped and asked faintly, "Is the lady well?"

"She is, now," replied Tembujin. "I suppose you are not to blame for the death of our child or of our bodyguard."

"Or of Lyris," Dana said through her teeth.

A tremor of guilt moved in Rue's face and then faded. "I serve the lord Eldrafel," she said, repeating a catechism. "I promised Sumitra nothing; why should I not have her ruby? It was Chrysais who thought I had earned it by telling Sumitra her husband had come." She shut her mouth with a snap of finality.

Sumi knows I am here? She plays to summon me? "Where is she?" Andrion asked. Rue looked sullenly past him.

Dana finished with Jemail. "The woman is a slave," she said scornfully. "A puppet. Leave her what shred of dignity you can, her loyalty, and settle the score with the master who manipulates her." She cleaned her hands of dirt and blood, and of animosity toward Rue, and threw the rag away. Her lips were clamped tightly shut, as if she had swallowed something slimy and struggled to keep it down.

"But I am no slave. And I will not be treated as such." Jemail pulled himself to his feet and stood at shaky attention.

"I will take you to your lady wife, my lord, if you will accept my service freely given."

"Traitor," Rue said, flat, into her lap.

"Treachery," Andrion told her, "is in the definition. No doubt your brother Rowan, gnawing his treacheries in Sardis, justifies his betrayal of me by believing he serves someone greater."

Rue shuddered, her head bending, her shoulders contracting until she was curled into a ball. Protecting her soft belly, Andrion told himself. "Keep the jewel," he said to her spiny shell. "You have paid for it." And to Jemail he said, "I accept your service, Captain, with thanks."

They walked away, following Jemail's lead, leaving Rue stiff and silent. The labyrinthine corridors closed around them, twisting this way and that like a rat shaken by a cat. The air, what air there was, was cold and damp and stifling. You could hide a body here, Andrion thought; in only days it would molder into an indistinct blotch of fungus, its humanity consumed. And he thought, Sabazians burn their dead, purifying the worldly flesh. . . . He shook himself. Really, this oppressive place produced the most morbid fancies!

After what seemed like years they came to a staircase. At its top was a closed door. Jemail signaled them to wait and slipped through. Andrion peeked out and was relieved to see that it was the same evening; the sun had set, leaving the sky appropriately blood-tinted.

"Is Rue enspelled to her treachery, do you think?" Tembujin asked Dana.

Dana snorted. "You saw her face as Eldrafel played with her. It was not as she had dreamed, to be so blatantly used by the one she craves. I would say the spell that holds her is much more subtle, that of the heart."

"I wager," Andrion said half to himself, "that it was Chrysais's jealousy that earned Rue her punishment, not the ruby." His sister's cruelty was unsettling. So was the obsession with Eldrafel which spawned it. That disturbingly elegant figure lurked behind everything, no doubt, greedy for power.

Jemail returned and waved them onto another terrace. This was shabbier than the one from which they had started, edged with neglected myrtle bushes. Glancing over his shoulder, Andrion could just see beyond the intervening rooftops the terrace and lotus pool outside their chambers, shrouded in the gathering dusk. Sumi, then, could well have seen him from here. His mind drifted like a lotus petal on the smooth cascade of her music.

The body of a guard, his neck twisted at a bizarre angle, sprawled outside another doorway. As relieved as Andrion was to find a guard somewhere in this strangely deserted place, he still had to say, "Jemail, you did not have to kill him."

The hawk-nosed Minran hoisted the corpse's spear. "It would never do to have one of my mates report that I now serve you."

Easy to catch someone by surprise, when you are a friend. But it was too late to be squeamish now; they were inside the corridor. Tembujin's head went up, listening. "I hear it!" he exclaimed.

Before the words were quite out of his mouth, the music stopped. And yet its resonance still hung on the air, echoing in the ear or in the mind; it did not matter. Andrion told Jemail to watch the outer door. Before him were three barred cells. Unerringly he went to the farthest one and placed his hand on the wood. It was warm to his touch, vibrating through his entire body.

He released the bar and flung open the door.

The room was filled with spiraling gold and silver motes like the last remnant of sunset. In the midst of the brilliance was a shape, not a shadow but somehow the opposite of a shadow, a form molded of light itself. Even as Andrion squinted through the glorious radiance it ebbed, absorbed with a slow sonorous hum into a disk and a crescent, and into the body of a woman.

Sumitra sat on a narrow bed. The strings of the zamtak on her lap still thrilled beneath her fingertips. Tears hung in shining strands upon her cheeks. Her dark, lambent eyes touched Dana without surprise, met Tembujin with pleasure, and fixed upon Andrion. They flooded with serene joy, the fear and doubt of her ordeal forgotten. He had come. He had cared enough to come.

The room was gone. The entire world was gone. Andrion saw only Sumitra. His feet did not even touch the floor as he rushed into her embrace. Her warmth seeped through him, and jasmine and apricots flooded his senses. He had not realized until now just how parched he had been. His pride was only an affectation, his rank insignificant, it was her touch that mattered—but without his rank he would never have known her, and his life would have been a withered leaf tumbling aimlessly in the wind. . . .

The wind. He saw then, beyond the soft hair pillowing his cheek, Dana watching him hold his wife. Her face was raw with a regret made doubly poignant by her denial of it. The floor rose suddenly beneath his feet and jarred him back into reality. The game was not over, the players still ranged themselves in intricate patterns, the rules were still maddeningly subtle.

Dana's expression was gone, wiped away by resolve, before he could respond to it. She did not want him to respond. She thrust out her chin, tilted back her head, lifted the shield that lay at her feet and clasped it in a passionate grip. The great disk flared in her face. Turning away slightly, retreating into her close-fitting carapace of law and duty and desperate righteousness, she searched the shield as if its shining surface were the liquid in the bronze basin of Sabazel. "Mother," she whispered, "Astra. Kerith."

Sumitra's face pressed against Andrion's shoulder, her hands kneaded his cloak. "Purple becomes you," she said. The movement of her lips against his skin was ripple after ripple of a delight that was almost, but not quite, unalloyed.

Tembujin, glancing uncomfortably from Andrion to Dana and back, bent and picked up Solifrax. He hefted it, curious but clumsy. Sparks rushed along the crystalline blade to shower over Andrion.

With a shrug and a bow, Tembujin surrendered it to its owner.

Bliss. The hilt of Solifrax tingling in his hand, and Sumitra snug in the circle of his arm. . . . Dana still bent over the unyielding rim of the shield. All they had done was to complete one set of the never-ending game. The conclusion was distant as ever. Andrion's exultation drained away, leaving him light-headed. He stiffened himself and asked the necessary question, "Now what? Do we flee across the island and find a ship at Akrotiri to take us home?"

"Yes," Dana replied. Her features were harrowed by more than the effort of translating the images in the shield. "Or we can hide until Miklos comes looking for us."

"Hide?" asked Tembujin caustically.

"You would suggest we attack?" Andrion retorted. "We would surely be caught if we searched for a ship here. If we came to the dye works by sea, not by land, we could rescue Niarkos and the others without raising too much of an alarm.'' And stir the pot of the gods ourselves this time? That would remain to be seen. One whole hell of a lot remained to be seen. He offered Dana and Tembujin a slightly crazed smile; they exchanged a wary glance and smiled back, like prisoners pretending bravado before their executioner.

Harus protect us! Andrion swore, and managed to belt on the sheath of Solifrax without releasing Sumitra. She clung to him, her hands taproots into the soil of his flesh—the shape of her abdomen was hidden under her gown, and he would not grope for it before the others—gods! she would have to walk across the island, would she not? Well, his own mother had been further along in pregnancy when she rode to Iksandarun—and you were born early, some nagging thought told him. No choice, he told it, and stilling the whirlpool of his own mind, he led the way out of the cell and down the corridor.

The clear evening had bleared into hazy night. The wind was already stained with a scent of spoiled fruit; an eerie chant floated from the arena, like a creeping fever distorting the perceptions and revealing hideous images in the depths of the mind. ''Captain Jemail,'' Andrion said, trying to ignore scent, chant, and fever, ''take us to Akrotiri.''

The soldier opened his mouth, but Andrion's glinting eye, and the sword glinting as brightly in his hand, stopped any comments in his throat. He made a smart about-face and headed toward a narrow stairway.

Tembujin, carrying Sumitra's zamtak, eyed the somber darkness. Dana's dagger glimmered, reflecting the faint glow of the shield. Andrion, his left arm still securely around Sumi, raised Solifrax like a lantern with his right. The blade shone with a pure white light.

Which illuminated a shape skulking behind the myrtles. Jemail leaped, and after a brief struggle deposited the form of a boy at Andrion's feet. The luminescence of the sword polished Gard's gray eyes into silver mirrors.

Andrion was not quite sure whether he was pleased to find the apparent ambush only a child. ''What are you doing here?'' he demanded.

''Following you,'' the boy answered with disarming candor. ''I went to my mother's chambers after my lessons, but

she was making love with Lord Eldrafel." He grimaced as
though dosed with bryony.

Sumitra chuckled. Andrion had to agree, physical love had
its ludicrous moments. But Tembujin said indulgently, "When
you get older you will change your opinion."

"Everyone says that," returned Gard, not believing a word
of it. And he looked with interest at the sword and the shield
and the woman held so tightly against Andrion's side. "Is she
your wife? What did you do to Rue; why is she in the cellar
bawling? Is that sword yours? Is that shield hers? Are you
escaping? Will you take me hostage?"

"We did nothing to Rue," Andrion said, briefly giddy at
the barrage of questions. "This is my wife Sumitra, and my
sword Solifrax. The shield belongs to Ilanit of Sabazel, of
whom Dana is a deputy. And I think you can simply return to
your room." The chant from the arena seemed to grow
louder, emanating from every direction at once, surrounding
them.

Gard drew himself up; his head came just to Andrion's
ribs. "If you send me away, I shall go straight to my mother."

Jemail's face went ashen. Andrion quelled an impulse to
shake the boy until, like milk coagulating into butter, his
bravado became an appreciation of the situation. But then,
with his limited experience he could probably never appreciate the situation. Innocent? Perhaps, but Gard was nowhere
near as naive as Andrion had been at that age. Iksandarun had
had its intrigues, but it had hardly been a sensual hothouse
like Minras.

The boy's threat was not an idle one. He did not lack
courage, to follow them alone through the gibbering shadows
of the cellars.

Andrion glanced at Dana, brows raised. Was it ill-considered
to try and throw their tormentors off balance? He could not
visualize Eldrafel's lithe body ever losing its balance. But
Sardians, Khazyari, Sabazians did not wait like dumb bul-
locks to be used. Dana offered a brief shrug, a crimp of her
mouth, a sound that was part laugh, part groan. Do it; we
have no other choice.

Harus! Andrion exclaimed to himself, and to the boy he
said sternly, "We will only take you with us if you behave
yourself."

"Yes, yes," Gard agreed with a solemn nod, but his eyes
danced.

"Gods!" protested Tembujin. "Instead of having half the army of Minras after us, we shall have it all!"

Gard seemed even more delighted at that prospect. With an exhalation of aggravated amusement, Tembujin handed the zamtak to the boy and set an arrow to his makeshift bow. Gard obediently shouldered the instrument.

"Let us go," said Andrion, and they went, led by the shimmering crescent of the sword and the gleaming circle of the shield. The chanting swelled and died away. The wind muttered uneasily across the sky, the moon and stars cold, sputtering lamps in its depths.

Rue stood in the doorway leading into the cellars. Her eyes were red-rimmed with bitter cunning, her small mouth was circled as tight as a clenched fist, hating those who deigned to pity her. Her baleful glare followed the shadowed figures until they were absorbed like ghosts into the unforgiving night.

Chapter Ten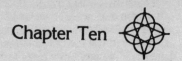

CHRYSAIS'S AND ELDRAFEL'S bedchamber was not appreciably darker at night than it had been during the day's gloom. The lamps cast a brazen aura that only emphasized the shadows lurking in the corners and at the top of the staircase.

Rue lay prostrate upon the marble floor. The ruby in her nose winked as if struggling to detach itself from her. Her liquid eyes, muddied with cunning, gazed up through her lashes at Chrysais.

The queen sat huddled in the midst of the bed, rising from the churned bedclothes like Zind Taurmeni rising from its cracked and fissured slopes. Perhaps smoke hovered around her as well, or perhaps it was merely the floating strands of her tousled chestnut hair. Her mouth, pale and sulky without its crimson paint, was turned so severely down at the corners that creases marred the softness of her chin. Her slightly smeared face seemed imperfect, and therefore more human than her gaudy mask. "They took Gard," she essayed.

The slave cast a wary look at Eldrafel. He sat on the edge of the bed, wrapped in a loose robe whose folds were at once careless and artfully draped to set off the smooth, strong lines of his torso. His hair was as sleekly contained by the fillet as always, his face the usual unconcerned facade. His gleaming eyes rested on Rue; intercepting her glance, they stirred, very briefly, and his brow rose, just a bit. He might have been amused that she had dared to return, or that Andrion had dared to free Sumitra, or most likely that he himself dared to stay within an arm's length of smoldering Chrysais, goading her with his coolness.

Rue licked her lips. "And, and they know about Rowan in Sardis."

Eldrafel nodded. His other brow twitched.

"Is that all?" Chrysais demanded.

Rue stared at her a moment. "I have told you all I know, serving you faithfully although—"

"Although you are Lord Eldrafel's slave, and mine only by default?" Chrysais's eyes were sapphire projectiles.

Rue tried to bury her forehead in the floor. "The Lord Eldrafel has promised my brother and myself freedom, if his plans are brought to fruition."

"True," said Eldrafel. "When my plans are brought to fruition."

Mollified, her mouth relaxing a little, Chrysais repeated, "Is that all?"

The woman nodded.

"Then go now, and anticipate your reward."

Rue went. The door shut with a snap. Eldrafel rested his chin in his hand, contemplating a blot of shadow across the room.

"They took Gard," stated Chrysais. With an extravagant breath, part sigh, part moan, she rolled off the bed, hitched up her robe, and began to pace up and down. Her feet kicked aside the chamomile, leaving moist prints on the floor.

"So they did not succumb to the drug," said Eldrafel. "So the emperor proves his mettle—and his rashness, I wager. I had intended something of the sort, of course." His expression wavered, indignant that some facet of his plan had gone awry, pleased that the game had taken a more challenging turn. But he seemed to find pleasure the more profitable.

"They took Gard!" insisted Chrysais.

"Do you think that proper little prig Andrion would actually harm the boy? Be pleased to have . . ." Eldrafel looked up at Chrysais with a slow smile. ". . . the little bastard out of the way for a time."

Chrysais flushed an ugly mauve. "How can you say that?"

But Eldrafel, inspecting his pearly nails, said, "Interesting, that the brown dove, the wife, could rouse the power of the weapons to such a height. By the living god, I had to bear that infernal music ringing in my head all day!"

Chrysais did not seem particularly sympathetic. "But you did not take the sword and the shield from her. And now they have them."

Eldrafel nobly forebore to point out that he had been occupied with Chrysais herself most of the afternoon. He continued to stare entranced at his own hands.

Chrysais flounced away across the room. She lifted and
turned in her hand the miniature plait of hair she had laid
down earlier. "So they have their weapons again. But where
can they go?"

"Exactly," Eldrafel said with mocking approval. "You
begin to appreciate their problem. A bold gesture; that is all.
Let them have their moment of triumph. Such spirit will be
more acceptable to the god than if they walked like oxen to
the slaughter."

The plait snarled among her fingers, Chrysais said hesi-
tantly, "Eldrafel, my love, is it really necessary . . . ?"

He looked sharply up, and she flinched in the glitter of his
eyes. Not anger, but a ruthless intelligence shaded with the
faintest hint of disappointment.

By rote Chrysais patted her hair, raised her bosom, bit her
lips to redden them. She offered her husband a sly half smile.
In her deepest, sweetest voice she said, "Yes, yes, of course."
And brandishing the strand of black hair, she said, "Shall I
use this to guide them?"

"Ah!" exclaimed Eldrafel. In one fluid movement he rose
from the bed; in another he embraced his wife and escorted
her toward the stairway. "Very good, my dear, very good."

Her cheeks flushed again, becomingly pink this time. She
leaned into his arm as they climbed the stairs. When they
opened the door a cloud of incense billowed out, surrounding
them. Fingers of shadow, cast by the flickering lights inside
the tower, reached across the ceiling of the bedchamber.

Then the door shut, the shadows steadied, and the only
sound was the reed flute of Eldrafel's voice singing in a
minor key, so quietly that it seemed almost to come from the
darkness, from the stone of the palace itself, and not from a
human throat at all.

The moon slid down the western sky, drawn by the indigo of
the night, as pink and coral clouds swarmed up from the east.
Even though Andrion was so tired that the jagged rock he
leaned against seemed as soft as a down pillow, he was so
tense he could not quite catch his breath, let alone rest. Those
hours of paperwork, audiences, and councils were taking their
toll upon his body, he told himself. Tembujin lived a more
active life upon the moors and was already asleep, his hand
protectively near Gard's snoring form.

Jemail sat nearby, dozing over his spear. Did he actually

expect reward for his service? Andrion Bellasteros, Emperor, King of Sardis, would certainly reward him. And poor ensorcelled Niarkos, for that matter. This cold, hungry, hunted man was in no position to reward anyone. Embarrassing, that not one of them had thought to forage in the storerooms for food and blankets. Gard had been quite indignant when he realized his adventure would cost some discomfort, but Tembujin had told him in no uncertain terms to hold his tongue. With alacrity unusual in a child, he had.

Another lesson in humility, Andrion told himself. Harus, Ashtar, whoever and whatever you are, must you be such implacable tutors?

He closed his eyes for a moment, trying to remember their path from Orocastria, failing. Jemail had led them out of the city on the main road, he was sure of that. But then they had followed a maze of paths through the countryside, by low walls that dimly defined groves and vineyards, and along paths hacked up treacherous screes, kept from sliding only by thorny scrub. The setting moon, damp and insubstantial in the perpetual haze of Minras, had afforded almost no light; the stars had been veiled into mere blots of phosphorescence; the wind had offered only brief, odorous puffs, causing leaf and branch to whisper mockingly. A waking nightmare, Andrion thought, a shadowed journey from nowhere to nowhere, serving no purpose.

No purpose? Sumitra lay folded against his side, her zamtak across her lap, watching in drowsy bemusement as Dana stroked the glowing surface of the shield. Did Sumi cling to him all the more tightly because Dana was there? Perhaps; but they were all too polite to take notice. Solifrax rested, murmuring of latent power, along his thigh.

As usual, his wife sensed his thought. "I sang to the shield and to the sword," she said into his throat, her breath sparking his necklace. "I called them, and they answered. Such power, it is . . ."

"Frightening?"

She nodded. "My zamtak speaks, and yet it cannot speak without me. It has never been anything other than a musical instrument. I understand now, Andrion, why you wonder whether the strength is in you or in the sword itself."

He waited, but she did not question further. Thank the gods that her serenity was undamaged; if only he could share some of it. Surely the gods would not have given Sumi such power if they intended to deprive her of the child. Or would they, thinking that the power of the music, of the sword, was compensation for such grief? He snugged her a little closer against his side. Her head became heavier and heavier, and he realized she was asleep.

He smoothed her gown around her, letting his hand linger for a moment on her belly. Yes, it was tautly curved, like the surface of the shield.

Dana, too, sensed his thought. With a long exhalation she at last laid the shield down, turning a drawn and yet gentle gaze onto Sumitra. "She was not surprised to see me here with you."

"She knew you would come for the shield."

"Such certainty," said Dana, so quietly he hardly heard. "She is the perfect foil for you." She must have been exhausted to let such an admission slip. She arranged herself for sleep as if she had said nothing, presenting Andrion with only the angle of her shoulder as she curled about the shield.

Loving them both, Andrion thought, his cheek against Sumitra's hair, his eyes on Dana's back, was like speaking two different, almost complementary languages. It could be done.

He should have felt secure, Solifrax on one side, the zamtak on the other, the shield before him. But he did not.

As Sumitra tried to catch her breath, she indulged herself in an examination of Andrion's aquiline profile, Sardian granite chiseled by the clean wind of Sabazel.

He stood with his hand comfortably on the hilt of Solifrax, surveying the brooding landscape. It was raw and unfinished, jagged rocks piercing the soil, and yet was at the same time immeasurably old, stark chasms cleaving layer after layer of weathered dirt and stone. Sumi wondered what it would look like in spring, when the now dormant groves and vines put on green leaves, when the oranges and almonds blossomed. Now the land was gold and gray, the sky a lacquered eggshell blue. Sea birds floated impassively across its dome, and yellow songbirds trilled from a stand of wizened pine.

Minras, she thought, was a tapestry woven of sensuality, sorcery, and a certain weird beauty. The air itself panted, straining toward some mysterious conclusion. The reek of sulfur and rot was inescapable. Three days' walk behind them Zind Taurmeni was lost in its vaporous shroud; an equal

distance before them Tenebrio solidified into a black hulk.
Beneath Tenebrio was Akrotiri, both Jemail and Gard averred
in their mouth-filling accents. Akrotiri, where Eldrafel had
been born. Perhaps he, too, was inescapable. Sumitra shuddered, and remained short of breath.

In a fold of land suitably far from the main road, Tembujin,
Gard, and Jemail searched for food while Dana started a fire
beside three great rocks tilted together like a tomb. The
Sabazian was so efficient; she hunted, built fires, and slept
easily out of doors. Sumi had never slept on the ground, and
even in Andrion's arms she lay awake wondering how many
spiders and snakes and other silent night creepers were scouting the pleats of her gown.

More than once she had glanced at Dana to see Dana
glancing at her, not angry or resentful, but somehow puzzled.
At how, Sumi told herself, Andrion could care for two women
so different. But Dana's gaze had not once been belligerent or
even hurt; her eyes would slip into their guard towers, and
abandon the problem as irrelevant. She would have to believe
it irrelevant, rather than insoluble, in order to serve her own
certainties. . . . Or so Sumitra thought, being rather vague on
Sabazian protocol.

She looked back at Andrion to see him frowning. He no
doubt found the lack of hue and cry worrying, almost
annoying—they had Gard, after all—but she could do nothing
about it. A few moment's respite from worry; she could
manage that for him. It was really quite stimulating out here,
no walls, no clustering attendants, no need to sit quietly,
hands folded. . . . An adventure.

Down the slope behind her was a valley, a surprising rift of
lush green in the blasted heath of the island's crest. It was
curtained by clouds of steam from several hot springs. Ferns
and flowers thrived in the moist warmth, and bees gamboled
drunkenly above them. A brilliant orange-and-black butterfly
lit on Sumitra's shoulder. Laughing, she tried to get it to
perch on her finger.

Andrion, startled by her laughter, looked around just as the
butterfly tired of the game and wafted away. His frown
evaporated as he, too, glanced into the valley. "No harm in a
bath," he said, "even though Gard would call the warm
pools 'the blood of the god' or something similarly unappetizing."

"The child," she replied, "is really quite engaging,

Chrysais's charm without the flavor of corruption.'' And she allowed herself to wonder if their son would resemble his impish cousin.

Andrion handed her down the slope as though she were as fragile as the butterfly. A pool lying amidst blowsy frills of celandine and myrtle was the perfect temperature; for a time they soaked, letting the heat mend the sores and strains of the journey.

''Bright shone the sun as we lay . . .'' Sumitra sang softly. Andrion stared into the sky as though it were a parchment listing commandments of chastity, his features stern but wistful. Gods, the man's nobility could be downright aggravating! Grinning, Sumi splashed him. He splashed back. She pushed him under the water. He surfaced with a grin of his own.

After a brisk wrestling match, moist skin against moist skin, the soft grass beside the pool was undeniably inviting. Steam drifted in scintillant veils around them, the sword lay exchanging resonances with the zamtak, and the bees caroled overhead. Sumi giggled as the coppery stubble on Andrion's cheeks tickled her throat, her breast, her flanks. He was much too busy to giggle. His body was an intoxicating paradox, strength tempered by tenderness; to Sumi nothing else mattered, and she succumbed to blessed drunkenness.

They clung to each other and to oblivious contentment, limbs woven tightly, belly crushed to belly. Then suddenly Sumitra felt a brief, delicate movement deep in her body. Her skin chimed, and Andrion started. The child had stretched its tiny body, awakening much earlier than expected to make this moment utter perfection. ''He acknowledges his father!'' she exclaimed ecstatically.

Andrion's face was transfigured by delight. But then his innate honesty had to raise its annoying head. ''Actually, it is my place to acknowledge him. If it is a him. What if it is a her?''

Sumi's ecstasy tarnished.

Andrion grimaced and went quickly on, cajoling, teasing. ''If it is a girl, we shall start a new fashion. An empress, taught by Sabazian tutors, riding with the Khazyari. We shall find a prince of the Mohan for her to wed. The only worthwhile thing my councilors have ever done was to choose a Mohendra princess for me.''

She had to smile at his recklessness and at the affection that inspired it, even as she knew the moment was indelibly marred. Indeed, something was hovering like smoke in the interstices of her mind, something that must have seeped into her awareness during those unguarded minutes of physical and emotional surrender. Already the cutting edge of her thought grew dull. I am only tired, she told herself. Very tired.

"I mean that last," Andrion told her, trying to keep her smile from fading. "About my councilors, and you—I missed you terribly, Sumi."

She clung to him fiercely then, frightened that so much as a hair might come between them. But her smile was gone, and contentment was stalked by unease.

Dana was sharpening a stake to impale the scrawny hare Tembujin and Gard had produced, when she saw Andrion and Sumitra returning. They walked close together, understandably reluctant to lose whatever peace they had found this afternoon. All lovers deserved moments of peace, did they not?

Her dagger slipped and sliced an ugly gash in her left forefinger. Clumsy! she shouted at herself. Fool, to let too many different strands of concern trip you up!

With a small sympathetic noise Sumitra ripped her already tattered gown and set about binding the wound. Her eyes avoided Dana's. Embarrassed to be caught loving him? Dana asked herself. Or greedy, wanting to keep her image of him to herself? But such a thought was unworthy of them all.

Dana tried to speak and her words curdled in her throat. Sumitra tried to speak and emitted only an awkward mumble. The constraint was hideous, unwanted but impossible to deny. Andrion watched them, his face a wound scabbed into numb expressionlessness.

Jemail appeared with a crust of bread and a moldy cheese rind begged from a farm. Andrion, as usual, insisted that most of the food be given to Sumitra and Gard. When she protested, when the child wrinkled his nose in distaste, one strict if fond look from the shuttered eyes of the emperor and they ate.

As night fell the stars and moon were swallowed in fog. The huge rocks that sheltered them seemed to grow taller and lean menacingly over them. Sumitra plunked idly at her zamtak while Gard, the only animated figure in the group, frolicked about the fire. He tried to draw Solifrax, to hear its warning hiss, and an impatient gesture from Andrion brought him to heel with the self-satisfaction of a child wanting his elders to notice his amiability.

The boy threw himself down beside Jemail, and Jemail flinched away from the chestnut hair and the gray eyes. Muttering something about standing guard, he hoisted his spear and disappeared into the darkness.

Dana sifted her thought for some reminiscence she could share jokingly with Andrion and Tembujin, but all the lighter moments of their campaign seven years before had been exhausted on the previous nights; the dregs of memory left her feeling old and used. And it was unfair to keep firing bolts of reminiscence past Sumitra's serenity, reminding her that her husband had lived a lifetime before he ever knew her.

Serenity? Dana repeated. The jangling zamtak, the tongues of sickly sweet fog lapping at the borders of the firelight, the dejected quiet of the group, set her teeth on edge. So did Gard's eyes, like and yet unlike his cousin Eldrafel's. "How did Gath die?" she asked, thinking aloud.

Andrion and Tembujin stiffened. Gard said, "He was drunk and went to bathe, and the water was too hot and cooked him like a lobster."

The silence was so thick that when a string on the zamtak suddenly broke, its ping reverberated like a bow shot. Sumitra swore under her breath, at the string or at the boy's callous words, or at both. But to him Gath had been a stranger, the object of a cautionary tale, not real.

Andrion cleared his throat and said, with heavy-handed jocularity, "You seem to enjoy being a hostage, Gard."

"I was to have been one before," returned the child. "Traded for the son of Melkart of far Dibourti. But when Melkart came to arrange the details, he was taken suddenly ill and died, and the little boy became king—with our help, of course."

With Minran help, indeed, Dana said to herself. Near that dusky garden of herbs sudden illness and death must be commonplace. Nothing is safe here.

Conversation languished. Each form lay wrapped in its own prickly mantle. Dana, her head resting upon the comforting quicksilver chime of the shield, did not think she could sleep. And yet she did.

She knew the vision that took her was unequivocally true. She stood on the hard, cold marble floor of a corridor, just inside the shadow surrounding the guttering lamp. But the guard outside Patros's and Kleothera's bedroom door looked right through her, not seeing her. The silence of the early morning hours was broken only by a distant hollow ringing like the sea. By the rumble of chariots in the streets. And by footsteps.

The guard peered into the darkness. Apparently he saw nothing. But Dana could see the young priest, his eyes rolled back in his head, holding a knife half concealed in his robes.

The guard yawned. The priest lunged. The soldier's open mouth was frozen, gaping, as his eyes gaped in death. The priest lowered his body soundlessly to the floor.

Dana tried to move. She could not. She strained forward, struggling to make her oddly numb limbs respond. Then she realized that she had no body, only eyes to see, a mind to understand.

The priest slipped through the door. His eyes in the lamplight glittered crazily, the pupils as tiny as poppy seeds.

Dana's thought leaped. The walls dissolved before her. She saw the bedchamber, the wide bed with embroidered hangings moving gently. The wind was fresh and cool off the Sar, and a frail moonpath shimmered on the floor, kissing the cradle beside the bed.

The bloody knife lifted the hangings. Patros lay, smiling slightly, his arms wrapped around Kleothera's body, holding her against him. She was a perfect fit.

Black flame flickered about the knife. Dana writhed, her thought twisting about the spindle of her desperation, tighter and tighter. Abruptly, with an expulsive wrench like a birth pang, her mind broke free. The cradle beside the bed shuddered as Declan emitted a shriek.

Kleothera started awake, saw the priest, the knife, the black fire, and shrieked in turn. Patros, instantly alert, rolled out the far side of the bed and pulled her with him. The priest staggered, struck blindly at the bedclothes, then turned toward the cradle.

In perfect synchrony Patros and Kleothera threw a blanket over the priest's head and bore him down. Patros twisted his wrist until the knife fell clattering onto the floor. Kleothera hurried to the cradle and swept up the baby.

Declan's wails subsided into little breathless hiccups as he burrowed onto her shoulder. I am sorry, Dana cried silently, that I had to wake you—with a pang she realized that she had indeed touched him across the leagues between them. Her son had her Sight. If she had kept him—no, not even Danica could keep a son. And without Declan's warning, Patros would be dead—although by the laws of Sabazel Dana should not have even known Patros, let alone cared for him. . . .

Astra was her heir. It was she who counted for everything in the closed world of Ashtar.

Guards were clanking down the hallway. Torches flared, driving away the darkness and the moonpath as well. For a moment it seemed to Dana as if Patros saw her, or sensed whatever part of her was with him. Gravely, if somewhat puzzled, he nodded his thanks. But his image was already dwindling, then was gone.

Dana stared upward into the enigmatic Minran sky. She had been in Sardis; she had no doubt of that. She wanted only to go home to Sabazel. All the seas and all the skies between her and Sabazel were an aching void in her heart.

Andrion's dim form loomed over her. "You were moaning; was it a vision?"

She sighed. "A priest, no resemblance to Rue, tried to kill Patros tonight. Thank the goddess I was able to warn him through little Declan."

He scowled. "Does Rowan have enough power to direct the priests of Harus to his own foul ends? Patros would indeed stand in their way; his loyalty cannot be bought. I only hope it cannot be spelled." And Andrion, too, sighed. "I do not suppose you could message Nikander to return to the north?"

She shook her head. "Sorry."

Andrion settled down beside her. For a time they spoke of the Sight, and of Sardis and Sabazel; she could see only Sardis, he suggested, because the tangled threads of Chrysais's, of Eldrafel's plot, had not yet tightened further about Sabazel.

That was not any less unsettling. Perhaps she simply could not sense happenings in Sabazel, or . . . "What I fear the most," she concluded, too weary to dissemble, "is that I am not interpreting my Sight correctly, and instead of leading us to freedom, I lead us deeper into a trap."

"We would be entrapped in any event," Andrion returned, struggling against bitterness. "It is my choice, too, to search out the snare."

"As Gath did? As that other king—Melkart?"

He did not reply. He knew the limits of her Sight as well as he knew his own limits; he might condemn himself, but not her. For too long had they woven a fabric of experience that was theirs alone. Now, in this dark hour, they did not even touch, because they did not have to.

Sumitra, Dana realized, was not asleep. Her eyes were jet slits, hooded by her lashes. Not jealous of her husband's intimate colloquy with the Sabazian; that was a word Sumi did not know. But still a shadow drifted over her expression as she watched them, as if the effort to be tolerant cost her more emotional currency than she had to spare.

Something, Dana fretted suddenly, followed them across the interior of the island, some invisible hound of hell sniffed at their heels, until, tired as they were, they could not rest but waited, poised and wary, ready to leap aside from a bite that would not come.

The fog drifted like a rent curtain across the moon, but its clammy gibbous face held no counsel and no comfort.

Andrion squinted upward. A falcon, the first he had seen since arriving on Minras, lay against the arch of the evening sky as if painted upon it. "So you come at last, Harus," he said to it. "You would be better advised to protect your chosen city and leave me to find my own fate." The bird remained impassive. The air was torpid, as foul as a drunkard's breath, reeking of brimstone and corruption.

Andrion scratched his chin beneath its coat of coppery stubble. Dana's lips were a tight fissure, he noted, and Tembujin's cheekbones were axe blades. He did not have to turn around to see that Sumitra's eyes were sunk deep, their brightness dulled. But she seemed uncharacteristically tense rather than tired. Had she been that way ever since those moments of delirium in the hidden valley? But hunger and weariness and worry made his own mind spin tauntingly with a frenzied dread, and subtlety was beyond him.

He peered down the boulder-strewn scree before him toward the small whitewashed boxes edging a harbor that was Akrotiri. The water was so clear that the fishing boats upon it seemed to be suspended in blue-green crystal. As the sun sank farther into the west, the shade of the cliff poured over town and harbor, blotting up the colors. The road downward, a gold ribbon strung from thorn bush to thorn bush, disappeared.

A dangerous trek in the dark, Andrion mused. And even if they arrived safely in Akrotiri, their clothing, stained and torn by their journey, could not have distinguished them from beggars. Except for Andrion's now dirt-mottled purple cloak, and the clear unsullied light of the sword he bore, and the purity of the light of the shield Dana bore beside him. None of which would buy them a boat.

They could steal one, he thought, and send payment later. Although none of them knew how to handle a boat, perhaps they could at least sail a small one back to Orocastria to free Niarkos and the others, evading pursuit by doubling back on their tracks.

Pursuit? What pursuit? That was reason enough for nervousness. They could not wait for Miklos to come and find them. They had to get off this haunted island!

With a sharp gesture Andrion turned around, Dana and Tembujin with him. Sumitra was gone. His heart, already racing, palpitated painfully. Unlike her, to wander away by herself. Gard pointed, Jemail gestured with his spear, and they turned up a path leading away from the cliff toward the beetling mass of Tenebrio. It had once been a paved road, but now the flagstones were settled crazily, overgrown by tiny creeping plants.

There she was, just entering a grove of trees; cypress and yew, shivering despite the still air, sifted the sunlight into cobwebs of light and dark. When Andrion stepped beneath the heavy branches, the hilt of Solifrax writhed in his hand. The shield swirled, its light sickly. The zamtak on Gard's shoulder jangled. Tembujin cursed. Jemail stopped dead, his eyes huge and frightened. "Wait here," Andrion said, not without sympathy, and they left Jemail behind.

Beyond the trees they plunged into a wilderness of grotesquely shaped stone. Worked stone, weathered over a millenium, until the toppled columns, the blind lumpish statues, were parodies of their original shapes. The road led between pillars that still stood, some square, some round, carved from porphyry, travertine, marble—even, Andrion swore, Sardian granite—all arranged like tributes to some ancient ruler.

Tenebrio filled the dusk. Its slopes were billow after billow of shining black stone like petrified waves threatening to inundate the heavens. Its crest blunted a rose-quartz sky and cast a smoky lavender shadow over the ruined . . . town? Temple? In the purple-tinted translucence every texture was accentuated, every shape crisp, every sound uncannily clear. Sumitra's footsteps, echoing from the rocky slopes of the mountain, were magnified into the marching tread of an army.

"I did not know we were so close," Andrion said to Dana, gazing warily up at the bare-branched vineyards and drystone walls upon the mountainside.

"It jumped out at us," she returned. Cold sweat stood like beads of ice across her forehead and she gasped for breath.

Andrion's nape crawled. This place was filled with an effluvia of sorcery, like a whirlpool sucking down all the evil air of the island, circling, circling. . . . "Sumitra!" he called, and the name, too, echoed, repeated again and again in a mocking torrent.

Sumitra walked on. Gard plucked at Andrion's cloak, whining to go back. Tembujin set an arrow to his bow. The string glinted gold and ebony.

Some presence was behind him. Andrion spun about. Solifrax flared from its sheath, slicing through the gathering violet shadows. A spectral moon hung above the sea, its slightly ovoid shape imperfect, incomplete; it would not be full until tomorrow night. To Andrion its face was a baleful glare. But I am your son! he protested. It gave him no sign. His necklace was heavy on his throat, choking him; he could not fill his lungs in this accursed air.

Sumitra swayed and sank to her knees among the ash-dusted bracken. She buried her face in her hands and crouched, waiting.

A shape stood atop a low wall, where none had been a moment before. One last ray of sun cast a dense shadow before it, like a hand reaching across grass and stone, right to the knot that was Andrion, Tembujin, Dana, and Gard. Then the sun was gone, as was the shadow, but the eerie rose twilight lingered.

The shape leaped down from the wall. A man, inhumanly agile, immaculately gold and purple and silver. Eldrafel.

Andrion stood frozen, Solifrax upraised, his hand cramping on the hilt. The fevered urgency of the air coagulated around him and time stuttered to a halt. It seemed as if he had been cast into the depths of the sea. Eldrafel's movements were slow and distinct, and the soldiers he beckoned swam like will-o'-the-wisps across the stone wreckage. Their broad, leaf-bladed spears glimmered like rippling seaweed.

Eldrafel's eyes shimmered with a fell pleasure, his turquoise and amethyst and jade necklaces clanked musically against his chest. "So we meet at last, my lord emperor." His voice fluted, making of Andrion's title a jeer. "I am so pleased you can keep your appointment with Taurmenios Tenebrae."

Appointment? They were meant to come here all along? Soot swirled through Andrion's mind, coating every nodule of rage, of fear, of anguish with black despair. Betrayed, yes, betrayed by his own pride and by the gods themselves to some greater purpose indeed. . . .

"Gods!" Andrion exclaimed. Desperation snapped his stupor. He lunged, wanting nothing more than to destroy that smug malevolence. Solifrax flared. For an instant even Eldrafel's gilt features blanched in the light of the sword.

But the priest did not move aside. He made one languid gesture. Black fire erupted from his fingertips and seared Andrion's hand. The sword was ripped away; leaving an arc of radiance like a comet's tail, it landed with a puff of ash at Eldrafel's feet. Its light winked out.

The ground trembled. Andrion's mind splintered. A turquoise shard was Gard, hoisted by a burly soldier, carried screaming and fighting to—amethyst, that was Chrysais, clutching her son convulsively, his moist face buried in his hair, his disgusted face buried in her bosom—no, she could not be crying, not those cold-blue faience eyes. . . . Her eyes were fixed on Andrion, drowned eyes, fathomless depths of emotion, power, and fear—yes, fear.

That gold and ebony shard was Tembujin, pinioned between two soldiers, his head lolling, a purplish bruise marring the angle of his jaw, his own hair a garrote round his neck. His bow lay broken in the dirt, where the zamtak lay pristine, as if carefully laid down, its strings humming. Sumitra was a dim shape in the dirt, sobbing rackingly, beyond reach.

Andrion strained to move toward her, strained to move toward Eldrafel. The world expanded and contracted again, man-shapes elongating and shrinking. The ground twisted and threw him to his knees. "Yes, yes," Eldrafel laughed. "I accept your homage."

And Dana—and Dana, her stricken face bleached as white as a skull by the ghastly pallor of the shield, her dagger in her hand, menaced at least five soldiers with light and sharpness and the frantic malachite shards of her eyes. Her thought howled so violently Andrion could hear it: "I have betrayed us all; Ashtar take me!"

"No!" he shouted, "it was I!" But his lips were numb and ash clogged his throat, and his knees seemed planted in the gritty dust.

"Sabazel!" she cried, and sprang forward, straight for Eldrafel. With horrible slowness a bronze spear turned the rim of the shield and buried itself in her side.

Her face did not change expression. Her eyes widened, seizing upon sanity, losing it again. They closed. She fell onto Solifrax, still holding the shield, and its metal clanged against the metal of the sword. Its light hissed and sputtered out beneath the sudden spate of carnelian blood.

In perversion of the clear ring of sword against shield, the harsh blast of a bull's horn rent the air. Torches leaped up, marking a stairway up the side of the mountain, charring the lavender twilight into impenetrable night.

Andrion could not move, could not feel, could not think, not even when soldiers seized him and dragged him off. Every nerve had been sheared away by the closing jaws of the trap.

Chapter Eleven

DANA SEIZED A vague tendril of memory. Amid sorcery-clotted ruins, Eldrafel, beautiful and malignant, gestured. The mass of Tenebrio gathered itself and fell upon her.

She drifted in a misty otherwhere, a being of thought, not of skin and bone. A Sabazian lullaby summoned her, a melody of moonglint on Cylandra's ice crown and the scent of anemone on a purling wind. Surrender to that song, whispered her thought, release that last strand of awareness, and slip peacefully into oblivion.

How tempting to let go, to be free. But something held her back. A task, a task had to be done that only she could do. She could not leave that task undone. That would be too easy.

She struggled through the mist as she had struggled through the blood-warm sea, fighting toward the border of air and water, of light and dark. . . . She realized she was surrounded by candles. The multitude of lights, reflected off stone walls, was too bright. She squinted, her lashes draping the lights with inky lace. Voices rose and fell like the susurration of the sea—Tembujin, Sumitra, Andrion. She was dead and laid on a bier, and these were her only mourners, for she was in an alien place.

Her awareness was rewarded by pain, waves of agony pulsing in her gut like the labored beating of her heart. She was not dead; she hurt too much to be dead. She remembered the bronze spear that had felled her. Fool, she chided herself, to be taken unaware. It was dying that was too easy.

Her hands and feet were cold leaden lumps attached to the tatters of flesh that were her limbs. Her breath rasped in her throat.

Andrion's face materialized before her, the skin stretched into a glazed mask. My fault, she wanted to say, but her icy lips would not move. Trembling hands touched her, a cloth swept across her brow, Sumitra's dark eyes swam before her. The eyes were dull, smudged windows behind which something struggled to be free—Dana saw Sumitra's hair rise from her head and wind tightly about her body, binding her to some terrible deed.

Vision, she told herself, only vision. The room faded, the candles blurred, the faces grew transparent and wavered out. Behind them was another form, not a person but the shade of one.

A young woman, elaborately coiffed and dressed in an open-bodiced dress, bedecked with amethyst, lapis, malachite. The jewels faded and brightened like drowsy eyes yearning to sleep but waked repeatedly by some consuming worry. The woman wrung her hands, and her body trembled so fiercely that her flounces and ringlets rustled. Her mouth was drawn tight, teeth glinting between red lips, and her eyes stared like a cornered animal's.

A ghost, Dana realized. The living woman had known such anguish that her mind snapped rather than believe and bear it. The phantom unclasped her hands and laid them over her face. She crouched, swaying. Proserfina, said some echo in Dana's mind. Her name had been Proserfina.

The great empty eyes looked up. Gray eyes, disturbingly clear, holding horror no longer, holding no trace of any human emotion. Those eyes were Eldrafel's, gnawing this once youthful face like worms behind the surface of a blush-fresh apple.

Then, as through a dark gauzy curtain, Dana saw Sabazel. At first she thought she was looking at the paintings on the walls of a sacred cavern, attenuated figures dancing intricate steps of life and death. . . . No, she saw Andrion clasping her own nubile body, performing a rite more ancient than any other. But even as she grimaced with both joy and regret at the memory, their bodies withered and were separated and swept away by a great ocean wave. Andrion!

She saw Ilanit sitting amid dead leaves in her garden, her gaunt body held as straight as a blade. But her face, too, was gnawed, her green eyes dull. Kerith paced up and down beside her, too tired to sit still, stamping and turning as if she alone guarded Sabazel. The child Astra sat beside her tiny quiver of arrows, but she did not see them; her eyes, the depths of the sea, reflected: Sarasvati running down the Royal Road, spec-

tral chariots painted with phosphorus pounding right behind
her. The skulls spoke with voices that were and yet were not
Bonifacio's, the priest's words vibrating with an uncharacteristic
vigor: "The living god comes from the sea, and by him shall
we be redeemed. . . ."

A vast shadow loomed behind Bonifacio like a puppet
master behind his toy. Upon its arm glinted a winged bull.

The images spun away, the candles reeled. Dana was alone
with the agony of mind and body; *we were meant to come
here, and I led us!* She would scream, expelling the frustration and pain. Her throat emitted a whimper. *Be silent then,*
she ordered herself. *Never whimper.*

The eyes above her were still Sumitra's, but now they were
lucid, dark and deep, surveying some terrible truth with a
somber and sober calm. Her hair was bound neatly atop her
head, leaving no image strands about her body. *A spell. She
had been under a spell, and now it was broken.*

Shadows beckoned seductively from beyond the candlelight. Dana tried to turn away from them, to ignore them, but
they swarmed ever closer. Her nostrils filled with the scent of
asphodel.

The window was an arrow slit in the massive stone wall.
Andrion blinked and peered through it as if waked from a
deep sleep. The moon had been dirtied. Thin black clouds
coiled like questing worms across its death's head of a face.

He had been dragged through a portal in the mountainside
and along labyrinthine stone corridors. All he remembered
was the rough-hewn walls rippling in the torchlight like the
grasping tentacles of a kraken; his mind had been flaccid, the
kraken's gutted prey. But rationality was returning, cauteriz-
ing his daze, searing mind and spirit with an agony he would
have thought impossible had he not felt it.

His bloodied hand reached for his belt and found the
sword's clasp dangling empty again. The sheath lay forlorn
on the floor. His hand clenched and crashed against the
windowsill.

We were meant to come here. Led by the ambiguity of
Dana's visions, or by my own impatience, or by some greater
force. *We were meant to come to Minras. But no!* his mind
howled, *I cannot, I will not believe that my life is only a
thread in the evil tapestry of Tauremenios Tenebrae. No, the
game is more subtle than that! It must be!*

His necklace sizzled against his throat. The merest breath of wind entered the narrow window to stir the room's cloying odor of incense and overripe fruit, mildew and blood. Do not test me, he told the gods. Do not taunt me. I defy your destinies and claim my own.

Andrion turned away from the window, into the central chamber of a comfortable, if not luxurious, suite of rooms. Again they were pampered like choice stock; it would have been considerably less disquieting to have been tossed into a dank and moldy crypt. A place like this had to have a crypt.

Tembujin huddled in a chair, rubbing his bruised jaw and fending off the damp cloth offered by Rue. "A camel is dancing inside my skull," he snarled. "You betrayed us again, did you not? If Dana dies her death is upon your head."

Rue, her presence probably one of Eldrafel's mordant jests, sat back amidst her baskets of clean clothes, food, and soap, averted her face to shield it from Tembujin's threatening gaze and said nothing.

"She is but a pawn," said Andrion between his teeth, "providing Eldrafel with only the details of the escape we were meant to make." And Jemail? he asked himself. He could well have made a mistake trusting Jemail. But the child Gard was untainted, he would swear to that.

Tembujin grunted. Rue did not move. The candles wavered and the jewel in her nose winked.

So this, Andrion thought, is what a mortal wound feels like, the heart oozing slow viscous drops like molten iron. . . . Sumitra was seated by Dana's couch. She had been used, callously, fiendishly, as bait; first kidnapped, then enspelled to lead them here. Andrion realized that now, too late, too late.

But even as his eye fell upon her Sumi straightened, lifted her zamtak into her lap and turned her lovely, guileless face toward him. Summoned, he went to her and set his hand upon her cheek. Like a sudden ray of sunlight glancing through cloud, he saw that her eyes had cleared and her manner had steadied into cool serenity.

The enchanting thread had broken. Chastening, that he had not been able to break it; more chastening still, that she should never have asked him to. But she had carried the burden of the spell alone. How could I have been so complacent, Andrion demanded of himself, to think we could not be ensorcelled? And he asked himself, Will you wallow in guilt and let your heart's blood drain away? Will you wait like a dumb animal for the bludgeon? Or will you act?

Dana whimpered, as faint as the mewing of a newborn kitten. Her fingers groped in the air. Looking for the shield, no doubt, but that, too, was gone. Andrion seized her hand and she grasped his feebly. Dana, feeble? Desperate enough to cling to him at all, let alone before his wife? Perfidious gods, to bring her to this!

Surely it was not her body, with its familiar tastes and textures, that lay upon the narrow couch like a side of meat. His cloak was snugged about the gash in her side; he could not remember placing it there. Seeping blood had colored the purple cloth scarlet. Her hand in his was marble cold, her face so pale as to be translucent, and her parted lips were the amethyst of Chrysais's jewelry. Only her will kept her alive, and that was ebbing. No, she cannot die, she cannot! Andrion's body shook in a paroxysm of grief, rationality shattering; act, act how, when what?

Sumitra turned her lips into his palm and kissed it, sending a thrill up his arm not unlike that of the waking sword. Her shining face damped his anguish, counseling hope.

Hope, yes, Andrion thought, I will seize upon hope. She refuses to regret her enchantment, she determines to make amends for the damage it has caused; she has always been willing to pay debts incurred by others. "Sumitra," he began, "Sumi, my lady . . ."

Someone moved at his back. He spun about. Gard stood just inside the room as a soldier slammed the door behind him. He announced defensively, "No one sent me here. Is she dead?" The boy's face was shadowed by the thicket of hair. Chrysais's chestnut hair, unfussed, waving free. Eldrafel's gray eyes, their clarity smoked by concern.

"No," replied Andrion. Odd, his voice was quite calm.

"Forgive me. They chased you to regain me."

"No," Andrion said, more harshly than he would have liked. "Your being with us made no difference to them at all."

Gard's eyes glinted. His lower lip stiffened. From his belt he produced a coil of black hair and said with a nod toward Sumitra, "I found this woven into my mother's tapestry. Your image, lady, made from your own hair. Bent across the shield of Sabazel."

"As if broken upon it," Andrion concluded. That, too, had been one of Dana's visions. He had thought it only symbolic. He thought too damn much. He seized the coil and held it in a candle flame until the stench of burning hair eddied through the room. No wonder the spell had been broken.

"The tapestry is here?" asked Tembujin.

"I suppose they need it for their magic," Gard replied.

"Sorcery," Sumitra corrected.

Tembujin looked narrowly at Gard. "But how could you touch the cloth? Dana tried to touch it with her dagger and it shot fire at her."

Gard shrugged. "The witch-fire only tickled me."

"An advantage then," said Tembujin acidly, "to being witch-spawned."

Gard's mouth stiffened even further. "Here. This was lying nearby, already threaded upon a needle. I brought it to you because I thought you liked me." He threw down the bowstring made of Tembujin's and Dana's hair, carefully separated into black and gold. The Khazyari pounced upon it and set it afire so quickly he burned his fingers.

"We do like you," Andrion told Gard's crestfallen face. "Thank you." And he thought, We victims of capricious gods must work together, seizing hope and defiance beyond reason.

Tembujin, contrite, added, "You were very brave to bring these to us."

Mollified, Gard turned and collided with Rue's indignant gaze. He quailed. Andrion pulled the small body against his side and said evenly, "Rue, if you tell Eldrafel that Gard brought us the hair, he will surely be punished. Do you really want to be the one who harms Chrysais's son?"

The serving woman's cheeks blanched at Chrysais's name. She nodded understanding.

So much easier not to care. But nothing should be easy. Andrion released Gard with a rough caress. He took Dana's hand and looked at Sumitra; equal tenacity, equal courage. A slight smile curved the fullness of Sumi's mouth, a decision made and accepted. She stroked the zamtak, and a trill like a flight of arrows fell into the silence. Dana's eyelashes fluttered, revealing a tiny slit of dull green.

Andrion's heart so stammered with love and hope that it felt like a knife blade turning in his chest. Sumitra's fingers moved again. Music cascaded over Dana's body. Her lips blushed pink. The green sparked. Ah, Ashtar, the unguarded depths of those eyes!

Ah, Harus, the sudden pallor deadening the glow of Sumitra's mahogany cheek—Andrion's knees buckled and dropped him on the edge of the couch. "Sumi," he breathed, hope rent by anxiety, "do not risk . . ."

"It is a matter of honor," Sumitra replied. Her demeanor was annealed of steel as pure and strong as the blade of Solifrax. "Your mother healed Dana's father of a similar wound while she carried you. Such magic marked you, but not for ill."

His necklace murmured against suddenly damp skin. "Yes, but I . . . Ashtar, Harus, have mercy." His voice shook. He compressed his lips so that he would not speak again. He tensed, every sinew in his body as taut as the strings of the zamtak, quivering like them to Sumi's touch.

Another rivulet of music, and another. Gard and Tembujin drew closer. Rue rose to her knees, her brows sceptically tight, wondering what trick Sumitra played.

Sumi's face glowed from within, her eyes widened and shone with a dark luminescence. A wind stirred in the chamber, fluttering the candles and sending shadows leaping up the rock walls, lifting strands of Dana's hair which seemed, in her extremity, to be spun not of gold but of brass.

The wind was the music, or the music the wind; Andrion could not tell. He knew only that the melody was as clean and precise as the wind that danced among the anemones in Ilanit's garden. That Sumitra had never seen.

A faint odor of asphodel eddied through the room. The hair rose on Andrion's nape and his necklace tugged at his throat, not in fear but in sudden exultation. Hope, healing, love, yes! He kneaded Dana's hands and bent his face almost to hers, calling her name softly but urgently. His body strained toward hers, summoning her flesh that was his own. Come back, the world is cruel, yes, but in it are those who love you! Her grasp tightened. Her lashes parted and her green eyes, faceted like cut emeralds with strength and vulnerability, looked up into his. For a moment he was giddy, slipping down a long, smooth slope into her awareness; Sabazel, set in the devotion of its people like a jewel in a royal crown. . . . He caught himself. I am Andrion, King of Sardis, Emperor. I am, blessedly, Sumitra's husband.

Sweat gilded Sumi's forehead. Her fingers moved even faster on the seventeen strings of the zamtak, the melody quickening, transposing itself from a minor key into a major. The candlelight shredded, the room filling with dancing light motes that consumed the shadows.

Muttering something that might have been a prayer, Tembujin knelt beside the couch. Andrion hardly noticed. A quicksilver warmth flooded Dana's hands. The cushioning mass of her hair flared gold. Her eyes gleamed and her mouth set itself with resolve. Andrion's heart reverberated with the beat of hers. His cheeks blazed.

The bloody cloak bled in turn, the dark crimson blotches brightening into red, then fading. Odd, Andrion thought with one stray tendril of his mind, Tembujin's hands were trembling as they unwrapped the bandage. He had not known Tembujin could tremble.

Between the rent edges of her dress Dana's skin was whole, marred only by a long pink scar. Even the gash on her finger was healed. I saw such magic, Andrion sighed, when I was in my mother's womb. Gods! Is it divine grace or human strength, only caprice to you but heart's blood to us?

Dana blinked, amazed, and inhaled so eagerly of that fresh wind her ribs expanded like a fan. Then Sumitra's hand slipped from the zamtak in a quick skittering trill and she fell from her chair. With a discordant clang the zamtak crashed to the floor beside her. The wind fled, and the candle flames stood unwavering in the still, dank air of the prison. The light motes winked out, leaving shadows etched beside every object.

"Sumi!" Andrion released Dana, leaving Tembujin to raise her from the pillow, and plunged to his wife's side. She cannot have hurt herself or the child, his mind gibbered . . . is Dana's life worth such injury, is Sumi's health worth Dana's death. . . .

Sumitra's shoulders shook, her hands concealing her face. Tenderly Andrion pulled her into his arms and rested her head against his chest.

Her eyes glinted between her fingers. She laughed and wept at the same time, exalted and exhausted. "I have power," she stammered. "I never asked for power. I would rather be home in Iksandarun."

Andrion rocked her against his shoulder; her flesh, her spirit, precious indeed. Through the mist blurring his eyes he saw Dana sit up, inspect her body, turn toward Sumitra so completely disarmed that awe and bewilderment and gratitude were plain on her face. The two women shared a long look, a tangible thread pulled taut past Andrion's face, finding their own common fabric.

Andrion's hand on Sumi's abdomen detected a tiny twitch, the baby somersaulting joyously beneath his fingertips. Only then did he grin and lay his cheek against Sumitra's sleek black hair, letting the women's thread of understanding spin without his interference, letting his own mind spin into thoughtlessness.

After a time he saw Gard sitting on the floor crying, trying in vain to conceal his tears. Andrion swept him into his free arm and held him close.

Rue's eyes were huge shocked blotches in her face. She lurched to her feet, threw herself against the door and pounded until a guard, frowning suspiciously, glanced inside. He slammed the door in her face. She turned her back to it and slithered bonelessly down the panels until she huddled again on the floor.

Tembujin seized one of her baskets, tossed aside some flat rounds of bread and found a carafe of wine, which he tilted to Dana's lips.

She abandoned Sumi's eyes, and with a faint, soft smile drank. "How," she croaked, "could I have so misinterpreted my visions?"

She did not accuse the visions of misleading her. Andrion replied, "You served some greater purpose, as Sumitra did, as I did, in bringing us here. Galling as it is, we have had far fewer choices in this matter than we thought."

"I tire," said Tembujin, "of toiling like an insect for some greater purpose which might just as well be a vile jest."

"If we do not know Eldrafel's purpose," Sumitra said quietly, "how can we know the gods'? And they must have a purpose."

Dana nodded. "I would believe that. Truly, I would."

"But we do know Eldrafel's purpose," stated Andrion. "I have known it, I think, ever since the attacks on Tembujin in Iksandarun. He wants the Empire, and has not scrupled to use both Chrysais and Gard to gain it."

The boy looked up, startled, the tears drying on his face. He might as well hear it now. "Of course," Andrion continued, "we do not yet know just how Eldrafel will implement his plan. Why this elaborate toying with us, when he could have killed us right at the beginning and presented Patros with both Solifrax and a legitimate heir?''

Gard's gray eyes were burnished with horror, not glee, Andrion saw with approval. So the boy had never realized that until Sumitra bore a son, he was the heir of the Empire. He shrank away, his face clotted with dismay; how could his new friend snatch his childhood so imperiously away from him? He cast about until he found the door, brushed Rue away from it, and ordered the guard to let him out. Frowning, Andrion watched the door shut. Perhaps he should have watched his tongue. But even a child should have knowledge of his fate, especially when it was likely to fall upon him soon.

Sumitra smiled against Andrion's necklace, causing it to trill faintly. ''Gard will surprise us with his strength, I wager.''

''As Andrion surprised Lyris,'' said Dana. He shot her a sharp glance; yes, she was teasing him. Her humor was like rain after a drought. They shared a brief, unashamed smile, and parted yet again.

Tembujin distributed the food from Rue's baskets, even offering some to the woman herself. With an abrupt shake of her head she refused. The moon crept beyond the edge of the window slot; the candles burned into heaps of gleaming tallow not unlike the heaps of rock on the slopes of Tenebrio itself. And here we are imprisoned in the belly of the shadow, Andrion told himself. At least we need no longer pretend to be guests.

The food was tainted with a slight flavor of sulfur, but still it was marvelously strengthening. After a time Sumitra wiped her lips and asked Rue, ''Is this the shrine you served before Eldrafel married Chrysais and took you and Rowan to Orocastria?''

Rue seemed to think that if she kept her eyes stubbornly downcast and her arms wrapped tightly about her body, her fingers caressing her arms, Sumitra's knowledge would evaporate.

But Dana ordered, simply and strictly, ''Answer her question.''

As if summoned by a drill master, Rue's eyes started up. Andrion suppressed a grin.

''Yes,'' the woman replied. ''My brother and I were born to serve the high priest, now the king, here in the shrine of Tenebrio.''

"But what of Taurmenios?" Andrion asked, envisioning the magnificently haughty statues guarding the harbor.

"Taurmenios is an upstart, a servant to the god who rose above his station and usurped the city of Orocastria."

"Ah," said Dana, "no wonder they were sacrificing bulls. In the older rites one sacrifices what is most valued."

"Is it too much to hope," Andrion interjected, "that it is Eldrafel who is most valued here. . . ." A chill, like the touch of cold fingers, stroked his nape.

"But Eldrafel," said Tembujin, "said something about the rites of Taurmenios Tenebrae, as if the gods were one and the same."

Rue's thin mouth thinned even further. "A pretty story to amuse the peasants, who would otherwise think Tenebrio old and weak, supplanted by the usurper. But the Shadow never fades."

The Shadow, Andrion repeated silently. An appropriate appellation for the god of this dark place. "And the rites that Eldrafel spoke of?"

"Once a year."

"Here?" asked Sumitra with some alarm. "Now?"

Rue wrapped herself even more securely with her arms. Getting information from the woman was like carving granite one chip at a time. Or like pitting olives, close labor for just one morsel.

"No doubt," growled Andrion. "How cleverly, how daringly, has Eldrafel timed his plan, to have us here when he wants us."

Dana went, if possible, even paler. "To have *us* here," she murmured. "Why us?"

Tembujin, with a sigh of aggravation, said, "I take it, then, that Eldrafel serves Tenebrio, not Taurmenios? He was dancing with the shadows around the altar in Orocastria even as the bulls lay dead."

"I would imagine," replied Andrion, "that Eldrafel works for himself."

Rue glared at him. Of course, he reflected, squashing her glare with a stronger one of his own, everyone uses the names of the gods as convenient. . . . What had Gard said about Eldrafel's birth? "Eldrafel, I hear," Andrion essayed, "was fathered by Tenebrio."

Rue loosened a bit. Her eyes gleamed, not with cunning

but with zeal. "Yes, yes indeed. His mother was Gath's sister Proserfina."

"Proserfina!" Dana exclaimed, so vehemently that everyone except Rue glanced warily at her.

Rue warmed to her tale. "Taurmenios, trying to break the loyalty of the royal family to Tenebrio, cursed them with childlessness. But Tenebrio cares for his own. Proserfina was not the first king's sister to conceive her child here, in the embrace of the god himself."

Andrion almost snickered; Eldrafel was just smug enough to genuinely believe himself the son of a god.

"What a shame," Rue continued, "that Proserfina's husband had died a month earlier, so he could not participate in the rites."

Tembujin did not even try to suppress his grin. "So the elegant creature really is a bastard." And at Andrion's caustic glance, "Of course, some of my best friends are bastards."

Rue shot Tembujin a withering look. He refused to wither.

Dana was listening again to that compelling inner voice. "Proserfina haunts these chambers," she said softly, "a specter of horror and regret. Perhaps she did meet a living god, although if so . . ." She grimaced. "I know not. Again my visions play with me."

An icy breath stirred the air. Rue spat, "You lie."

"I do not," snapped Dana. "Proserfina was here moments ago."

Rue stood up, her hands clenched before her as if ready to ward off any attack, ghostly or otherwise. "Why should Proserfina regret being favored by the god any more than Chrysais has?"

"Chrysais?" demanded Andrion. "She conceived Gard here?"

One corner of Rue's mouth twisted in a half leer, half smile. "Yes, your nephew has sacred blood, much better than the falcon droppings you claim. Tenebrio is strongest of all." Again she pounded on the door, and this time when the guard opened it a crack, she managed to slither out.

The room was so silent that her retreating footsteps seemed to vibrate in the rock itself. At last Sumitra said, "She chooses to lash out at us. Do you suppose we have managed to plant some doubt in her mind?"

"If anyone has, you have," Andrion told her.

Sumitra shook her head modestly. Over her smooth crown

of hair Andrion met Dana's and Tembujin's eyes. Truly Eldrafel's plot was as knotted as the maze of passageways, here and in Orocastria, in which he lived. His aim was power, of course. But how did he plan to achieve his aim? And why did those aims seem to be only the warp of a complex tapestry, its weft the incessant rumors of ancient, repellent rites? Gath dying in his bath, too soon for his death ritual—Eldrafel was not squeamish about taking the will of the gods into his own hands. And I am? Andrion asked himself.

"Now what?" asked Tembujin.

Andrion tried to shrug, but his shoulders were too tense. "Soap and water, I suppose, and clean clothes and sleep. If the rites of Tenebrio are held at the full of the moon . . ."

"Sacrilege," muttered Dana.

"Then all will be revealed to us tomorrow night."

"My lord," said Tembujin, standing and stretching, "you do not comfort me at all."

Andrion vented a short laugh of agreement.

The candles burned down to guttering nubs, unable to dispel the sooty darkness oozing in the window. The room was thronged with shadows—those cast by the four living bodies, by the specters of the past, and by some malign purpose that loomed larger and darker over them all as its time drew near.

Chapter Twelve

THE ROUGH GRAY walls of the room mocked its luxurious furnishings. The tapestries meant to conceal the stone only emphasized its harshness; their images swirled demonically beneath a patina of soot. The window slits were as empty as gouged eyes.

Rue cowered at Chrysais's feet. "You lie!" the queen said, with a vicious twist at the serving woman's hair.

"No, no," whined Rue. "I saw it. Sumitra healed the Sabazian with her music."

Chrysais thrust her away with a shudder of disgust. Her eyes glinted the shallow lavender of old bruises. The wine cup in her hand was half empty, her fingers still redly scabbed from the bite of Solifrax.

Eldrafel sat with his usual cool composure amid the silk and samite pillows of the bed. Above him hung a filigree lamp, gathering the shadows like supplicants around it. His bearded face was cast in a pale gold, rich, smooth, hard; his hair, bound by a silver fillet, gleamed. "Simple trickery," he stated expressionlessly. "As one might expect from the minions of inferior gods."

Rue opened her mouth, shot a quick and cautious glance at Chrysais, closed it again. She sidled toward the door. Eldrafel gestured airily, dismissing her. Rue turned, staggered slightly, and with her arms folded around herself disappeared. In the draft from the door the wall hangings shifted and emitted a fetid breath.

Chrysais watched Eldrafel with a hunger saved from maudlin only by the dignity innate in her blood. Eldrafel's eyes sliced through Chrysais and discarded her. They fixed far beyond the stone walls, surveying the world like a gameboard set in a significant pattern.

Chrysais's white teeth bit deep into the lush crimson of her lower lip. She jerked her gaze away from her husband. The great sorcerous tapestry from Orocastria reposed in a darkened alcove, so tautly rolled upon its frame that it seemed to strain to free itself. Its colors were unmuted, purple, coral, and silver in delirious juxtaposition.

Where Sumitra's hair had been sewn was now ordinary black silk. Chrysais looked back at Eldrafel, her sudden caution exaggerated by the wine into outright fear. Her mouth tightened stubbornly; if her quick intelligence knew who had removed the hair, her pride would not recognize why, and would deny it. But either Eldrafel had not noticed the change in the tapestry or it did not suit his purpose to care.

Chrysais drank and lifted a waiting carafe. "A shame," she essayed, "that it was not Sumitra who was wounded; she would have died. Pregnant, she becomes not a decoy but a threat. Even if the child is a girl, those crazed Sabazians might support her."

Eldrafel stretched, his muscles moving beneath his skin like those beneath the coat of a leopard. "Sumitra has her uses, as does her child. Her . . . powers only make her more valuable. How obliging that she has restored the Sabazian to health for us."

"The Sabazian is her husband's lover," sulked Chrysais. "I would have let her die."

Eldrafel's brows tilted in salty amusement. "Yes, I daresay you would, indulging your petty jealousies and ruining a greater plan."

Chrysias flushed and drank again. Eldrafel rose from the bed, began to pace across the floor, caught himself and changed his gait to a negligent saunter. He lifted an odd-shaped object from beneath a particularly dark and moldy tapestry.

Chrysais closed her eyes and then opened them again, as if hoping the object would change shape. It did not, even as Eldrafel held it at arm's length and turned it around and around, his bland expression tightening for a moment into puzzled resentment.

The shield of Sabazel, held on Dana's arm as she fell, had struck fallen Solifrax with such supernal force that the sword had been driven right through it. The crystalline crescent of the blade cleft the embossed silver star in perversion of Andrion's necklace. Blade and star alike pulsed with luminescence like a slow seeping of power. Or perhaps it was a burgeoning, the strengths of shield and sword combining in wary truce.

Eldrafel laid the bizarrely mated objects on the bed, set his foot on the rim of the shield, and pulled at the sword's hilt until his gilded features purpled. But Solifrax did not move.

Eldrafel released it with an oath. The flesh of his palms, delicate vellum, were seared scarlet by a deeper cold than their own. For a moment he stood regarding the jointed weapons, smiling narrow-eyed in an expression that in anyone else would have been an angry frown. Then he said, his voice coated with hoarfrost, "So, they shall serve as they are, an offering to Tenebrio and evidence of our power. It is no great matter."

The lamp flickered in a brief, musky breeze. Chrysais's painted face was suddenly featureless, her eyes hollow. But Eldrafel's mother-of-pearl radiance was undimmed. She reached for him, hand open like a penitent before a shrine.

He looked her up and down. His fingertips explored her chin, her breast, her belly, not in a caress but in dispassionate evaluation. "Ah, my dear," he murmured, "you know that the high priest must abstain from carnal contact before the blood rite of Tenebrio. As the king must now greet the dawn from the upper temple, and as you have your role to play later."

"Yes," she responded dully. And stood dully while he threw his lustrous purple cloak over his shoulders and glided from the room.

Again her teeth pressed into her lip, so far that the red paint deepened with blood. Her slightly unfocused eyes ranged around the room, regarding each tapestry, new and old, groping for counsel. She set the cup down with a crash and watched with interest as the wine splashed onto the tabletop. But neither did the crimson stains hold a message.

With a smile uneasily mingled of wistfulness and lust, Chrysais sat down on the bed and began to stroke the sword, up and down, as if it were a man to be aroused.

Andrion's sleep was tossed on the horns of uncertainty. The capture among the sorcery-clotted ruins had not fulfilled his sense of foreboding, it had increased it. The bated breath of Minras had yet to expel itself in that ultimate scream of horror, sigh of defeat, shout of triumph. . . . He wanted to writhe among the bedclothes. But Sumitra lay beside him in a tranquil sleep, her lips curved gently with the beauty of her compassion.

The darkness ebbed; beyond these thick walls dawn crept across the sky like a blush up Sumi's cheeks. Andrion dozed and woke, his senses rippling with a faint but undeniable awareness, like a distant sound that is overlaid with the noises of the day and only becomes apparent in the depth of the night when all else is silent. He felt Dana's body touching him, enclosing him, nourishing him even as he fed her. . . . This was embarrassing.

He tried to quell the sensation; wrong time, wrong place, wrong woman, by the tailfeathers of the god! But he was stirred not by lust but by an ineffable awareness of unity, as though his necklace had transformed itself from symbol to reality. And yet something about that unity disturbed him. The moon and the star existed side by side, not in one.

Andrion kissed Sumi very gently, not wanting to wake her. He rose, shaved, and dressed in a clean kilt and cloak. He found Dana staring out the tiny window toward a sky inspiringly clean of soot, the infinite azure of Ashtar's eyes restored. It was, it seemed, early afternoon.

"I could perhaps squeeze through the window," Dana said in greeting.

He laid his hand on her shoulder, where the sinews sang like the strings of Sumitra's zamtak. "And do what? They have taken even your dagger. No, we must wait, playing dumb, storing our defiance until it can be used to best effect."

She laid her hand on his, allowing him an affectionate if exasperated smile. The touch acknowledged that odd congruence of sensation without exploring it. "These rites," she began. "I would expect any rites committed here to be as dark and twisted as the place."

"True . . ." A guard opened the door. Andrion noted three others outside; if they managed somehow to overcome those four, he wondered vaguely, would eight guards appear next time?

It was he who was summoned, and separated from his companions. He managed to counter Dana's frown with a brisk nod toward the omen of the sky. Setting his jaw, glancing reluctantly toward sleeping Sumitra, he followed the soldier.

The rough-hewn corridors twisted and turned past dark

niches, shadowy stairways, and bolted doors. Andrion could imagine the creatures lurking behind those doors, but chose not to. The air itself was volatile with a chill sentience that yearned to escape the confining stone and flood the sky, extinguishing the sun.

Andrion was thrust into a room and the door slammed behind him. The light leaking through the interstices of a large filigree lamp illuminated luxurious if somewhat decayed furnishings. Dingy tapestries, their stitched scenes skewed just enough from reality to be nightmarish, undulated along the walls. A tiny pot of incense—no, by Harus, of lethenderum—burned on a table, valiantly attempting to dispel the pervading scent of rot. His muscles tightened into a sustained shiver, and when a shape moved in an alcove, he crouched.

It took him a moment to recognize Chrysais. She wore a simple linen gown almost like a shroud, swathing her body from throat to ankle and masking its lushness. But her face was unmasked, pale and strangely indeterminate without its paint and powder. Her hair hung loose down her back. She assumed an attitude of tipsy flirtatiousness, and said, "Welcome, little brother. Or is it half brother?"

"Half brother," Andrion responded. Well, he thought, she is certainly never boring. She extended her hand. Her fingers were red and swollen around the scab of what looked like a knife cut. He cultivated a mote of sympathy, bowed and gallantly kissed the proffered hand.

She inhaled, sharp and shuddering, as if he had made a much more intimate gesture. He started back. Already the lethenderum was distorting his senses, as if his senses had not burden enough. Dana, he thought, a reluctant bud flowering in season; Sumitra, shy discretion, a bloom plucked and cherished; Chrysais—Chrysais was all bold subtleties.

Her lashes fluttered, butterflies swooping around the shining blue-violet pools of her upturned eyes, luscious, lustrous drowned eyes. Her hand splayed against his chest, just below the arc of the necklace. Her flesh was hot. The necklace hissed.

So, Andrion wheezed. She had searched her sexual arsenal for whatever blandishments would tempt him and had come close to the answer; not blatant eroticism, but vulnerability. And yet her vulnerability, unlike Sumi's, unlike Dana's, was not edged by strength; even the challenging sexual sting he had felt so clearly at their first meeting had been blunted.

"Do you set the price of my freedom?" he asked. "Or is this, too, simply part of Eldrafel's plot?" It would be funny, in a mordant way, if it were not so repellent. Repellent because, damn the lethenderum and his own importunate body, she was tempting him.

But Eldrafel's name took her aback. She faltered. Andrion wrenched himself from the creeping tendrils of her fingers and saw behind her, filling the alcove, a tapestry with colors as raw as fresh meat. It had to be the one Dana and Tembujin had found. The ship, Bonifacio, Niarkos, Sumitra laid across the shield in the ancient temple where she had led them; his gorge rose and his heart hardened.

Chrysais followed the direction of his gaze and raised her chin in arrogant modesty. "Evidence of my power," she murmured.

As one can see the vanished beauty in an old woman, something in the line of the cheekbone or the tilt of the head, so Andrion saw suddenly the crone implicit in the sag of Chrysais's cheek and the fragile skin around her eyes. The power that has drained you? he asked silently.

His thoughts wriggled in his grasp. He straightened, folded his hands behind his back and said sternly, before either his sister or his body distracted him again, "I hear that the royal line of Minras suffers from sterility. Perhaps their god is failing."

"Failing? How little you know of the special favor granted to us."

She said "us," he noted. "How the god Tenebrio visits the barren wife and fills her?"

Chrysais flushed mauve. "Rue, that blabbering wrench."

"It sounds quite distasteful to me," Andrion said. His veering thought reminded him that Bellasteros had supposedly been sired by a god—under the purity of the Sabazian moon, he asserted, not in these ugly, unhealthy passages; summer king, winter king, and the natural cycles of the world. . . .

"How would you know?" Chrysais retorted. "The touch of a god is—is like standing unburnt in the midst of a bonfire." The mauve faded to an attractive pink. "Proserfina could not bear the intensity of such a touch, and died at Eldrafel's birth. I not only bore it, I gloried in it!" Her eyes gleamed, but her lips crimped defensively. If she had private knowledge, it both elated and disturbed her.

Proserfina, Andrion thought. If she had died so young,

how could she have known what her son would become? But if she did not know, why did she haunt these dim galleries, gnawed by horror?

His thought raveled, and as he grasped at it, suddenly knotted. Gray eyes, mirrored with perception. "The god in the person of a man?" he asked. "Was Gard fathered by Tenebrio or by his high priest, Eldrafel?"

Chrysais deflated so abruptly, her features blanched so white, that he thought she was going to faint. He took her shoulders and set her an arm's length away on the bed. "The priest is transformed by the god," she recited. "The priest becomes the god."

So it was true. Please, do not let the boy discover it too soon. "Tell me," Andrion demanded.

"What could I have done?" she began. "Go home to the god-king Bellasteros, whining that I hated my husband? Oh, Gath would have sent me back, dishonored, if I had not had his son; I could not have borne that. So I agreed to visit Tenebrio."

"Bellasteros would not have scorned you for returning."

"Would he not?" Chrysais drew herself up and fixed Andrion with an acrid glare. "He put aside my mother in favor of that Sabazian whore—"

"My mother," stated Andrion, but she paid no attention.

"He cared nothing of real women, only of those trousered hellions."

"Who are free to take or reject a man as they choose?"

Her mouth twisted, but she would not take the bait. "I learned here what a woman has for power. And I helped Gath, oh yes, for his power was mine. I won for him the fealty of the far sea, first with my charm, then with my herbs. I knew many men, but I found none I could . . . respect. Who would respect me."

Andrion had to listen intently to understand her words, her body spoke so much more urgently. Even without her cosmetic weaponry, Chrysais's flesh was rich enough to pour, her manner experienced to the point of jaded. She leaned toward him, face upturned, lips parted and moist, a lodestone turning ineluctably to the north, any north at hand. Power indeed, burbled Andrion's careening mind. Voluptuousness as power. It must have been the disorienting effect of the lethenderum that made him shove her gently away instead of throwing her down.

"Eldrafel was only a child when I came to Minras," continued Chrysais. "I saw him now and then; he was almost as bright and handsome as Gard. But that day I came here to Tenebrio to prepare for the rite, I saw him as a man.

"Supposedly it is the supplicant's husband who impersonates the god. But this time . . ." She chuckled huskily. "We gave Gath an elixir of hemp and spiced honey, so that he dreamed he was with me. But he was not."

Her eyes, soft-focused with lethenderum, seemed to see some distant romance. Romance only in retrospect, idealized by the veil of time and self-deception. She draped herself over Andrion like a soft fur, and again he removed her, somewhat less gently this time. Her lotus scent mingled with that of the lethenderum, and the blood pounding in his head dizzied him.

"Of course," she continued, her sultry voice crisping, "I could not hide that I had indeed met a god. But Gath had none of Eldrafel's style. When he suspected how matters truly lay, he moved against us, direct but clumsy, as was his manner. We moved first."

Andrion felt a sneaking sympathy for Gath, hopelessly outclassed by the deviousness of Chrysais and Eldrafel and their innumerable spies. "What happened?" he prompted, remembering only too well Gard's account of his . . . mother's husband's death.

"The time had not yet come for Gath's death ritual," said Chrysais dreamily. "The moon must dance along the tops of the columns, you see, stirring the shadows in the temple, or Tenebrio cannot drink the blood we give him, and with it nourish the soil."

Andrion shuddered. Shapes moved in the cellars of his mind—the dark god drinking and then excreting blood—a horned figure dancing on stone walls. . . . He chased the images, but they eluded him.

"So we staged a ritual of our own. We fed him ergot, and when he went mad from it, screaming that his flesh was burning, we led him to the bath. It is easy, really, to drown in a bath when careless. Only a few servants were executed for overheating the water." She drooped against Andrion's side, eyes closed, mouth slack, her lips in repose curving sadly down. "Ah, Eldrafel," she sighed.

Was she remorseful? Andrion wondered. Or merely tired? At least she did not gloat, as Eldrafel no doubt did, over their crimes. As Gath had. Her pride had worn thin indeed, to lead her to talk so freely. Or else, he reflected in a moment of cold reason, with the fulfillment of the plot it no longer mattered what he knew. He was here, they had wanted him here. . . .

He could not hate her. He hated the men who had corrupted her, Gath and then Eldrafel, even as he knew she had allowed herself to be corrupted.

And suddenly, like a great reptile surging up from the depths of a swamp, the memory struck him. The cavern, damn it, the pictures on the wall of the cavern, Ashtar's shrine in Sabazel; a clean, blue cave, sacred, not profane like this place that fostered the darker passions.

With an effort he seized the idea before it spun away. The death ritual of the king, the sacrifice that won the health of his land. An ancient custom no longer followed in Sabazel or Sardis or the Empire, thank the beneficent gods. And yet, he asked himself giddily, are those not the same gods who once demanded my death in place of Bellasteros's, and at last demanded his death in place of mine?

An ancient custom still observed on Minras, under the eye of gods who amused themselves by moving kings and queens upon the gameboard and then devouring them. . . .

Chrysais's fingertips crept up the inside of Andrion's thigh, and he gasped. Rationality frayed. The tapestries waved, liquid rather than cloth, the lamp spun and emitted a trail of sparks, the windows winked and leered.

Chrysais entangled him, pulling him down into a miasma of lotus and sweat. He had just enough sense to be grateful for the layers of cloth crumpled between their bodies. Her lips moved against his—yes, he had been right about the taste of her mouth, sweet wine with an aftertaste of vinegar.

He wrenched himself away, muttering, "By all that is holy, woman!" But even the definition of holy was worn thin. His addled senses left him lying between her linen-wrapped legs, the heat of her body drawing him like a moth to the flame. Gods, even his body used, abused, violated. . . .

But she did not pluck at his clothing. She clutched him like a child, her erotic lures suddenly irrelevant. Her voice pleaded, very nearly sobbing, "Love me, love me, love me."

What? This plea was not at all what he expected. Andrion froze, his heart pierced by an exquisite pity. How could Chryse and Bellasteros, who had raised Andrion and Sarasvati with strength and humor and understanding, have failed so utterly with this child of their adolescence? But how could he condemn them for the choices she had made?

"Please, love me," her breath shuddered in his ear.

He rocked her in his arms, murmuring distracted endearments, as the room stuttered and demon images clambered down from the tapestries and danced. As the door opened and Eldrafel led in a procession of dark-robed figures.

Andrion struggled for coherence. Would they accuse him of rape or incest? But no, that was much too easy, for the warp of the tapestry was only loose threads without the binding weft. . . .

The soft bed and Chrysais's billowing body fell away. Andrion reeled. Supported between two priests, bracketed by their black and glittering obsidian knives, he saw only Chrysais's eyes flood with tears.

"Forgive me," she said, seizing some last thread of composure from her lethenderum-laced snarl of truth and falsehood. "You see, Eldrafel could not die as king, for he is high priest and must perform the ceremony. . . ." Her words drifted away in an attenuated sigh.

Even now he could not hate her. Even as his mind coagulated and he remembered that according to the ancient traditions the king must come freely to the place of his death. And he, more a king than Eldrafel could ever be, had indeed come freely to the bowels of Tenebrio—too innocent, or too civilized, or simply too stupid to realize what he was doing— manipulated, god's beak, manipulated!

Eldrafel's smirk he expected. It was Chrysais's naked face, turned up to her husband, begging for the love his evil perfection could not comprehend, that seared away Andrion's inebriation, that stiffened his spine and led him to lead his own escort out the door.

Chapter Thirteen

ALL TOO SOON the effect of the lethenderum wore off, leaving Andrion's perceptions disconcertingly clear. If the priests had hustled him straight from this life to the next, he reflected glumly, he would by now be mercifully finished with reflection. But mercy was a concept alien to the nature of Minras. The priests had returned him here, giving him the leisure to fear not death itself but dying with his tasks unaccomplished.

The remote, unattainable vault of the sky darkened into the transparent teal blue of evening. Andrion's hands lay spread in a placatory gesture upon the cold stone windowsill. He clenched them and turned away from the free air of heaven back into the dim, clammy chamber, determined to placate neither god nor man.

His bald account of the scene with Chrysais shaped Dana's expression into contempt edged by pity; Sumitra's into pity edged by contempt. His equally bald revelation of Eldrafel's endgame sent a spasm of fear, then disgust, then defiance across each face before him, until at last he watched appreciatively as three masks of courage settled into place and three sets of gleaming eyes turned to him for direction. Surely he had direction to give. . . .

Tembujin shook his head. "You almost have to admire Eldrafel's audacity," he said, outraged by his own admiration. "He has found a way to avoid his own death and in the avoiding win an empire for his evil god."

"You cannot know a god by his followers," Sumitra said.

Dana glowered, arms folded. "Indeed, I can believe that Sardis was once led to excess by youthful zeal, not by Harus's true wishes. But Minras stinks of a demonic influence, not divine."

Andrion sensed her presence rather than hearing her words,

still caught in that odd unity with her, an intimacy that was both intriguing and intolerable. There must be a reason, this all must have a reason—wait, wait. . . . He could not take a deep breath; he was panting, they were all panting, chattering like magpies to keep from screaming.

"What was the purpose of that charade with Chrysais?" asked Tembujin.

"According to some customs," Andrion replied, grateful for a brief intellectual exercise, "the king must be taken from the queen's embrace to the death ritual, affirming his role as—you could say the generating principle. I do not know whether Chrysais actually intended to, er, consummate her embrace with me; perhaps she meant to at first, and then realized that kind of embrace was not what she really wanted." He sighed; Minras did not lend itself to intellectual exercises.

"Eldrafel," said Tembujin scornfully, "would not have cared one way or the other. Just as long as the letter of the ritual was observed."

"As we fasted when we crossed the island," Andrion continued. "For lack of food, not in preparation for a ceremony, but we fasted."

Dana fingered her new shirt and trousers. "They have even made an attempt to dress us in our usual garb. We needed new clothes, yes, but . . ."

"Style, not substance," said Sumitra. "Appearance is all." She lifted her zamtak and plucked idly at it, as if seeking some magic combination of notes that would open the portals and free them. But the door did not budge.

Andrion glanced again out the window. His own rangy body, while clad again in a chiton and cloak, seemed naked without the lost falcon brooch, seemed hideously vulnerable without Solifrax. But the power of the sword is in me, he reminded himself. That is why Eldrafel has waited until now to kill me—try and kill me, he amended hastily.

"Is my image still sewn on the tapestry?" Sumi asked.

"Yes. But without your hair it seems to have no power over you. Your strength amazes me, my lady." Andrion smiled at her, in wan apology for ever having measured strength by force of arms.

Sumitra asked with her own swift logic, "But is your image, and Dana's and Tembujin's, not on the tapestry at all?"

"No, they are not. I suppose because as monarchs we must move freely, drawn only by trickery."

"Then you think we are to be sacrificed with you?" demanded Tembujin. "Surely we are meant to be more than just bait."

"I assure you I have no intention of being sacrificed," Andrion retorted, his dark eyes kindling, "not to Tenebrio, and certainly not on Eldrafel's behalf."

Dana turned, stamped away a few paces, spun back again. "Chrysais is no doubt enjoying the humiliation of Sabazel's children."

"Not as much as she thought she would," said Sumitra. The zamtak warbled. Dana gesticulated to heaven, refusing any sympathy for Chrysais.

Andrion said, "Evidently they do not make such drastic sacrifice more than once a generation. Perhaps the rites vary from time to time. Perhaps no one really knows the rules of this game." He realized his fists were clenched again, and his jaw was set so tightly his ears ached. "If only we can return safely to Iksandarun, by Harus, by Ashtar, then I vow never to complain about paperwork again!"

Tembujin's brows, black wings against his bronze skin, shot up under his hair. "Indeed, my camel herd looks quite appealing."

"I would gladly weed Danica's garden all by myself," offered Dana, "and clean out the dove roosts in the temple to boot."

Sumitra drew a flourish from the zamtak. "Ah, the interminable receptions for the councilors, the squirming courtesies of their wives. I would greet them all with open arms!"

The door opened and a company of soldiers jostled in the doorway. The moment burst and emitted a cloud of apprehension.

One soldier took Sumi's zamtak from her hands and set it aside. The others ushered the four—victims? Andrion asked himself, and he answered, never—into the corridor. A corridor that coiled like a worm through walls of moldy rock, through air that thrummed with a chill and malignant vitality. Too many guards escorted them to even think of escape. Even if they had somewhere to go.

Sumitra set her hand on Andrion's arm as if they were entering a state reception, and he laid his own hand on hers. How could he leave her sweet jasmine kisses, her body, which was opulent without being in the least jaded, her placid spirit, and her steel-braced demeanor? Perhaps they would be rejoined after death—he had always believed that somehow Danica and Bellasteros had at last found peace together.

Do not be ridiculous, he told himself. You are not going to die.

Tembujin offered his arm to Dana. She refused it with a look that would have dropped one of his camels dead in its tracks. If I must die, her manner said, it will not be on a man's arm.

Amid the dank, uneasy air another breath stirred, a distant memory of free wind. And suddenly they emerged into the outside, into a breeze fresh from the sea. Andrion inhaled, thinking for a moment he could taste anemone and asphodel. The wind caressed his warm cheeks, lifted his hair from his head, murmured sweet nothings in his ear.

On his other side Dana's nostrils flared, and she almost smiled. And you, Andrion thought, blood of my blood. . . .

The wind curdled and died, overcome by the chill reek of sorcery, sulfur, and decay. But that brief freshness, like the clarity of the sky, was a good omen. He would believe that. He had to believe that. He exhaled the scent of Sabazian flowers and felt his chest constrict.

They were in a basin in the mountainside, an amphitheatre roofed by a vast pink and violet sky. The peak of the mountain brooded blackly behind them; before them columns ringed the rim of the basin like fingers groping at the twilight. In the uncanny light the rock seemed only a daubed backdrop in a theatre.

Andrion and Sumitra, Dana and Tembujin, were installed on a dais to one side of the amphitheatre's floor. Of the various soldiers standing about, spears dim gleams in the gathering darkness, none seemed to be Jemail. Maybe the man had not been a spy after all, and had already been put to death. Maybe he had escaped. Maybe he would come rushing in at the last moment and save them all. . . . No, Andrion thought, the man was too intelligent to throw himself away so rashly.

The sky darkened into polished indigo studded by stars. A faint silver glow in the east presaged the rising of the moon. Eyes glinted amid the columns as if the temple was a beast stretching and awakening; Andrion realized with a start that the basin was surrounded by spectators clad in indistinct

ash-gray robes. A slash of charcoal on the opposite side of the
floor deepened, becoming a fissure like an axe-cut dividing
the temple into two halves. A narrow bridge without handrails
arched from one side of the cleft to the other.

A figure stood upon the bridge. That chased-gold hair and
beard, that marble face were unmistakable; Eldrafel bowed
tauntingly to his erstwhile guests and made a grand, sweeping
gesture to the sky.

The full moon rose slowly, ponderously, over the rim of
the world, reluctant to be called by such as he. But it came
nonetheless. Its light painted the temple and the mountain not
with Sabazian quicksilver but with a livid phosphorescence.
The stars faded, the sky turned a pallid slate gray. Under its
pitiless gleam the shadows were refined into dense, black
shapes, tangible nothingness.

Dana shuddered, sickened. Andrion's necklace muttered
against his throat. Evil upon evil, he wanted to scream,
perverting the moon, making it not a symbol of light but of
darkness. . . . His cry gurgled in his throat.

A bull's horn sounded in a low, eerie wail. The frieze of
faceless watchers responded with a chant.

Eldrafel gestured again. Robed figures staggered forward
bearing a huge krater. The caldron was incised with turbulent
scenes of war and death. Gorgon faces leered from the han-
dles, tongues lolling, eyes rolling in drunken spasms. One
priest produced what looked like a goblet, ladling into it
liquid from the krater; Eldrafel took it, threw back his head
and drank. He held a skull, Andrion saw, cunningly sheathed
in silver.

Sumitra trembled on his arm. Tembujin swore under his
breath. The necklace hissed, tugged, fell back. Yes, the
guards were intent on the ceremony, not on their prisoners,
but how . . . The watchers began to file down from their
seats and past the krater. Each received a clay cup of liquid.
The chanting harshened, achieving a note of menace that
curled the hair on Andrion's neck. Every fiber in his body
contracted in response.

Two priests carried cups to a particularly opaque shadow at
one side of the floor. As the moonlight crept onward, the
darkness parted like a curtain. Chrysais sat on a throne carved
with weathered winged gargoyles, Gard on a stool at her feet.
One of her hands rested like a claw on his shoulder, whether

protecting him from the evil ritual or trying to thrust him into it, Andrion could not tell.

The boy was stiff with sulky compliance; his teeth seemed to have turned to granite, so tightly did he hold his jaw. Turquoise and amethyst weighted his narrow chest. Andrion thought, it is he who deserves pity. But something in the boy's attitude refused pity.

As if aware Andrion watched him, Gard glanced up. In the moment Andrion had the boy's attention he winked at him, wondering as he did so if he promised something he could not deliver. But the boy loosened, forgiving the emperor for being related to him—not surprising, considering his meager choice of relatives. His pallor ebbed to an excited flush.

Andrion laid his hand on his necklace. The moon and the star thrilled against his flesh; a message, but what, gods, what?

Grudgingly, Andrion looked at Chrysais. Beneath her gaudy mask her face had shriveled; that youth he had once seen in her was now only cruel illusion, ravaged by passion. Perhaps she grew so weary that peace would be more welcome than any passion. But her eyes were anything but peaceful, darting in flat blue gleams from Andrion to Eldrafel to Gard and upward to the glaucous face of the moon.

The many portals into the mountain emitted breath after cold breath. The sky glazed over with frost. The chanting was the moan of a winter storm, and yet no wind stirred; each robe and each shadow hung like carved drapery in the pallid light.

Eldrafel swaggered forward and flourished the skull before the prisoners. "One of your earlier victims?" Andrion asked evenly.

Laughing, Eldrafel drank again. Crimson liquid sloshed through the eye holes, gaping in a spasm of terror. A miasma of herbs and honey drifted from krater and skull alike. Dana sipped warily at a cup offered her by an anonymous robed figure and spat. "Wormwood, henbane, belladonna, thornapple, fermented honey. A witch's brew, if ever there was one." The spittle at her feet spun a thread of smoke into the cold air.

Everyone, even the soldiers, drank deeply. Except for Eldrafel, who threw the skull carelessly into the krater, and Gard, who reached for his mother's cup and had it snatched from him. Despite the potency of the brew, Chrysais's rouged cheeks grew paler, not pinker, as she drained her cup.

Priests set crowns of crimson amaranth on Andrion's and Sumitra's hair. Ice flowers, as heavy as bands of iron. Sumitra winced; Andrion took her garland from her head, was prevented from throwing it down by flashes of obsidian and bronze from the hovering priests and guards, compromised by placing it upon his own head. His neck started to bow under the weight of the two wreaths, and with an oath he straightened.

Eldrafel pinched Andrion's arm, testing his ripeness, perhaps, and wiped his hand on his robe with a supercilious sneer. "Here is your sacrifice," he announced to the gathered crowd. "Andrion Bellasteros, King of Sardis, Emperor, brother of Queen Chrysais, who comes here of his own will to give himself to Tenebrio." The chanting quieted, but remained a drone beneath the singsong rhythms of Eldrafel's voice.

"And another sacrifice to the glory of the lord of darkness: Andrion's son and heir."

Andrion ground his teeth. Very tidy, to eliminate not only the current occupier of the throne, but any potential rivals. Sumitra shuddered, melding herself to Andrion's side. He wrapped an arm around her. *Sumi, my shield. . . .* His free hand flexed, but remained empty. Despite the cold his face flushed hot; his mind spun, striking sparks from the flint of his will.

Gard started, struck by one of those sparks. *Of course,* Andrion told himself, *we, too, are of the same blood.* He nodded to the boy's grave eyes; *something will happen soon. I will make it happen.* His jaw ached, set as tightly as Gard's. The notes of a flute slithered among the columns, repeating the storm wail of the chanting. But still the wind was silent.

"These lesser rulers," announced Eldrafel, "Khazyari and Sabazian, shall be sacrificed to a lesser god: Taurmenios, in the arena at Orocastria."

Dana's reply was a muttered epithet, Tembujin's an obscenity. *So they were not in danger here and now,* Andrion told himself. *A mote of relief.* His necklace coiled on his throat, amid the nervous sweat that should surely have turned to snowflakes by now, but had not.

Eldrafel turned away from his captives. He cast his robe down. His body in the moonlight was a gilded idol, his jewels blue, purple, and green ice, his armband shining coldly. He wore only a codpiece and belt, but did not shiver. His languor fell away like a snakeskin as slowly he began to dance.

"Hail, leader of souls," shouted a slurred voice. "Hail, lord of the dance." Eldrafel's cool mien did not change. He stepped and spun, sewing light to shadow in a litany to his dark lord. The muscles coiled and loosed in his buttocks. Andrion stared, fascinated and repulsed, and fascinated by his repulsion; Dana made a sound part moan, part snarl. It was degrading to be compelled by beauty so flawed, and Eldrafel knew it.

The music rose and fell, the piercing wail of the flute underlaid by a chanting so deep as to be barely perceptible. But the very stones beneath Andrion's feet reverberated with the melody. It was just imprecise enough, making just enough irrational loops and glides, to be inhuman. The columns themselves seemed to shift, following the pattern of the dance. Step, step, turn. Step, turn, step.

Andrion squinted. The temple was a bowl of cool, indifferent moonlight. The stones, the people, the krater and its contents, were the translucent gray of Eldrafel's eyes. Only the shadows were real, thronging behind the priest as he danced, linking arms with him, repeating his steps.

"No," Tembujin said suddenly in Andrion's ear. "He is dancing alone. Only illusion, that the shadows dance. I—I can tell."

The frieze of glittering eyes dimmed, the insubstantial bodies swayed. Creeping hallucination, Andrion thought. Part sorcery, part drink. Chrysais sat motionless in her chair, eyes fixed unblinking on Eldrafel's form as it threaded light to darkness. But Gard shifted restlessly, watching Andrion as if for some sign. Andrion should have felt foolish, standing there helpless. But his body was warming with a grim, lucid determination, his sinews winding tightly, his necklace dancing its own dance against the pulse leaping in his throat.

Suddenly harsh bellowing blotted the music. Eldrafel beckoned. A huge strong-shouldered bull with long polished horns was led onto the floor, struggling with the six soldiers clinging to its halter. Behind it came a troupe of human figures, leaping and dancing, surrounding two shambling men which Andrion's cold-annealed perceptions recognized as the two guards he and Dana and Tembujin had overcome just before they freed Sumitra. "Harus!" he swore under his breath.

Whether the dancers were men or women he could not tell;

all were kilted and draped with necklaces and bracelets, all in the harsh metallic moonlight were drained of individuality. They were very young, he decided, still in that smooth and slender early adolescence before the necessities of the flesh molded them into male or female.

The music continued, blending with the bellows of the animal as its handlers abandoned it in the midst of the floor. Its eyes were bright pinpricks of madness. Its nostrils fluttered. Eldrafel pirouetted so close before its face that his hair brushed its horns. It charged.

Eldrafel was not there; he stood again upon the bridge, watching with proprietary interest as the dancers ran forward. Surely they, too, had been drugged, for with ecstatic leaps and hand clappings they threw themselves at the raging animal. The two guards were carried along in the rush. They jumped and clutched, and the sharp horns threw them aside like fish yanked flailing from the ocean and dashed against a rock.

Their screams were short and sharp and suddenly ended. The screaming of the bull crashed like a tidal wave against the columns and resonated in Andrion's head. Sumitra, with a short cry, turned her face into Andrion's chest. The temple shuddered.

Gard blanched and hid his face. Gods, Andrion wailed, what kind of parents would force a child to witness this savagery? Chrysais stroked Gard's hair absently, sadly, knowing she could not soothe him.

The troupe of dancers whirled. The bull stamped, head lowered, great shoulders hunched. Someone ran forward and seized the horns. The animal convulsed. A slender body flew through the air and struck the floor with the terrible moist sound of a melon cleaved in two. The others seemed not to notice, continuing to weave patterns about the huge bull, the embodiment of Taurmenios, the embodiment of the madness of Minras. . . . Another leaped, seized the horns, flipped and landed upon the animal's back. Again the bull contorted itself; the acrobat slipped, fell, and was trampled.

Prisoners given a chance for reprieve? Andrion wondered, his head spinning. Children dancing into the afterlife, believing that this ghastly spectacle pleased the gods? But then, it certainly pleased Tenebrio. His stomach heaved, and he closed his throat on bile and outraged cry both. He clutched Sumitra even more closely against his chest.

The dancers twirled and gestured, throwing each other toward the bull. Andrion blinked, looked again; still the forms darted through the moonlight like silvery flying fish skimming the ocean waves. They flashed, and the horns flashed, and the smooth and graceful limbs became ugly dark-mottled meat upon the implacable stone.

They were all gone. A low, predatory murmur came from the crowd, the dark god not yet satiated. Eldrafel's tongue passed lovingly between his lips. He stepped over the mangled bodies toward the bull. Its chest heaved, its horns sagged; then, crazed by the sickly sweet scent of blood, it charged again. Oblivious to and yet preeningly aware of the watching eyes, he seized the bull's horns just as their red, razor-sharp tips touched his chest. The bull jerked its head up. Eldrafel rode the horns, his body curving into a somersault, landed on the bull's broad back and somersaulted again. He leaped with infernal grace to the stone floor, not even out of breath. Exalted by sorcery and death, he laughed. His upraised hands were stained with blood.

"Khalingu!" exclaimed Tembujin. "He really did that!"

That was what all the acrobats were to have done, Andrion realized. But they were mortals, not demons. Mortals whose sensibilities had been long eroded by the lurking evil of this place. His spine contracted, his body trembled, and sternly he quelled the weakness of his own flesh.

A mob of priests and soldiers rushed forward. Obsidian and bronze winked. The bull's bellows ceased abruptly. A pool of dark carnelian spread bubbling and seething across the stones.

The music stopped. The frieze of watchers shattered. Robed figures swarmed, bathing in the blood of man and bull like sharks in a feeding frenzy. Andrion's appalled eyes recognized Rue, her hands and cheeks matted red, her curious liquid eyes swirling with an uncertainty only heightened by drink and hysteria. She plucked at the elegant figure of Eldrafel, pleading, perhaps, for some reassurance. Mockingly he fondled her and wiped his hands on her robe.

Chrysais lay back on the cold lap of her throne, eyes closed. Gard huddled on his stool. From the spilled blood rose a mist, tentative at first, then thickening into a frost-faceted veil. The reek of sorcery intensified until Andrion choked on it. The moon was as sickly as Sumitra's face, which peered up at him—I am frightened, forgive me. . . . We are all frightened, he told her silently.

They stepped back, away from the gasping, heaving mass of bodies. Sharp if somewhat wobbly points pricked them back onto the dais. Defiantly Andrion dashed the amaranth crowns to the floor. The petals shattered, skittering across the stone like beads from a broken necklace. The drunken, distracted guards did not protest. Andrion's brow tingled as if touched by the diadem.

Eldrafel turned. One gesture sent the robed figures scurrying back to their places on the rim of the basin, like columns amid the eddies of mist, now concealed, now revealed. Their eyes burned red as the eyes of hunting wolves. Another chant began, quick guttural words like racing heartbeats vibrating in the belly of the mountain.

Several guards dragged the pitiful remains of men and beast to the edge of the abyss and threw them in. A light flickered in the depths to receive them, not pale, like that of the frozen moon, but a florid luminescence that welled upward and tinted pink the drifting coils of mist.

Eldrafel danced along the edge of the cleft and across the narrow bridge, leaning perilously far, pulling back. The mist grew opaque, becoming smoke lit from beneath by tongues of sullen flame. And yet the air remained stiflingly cold.

Eldrafel leaped onto the dais, his eyes mirroring the crawling scarlet light of the chasm, grinning in an ecstasy of evil. Tembujin's glance darted from abyss to Eldrafel and back. He frowned.

"Now it is your turn," Eldrafel said. "Tied and torn and cast into the depths; I shall give you a few more moments to anticipate." He pulled Sumitra close and planted a lingering kiss upon her mouth; before she could react, he released her and kissed Andrion as well. His body stank of rich unguents and sorcery, but not, despite his exertions, of sweat.

Sumi spat, as Dana had spat out the poison drink, her face convulsed with disgust. Andrion's lips burned, violated by venom. With a furious snarl he wiped his mouth on his hand and struck out, but Eldrafel, unperturbed, had already pirouetted away.

To where two waiting figures held a linen-wrapped bundle. Eldrafel pulled the cloth away. He raised high the shield of Sabazel and its consort, the sword Solifrax. They glimmered faintly, not reflecting the ghastly light of the sky or the bloody light of the depths, but for just a moment gleaming with the radiance of a free sun and moon. Then they faded into dull lumps of metal.

Andrion quivered as if his own body were transfixed by the sword. Behind him Dana emitted a low cry of rage and despair. In Eldrafel's hands the joined weapons were an image of sexual brutality, their purposes mocked, Andrion's love for Sabazel blasphemed.

And yet, Andrion told himself, forcing a breath from the suffocating air, leaning forward like a runner before a race, and yet he was almost relieved to see the two so combined. Now he understood the odd unity he felt with Dana. Now he understood what it was he could, he must do.

Flames leaped from the chasm, casting fantastic shadows across the temple. Eldrafel laid the shield and sword at Chrysais's feet, responding to her outstretched hand with a bow so exquisitely courteous it was a jeer. He turned and began to dance again with his wraiths of smoke and sorcery. The chant swelled; the mountain festered with it, lurched and spun like a whirlpool around the solitary figure that danced a litany to a dark god.

Andrion held Sumitra. Dana's hand pressed into his back. Tembujin at his left muttered, "I can tell what it is he intends us to see, and yet I can see that it is not there. No flame, no smoke, just the dark chasm and a few strands of mist like will-o'-the-wisps."

"Thank you," Andrion said. If Tembujin could not be sucked into hallucination, then neither would he. His mind danced, each thought, each sight, each scent a crystalline bubble prismed with implication. Wonderful, he told himself, how peril concentrates thought. His necklace purred agreement.

His companions were profiles chased one after the other upon frozen moonlight and lurid flame; Dana an edged weapon, Sumitra a newly minted coin, Tembujin an exotic and yet familiar statue. Silver-rimmed faces, too precious to waste on the sickly paradoxes of Minras.

Sumitra, he told himself, has been bait to draw me here. If I were not here, she would be bait again. Dana and Tembujin only become lesser rulers when I am here as a greater one. Eldrafel can only use them as threads in his evil tapestry when I am his needle. One chance, all I need is one chance to kill him—I, too, am corrupted, he thought, writhing, wanting to so cold-bloodedly kill!

Andrion looked again at Gard's ashen face. And Eldrafel

needs him, too, for now; but the time will come when Gard dies of some mysterious disease. . . . I must save the boy, I must commit him to saving himself by giving him the chance to refuse corruption.

The sword and shield lay on the floor by Chrysais's feet. By Gard's. Eldrafel could not turn the weapons to his own use, but he could flaunt them, denying their power to those people to whom they were so much more than weapons. Such appalling profanation would win battles more handily than if he did control the power of shield and sword.

Eldrafel, self-absorbed, pranced along the rim of the abyss, across the bridge, back again. Chrysais's features were blotched clay, resenting the satiety she had craved. Several priests, armed with daggers and ropes, stepped toward the dais. The chanting reverberated in succeeding waves through the rock, echoing upon itself.

Gard looked up, summoned by Andrion's fierce resolve. And his face ignited to his uncle's command. Andrion tore the necklace from his throat and pressed it into Dana's hand. "Ah!" she gasped, as if he had struck her in the stomach. But that link between them tautened and held. "Andrion!" Sumitra wailed. Dana seized her shoulders, holding her back from following as Andrion leaped from the dais.

Gard jumped from his stool, at last unleashed. He swept up the sword and shield and almost dropped them, startled by their weight. The priests shouted. Eldrafel stopped in mid-gesture, limbs held in elegant angles, head tilted.

Gard threw the weapons. They flashed, frost and fire mated, and Andrion picked them effortlessly from the air. His hand fit the hilt of Solifrax; Daimion's sword, Bellasteros's sword, his own sword that he had won; smoothly he pulled it free of the shield. Chiming, the silver metal of the shield flowed together and the wound in the star healed itself.

Sword and shield rang as one, a long sustained note like a plucked string of the zamtak. The sound was not loud but incisive, cutting the chant in mid-phrase and shivering on through the sudden silence. The smoke wraiths fled. The watchers drew back. Chrysais jerked erect, her mask thinning suddenly to reveal—not quite relief, not quite disappointment.

Gard's laugh of delight, pure and unaffected, cleared the miasma of sorcery as surely as did the ring of the shield.

Andrion set the shield upon his own arm. It was strangely light, carrying itself, permitting him only to guide it. Its emblazoned star pulsed, reflecting the clear radiance of the sword and doubling it. But the odd unity with Dana continued, no longer uncomfortable but as easy as the curve of the shield fitting the curve of the sword.

The watchers huddled with tiny gibbering noises, their eyes not feral gleams but moist drunken blurs. Guards gestured ineffectually around the dais. Cold flame licked the rim of the chasm. The spinning world halted abruptly and even the bleak face of the moon steadied.

Dana clutched the necklace to her breast. Did she cry aloud, or was it only a tendril of her thought that lashed Andrion's mind like a whip: My shield, by Ashtar, my shield; gods, what other man save him can raise my shield!

Sumitra stood with her hand pressed over her mouth, her great brown eyes glistening with shock. By all the gods, Andrion howled silently, Sumi, I cannot leave you—I must leave you—I vow in the name of Harus, of Ashtar, I shall return for you and for our child and for the Empire that is mine!

Tembujin twitched as if he meant to leap forward and help Andrion; the guards seethed clumsily around him, Sumitra swayed, and he grasped her instead. Andrion could sense his thought, too; do something, you idiot, before someone realizes they can threaten us and force you to disarm!

Eldrafel stood before him, his lips drawn back in a snarl, his teeth glinting like ice pearls. He raised his hands and a sudden force like a blast of black fire lanced through the mist. But Andrion was expecting that. The shield leaped up, turning the blast with another ring. Did the demon priest's perfect features warp with surprise? Good. Very good.

Andrion edged to the side, toward the abyss and its gelid flame. Illusion, he reminded himself. The fire is illusion. My mother once told me of a fiery chasm and how her shield protected her.

Eldrafel spun about to see Gard's small fists gesturing triumphantly. The priest hissed like a striking cobra and slapped the boy sprawling.

Chrysais jumped from the throne, stumbled, swept Gard into her arms. Her face was hidden in his hair; his face, a pale oval smeared with blood from a cut lip, stared up at Eldrafel in unalloyed hatred.

Andrion winced. But perhaps it was just as well for the boy to realize he did not watch an impersonal melodrama.

Eldrafel was upon him again, hands raised. At last. Andrion lunged for his heart, Solifrax slicing a shining arc through the smoke. But the blade turned suddenly, twisting in Andrion's hand as if meeting some resistance thicker than flesh, and slipped along Eldrafel's ribs leaving a gory but shallow wound. Hellfrost and damnation, is the man invulnerable!

The shield emitted a shower of light. Eldrafel's upraised hands remained empty. His face opened in amazement. His chest was streaked with blood, slow ruby drops oozing over the smooth beauty of his abdomen; good, Andrion thought, you can bleed, you bastard!

It was Andrion who grinned now, in a fierce joy. He stepped backward, without any grace whatsoever but with a great deal of caution, onto the narrow bridge. Fire licked at his feet, but he felt no heat, only a chill breath from the abyss. And what was down there? The corridors of Mount Tenebrio were as tangled as those of the palace in Orocastria. The mountain, too, must have a basement. If not, Andrion thought with a shuddering sigh, I die on my own terms, with the symbols of Empire and Sabazel in my hands.

Suddenly, in answer, a wind pealed down from the indigo-dark vaults of the sky. The moon spun amid clouds of star-stuff. The shield and sword blazed with an unsullied white light.

Eldrafel stepped onto the end of the bridge. The black force lanced out again. Again Andrion turned the blast, this time back into the priest's face. Like an ugly sea creature hidden in the heart of a gleaming nautilus shell, something moved behind Eldrafel's gold and marble facade, some vile inhuman shadow.

Andrion blinked. The vision vanished as fast as it had formed. Eldrafel glared at him, spitting curses, his clear gray eyes mottled with flecks of vermilion, his hair knotted by the wind.

With one last desperate glance at the three moon-gilt figures on the dais, Andrion stepped off the bridge. The light of sword and shield bore him up and the wind sustained him, so that he floated into the red depths as light as a falcon's feather. Was it blood that rushed in his head, or the flutter of wings? Whichever, the flames of illusion parted before him.

"Gods," he muttered between teeth locked in a spasm of courage and fear, "gods, make sport of me if you will, but protect mine!'' The pale mark of the necklace on his throat throbbed.

A sound like the howling of jackals eddied down the cleft. ''Throw them all in!'' shouted Eldrafel, his voice no longer melodious but burred with fury.

Chrysais's bitter scream was louder. ''No, we must keep them to draw him back!''

''This insult to Tenebrio must be avenged!''

Chrysais laughed, high and shrill, flirting with hysteria. ''Tenebrio has tasted your blood tonight, my king; yours and this your son and heir's. That will sate him for now.''

And Gard's wail pierced the darkness, ''His son? His?'' The hatred in his voice rusted into anguish.

The wind died. The voices faded. Andrion was surrounded by hollow silence. The flames shredded into nothingness, consumed by a cerulean twilight that was neither light nor dark, neither victory nor defeat, but continued struggle. . . . He was floating, he realized. He could not really float.

In that moment of doubt stone came up to meet him and struck him senseless.

Chapter Fourteen

AS SOON AS the door shut behind him, Eldrafel seized a water pitcher and dashed it against the wall. The smash, and the clattering rain of shards, was not enough to restore the shine to his tarnished features. He proceeded methodically to destroy every breakable object in the chamber.

Chrysais stood flat against the wall. Her dress was smeared with blood from Gard's lip, her chin quivered from his agony. He had thrust her away from him, calling her names he should have been too young to know.

She had left the sobbing boy with a Rue so subdued as to be stupefied. Now Chrysais's hands clutched only at the sardonyx figurine choked between her breasts. She watched her husband's rage with bleak, dry eyes. If his fury had not been so cold and silent she might have screamed at him, berating him for botching the sacrifice, or wept in anger at their plan going so wrong. But before this supernal rage she could only wait.

Her various pots of paint and perfume left fragrant multi-colored blotches upon the floor. A wine carafe splattered crimson across an old tapestry, blotting the writhing figures in a tide of blood. The images on the new, incomplete tapestry seemed to dance mockingly.

Eldrafel stood breathing hard, lip curled in scorn, watching it. Only the images of sword and shield stood out clearly from the canvas, their stitches winking to each other. With a growl Eldrafel picked up a long needle and thrust it through the picture of the shield as Solifrax had so lately penetrated the real object. But the silvery twinkle, as of distant laughter, did not abate.

Chrysais said dully, "We cannot enspell either sword or shield. I doubt if we can enspell Andrion or any of his minions. They are strong, much stronger than we thought."

"Than we thought?" Eldrafel mimicked. "Speak for yourself, woman; it is your powers that have been defeated, not mine."

"Defeated?" replied Chrysais. Her face began to crumple, the mask slipping. "We are not defeated. Andrion lives, yes; the shine in those images proves that, if nothing else. But we have the others, and he will come for them. He must."

"Then he must come to Orocastria," Eldrafel snapped. "Tenebrio did not receive his sacrifice. His full sacrifice," he amended, glancing with distaste at the gruesome furrow Solifrax had sliced in his own flesh. "And now the full moon is setting; the proper time is passed. Taurmenios now must receive his due, at his festival in the dark of the moon. He has been restive lately."

Chrysais brightened a bit. "We can use the rites of Taurmenios to placate Tenebrio as well."

"Yes." Eldrafel tried to smile his usual smile of sublime confidence, but his mouth merely tightened without curving. His eyes turned again to the tapestry and chilled.

His eyes were fixed on the image of Sumitra. Chrysais started forward with a jerk. "Would you like more wine, my love? I can send for food, if you are hungry. . . ."

He turned on her. "I would like to think that you replaced Sumitra's hair with silk because she has already served her purpose. I would like to think you destroyed the bowstring because we have Dana and Tembujin already in our power."

Beneath her paint Chrysais's face went stark white.

"Do I think correctly?" His voice seethed. "Or are you protecting someone? Someone who might have fallen to the blandishments of that snot-nosed prig your brother?"

"I destroyed the hair," mumbled Chrysais, looking at her feet, concealing her eyes and with them the truth, "thinking that free sacrifices would be more acceptable to Tenebrio."

Eldrafel said nothing. The room was so silent that a faint sigh from the hanging lamp sounded like the hiss of a cobra. The tapestries hung lank, the scattered bits of porcelain lay like the pieces of a game abandoned as too intricate to play.

Then Eldrafel stretched. Perhaps his anger was assuaged. But still his eyes glinted adamant, and his body was not indolent but tense. "Come," he said with a nod toward the bed. "Let us enjoy ourselves, my wife, and forget the disappointments of the night."

Chrysais hesitated as if he taunted her. But he was already

removing his scraps of clothing and casting them on the floor. His belt left a golden path through the blood smeared on his chest and abdomen.

She smiled, her cold wax face melting with relief, adoration, and a hint of gratitude. She moistened a cloth in the puddle of spilled water and went to the bed. "My poor darling. Let me clean that."

"Oh, yes," Eldrafel murmured. "Yes, you shall clean it." He seized her head in his hands, and despite her protesting squeak, forced her mouth down upon the wound.

She squeaked again, shuddering, but his hands did not relent. Her own hands coiled in the bedclothes. Her eyes pinched shut. Her red lips and pink tongue darkened to rust with dried blood.

Eldrafel lay back with a sigh of pleasure.

Sumitra could not tell whether the soldiers who had precipitously jostled her, Dana, and Tembujin back to their cell were more drunk or dismayed. Two of them even now glowered from either side of the door, as if proper supervision would prevent any more outrages like Andrion's escape.

Only three candles sputtered sulkily on the table; the window frame was tinted with silver, the last grace note of the setting moon and the wind that had scoured it clean. Dana looked longingly out the aperture, at the guards, around the dank room; she collapsed against the wall with her arms crossed and her mouth as hard as a fissure in the rock.

Tembujin stood staring into the shadows that ebbed and flooded darkly in the corners, intent upon some thought of his own; his features considered envy, anger, frustration, fear, and finally seized upon the slitted eyes and outthrust chin of resolve.

Sumitra sat down, stood, sat and again leaped to her feet. She did not want to worry about how close she had come to death, how narrowly she had been saved by Andrion's daring and perhaps rash leap. She did not want to worry whether he were alive or dead, whether he would come to save her, whether she was kept as elaborate bait. She had already worried, and her mind was rutted deep.

The terrible scenes in the temple, the terrible emotions, crawled like leeches through her senses and drained her of strength and will. More drab, dark days of waiting and praying and hoping lay ahead. . . . By the six arms of

Vaiswanara, she screamed silently, I grow sick to death of waiting!

The zamtak lay nearby; as she reached for it, her last consolation, she saw a quick gleam in Dana's hand, something touched by a last ray of moonlight. But the moon was down, and the object shone on.

Yes, Andrion's necklace. Her mind dashed away the memory of him pressing it upon Dana. "Give it to me," said Sumitra quietly, aware of the guards, but with a low intensity that brought Tembujin up with a start.

Dana was not at all startled. Curtly she said, "I am of his blood. I shall keep it."

Sumi laid her hand on her stomach. "And what do I carry here, a melon? The necklace is mine, as he is mine."

Dana drew herself up to her full height, almost a head taller than Sumitra. "I bore him a child; Astra, the heir to Sabazel."

"Signifying nothing," snapped Sumi, "in the real world."

"He gave me the necklace and I shall keep it!" Dana retorted.

"Dana," said Tembujin, "shut your mouth."

Dana scowled. "How dare you—"

"Arguing solves nothing," Tembujin interrupted, laying a mollifying hand on Dana's arm. She wrenched herself away.

Sumitra groped for calm, for certainty. Dana's tight white face was still before her, the glittering eyes still pinioned her. And yet something moved in those eyes, some reluctant shade of remorse. The remorse must be mine, Sumi informed herself; if I hate her, I am unworthy of him. With an effort she said, "This evil place would drive me to forget my manners. Yes, Dana, he gave you the necklace, you must hold it until his . . . return. . . ." Her voice strung the last word over an entire octave, and she sat suddenly in the nearest chair.

Tembujin shot a wary glance at the guards. They stood immobile, their eyes rolled back so far that only slits of phosphorescence were visible between their lashes. With a snort of humorless laughter he knelt beside Sumitra. "Look," he murmured. "Look over there—inconspicuously, mind you—by the inner door, where yesterday Andrion laid the sheath of Solifrax."

Both women glanced cautiously around. The snakeskin sheath seemed at first to have simply slipped down onto the flagstoned floor. Then Sumitra realized that the shadows hanging about it were not shadows at all, but a darkly gleaming mist. She leaned forward, her hand on her heart to keep it from leaping into her throat.

The sheath wavered behind its obscuring cloud, flowing across the floor as if it were serpent again, questing for its burrow. And like a serpent, in one smooth motion it oozed between the stones and disappeared. The mist thinned into omnipresent shadow.

"Ashtar!" exclaimed Dana under her breath, even as the necklace flickered and faded in her hand. "It goes to him; he is still alive."

"He gave you the necklace," Sumitra whispered. "You are blood of his blood, you have known him always, you have the Sight."

"No, lady," Dana insisted with bitter courtesy, "you are closer to him than I can ever be. And you can control your power. Here. Keep it safe, for it will belong to your child, not to mine."

Tembujin snorted again; the women's kindness was sharper than scorn.

Sumitra gazed at the gold chain, the moon and the star Dana dangled before her, but made no move to take it. "I did not heal you just to show my power," she said. "I did not heal you just to make you owe me."

"I know that. Here, take it."

Sumitra took it. It lay across her palm with a warm tingle, dispelling the chill of the night. The window flushed golden pink, presaging the rising of the sun. "We shall share it," she said, and she laid the necklace along the zamtak, so that its chain seemed another string. And quietly but unmistakably the zamtak began to hum, quivering as if in a slow heartbeat.

"Ashtar!" Dana exclaimed again, and suddenly smashed her fist against the stone wall. The guards woke and stared at her. She regarded her bleeding knuckles as if they marred someone else's hand. "I am a fool," she muttered, her voice no longer sharp but husky. "As long as Andrion bears my shield I am with him. I did not need to hurt you, Sumi."

"Nor I you," said Sumitra, with a sad shake of her head. Her throat clotted and her eyes burned; gods, do not make me weep before this warrior!

The warrior turned and fled into the inner room.

With a shivering intake of breath Sumi lifted the zamtak and stroked the strings. A tear spilled from her eye to trace a shining path down her cheek. The child fluttered briefly, deep in her belly. "I am tired," she said, her voice very small. "Forgive me." She was not sure of whom she asked forgiveness, herself, most likely. All will be well, she told herself. All must be well.

Tembujin sighed, hugged her, rose and began to prowl the room, up and down, a lion in a cage.

The necklace gleamed amid the strings of the zamtak, beneath Sumitra's hand. Upon the tide of music her serenity returned.

Andrion sensed hard stone at his back; the air against his face was still and cold, smothering him with malignant tension.

He was bruised and battered; the briefest movement made him wince. But the hilt of Solifrax lay in his right hand, and his left arm was thrust through the straps of the star-shield. Their combined whisper stirred the hollow silence around him.

He had thought himself lucid, there in the temple. Now he was not so sure. Had it been some tendril of sorcery that had urged him to make this gamble? Sumitra, Dana, and Tembujin could well be dead now. Sumitra and the child, he reminded himself with a pang like a spear thrust through his heart.

His feet were frosted lead. He drew up his knees. He parted his lashes just enough to see the eerie twilight around him, neither day nor night but some uneasy combination of the two. The aura that emanated from sword and shield illuminated the pitiful piles of meat beside him that had only hours before been human beings and a bull. Thank whatever mercy of the gods eked out to man that the faces were turned away from him.

Thank the merciful gods that only scattered bones lay beside the bodies. Andrion closed his eyes again. Had he been selfish, to run away and leave them? Or would it have been more than selfish, blatantly stupid, not to risk them?

He had been strong enough to escape, but not strong enough to kill Eldrafel; that black force the man carried about him, turning the invincible blade of Solifrax . . . The ordeal would continue, eternally, and he was sick to death of it. He groaned, "Harus, why?"

Images formed in his mind. Fancies, he told himself. Lingering hallucination. But the vision was as clear and precise as Dana's face.

The gnarled branches of a tree danced amid drifts of wind-tossed leaves and globes of golden fruit. A fresh, cool wind purled down from Cylandra, scented with anemone, asphodel, and appropriately enough, jasmine. An old woman in a blue hooded cloak stood beneath the tree, leaning upon a staff twisted by a serpent.

The image wavered, seen through water like the shapes formed by the tiles in the pool in Ashtar's temple. Then it stood out bright and firm.

The woman held Solifrax upright in its snakeskin sheath, the familiar gold filigree hilt defined in intricate detail by her hand, as if her hand were a transparent lens. The wind fluttered her hood, allowing just a glimpse of omniscient sky-blue eyes. A falcon soared around the tree and dropped swiftly down, its raucous cry stirring fruit and branch alike, and landed upon the woman's arm as delicately as a falling leaf.

The hair rose in questing tendrils on Andrion's nape, and a shiver not of cold but of awe tightened his spine. Ashtar, with Harus upon her arm, a vision his father had seen but once, and he himself had seen only intimated upon a battlefield. A vision that promised and demanded much.

God-beloved Andrion, god-haunted Andrion, tested and sported and tested again. . . . He stared up, open-eyed, into the cerulean twilight. A figure looked inquisitively down upon him. If it was a figment of dream, it was the most genuine figment he had ever experienced.

The man was fully mature, in vigorous middle age; his sturdy torso and long, wiry limbs were clothed in a meticulously draped cloak. His hair lay like russet-brown feathers across a high forehead, his nose was a magnificent beak that put even Jemail's prow to shame and eclipsed Andrion's aquiline profile completely. His eyes were bright and probing, now amber, now as dark brown as Andrion's own; they were of a pellucid lambency Andrion had thought never to see again since Bellasteros's eyes had closed in death. Eyes like those could see through walls, across leagues, into other dimensions.

In the strange light of the cavern the man emitted a faint light of his own, an untainted luminescence like that of sword and shield. Manners, Andrion told himself, spurring his sanity; he staggered to his feet.

"My lord Harus," he croaked through parched lips and throat. Shakily he saluted, sword and shield clattering. Solifrax flared. The star-shield was rather more cautious, but gleamed in polite greeting nonetheless.

The god, if it were a god, smiled. His face seemed to crease naturally in lines of wry humor.

"My lord Harus," said Andrion, more steadily, "how may I serve you?"

"I have come to serve you; you called me. Although," Harus added with a furtive twinkle, "you have not called on me overmuch of late."

With a shamefaced nod, Andrion said, "If you are indeed a god . . ." He stopped, gulped, continued, "If you indeed the god, you can see my heart and read the doubts there. You can feel my bruises."

"Ah," said Harus, frowning in mock severity, "if you did not doubt, you would not be Andrion. You would not be Bellasteros's son. You would not be my—" He stopped, his frown cracking into a wide grin.

Andrion essayed a bewildered grin of his own. The man's— the god's—voice was not soothing but bracing, indeed like the compelling cry of a raptor. "Tell me," he asked, "are we indeed shadows dancing at the whim of the gods? Or are the gods the shadows of our own desires?"

Harus's auburn brows, feathered like arrows, quirked with an indulgent irony. "Whatever I told you, would you believe me? Would you not continue to struggle with your own conscience and your own will?"

"Probably," Andrion admitted, looking down at his feet. He stood on gray, crumbling bones.

"Few mortals even think of such questions, let alone try to answer them," Harus said gently. "One of the hazards, the burdens, laid upon the child of a god. Like Bellasteros. Like Eldrafel."

"How can you say those names in the same breath?"

But Harus was looking beyond him, lips compressed, as if the stone were as clear as a window. "Your attraction to Gard has a purpose, Andrion. He needs your help. You, too, are the grandson of a god."

The dimness sparked and swirled. Andrion shook his head, but he remained slightly giddy. "The stories told to explain why Bellasteros was a nine-month baby born in seven months. Very convenient. We know the truth, that my grandmother Viridis celebrated the rites in Sabazel and that my grandfather is some . . . red-headed stranger. . . ."

Andrion heard his own voice fade and die. Such cynicism ill suited him. Harus was waiting, head cocked. Slowly the blood mounted into Andrion's cheeks until they seemed to steam in the chill darkness.

Again Harus released a broad grin, adding a chuckle at Andrion's discomfiture. He touched the star-shield, drawing from it a burbling chime almost like a woman's low, delighted laugh. "I, too, know the beguilements of Sabazel."

"Ah," said Andrion faintly.

"Bellasteros's mother," Harus said, "may she live forever in my affection, had to be an outsider so that he would not be related to Danica. Dana is almost close enough to you for your own passion to be forbidden."

Andrion gulped. Dana, the daughter of his half-sister Ilanit; Eldrafel could almost with justification accuse him of incest. But not quite. His mind spun again, and the ground rocked subtly beneath his feet. "Eldrafel?" he asked. "Also the son of a god?"

Harus sighed. "Another convenient lie that is simple truth. Proserfina came here to lie with a god. What took her, sadly, was a demon."

Dana had sensed Tenebrio was a demon, practicing malevolent sorcery, not a god sharing beneficent magic; that explained much. That helped nothing, however.

"Tenebrio," said Harus gravely. "An ancient god whose time is long past, as someday my time will be past. But he would not go peacefully into the long twilight; struggling to continue, he became a demon, and lingered into the reign of his successor, Taurmenios. And now they feud." He stopped with a grimace of irritation. "Tenebrio sent Eldrafel to restore him to power. But Eldrafel has ambitions of his own, and has corrupted even Taurmenios. It is this island that shall suffer."

Andrion's neck crawled again. No wonder the air of the island was so charged with foreboding. It had become the dueling ground of gods.

Harus watched Andrion as if his every thought was painted in garish colors upon his face. And he actually seemed to approve those thoughts. "Through your mother you are descended from my consort Ashtar, through your father from me; truly you are beloved indeed." The god's face grew wistful. Emphatically he cleared his throat. "Here, I have something for you." He held out the snakeskin sheath of Solifrax.

The sword sparked. The scales on the sheath rippled, one after the other, like a glissando played upon the zamtak. "Thank you." Andrion took the sheath, hooked it to his belt, slid Solifrax into it. The sword sighed with a sensuality that was downright embarrassing.

Harus 'aughed at Andrion's expression. "No, I do not peer over your shoulder at every moment."

"But have you not been telling me that, as I feared, as I hoped, all my life and my parents' lives have been lived to your direction?"

The god shrugged. "Would you believe me, Andrion . . ."

"If you told me?" Andrion amazed himself by laughing. "Very well then, what else can I do but turn my own stubborn will to the task at hand, preventing Tenebrio from extending his shadow over Sardis and Sabazel and the Empire."

"Indeed." Harus saluted the King of Sardis, Emperor. He then enfolded his grandson in a rough embrace and left a kiss upon his brow. "Whether you or I make your decisions and guide your destiny, those decisions and that destiny remain the same. Because I trust you to choose correctly."

He winked, an affable conspirator, and with a rush of wings he was gone. Andrion stared open-mouthed into a cavern that now seemed doubly dim and empty. The mark of the god's lips on his forehead burned like a brand. "But I had more questions," he said lamely. "The history of Sardis, the borders of Sabazel, intent and belief and reason. . . ."

Surely a god should manifest himself in a glory of trumpets and incense. How could the fierce falcon god be so ordinary? Had the god diminished his power to fit Andrion's limited perceptions?

Or had Andrion, floundering upon this shore between dream and reality, created the entire scene? In his desperation he had gone so far as to claim descent from a god, even as the god's mundane appearance only proved the poverty of his imagination. . . . And yet Harus had worn the numinous cloak Bellasteros had worn, which Andrion at times felt draped over his own shoulders.

"But you probably would not answer those questions either!" he called. "That would be much too easy!" His voice reverberated into the distance. Perhaps he caught a remote flutter of wings; perhaps not.

No. Only his own god would bring the sheath for a weapon and no food or drink. Only his own god would speak of cosmic issues and neglect to say whether his wife and child were alive or dead.

You are incorrigible, Andrion told himself.

The white line around his neck, the mark of the moon and star upon his tanned skin, suddenly tingled as if the necklace still lay upon it. The shield tugged gently at his arm. He heard the notes of the zamtak, a shower of shining gold through the oppressive air.

They were alive. They were waiting. The ordeal continued; his duty lay clear before him. He would accept the vision, savor the enlightenment it brought, and struggle on.

He hoisted the shield, settled the sword at his thigh, and looked around him. Several black fissures rent the peculiar luminescent walls. Andrion certainly did not want to return to the labyrinth of the temple, but he had no way of telling where each opening led.

Danica, he remembered, had once followed a quest underground. He raised the shield and blew upon it, as she had. It flamed at his breath, emitting a clear light, tugging him toward one particular opening. "And thank you, Ashtar," he said, with a polite bow aimed at nothing in particular. He entered the fissure and stone closed around him.

Beneath the mountain of Tenebrio the earth was scored like an ancient face. And indeed Tenebrio was ancient, Andrion reflected as he trod warily through a pool of black, slick water like liquid obsidian. Mankind had abandoned such violent gods, leaving Tenebrio to gnaw his malevolence. These oppressive caves, now dim, now dark, but never light, were a catacomb not for human burial but for the burial of a dead belief.

Almost dead. Eldrafel, a like green leaf on the hoary, partly decomposed trunk of an olive, was indubitably alive and seeking to reanimate the cadaver of his infernal ancestor.

The passages looped back on themselves like a tangled thread; more than once Andrion came upon the prints of his own feet. At least he hoped they were his own feet. More than once he glanced behind him, certain that something followed him. But he saw only darkness gathered about him and the glow of the shield, dancing and jeering in the corners of his eyes. The rhythm of his breath was magnified by the enclosing rock until it became a wheezing bellows, echoing again and again in rushing waves of sound. The stone pressed down upon him, the great diabolical mass of Minras crushed him.

He staggered, clutched the shield closer to him, and forced himself to breathe slowly of what little air there was. There, the sound abated. His sense of following evil did not.

His mouth was as dry as a mummy's; he dared a sip from a stream of water dribbling off a gargoylelike projection. It eased his thirst, but its weedy flavor left his throat gummed and his teeth furred. Around another corner, sideways through a crevice, and he found stone lying in billows like a petrified wave. Upon the rock grew uneven ranks of mushrooms, their plump white caps glistening obscenely. He was hungry, but not that hungry. He moved on.

In the silvery gleam of the shield he saw the ceiling of the passageway fold in upon itself and crack into nobby stalactites. The floor sprouted corresponding stalagmites. Andrion had to move adroitly to keep from sliding in the dripping slime, but the weight on his shoulders lifted a bit. A faint echo of falling water stirred the silence; this cavern was, indeed, very much like the cellars of the palace in Orocastria. And the stalactites reminded him of the pillars decorating the facades of the Orocastrian houses. Taurmenios Tenebrae, indeed, the elder god consuming the younger.

Footprints smeared the floor, small female feet and a bull's hooves intermingled. He stopped, quelled a shiver, went on. Sickly fungus plastered the scoriated walls. Even as he choked on their musty odor, he could swear the air was a little lighter.

Andrion emerged into a vast underground chamber. The ceiling arched high overhead, lost in violet-blue depths like Chrysais's eyes. The walls receded into a shimmering gloom. A faint muttering of voices came to his ear; he drew Solifrax before he realized that it was the sword and the shield themselves murmuring. Their glows sent shadows skittering away across the hummocked floor, surrounding Andrion with wraiths. He took a cautious step and something crunched moistly; startled, he saw bones and flowers falling to mold beneath his feet.

The hair on the back of his neck prickled. Someone was indubitably watching him. He spun, sword upraised. The blade flared, an arc of fire in the dimness.

A brief whisper of movement in the uncanny light; a woman, the hem of her dress a ripple of nothingness above the floor. Her flesh, revealed by the Minran bodice, was as gray and hazy as the Minran sky. Her jewels were facets of darkly gleaming flint. But her eyes—her wide, white-rimmed eyes—were quite lucid, as sharp as flensing knives.

Andrion lowered the sword. His breath was a scintillating cloud of steam. Proserfina's skirt wavered and fell lank again. "May I help you?" he asked.

Her voice was an echo of an echo, elusively faint. Andrion had to strain to hear it, but hear it he did. "Eldrafel," she sighed. "You must destroy Eldrafel."

"I intend to," he replied, even as he thought, What horror, to seek the death of your own child. Andrion envisioned Proserfina confined in a stony cell, gazing out a window like a stubbornly slitted mouth, pleading and dreading while her belly swelled.

She sensed his thought. "Yes, I prayed that my child would be as other children. But I was betrayed. By Taurmenios Tenebrae, whom I had faithfully served." The air shivered with bitterness. The frail woman shape faded, so that Andrion could see stalagmites through it, and then solidified again. "It was a demon who came to me, who used me, not a god. I should have sought death that very night, but . . ."

"We all must hope," Andrion offered. How could he soothe a phantom?

"My baby's eyes were colorless," whispered Proserfina, "like mirrors, the eyes of the demon. And I realized then that god and demon were one. Eldrafel—the demon's spawn— laughed at my credulity, in a laugh that was not a child's." Her voice thinned and broke, swallowed by the silence.

But her words went on, falling one by one into Andrion's mind like the tones of the zamtak. "I stole away from my serving women and found Gath's store of herbs. A posset of aconite, I thought, and I would know no more of what I had done. But I cannot forget; the memory sustains me."

"How may I help you to rest, lady?"

"The priests greeted my baby's arrival with rites such as those you escaped. To render him invulnerable they bathed his tiny form in the mingled blood of bull and man, and their own blood, as well, for they committed ghastly mutilations upon themselves in worship of the dark god."

Andrion cringed, his body shrinking at the image. And he thought, No wonder the demon priest had resisted the thrust of Solifrax.

"But those who anointed him were drunk on herbs and pain and power. They did not realize that the places where they held him could not be touched by the blood."

"Ah," said Andrion. "The marks of their hands upon him. Where?"

"The nape of his neck, and the back of his right thigh. There he is vulnerable."

Andrion closed his eyes and opened them again. The feminine form hovered, waiting, still waiting. "My most humble thanks to you," he said with a bow. "I shall do my best to dispatch Eldrafel."

"Yes . . ." The sibilant was a sudden breeze through the cavern. The phantom thinned again, became only an image sketched upon gauze, and then shredded completely away.

The breeze stopped as suddenly as an intake of breath. The nape of his neck, Andrion repeated with a grim smile, and his right thigh. . . . The dim lavender light went out. A deep if distant bellowing boomed through the darkness. A phantom bull, thought Andrion. A skeleton, bones lime white and mad eyes glittering, roaming the tangled corridors, screaming its own agony.

He told himself firmly the noise was only an air current rushing through the snarl of passageways, drumming in the rock. But he knew it was not. These caverns were so filled with sorcery that even he could sense the spectral otherworlds, good and evil both. This was what Dana suffered, he thought with a catch in his heart, trapped in some shady place where those worlds met and mingled.

A susurration of voices, a threatening echo of the temple chant, stirred the darkness. Sword and shield gleamed, murmuring in return. "Ssh!" Andrion commanded, trying to ascertain the direction of the sound. Solifrax fell silent. The shield muttered truculently and quieted.

No good; the sound surrounded him. A miasma of cold crept up from the ground and sucked at him. Dizzied, he swayed.

Then the shield spurted light and almost jerked him off his feet. He shook himself and followed its lead. I must not panic, he told himself. I must walk carefully through the slime. . . . Slime. He raised the shield over his head. Its radiance swept the ceiling of the cavern, picking myriad tiny red pinpricks from an undulating carpet of blackness. Bats. An opening to the outside world must be nearby.

The bat slime beneath his feet chittered and crawled. Something nibbled at his toe. He leaped and almost fell. The shield, impatient, pulled him on, a thread of light almost but not quite dispelling the horror.

Footsteps squished behind him. One hoof, then two, in an uncanny manlike rhythm. It might really have been the thudding of his own heart, but he did not wait to find out. He stumbled on, his head so light that the aureole about shield and sword danced around him.

A streak of brilliance curved down the darkness. He squinted; it was daylight. His nerves frayed and snapped at last. He ran for the cleft, thought for a ghastly moment he could not squeeze through, thrust both shield and sword ahead of him and burst out into sunshine. Thin, watery sunshine, but blessed even so. The free air, tainted though it was with the sweat of Minras, tasted like new wine.

Something threw itself at the cleft behind him, scrabbling at it, trying to burrow through. Andrion did not stop to consider. Ignominiously he fled, leaping down the rocky crenellations of the mountainside until the cleft was only a dark line among the weathered boulders behind him.

Then he stopped and leaned dizzily against a stone which despite the sunshine was cold. "Something objected to Proserfina's message to me," he gasped. "Terror is as good a weapon as any." Well, yes, he had run away—but his business was out here, was it not?

With a snort of derision modified by a wry crimp of his mouth, Andrion stood. He was still light-headed, it seemed; the ground heaved beneath him.

And he smelled roasting meat. Really, these hallucinations were becoming annoying. Ignoring his stomach's importunate rumble, he thrust Solifrax into its sheath and offered the shield an appreciative stroke of his fingertips. It sparked, sighed, and faded into quiescence.

Andrion continued to smell meat. With a muttered oath he turned and began picking his way much more carefully down the scree, drawn by the tantalizing odor. He passed withered vines, half-collapsed stone walls, meadows overgrown by thistle and nettle. An occasional abandoned olive made its tortuous way through the black rock, and a mottled lizard or two lay hopefully in what passed for sunshine. No wind, no singing birds, no evil chants; Andrion's own breath seemed as loud as a gale.

At the side of a wizened tamarisk a solitary thread of smoke spiraled upward to join the hazy gray sky.

He was on the far side of Mount Tenebrio, he realized. He crept closer to the tiny fire and the figure that bent over a spitted hare. From here he saw the blurred suggestions of field and farm, the interior of the island, flat as painted miniatures under the brooding hulk of the mountain and the lowering sky it anchored. The sea and Tenebrio's two temples, sinks of malignancy, were behind him; Zind Taurmeni was an obscure blot ahead.

His stomach flopped loosely under his ribs, and his foot dislodged a pebble. It bounced downward with all the noisy abandon of a ballista shot.

The figure by the fire leaped up, seizing a spear. Most of his face was obscured by a fuzzy black beard, but the arch of the nose and the belligerent glare were quite familiar. Andrion stepped out from behind the boulder, flipped his cloak jauntily over one shoulder and said, "Greeting, Jemail. I am pleased to see you alive and free."

The man stood staring at face, sword, and shield, his beard bristling in indignant disbelief. "Have you returned from the dead?"

"Almost." Andrion sat rather abruptly onto a small rock. "Are you not going to offer me some of that hare?"

Jemail shook his head, muttered under his breath, turned to the spit.

Something clung to the hem of Andrion's cloak. He picked it off, considered it a moment, and broke into a laugh. It was the long russet pinion from a falcon's wing.

Chapter Fifteen

DANA SHIFTED AGAIN, but it was impossible to sit comfortably in a donkey cart. With a sigh she considered the desolate landscape crawling by on either side of the road.

She could not imagine Minras ever being softly green, even in the summer; now, in the midst of winter, the stony bones of the island were as prominent as those in an old, sick face. Only the distant cone of Zind Taurmeni seemed young and brash, thrusting aside the pallid crust of Minras and yet clinging to it like an ill-mannered child. Now its black slopes were textured with snow. Perhaps it was that odd inside-out shadowing that made its outline seem different.

Dana glanced upward, around the gaily, incongruously striped canopy. Billowing blue-black cloud stifled the sky, muting the daylight into a strange verdigris luminescence. The chill air stirred in gasps as impatient as her own thoughts. But her body was numb; the reek of sorcery and decay, although subtler here in the open air than in the temple, acted like a soporific drug. Perhaps the anticipated climax would never come, she thought wearily. Perhaps the ordeal would continue forever, into some eternal purgatory and beyond.

She laid her hand on her shirt, taking a morsel of comfort from the tingle of Andrion's necklace beneath. Sumitra had removed it from the zamtak two days before, when they had left the diseased caverns below Mount Tenebrio, saying, "In the confusion of the rites I doubt if anyone noticed Andrion give this to you. Here; keep it safe."

Dana had protested, writhing from her jealous temper tantrum, drained by the visions that had haunted her sleep.

"It is yours," Sumi had replied graciously. "He gave it to you in exchange for the shield, did he not?"

Of course he had. Even Tembujin's keen glance, Sumitra to Dana and back again, had acknowledged that. Dana had taken the necklace with embarrassing alacrity and muttered thanks.

Damn Sumitra's graceful poise, Dana thought now. Even huddled in the corner of this cursed cart, she sat placidly, her lashes casting a crescent on her smooth mahogany cheeks, her fingers playing as lightly with the strings of the zamtak as if she sat in her chambers in Iksandarun.

Sensing Dana's eye upon her, Sumitra looked up. A tightness at the corners of her mouth and a blurring of the depths of her eyes hinted that even now, nearing the midpoint of her pregnancy, the jolting of the cart might topple her back into nausea. But still she was calm.

Sumi's serenity had been forged in an ordered world, Dana thought, and turned always toward order. What strength to cling to such certitude even as it was inexorably rusted by the width of the sea and the degenerate dampness of Minras. But then, what courage to come halfway across the world to marry a stranger, making his people, his gods, and his complexities her own. Even if Sumi's stranger had been not Andrion but Gath, as Chrysais's was, the game would have been played quite differently. Or did Chrysais find her hand holding loaded dice? Dana dropped her eyes, shamed by understanding, knowing that she must understand. A matter of honor, she told herself firmly. My honor, and that of Sabazel. For Sabazel is not the only land that breeds honor in its daughters.

Tembujin crouched sullenly at the other side of the cart, his bright black eyes seeming to count each blade in the thicket of spears surrounding them, his brows as low as the lowering storm clouds.

"At least this time we do not have to walk across the island," said Sumitra. She strummed the zamtak, but the notes were blunted by the stagnant air.

"Damned island," Tembujin snapped. "No place to go."

Dana and Sumi shared a frown. Tembujin, child of the open plains, found it excruciating humiliation to ride in a cart. Probably he would have leaped from the vehicle and taken his chances, except for the conviction that his presence somehow protected Sumitra. Even though his presence could do nothing to protect her, and that, too, galled him.

Eldrafel came prancing by on a richly caparisoned gray gelding, as befit his androgyny. One hand was curled languidly on his thigh, the other directed the horse with the merest twitch of the reins. His eyes were silver polished with a tint of purple, reflecting nothing; his face wore a mirthless smile, unnervingly indecipherable. His languor was like a slap.

"We certainly have him at a disadvantage," muttered Tembujin.

Behind Eldrafel came Gard, plodding along on a pony, inching closer and closer to the car. His imploring eyes, as achingly large as those of a tormented puppy, fixed on Dana, Tembujin, Sumitra in turn. Then Eldrafel woke, spat an order, and reined in the boy as impersonally as the horse.

Eldrafel paused to lean under the edge of the canopy that sheltered Chrysais and Rue and say a few condescending words. Rue sat by the silk-wrapped tapestry, her body leaning away from it and Chrysais alike. But she and Chrysais looked up together, as they always looked up, at Eldrafel. Rue's gaze was like that of a mole cast suddenly into light, blind and unfocused. In Chrysais's moist blue eyes the tide was receding; they parched slowly into salt flats shaded by racing lavender clouds.

At the end of the procession came a company of anonymous hooded priests, their dark robes a moving shadow under the sunless sky.

Tembujin snorted in disgust. Dana fingered the linen of the shirt and the necklace singing between it and her skin. For the hundredth time these last days her mind unraveled, its fabric parting to reveal visions, omens, dreams, the patterns woven and rewoven. And yet these most recent images, while as clear as the vision of the assassination attempt on Patros, were much more remote. She could see them, hear them, taste them; she could not participate in them.

She saw Bonifacio, his small plump form like a toad in the shadow of a taller being—Rowan, his cloak carefully concealing an armband that bore not a winged bull but the leering gargoyle of Tenebrio. Eldrafel had no doubt deigned to use the winged bull only because it would be recognized by the Sardians as a symbol of Minras and draw them hither. A joke at the expense of Taurmenios; those evil legends penetrating even to Sardis were not of him, but of Tenebrio.

The shadow that loomed in turn over Rowan was Eldrafel's. That much was obvious. Dana could see the fields outside the walls of Sardis withering, could see vapors hanging over the city as pestilence spread through its streets, could see the countryside far into the depths of the Empire itself blasted like this heath of central Minras.

Sumitra was looking at her, concerned; more than once Dana had groped for words to explain her visions and had felt them slip like water between her fingers. She could offer no explanations, only the bare images, so that Sumi and Tembujin knew as much as she did.

Another wave of sensation, undeniable. A sere and desolate Sabazel. Sarasvati returning from Sardis, the mythical chariots at her heels. Sarasvati holding the diadem of the Empire.

It gleamed for her, the loyal daughter of Bellasteros, but her indigo eyes did not reflect its light. She spun about, holding it stiffly out to Ilanit and to Kerith, but they, too, could only stare, astonished and appalled.

Had Rowan hidden it in her baggage? Probably so. Dana squirmed, hearing the faint, compelling whispers that Rowan fed Bonifacio: the ills that had befallen Sardis and the Empire were caused by the evil Sabazians and their demon-goddess Ashtar—even the assassination attempt on Patros was proof of their perfidy. Had not the princess Sarasvati been corrupted by them, and Andrion lured away from his duties? They accepted the barbarian Khazyari at their mysterious rites, and had even forced a Khazyari advisor, Tembujin, upon Andrion. Ready the army, march upon the heretics. . . .

"Mother!" Dana muttered under her breath, "did not Danica secure Sabazel before my birth? Must we fight again and again?"

"Clever," said Sumitra, "to use Sabazel as a scapegoat, playing upon the distrust of an earlier generation. Was it Eldrafel's idea, do you think, or Chrysais's?"

Really, Dana thought in exasperation, Sumi's perspicacity was downright—soothing. She essayed a wan smile. Sumitra's lashes fluttered. Tembujin did not blink, perhaps waiting for Dana to explode like an overripe pomegranate from the pressure of her Sight.

Perhaps she would burst and spray them all not with seeds but with blood and tears. In a sudden gut-wrenching hunger she wanted Sabazel, the clean wind off Cylandra, the cooing of the doves in the temple, the small unimportant tasks of daily life. The company of women who were free of the stifling company of men. But Sabazel might not be there for her return.

Her head spun. Niarkos, splattered with garish purple stains, lifted and folded a vast square of purple cloth. Miklos paced up and down the seawall in Rhodope, gauging the size of the moon. Patros, beloved Patros, more gaunt and stern than ever, bent over the desk in his study; Kleothera's round face and Declan's tiny one hung beside his, defined by guttering lamplight; Valeria bent protectively over her sloe-eyed children. The shadows about them swirled with Sardian officers, their swords licking black flame, their eyes dazed, sucked dry of rationality as the land itself was sucked dry of life. Bonifacio's earnest drone hung heavy on air torpid with decay, "Sabazel must be destroyed. The living god, arrayed in Rexian purple, comes from the sea."

Dana shuddered. She clasped the necklace so tightly that if not for the material of the shirt, she would have cut her hand on it. Steady, steady, she told herself.

Tembujin and Sumitra were still watching her, sympathetic and uncomfortable both. "It is just as well that Andrion could not kill Eldrafel that night in the temple," she sighed. "He must live, so his plot can be revealed before the legions of Sardis, before Sabazel. . . ." Her voice roughened. Steady! she ordered herself.

"Bonifacio," said Tembujin with a curl of his lip, "is only clean when the pond in which he paddles is clean."

"He is simply not strong enough to resist Eldrafel's sordid intrigue," Sumitra pointed out. "No blame to him."

"He has not even tried to resist," sneered Tembujin.

The moon and star purred reassurance in Dana's hand. Andrion. He was still alive and armed. She had been with him on his journey through the cave, watching and hearing him like an actor playing on a painfully distant stage. But what he had discovered she now knew, and had shared with Sumitra and Tembujin.

She had not told them of her chagrin that Andrion was visited by Harus while she had never seen a manifestation of Ashtar. Unless the goddess fondly imagined that the visions with which she harrowed Dana were such appearances. Only my deity, Dana thought, would make such relentless intrusion a mark of favor. "If Eldrafel is really a demon," she muttered, disgruntled, "why do the gods not help us to defeat him?"

"Then the game would not amuse them as much," Tembujin replied.

Sumitra laid down the zamtak and folded her hands in her lap. "My cousin Rajkumar had a story about Vaiswanara. . . ." she began.

Tembujin settled himself politely to listen. Any distraction, thought Dana. Children's counting rhymes, anything.

"Once, many years ago, the Mohan's summer floods were much higher than usual. A man found himself sitting on the brush roof of his house, cut off by the rising water from the rest of the village. So he prayed to Vaiswanara to rescue him.

"The water was lapping at the eaves when a boy in a dugout came by and offered to take the man to safety. But he refused, saying that Vaiswanara would save him. The water was licking at his toes when two men in an outrigger came by and offered to take him to safety. But he refused, saying that Vaiswanara would save him."

Sumi's voice lilted, almost singing, her eyes filled with some distant vision of her homeland. "The water was sucking at his throat when a great sailing dhow swept up the river. The captain was already lowering a boat, but the man refused, saying that Vaiswanara would save him.

"So the water rose over the rooftop and he drowned."

Tembujin arched an eyebrow, wondering what the point was.

"The man came before the portals of Vaiswanara, shaded by the great bho tree where the sacred monkeys chatter. The god himself sat at his wheel inside the door, spinning out the lives of men. 'My lord!' cried the man. 'I prayed to you, but you did not save me!'

"Vaiswanara did not look up, but the third eye on his forehead blinked sagely. 'I sent you a dugout, an outrigger, and a dhow,' he said. 'What more could you want?' "

Sumitra glanced from face to face to test the effect of her story. And Dana laughed, a peal of sparkling merriment that turned not only the heads of the guards but the gilded crown of Eldrafel himself, gliding back up the course of the procession.

Sumi's mouth fell open. Probably, Dana reflected between the blessed gulps of laughter, she has never heard me laugh. But if I did not laugh I would surely go mad. Sumitra must herself be a favor from the mingled humor of Harus and Ashtar.

Tembujin, with an obligatory snicker, turned and glowered out over the landscape. "What do you see?" Sumitra asked.

"I am watching for a boat," he stated.

Dana emitted a giggling coda. "You idiot, we have our boat. We know a great deal more than Eldrafel thinks we know, about Sardis and about his sweet self. Our role now is to play dumb, to lull them into complacency. Remember, Andrion is free."

Tembujin fell back against the railing with a grudging shrug of assent.

Just behind him Eldrafel said, with his usual rancid courtesy, "I am pleased to hear you enjoying yourselves."

Sumitra dropped her gaze to her lap. Tembujin made a sound halfway between a growl and a jeer. But Dana met Eldrafel's jibing smirk evenly.

His eyes flickered. She had the sudden feeling that he could see through her clothing, not to the taut flesh of her body but to the necklace she wore concealed. Her chin went up, her eyes flashed and crossed his with an almost audible sound of blade against blade.

Eldrafel swore under his breath and spun his horse about. "See," said Dana bravely, irrationally, "we do have him at a disadvantage."

Tembujin groaned.

As Eldrafel cantered away, Gard slipped between the surrounding soldiers and leaned over the railing of the cart. "Is Andrion alive?" he hissed.

"Yes," said Sumitra. "Take heart."

The boy jerked at a peremptory shout from Eldrafel, his lower lip thrusting out even as his shoulders hunched, anticipating a blow. He edged away, just quickly enough to be seen to obey, just slowly enough to show stubborn defiance. Chrysais watched him as a prisoner would look through prison bars toward fresh air and sunshine, unattainable mercies.

A falcon coasted high above, drawing Dana's eye to a massive outcropping of stone like the crest of a rocky flood upon the horizon. The lumps of gray stone mounted upward into a corrugated gray sky, one indistinguishable from the other. The necklace tugged gently at her throat. "Andrion is there," she told Tembujin and Sumitra. "No, no, do not turn around. But he is there, and he watches us, waiting."

"Waiting," repeated Tembujin. "Yes, indeed."

Sumi, with a smile of strained serenity, lifted her zamtak and began to play. The notes pierced the torpor of the atmosphere and sang across the heath. "Green grew the willows along the sea strand/ Bright shone the sun as we lay hand in hand. . . ."

• • •

The odd light distorted the small shapes of the horses, and carts, and human figures, as if Andrion watched the procession through the depths of the sea. But he could easily identify the blond head and two dark ones beneath the canopy. He recognized Gard, Eldrafel, Chrysais, and Rue. "Well," he said, "everyone is on stage. Soon it will be time for the next act. But not soon enough."

Jemail's dark sideways glance pronounced Andrion's metaphor only further evidence of his doubtful sanity.

Andrion shifted restlessly and the shield scraped against leafless, thorny scrub emitting a squeal like fingernails over slate. Solifrax skreeed in response, setting his teeth on edge. The dense chill of the boulder behind which he crouched—worked stone, an old tomb, perhaps?—seemed to attract the oppressive air like a lodestone attracts iron, gathering a miasma that for a moment gagged him.

But the fitful wind carried one strand of purity, the faint but distinct melody of zamtak and voice; "I gave him my song, yes I gave him my song. . . ." The sound swirled away, but the sword and the shield continued humming in unison the rest of the verse.

He smiled. Then his lips compressed the smile into a grimace. Gard, he thought, struggling with a paradox of blood, descended from Harus and Tenebrio, Bellasteros and Eldrafel. Rue, her faith sorely tested. Chrysais, her every emotion seared away except faith, but not necessarily faith in a god.

Dana. He rolled over onto his back and lay flat in the gray ash and dirt, regarding the falcon swooping unconcernedly overhead. He tapped Solifrax beside him, stirring the dust to mist. Harus's kiss still burned on his brow; had he been given a third eye like the one Sumitra attributed to Vaiswanara? But it was his mother Danica who had been given godlike powers, the last of which she had expended to save his life, even though sons were purportedly of little account to Sabazians.

He cleared his throat hastily and looked again out over the heath. The procession was disappearing around a corner of the road, the faceless hooded priests shuffling last in line like the evil presence that had tried to follow him out of the cavern.

The shield chimed, glimmered, quieted. Andrion knew he shared its resonance with Dana, that she moved in his thoughts as he moved in hers; he had heard her laughter as surely as he had heard the grim news of events in Sardis. He sat up abruptly, regarding the shield in gratitude mingled with resentment.

Jemail had not moved. "Why come with me?" Andrion asked him.

"My wine cup would be empty indeed if I returned to Eldrafel," the soldier said.

True enough. "I shall reward you in time."

Jemail eyed the pale glow of Solifrax and star-shield. "Well, my lord, we shall see about that."

Andrion allowed himself a grim chuckle. The procession was gone. Zind Taurmeni lay ahead, its harsh features still brooding down upon Orocastria. But now it had snow on its peak, and its profile . . . Andrion squinted into the hazy distance. A mirage, surely, that the mountain's profile had changed. But he could swear it had bloated like a decomposing corpse.

Andrion sheathed Solifrax and slid down the scree behind him, collecting a patina of dust. Ten more days before the rites of the new moon, he reflected; by that time he would be so dirty he would be recognized only by what he carried, without sword and shield as anonymous as the faceless priests. . . .

Suddenly he grinned. Were there perhaps bales of old clothing in the palace cellars? "Jemail," he said, "what can you tell me of the priests and the rites of Taurmenios?"

Jemail's saturnine face lengthened. Yes, he seemed to think, Andrion was indeed mad, but the god-touched usually were. Or vice versa.

Thunder grumbled down the sky. Its low bass note struck a corresponding tremor from the ground itself. How, Andrion thought, can I possibly survive ten more days in this unwholesome place?

He turned and followed Jemail, plodding away from the rocks toward Orocastria and the new moon, carrying sword and shield, Empire and Sabazel, honor and family like a snail encumbered by and yet a part of its heavy shell. Ten more days, twenty, a lifetime—he had no choice but to survive.

Chapter Sixteen

WITH A SIGH of grudging pleasure Dana lowered herself into the warm water. Pleasure, to get a real tub bath after days of trying to wash in a basin. Grudging, for how could she enjoy herself when Sumitra and Tembujin and certainly Andrion himself were not afforded the same opportunity? And just why, she wondered darkly, had she been returned to the same chambers they had occupied when they first arrived on Minras, several lifetimes ago?

Her jaw hurt from grinding her teeth. They had slogged through watery sunshine and sooty rain until she had wanted to run gibbering over the nearest cliff; gods, they had walked from Orocastria to Tenebrio faster than the donkey train returned them! Sumitra had tried valiantly to amuse them, singing and telling stories, but even her resilient humor wore thin long before Orocastria. And Tembujin—Dana grimaced. Tembujin had been reduced to answering every comment with a snarl, his lively tail of hair hanging as limp as the gutted skin of a sable. At least the singing of the shield had followed them, at times close by, at times fleeing patrols, so distant as to be almost inaudible.

She was sure that Eldrafel had prolonged the journey just to torment his collected victims, Dana, Sumitra, and Tembujin, Chrysais, Gard, and Rue. But at last the old moon had pared itself to a wraith and disappeared, and they had gained the crazy-quilt palace in Orocastria. Compared to the pestilential air of the caverns, the atmosphere here was only ominously oppressive.

Dana let her hair fall over the rim behind her. She sank down until the water rose to her chin and wriggled her toes against the opposite end of the tub. At least the bath itself did not seem to be the danger. Although, she thought as she

peered resentfully up at the frescoed sea creatures, she preferred the stark stone walls of the cells where they were now
lodged, the same from which they had rescued Sumitra, to
these painted bulbous leers.

Her experience must be twisted indeed to consider a bath a
danger. Sabazel! her mind fluttered, like a caged bird beating
its wings against the bars of its cage. But not wings, no—
wings were an attribute of Harus.

Sabazel, demanding much, offering—well, not peace in
return for loyalty, but a certain propriety—which must be
passed on to Astra scrubbed as clean as the surface of the
shield—the shield could not be dirtied by this swamp of
passion and dread, it could not!

Dana splashed. The sound of water upon her outer ear
could not conceal the slow hum of the shield among her inner
perceptions. Andrion was here in the palace; he had somehow
managed to sneak past the innumerable sentries posted to
catch him. Perhaps Jemail was hiding him in the cellars,
where a legion could skulk unnoticed.

The door to the suite opened. Dana started up, causing the
water to rush over the edge of the tub and splat against the
tiled floor. Andrion? Ashtar, if he comes upon me now, like
this, I shall throw myself upon him like a starving man upon
food. But no man, not even Andrion, is more important than
the law—he knows that, I know that—he is Sumi's, not
mine. . . .

Eldrafel leaned against the doorway, a cup in his hand, his
gray eyes creeping like slow frost over her body. They noted
but did not linger upon her lean, taut flesh; fixing upon the
gold necklace encircling her throat, they glinted like the cold
blade of a butcher's axe.

Dana did not move. So, she thought, you brought me here.
You corrupt even my uncertainties. A flush of fury colored
her cheeks and moved so swiftly down the length of her body
that she half expected the water to steam.

Eldrafel's heavy-lidded gaze followed the pinkness. "I
wondered if the hair on your head had been bleached by the
sun," he commented. "But I see you are truly blond. As I
am."

Dana might not be burdened with coy self-consciousness,
but this was too much; she growled an epithet, heaved herself
from the water and threw on her waiting garments. Which

clung immodestly to her wet limbs. Eldrafel, relishing this effect, held out his cup. "Wine?"

"No."

"It is not drugged," he told her, smiling.

She snorted and dodged around him into the sitting room. He followed, and after a brief dancing skirmish of steps and turns, cornered her. He drank, deceptively lazy. The wine stained his lips but not one drop smudged the gleam of his beard. He seized her arm and pulled her close to him. "I see," he murmured, "why even proper Andrion lusts incestuously after you. I like strong women too."

"So you can weaken them?" Dana retorted, and wrenched away.

He set down the cup and seized her again, his hands like shackles on her arms. Seething, she struggled, but even though he was no larger than she, his strength was uncanny. When she moved to kick him he crushed her against the wall. His body against hers was as cold as stone and as unyielding, because it was she who was meant to yield. Between a rock and a hard place, she thought dizzily.

Eldrafel's voice was silky with grace and power. "And you like strong men, do you not?"

Her mind howled. No Sabazian was ever used by a man she did not want, why can I not break free, how dare he use sorcery upon me. . . . He kissed her, his mouth fermented like the wine, and to her abject horror her body responded. Gods, surely I never wanted him, surely his beauty has never blinded me to his evil! Her knees were weak, her loins drenched with desire, her love for Andrion horrendously perverted.

Then something in Dana's thought snapped like an arrow finding its target. No! You shall not humiliate me!

His hands crawled over her body, inspecting every crevice, plucking less at her garments than at her skin. She went limp. Her hands splayed against the breadth of his chest, sensing the slow susurration of his heart; her nostrils against his hair filled with a nauseating scent of musk. He laughed in triumph.

The nape of his neck, and the back of his right leg. . . . But she had no weapons save her fury and disgust. Suddenly she uncoiled and thrust him away with such force he fell sprawling. For one brief moment his face warped, affronted. Then it sheened with arrogance again. "I assume," he said, "that the answer is no?"

Dana cursed him, consigning him to the icy silence of the last circle of the underworld.

Eldrafel was unperturbed. He rose to his feet, brushed himself off, adjusted his purple cloak and kilt. "Well, then, basilisk, it is your loss." And with a sweeping, taunting bow he turned.

But not before Dana had seen the glitter of gold in his hand. She grabbed at her throat. The pulse leaped raggedly through her naked skin. Ashtar, she had been so overwhelmed she had not even felt him undo the clasp of Andrion's necklace. "No!" she screamed, "you cannot have it!"

He was gone. Dana raged, at him, at herself, at Andrion and Sumitra for laying the necklace upon her. Fool, blithering fool, this is what happens when you lower your guard! Her body was slimed by the tracks of his hands; she shuddered, as if she would crawl out of her own skin. She kicked at the wall but could not shatter it. The door opened and a platoon of guards swept her away.

The blue lotuses in the pool tumbled like acrobats. The somber sky wheeled overhead. A trireme creased the glassy swells of the harbor. Each passage, terrace, and doorway jumped out as if illuminated by a sudden flash of lightning. Thunder rumbled like the distant, inescapable roll of chariot wheels. I cannot bear any more of this! Dana wanted to scream, so loudly that the shriek would rend raw rock and worked stone alike and send them tumbling into the sea, so that the sea would roil and seethe and with its salt spume wash this infected sore of an island clean.

The guards threw her into her own tiny cell and slammed the door. In one stride she was at the window, looking down on the dim shapes of palace, town, and sea. Her fingers drummed on the sill. "Tembujin!" she shouted.

From the next window, an arm's length away, came a sullen reply.

"Tembujin! I want you to help me!"

"How?" he asked, with a note of interest.

Dana leaned out her window, eyeing his window and Sumitra's balcony beyond. She was gasping for breath, she realized, as the air of Minras gasped with fevered sensuality. "Listen," she began.

Eldrafel swaggered into the bedchamber. Gard sat there, with a damp clay tablet in his lap, a stylus in his hand, and his tongue caught firmly between his lips. Eldrafel snatched the tablet and glanced at it. "Too many mistakes," he announced. He pulled the necklace of the moon and star from his belt and considered it. "Hmph!" he snorted sourly. "The king must come of his own free will, as enjoyable as it would be to enspell him." He placed the necklace like a garrote around Gard's neck.

"That is Andrion's!" the boy protested.

"Indeed. Proof to Sardis that he named you his heir."

"But Andrion is still—" Gard shut his mouth with a pop and peered down at his feet as if his sandals held his next lesson.

"Still alive?" sneered Eldrafel. "Not for long."

The boy winced. Chrysais came slowly down the stairs from the tower room. "What is it? Oh!" She stopped dead, her hand on her own throat, when she saw the necklace. "Where did you get it?"

"From the Sabazian. They do indeed like men." Eldrafel smoothed his kilt and smirked lasciviously at her. Her lips pursed as if she sucked on a lemon. "I would like to see," he went on, "a more respectful attitude on the part of your son here."

At the word "your" Gard shot him with a resentful glance. Chrysais's complexion flooded mauve.

"Go away," Eldrafel told Gard. "If you take off that necklace, I shall beat you until you are the color of my cloak."

Gard nodded petulantly and fled, his gray eyes polished with what might have been either tears or the flash of a sword. Two guards roused themselves and followed him. He had not once looked at his mother.

"He is your son too," said Chrysais, almost before the door had shut. "He is descended from two gods."

"Is he? How can a man ever be sure that a child is his own, when women are available to all?"

"You know I have been faithful to you!" she protested.

"Do I?" Eldrafel responded. "You tried to seduce even your own brother." He danced a few steps. The dried chamomile rustled mysteriously beneath his feet.

She coiled. "Do not insult me! I am a king's daughter, a king's wife, a king's mother; I have brought you Minras and Empire alike."

"Minras was mine already," said Eldrafel, scathingly reasonable. "Gard shall bring me the Empire. It is the kings themselves who matter, my dear, not their women."

Chrysais stared at him, her lip outthrust haughtily, her knotted fists half concealed by the flounces of her skirt. Slowly her mouth wilted, her right hand loosened and reached out, palm empty. "Ah, Eldrafel, do we grasp too much, and lose ourselves?"

Her voice was as tremulous as a crone's. Eldrafel did not look at her but at himself, in the mirror of her dressing table. His image wavered slightly, as if it were a pupa responding to the proddings of the butterfly beneath. "I weary of your sniveling," he said. "It is too late now for your courage to fail. Go back to the tapestry and try again to draw Andrion and sword and shield here. I thought you had power."

"I do," protested Chrysais, perilously close to a wail. "Eldrafel, my love, please . . ."

He settled the fillet around his hair as if visualizing the diadem there instead. Thus reassured, he turned, glossy with pride and malice. "Try to do something right for a change," he told his wife. "As for me—I must be about my father's business."

"I have power," said Chrysais, the words dull hammer blows upon an anvil. But the door had already shut; he had not once gazed directly at her. She looked toward the stairway, eyes as flat as faience beads. She looked toward the door, and her eyes flooded. Viciously she gulped.

"I have power over you," she stated. She went to her dressing table. Slowly, ritualistically, she daubed herself with carmine and kohl, considering the reflection of the shapes and colors, not her face. With a coquettish if somehow astringent smile she patted lotus oil onto her bosom and the sardonyx amulet alike, and followed Eldrafel out the door.

Dana sat on her windowsill and joined her chain of rags, woven from torn bedclothes, to Tembujin's. She swayed precariously above the drop; he grimaced, but she remained calm, going so far as to hum under her breath. Sumitra hovered on her balcony, hands clasped, chin set.

"All right," Dana said. Tembujin tested the knot binding the rope to his bedstead and braced himself against the sill. Dana planted her feet against the stone and arranged the clumsy rope about her hips. "Go!" In great leaps she de-

scended the vertical wall and landed only a bit too precipitously among brambles and ash at the bottom.

Sumitra gasped. Then, as Dana waved, she waved back
with a relieved smile. Tembujin almost, but not quite, grinned.
Swiftly drawing the rope inside his room, he glared at the
muted outlines of the palace, accentuated by the occasional
glint of a spear, but no alarm was raised.

"Do not worry," Dana called quietly. "A sorcerous mirage still conceals this wing." As she looked upward, the
wall seemed to shimmer and shift before her, but the two
peering faces remained firm. Really, Dana thought, with the
first spark of exhilaration she had managed to kindle in ages,
that was not difficult at all. She and Kerith had made many
more complicated jaunts through the asphodel-scented fissures of Cylandra.

Kerith. Astra. The spark ignited into flame. Slowly, slowly,
she told herself: free Niarkos and his men now, arm yourself,
and Sabazel and Sardis will follow. She waved again and
crept away.

A fitful sea breeze so filled the afternoon air with the
stench of irex that even the lowering clouds were tinted
purple. An odd molten light seeped through crevices in the
overcast, every so often dispelling the gloom with wincing
glare. Dana warily retraced her steps to the lotus pool, avoiding the numerous guards, and slipped inside the suite of
rooms. She went out the far window.

The malignant tower still stood, if possible even more
askew than before, but the blue threads of light wafting by its
windows seemed drained of brilliance, as pale as thin milk.
The witch-fires extended too far? Dana asked herself as she
scurried toward it.

Guards clanked around a corner; she dived over a low wall
and crouched as they marched by with as much spirit as if
they moved through thickening honey. Andrion . . . No, he
was in some other part of the palace. He might know what
she was doing, but he could not grab her shirt and stop her.
But then, even he would no longer counsel patience.

She crept along the wall and peered through a lattice into
an alcove filled with fluid green shadow and evil whisperings.
The herb garden, stroked by an eddy in the reeking breeze.

Someone stood on its far side, by the pillared corridor
leading from Chrysais's chambers. Dana squinted. Sunlight
blasted the still figure and then just as quickly faded, but not

before it and its velvet-dark shadow were etched on Dana's mind; ornate chestnut curls, frills of silk and turquoise, richly curving breasts heaving raggedly with—terror?

Then Dana saw what Chrysais had been watching.

Two long white shapes lay beneath the sweeping fronds of the yew, more camouflaged than concealed by rippling shadow, like fish bellies flashing in a green-scummed pool. The tiny red jewel in Rue's nose winked and then was eclipsed by the luster of Eldrafel's hair and beard. She clawed at him, ecstatic, her limbs tangled awkwardly around his; his limbs were as gracefully arranged as ever. As when he danced, the muscles in his buttocks clenched and loosed, efficient, compelling, impersonal.

Rue began squealing like a pig, shriller and shriller; Eldrafel, always mindful of appearances, put his hand over her mouth. Even in the gloom Dana could see his cool smirk, not one hair disarranged, as Rue wriggled blowsy and sweating against him.

The nightshade rustled, the tainted rye hissed, and Chrysais was gone. Dana turned away, eyes and hands clenched, gulping the sudden acidic flood of her breakfast back into her stomach. Is that what it looked like? Were her piercingly bittersweet hours with Andrion, her cheerfully bawdy times with Tembujin, an image of this bestiality? Bad enough that afterward she reeked of their vital odors, not her own. . . .

Her thought veered into part vision, part deduction, and she saw what had happened there in the garden as surely as if an echo hung upon the inebriated air: Perhaps it was her disillusionment that led Rue to concoct a salad of hellebore and nightshade, although Dana was not sure if the serving woman had meant to eat it or serve it to someone else, Chrysais or Sumitra or Dana herself. Eldrafel found Rue in the garden, and as her eyes lifted to his smooth and elegant body, her sorely-tested faith saw one last chance to be vindicated. Her eyes, huge and liquid, dark brews of resentment, and fear, and a rapacious cunning. . . . She murmured something about Chrysais being weak, not a fit mate for a god, her whining lack of control unraveling all his plans. She mentioned her brother Rowan who worked so selflessly for Eldrafel back in Sardis, where the plot was still tightly knit. She indicated her own possible defection.

Dana heard Eldrafel chuckle through the muffled crescendo of Rue's squeals. Oh, yes, he could perform as beautifully on

a woman as everywhere else, but in the end, sex was to him
only another weapon.

She again choked down the bile in her throat. She leaped
up, plunged over the wall and across a roof, and clambered
like one of Sumitra's monkeys up to the same window she
and Tembujin had used to enter Chrysais's bedchamber. Again
it was unlatched. Protected by sorcery or overconfidence? she
asked herself. I do not care.

Quickly she searched the chamber, but the necklace was
not there. She bounded up the stairs. And halted at the top,
realizing someone was already in the tower room. Someone who
gasped and panted like a personification of the frenzied air of
Minras.

She looked through the door, dreading to see some other
scene of animal lust. But she saw instead Chrysais, a small
dagger held awkwardly in both hands, slicing the great tapestry into shreds of canvas and yarn that quivered like wounded
flesh.

The queen was a wraith of the lush figure she had once
been. Her lips were drawn in a rictus grin about clenched
teeth. Her face was chalk white beneath the gaudy paint and
powder, not human flesh but a staring mask of tragedy,
drained by sorcery and thwarted ambition and hatred of
reason and emotion alike.

The images of city and sea, human and animal, disintegrated into drab confetti. With a shriek the blue witch-fire
rimming the tapestry snapped and dissipated. The lamps before the tiny shrine went out, and the nephrite bull shattered
into heavy black dust. The odor of lethenderum and sorcery
seeped away. The chamber was only an old tower room,
floorboards gaping unevenly, walls splotched with fungus. A
cloud of ash drifted in the windows, carried on the fetid
drunkard's breath of Minras. The floor shuddered and subsided.

Chrysais spun about, sensing Dana's presence amid the
shards of her sorcery. "It is all your fault!" she spat.

"What did I ever do to you!" Dana retorted. But she
understood why Chrysais hated her, a woman free of masculine taint, even as she rejected understanding; she would not
let herself sympathize with this woman who had sold herself
not only to a man, but to a demon.

Among the wrack of yarn and cloth that shifted uneasily
across the floor Dana saw several unused skeins, their colors
still vivid, and a length of canvas completely bare of stitch-

ing. Perhaps these materials were particularly susceptible to enchantment. . . .

Chrysais stepped closer, the dagger circling. "Hold the blade the other way," Dana babbled soothingly to the blighted face and the eyes like discolored bruises. "Let the haft extend past your little finger, not your thumb. It is much more flexible that way."

Chrysais hissed epithets upon her, Sabazel, and every woman who had ever crossed its borders.

Dana stood her ground, hands extended placatingly. "Let me show you how to hold it."

Chrysais did not so much lunge as stumble forward. Effortlessly Dana caught her arm, twisting it until, with a cry, Chrysais let the dagger fall. She swept the weapon into her own hand.

But the queen of Minras stood immobile, her face hidden by hands that were mottled and blue-veined claws too frail even to sift the dregs of power. No longer aware of or no longer caring about Dana, she swayed back and forth, keening in a high-pitched wail of mourning.

Dana quashed the impulse to go to her, embrace her, and lay her head upon her breast as one would soothe a devastated child. Chrysais had bought, and now paid, for choosing to be suborned by a man. She seized the canvas and the fresh yarn, thrust the dagger into her belt, and started down the staircase. As she clambered out the window, she heard Chrysais blunder down the stairs and out of the door.

Dana landed lightly and straightened. Zind Taurmeni was an obscene protuberance over palace and city, purplish black and gray stone piled as high as the threatening purplish black and gray clouds. Which might as well be laden with ash as with rain; a gray patina bleared the giddy patterns of walls and terraces.

To Dana's horror, another patrol drove her crouching back to the lattice. Rue, thankfully, was dressing, her eyes glazed with smugness and zeal. But Eldrafel stood naked, a masterpiece of statuary draped by the odd flowing shadow, features distorted with furious consternation. He knew what Chrysais had done to the tapestry. Dana bolted.

She skirted patrols all the way back to the cells. The subtle, invigorating purl of the shield did not abate, but remained an undercurrent to her thoughts, goading her, teasing her.

She paused among the brambles at the base of the wall.

Here I am, she said to herself with a hollow laugh, armed and relatively free; I could find Andrion without too much effort, and together we could join Niarkos and the others—I did not even have to destroy the tapestry to free them, it was done for me—how subtly the gods, or demons, work. . . . She shook herself, trying to pin down her pirouetting thought. I must plan beyond today and tomorrow, beyond the rites of the new moon—I shall not leave Tembujin and Sumitra to face Taurmenios alone—Andrion will only know where they are by where I am. . . . Her thought knotted wearily. The fate of Sabazel is bound with that of Sardis, incessantly. Freedom? What is freedom?

I have no time to be tired, she informed herself. That cursed greater purpose still drives us all. Decisively Dana called, and a moment later Tembujin's swarthy face appeared over the windowsill. "Back so soon?"

"I did not linger to start any fights, as you would have!"

Between Tembujin's strong back and her agility, it took Dana only a moment to scramble back up the wall and catapult herself onto Sumitra's balcony. "Here," she said, "I have something for you to do." And she told them both about Chrysais and the tapestry.

From his window Tembujin vented a heartfelt oath. "So she turned against him at last."

"She need not have gone to him to begin with," stated Dana.

"No?" asked Sumitra gently.

Ignoring that quiet negative, Dana pulled the yarn and the canvas from her shirt and thrust them at her. Sumi fingered them, intrigued and wary. "Have you not been sewing a great tapestry in Iksandarun?" Dana inquired.

"Yes. The eternal tapestry. Valeria and I shall be working on it with our grandchildren. I hope."

At his wife's name Tembujin vanished. Ah, Dana thought, he has not mentioned Valeria or the children in ages; that wound must be deep indeed. He and Andrion both chose to mate themselves to cooing doves, while I, while I . . . have Kerith.

The wall reverberated, as if Tembujin smashed his chair against the stone in frustration. Dana exchanged a doleful look with Sumitra. The demands of family; the world in microcosm, the purpose of everything, surely. Sumi cleared her throat in silent agreement. "What can I do?"

"I see the pass at Azervinah," said Dana, "where the
Royal Road moves from the southern provinces to the north. I
see General Nikander and his legions turning about in their
march to Iksandarun, drawn back to the homelands of Sardis." She frowned. Her Sight had only led her so far; surely,
surely, Rowan would not dare to actually march on Sabazel.
"Azervinah," she sighed. "A good central point."

Sumitra unrolled the canvas, removed a clasp from her hair
and threaded a strand of silver yarn upon it. "The fortress
atop a mountain? The one that Queen Danica took for
Bellasteros before Andrion was conceived?"

"Yes," said Dana with a smile. Sumi was not, and never
had been, gulled by the official Sardian story of that campaign.

"Well, I do not know if I can—I suppose . . ." With a
stern nod Sumitra stitched the outlines of the fortress. She
threaded other clasps, leaving her hair to fall loosely about
her shoulders like a shining ebony curtain. Her eyes began to
gleam as she sketched a face, a falcon standard, marching
soldiers. Then she laid the various threads about the canvas
and picked up her zamtak.

Dana leaned against the wall, arms crossed, satisfied that
her impulse to pick up canvas and yarn was justified; in
response to the purity of the music the threads rose like
growing tendrils, dipping and weaving in an intricate dance.

Tembujin leaned upon his windowsill, his haggard face
slowly smoothing itself. Images formed on the canvas, the
lugubrious face of Nikander, flashing scarlet pennons, and
above them the outspread wings of a falcon.

Ah, yes, Dana said to herself. Harus, the falcon god; a
beguiling figure if ever there was one. Ashtar's consort. She
wondered with a sudden shudder if the gods mated as men
and animals did.

Men! Dana removed the dagger from her belt and tossed it
to Tembujin; he ran the edge of the blade over his thumbnail,
a wolfish grin transforming his features.

Men. The embraces of Ilanit, of Astra, of Kerith, were
unadorned and uncompromising. Dana slid down the wall and
sat on the floor. The music squeezed her as a press squeezed
olives, her body only the mortal husk, her mind the clear,
sweet oil. That was what repulsed her, she thought. The
grinding together of the husks to make dry and tasteless
power, unmoistened by the oil of love.

And stubbornly she insisted to herself, Danica did not sell

herself to Bellasteros for power, as Chrysais accused. I do not sell myself to Andrion. We follow our hearts and our gods.

The music floated away into the afternoon and dissipated. But still Dana could hear it, complementing the resonance of the shield. And she saw, suddenly, the necklace of the moon and star safely around Gard's neck. Of course, as much as Eldrafel would be tempted to enspell Andrion, he was bound by his own rules to leave him free. Justice, for him to be caught by his own game. She leaned back with a sigh of relief.

Sumitra's face shone, numinous as god-touched Andrion's, as she ran her fingertips over her tapestry and smiled like a delighted child at the vibrant image thereon.

Thunder grumbled, not in the sky, but in the earth itself. Dana looked up with a slight frown; something seemed to brush the back of her neck, some vague, unnamable dread to add to the all-too-familiar dreads she already bore. And are you as restless as we, Taurmenios, eager to be cleansed of the touch of Tenebrio?

Ashes wafted in the window, sloughing from the diseased skin of Minras.

Chapter Seventeen

ANDRION LAY PRONE at the edge of the roof, trying to look like just another decorative excrescence. The air was delirious with sorcery and decay. And yet this evening was different; the clouds moved sulkily off to the east, thrust by a faint but clean breeze. Andrion inhaled, wondering if he hallucinated that refreshing breath.

A shimmering twilight illuminated the irrational pile of the palace but only thickened the shadows in the arena. The scene of tonight's ceremony. At last, he exulted grimly. The waning of the moon and the nights of no moon at all had been an ordeal. Even the sword and the shield, exchanging brief resonances like the grumbling half sentences of an old married couple, had shed little light into the dimness of time and mind.

Andrion scratched his chin. His beard itched from the soot rubbed in it, as did the hair that was by now starting to wave untidily around his face. He had certainly become unrecognizable, emerging from his noxious subterranean sanctuary as dirty and disheveled as the lowliest peasant. Harus, even a Sardian garbage midden would smell like a garden after those cellars!

Jemail, huddled by Andrion's feet, exchanged beady stares with a passing pigeon. Thank the gods for the man's taciturnity, Andrion thought; if I had been sequestered with someone cheerful and talkative, I would by now have committed murder.

Suddenly the sun glanced out, a gaping wound between cloud and horizon spouting a path of bloody light across sea, harbor, land. The clouds billowed scarlet and ocher and coral tinted with purple. The two mountains, Zind Taurmeni squatting close by, Tenebrio a lowering blot on the far edge of sight, seemed to shift and frown at each other like armies jockeying for an advantage.

The mirage-blotted wing of cells where Dana, Tembujin,

and Sumitra were imprisoned was fronted by a squad of
soldiers. The terrace of the lotus pool was deserted, each
flower a tiny blue flame in the valedictory glare of the sun.

Then the sun was sucked into the sea. The lines of the
palace thinned and blurred. The clouds retreated. From among
a few pale stars peeked the faint, unbearably fragile crescent
of the moon. The shadow of the old moon nestled eerily
between the horns of the new; an ill omen, Andrion told
himself. But then, this entire place was an ill omen.

He scooted back from the edge of the roof and sat up,
arranging the dark, hooded cloak Jemail had found discarded
in the cellars. It was frayed and mildewed, but similar enough
to the ones worn by the priests, especially after dark. Although Andrion felt rather foolish masquerading like a char-
acter in one of Aristofanis's comedies, he and Jemail had
already walked right by two boredom-glazed sets of guards.

An owl hooted close at hand. More ill omen—for the
Minrans, he informed himself sternly. Had Dana really seen
Chrysais snap at last and destroy the sorcerous tapestry? He
could not quite believe the image the shield fed his sixth
sense. And he was vague about just what it was Dana had
asked Sumitra to stitch—something about Nikander—well,
he told himself, Niarkos is here now, we shall worry about
his brother Nikander later.

Andrion touched his throat; Eldrafel had his necklace, he
could feel that without intercession. But at this moment,
oddly, he felt no threat.

He settled the shield on his back, in its harness knotted
from several pieces of twine. Solifrax, tucked well back
under his cloak, muttered impatiently. The shield remained
stonily silent. Someone moved below.

Andrion and Jemail threw themselves flat upon the ashy
tiles. Eldrafel, gleaming like carved ivory, strode purposefully along the edge of the lotus pool and disappeared into the
suite of rooms. Ah, thought Andrion. He thinks no one sees
him, and does not bother to be indolent.

The door crashed open, the sound reaching Andrion's ears
a moment after the sight. Eldrafel emerged, dragging Chrysais
by her hair. The owl hooted again, the wind sighed, but from
the struggling figures came no sound. Despite her undignified
posture, Chrysais moved with the more composure of the
two.

Andrion tensed. She had tired of her husband, and he of

her, no doubt, but what—Eldrafel threw her down by the
edge of the pool, knelt over her, clasped her throat in his
hands. She did not fight, but lay back as gracefully open as if
receiving him as a lover, her hands caressing his chest and
arms.

Coolly, dispassionately, he held her head under the water.
Her body shuddered; her hands slipped from him and fell
slack onto the pavement.

Andrion started to leap up, and caught himself just as
Jemail's hand seized him. For a moment he thought it was his
own horror that caused the ground to rock beneath his feet.
But with a ripple of thuds a row of pillars swayed and fell,
and Zind Taurmeni belched a cloud of blackness that swelled
up and out, covering the sky with an opaque pall, blotting out
the last vestiges of light. The ground thrummed as if to a
giant pulse.

Jemail clutched the roof tiles like a flea clinging to a
scratching dog. Andrion lay petrified; the blood drained from
his face, leaving his skin clammy with terror. "So, Taurmenios," he muttered, with more bravado than at the moment
he felt, "you, too, are getting a belly full of Tenebrio's
priest."

But it was obscurely cheering to see the divine eructation
take Eldrafel, too, by surprise; he stared up at the mountain,
cautious and accusing, his hands still locked on Chrysais's
throat. Even here, apparently, the mountains did not as a rule
make comments on the evils of men.

Eldrafel threw Chrysais's body into the pool with all the
regard of a boy skipping a stone, wiped his hands on his
cloak, and with a backward glance not at Chrysais but at the
mountain hurried away. Perhaps his brisk stride betrayed a
hint of nervousness. So then, Andrion thought scornfully,
there are forces greater even than you.

Jemail cast a bleary eye toward Zind Taurmeni. The ground
remained still. The dark cloud lay like fog over the palace and
the town. Other concerns were more pressing than the god's
indigestion. Andrion clambered up, organized his limbs, jerked
Jemail to his feet, and sprinted down from the roof. He had
ample shadows to conceal him now, and in consequence
stumbled more than once over some step or angle of the
confused architecture. Behind him Jemail clattered and crashed
like an armored legionary mounting his chariot.

The lotus pool emitted a thin cerulean light. Andrion skid-

ded to his knees beside it, knowing it was too late to save
Chrysais. She floated among the flowers, her upturned face as
dewy and fresh as a child's. The sardonyx figure lay just
beneath her fingertips; in her other hand was a damp wad
of—yarn, Andrion realized. Her open eyes were turned away
from both, truly drowned by depth after depth of a blue
serenity unattainable in this world.

She had been a sorceress, yes, but also his sister, and the
blood of Chryse, Bellasteros, and Harus himself cooled in her
veins. Perhaps she had, in the end, saved herself. "Ah,
Chrysais," Andrion murmured, "I am so sorry." Jemail
ground his spear against the pavement, uncomfortable but not
entirely uncharitable.

A shower of fine gritty cinders rained down, leaving a crust
on the surface of the pool which eclipsed the light it emitted.
The wind eddied with decay. From the corner of his eye
Andrion saw an adder slip across the terrace and disappear,
following by several grotesquely scurrying centipedes.

"They are poisonous," Jemail hissed, shifting his sandaled
feet.

Everything here is poisonous. Andrion brushed the cinders
in a swirl away from Chrysais's face and closed her eyes
before the darkness could cloud their luminous stare. He
picked up the sardonyx gargoyle. Gargoyle? Had the amulet
not been an image of Eldrafel? With a frown he tucked it
behind his belt. He could not bring himself to disturb the
peace of his sister's body in any other way.

He rose, and was somehow not surprised to see, glimmering faintly in the gloom, the ghost of Proserfina. She floated a
handsbreadth above the pavement, as if the stones had subsided since the days her living feet had walked them. The
spectral image was drawn almost too thin to perceive; only
her eyes were hard and clear, illuminated by a cold flame.
Her days of waiting draw to an end, Andrion told himself. He
saluted her.

Jemail frowned, seeing nothing, relieved that he did not.
Torches sprang up along the terraces; their flames were densely
crimson, contracted against the onslaught of cinders and
shadow. The evening's hint of freshness was devoured by a
chill so profound it seared the nerves like heat.

Another snake slithered by the pool, which was now completely covered in cinders, swamping the lotus, burying Chrysais

as surely as if she were in a rock-cut tomb. A thin metallic piping began to wail from the arena.

Andrion turned toward it and stopped, his mind sliced by a sudden subliminal screech of the shield. Dana, Dana sat with her head between her hands, straining toward him, warning him. . . .

"Come," Andrion said to Jemail. They turned away from the arena and left the terrace to its ghosts.

I am a fool, Sumitra told herself. A blithering fool. So proud of that piece of tapestry, folded carefully around the zamtak; beguiled by my power as surely as Chrysais. . . . An adventure. Indeed. Her thought spattered and reformed. Never even thought to be wary, on this night of all nights, of my food and drink. Rue did not bring it, I was lulled into stupidity, I have been drugged.

The guards jerked the cloth-wrapped zamtak from her flaccid hands and thrust her into the midst of what appeared to be molten shadow. No, it was a line of black-hooded priests, avatars of the strange, palpably dark night.

The guards, moving with the sudden jerks and starts of restive horses, did not pause to puzzle over Dana's presence in Sumitra's cell; they tossed the zamtak away with a jangling discord, tore the makeshift rope from Tembujin's grasp, slammed both his and Dana's doors and shot the bolts, leaving Sumi with an afterimage of two appalled faces and the echo of an ugly Khazyari epithet.

We were supposed to go together! No, said one lucid memory. Eldrafel said only that Dana and Tembujin were destined for the arena in Orocastria. Unfair, Dana came back to the cells to help me. . . .

Sumitra's mind disintegrated into cinders. The wind, which had been so encouragingly tinted with freshness, now wheezed with the reek of sorcery and sulfur. She choked, on darkness and air alike. Hands grasped her arms and bore her stumbling across a pavement and up a flight of steps.

An owl hooted. A feeble strand of music coiled through the murk. The ground crawled with adders and huge centipedes, maggots infesting the rotting corpse of Minras. The guards skittered about, warding off the creatures, but the priests plodded on impassively. Perhaps they, too, were drugged, Sumi's mind gibbered; that was why two shapes vanished into darkness and then reappeared, subtly changed. . . . But the gloom revealed impression, not substance.

The palace was a tentative charcoal sketch. No, the drawing was of raw fragments, slabs, pinnacles of stone so dark as to be colorless. A slag heap, perhaps, abandoned by the gods at the world's completion. Perhaps a quarry, the gods building a tomb. Sumitra staggered on leaden feet, carried by hands like shackles on, and on, and on, into the feverishly icy gloom.

They were climbing Zind Taurmeni. But Andrion would be waiting at the arena, lulled by Dana's continued presence at the cells. He cannot save me, Sumi thought giddily. I am going to die, and our child with me; obliterated in this dark place, unburied and unmourned—no, I will be mourned, anguished, ached. . . . She was numb, and fear and grief were only words.

She gasped through the foul taste clotting her mouth, her cauterized mind so fixed on each inhalation and exhalation that only slowly did she realize she was standing still and the gloom was ripped by red light.

Red fire. Sumitra gulped, spat, squinted. A fissure in the rock, filled with seething crimson reflections, opened at her feet. It was so like the one cleaving the temple on Mount Tenebrio that for a moment she swayed, disoriented, wondering if she had been dragged across the entire island. But here the fire was real, a hot breath upon her face, breast, and belly in stark contrast to the chill at her back, drawing a shiver through her body and gooseflesh to her skin. How could fires feed on rock? Were there trees at the bottom of the cleft? Why were they not consumed. . . . Her skin contracted again. She turned.

Eldrafel, the evil genius of this place, stood upon a nearby promontory of rock. His hands were outstretched, his face was carved of rose porphyry, his jewels shone like drops of blood. He intoned a fell chant in a voice not hoarse, not harsh, but blasphemously pure and clear. Lord of darkness, lord of death, leader of souls; the god from the sea, shadow made flesh . . .

Sumi scrabbled for coherence. This cannot be happening to me, or to my child; I am asleep in my chambers in Iksandarun and will wake to Andrion's indulgent chuckle that I could imagine such a dream! She wrenched suddenly, breaking the grip on her arms. She spun. One step, two, and she tripped and fell.

Another pair of hands plucked her up. Strong, firm hands, long fingers, not shackles on her arms but protective vambraces. She looked up. A hooded face peered down at her, all angles and pale resolve, sooty hair and beard, dark eyes. Gods, the eyes were a pellucid brown, layer upon layer of lambency, unsullied by fire or gloom.

Andrion! she wanted to scream, always you return for me! But with an effort she did not. She sagged, faint with joy, but the hands held her up and pressed her into another, surly but resigned, grasp.

Eldrafel's voice stopped. In the silence the burble and hiss of fire reverberated in the abyss. A tendril of blinding blue flame snapped above the rim and fell back, leaving a spectral trail of lightning to play along the jagged rock. A crimson glow rose upward, illuminating the banks of cinders that drifted across the sky like black algae across a pond.

Eldrafel turned. His flesh and hair gleamed scarlet, but his eyes remained frost gray. His steady gaze fixed upon Sumitra, raked her, abandoned her and splintered into fangs of ice. His lip curled in a venomous snarl, uncannily aware of the interloper close at hand.

Sword and shield raised as one, Sumi thought, the light of sun and moon driving away darkness. As if drawn from her own vision, shield and sword glinted before her. A many-pointed star spilled rivulets of quicksilver, a crystalline crescent shone as bright as the sun. She winced as she would wince at the apparition of a god, awed and yet yearning toward it. The radiance cleared her mind like a gust of clean wind.

A guard rushed forward, and another, their spear points dull flames. The shield leaped up, chiming, and Solifrax sang. The flames were extinguished. The guards fell. The priests, rendered into one indistinct mass by the attacking light, quailed.

Cursing his soldiers, Eldrafel lunged alone toward Andrion. Blackness streaked from his fingertips and broke against the shield to mingle with the cinders swirling across the mountainside.

It was Jemail, Sumitra realized, who held her. He was drawing her away, as if he were a genuine priest loyally guarding the sacrifice.

The guards, goaded by Eldrafel's scorn, rushed again toward the weapons he desired, the man he named his victim. But it was more than a man, it was Andrion, Beloved of the Gods, who danced now, his gestures not elegant but precise, economical, deadly. The shining disk of the shield unspooled clean skeins of light; the glittering arc of Solifrax sewed them to darkness, mending it. The guards scattered, howling in fear.

Of course, Sumitra said to herself, Eldrafel had indeed intended to sacrifice me. But he had also intended to draw Andrion here, to kill him and take the weapons; amusing, that his only too mortal followers were stunned by a god-crazed audacity equal to his own.

The shield chimed, a deep note ringing against the lowering sky. The sword leaped and parried. Scattering a knot of soldiers, Andrion rushed Eldrafel's promontory. Solifrax shrieked, and jewels spewed from the priest's body, but his flesh remained unscathed.

Andrion did not pause; he raised the shield and thrust forward, pushing Eldrafel toward the abyss. But with a howl of frustration and rage and a backward spray of dark flame, the priest leaped, twirled in midair over the fiery chasm like over the shoulders of a bull, and landed gracefully on the far side, safe in the arms of darkness. His voice echoed, shouting curses which pelted down like stinging embers, and then was gone.

Sumitra would have shouted herself, her patience worn thin—he escaped yet again, his evils continued, the ordeal would never end. . . . Her tongue seemed too large for her mouth.

The ground rumbled and shivered. A blinding incandescence surged up the abyss, spilling liquid fire over the rim. Andrion jumped away, but two priests were not as swift. Flames licked out and ignited their cloaks, leaving them writhing and screaming among the rocks. Not one of their colleagues stayed to help them; the other priests and the guards rushed in a struggling mass down the mountain.

Andrion seized Sumitra. The honest radiance of sword and shield emphasized the starkness of his face, honed by days of short rations and worry. But his luminous eyes were unchanged, and the tight, lopsided grin he offered her was achingly familiar. She buried her face in the warmth of his chest, and he held her close in a moment of mute communion.

"Come," Jemail said, with a frantic shooing gesture.

Sumitra roused herself. "Come where?"

Andrion settled her in the angle of his left arm, in the light of the shield. The blade of Solifrax, held before them both, was unstained by the blood it had shed. Andrion regarded it with detached irritation. He had not killed for seven years now, Sumi knew, and all that sparring in the palace court-yards had been merely—no, not merely exercise. Incorrigible Andrion had never quite trusted fate to let him lie fallow.

The brilliance poured ahead of them. Sumitra felt as if her steps were buoyed up, by Andrion and light together, and she floated down the path up which she had stumbled only a short time before. "Come where?" she asked again. "To rescue Dana and Tembujin?"

"To the dye works," answered Andrion tightly, caught between duties. "We must reach Niarkos before Eldrafel has time to enspell him again. Then Dana and Tembujin."

Ah yes, Niarkos had been enspelled with the tapestry. Sumi had never seen it. "And Chrysais?"

"She is dead," Andrion said, flat.

"Ah. Perhaps not unrepentant, not quite unredeemed?"

Andrion clasped Sumitra close, fiercely possessive; unashamedly she clung to him. "We must part again," he murmured, "but not for long, love."

She would have protested, but she would rather be as strong as he, and play the celestial, the diabolical game to the end just as bravely. The glare from the wound in the mountain dwindled, but never quite died. Its truculent glow followed them as they crept down the far flank of the mountain. They avoided the torches of Orocastria, a swarm of tiny red insect eyes, and made their way toward the coast. Where the polished ebony of the sea heaved and stretched like a sleeper in the grip of ghastly dreams.

Chapter Eighteen

THE CLANGOR OF the abused zamtak lingered in Dana's ears all night, overriding the rise and fall of a piping just enough off-key that it scraped her nerves. As if her nerves were not already raw, the terrible vision of Chrysais's death had grated them into bloody shreds. Chrysais had been born with Bellasteros's contradictions, with Andrion's; yet she had been born a woman, with her own cloying courage. Dana could not find the will to deal with Chrysais, not now.

She heard the singing of sword and shield, and knew that her desperate message to Andrion had been received. Why? she asked herself; why had she so drained her strength to warn him of Sumitra's peril when he might have discovered it for himself?

The darkness around her eased a bit. Dawn, or a lessening of the cinder fall, or both? The tiny lamp had given up the ghost long since, but then, it could not have protected her from the odd tactile chill that sucked the warmth from her limbs and the steadiness from her mind. She had courted the cold, she knew, sitting with her back against the wall; she needed Tembujin's presence on the other side of the stone more than she needed physical warmth. She doggedly ignored memories of what his presence could at times mean.

"And now?" he called. His voice was a fiery liqueur.

"They found soldiers at the dye works." Of course, Eldrafel would have the Sardians guarded. He had probably had them guarded even when they were insensible. Being untrustworthy himself, he would trust no one else.

The vision poured into her, filled her, seared her like molten bronze.

Sumitra sat on a low stone wall, her knees drawn up, armed with a stick to push away the sinuous forms that stirred the shadows around her. Her eyes were lamps turning again and again to the buildings nearby.

Andrion pressed himself against a corner and peered around it. Torchlight, ruddier than the luminescence of the sword and shield he held, washed over his features and eroded them from the smooth visage of a god into the taut and weary face of a man. He frowned with calculation.

Human figures rushed among the pits and piles of the factory, into the low sheds and back again, fighting the centipedes and snakes. One small group hurried off toward the city, burdened with several large bundles that must be bolts of cloth; the rose shimmer of the fabric was an odd pastel note in a scene otherwise drawn in black and red.

The stink of the rotting shellfish was overwhelming. Andrion strangled a cough. Dana clung to her Sight, wheezing.

Seven Sardians were seated under an overhanging roof; the eighth, Niarkos, was a great black hulk exchanging insults with a Minran officer. Perfectly lucid insults, thank the gods, if as uninventive as most procreative and eliminatory expletives were likely to be. With a mirthless grin Andrion stepped into the torchlight.

Solifrax rang, and the shield chimed agreement. The Sardians leaped up with cries of joy. The Minrans stopped dead and spun about. The centipedes, unimpressed, continued to scurry among their feet.

Andrion shouted and charged as if he had a legion at his back. Niarkos felled the officer with one blow of his massive hand. The Sardians erupted, seizing spears and staves before the Minrans could recover from their surprise. They went about their task of subduing the guards with relish, settling a few grudges.

Dana leaped to her feet, staggered against the table, and began to pace back and forth, flexing her arms to draw the blood like acid back into them.

One guard stepped upon an adder, which turned and bit him. He yowled and danced, and a Sardian tripped him into a pool of slimy, rotting shellfish. His flailing emitted a miasma as palpable as the still-drifting ash.

The Minrans fell back toward a huge shoal of empty shells. Jemail lunged out with a cry. Expressionlessly, he cut and thrust with his spear, sending more than one of his erstwhile colleagues into the pile of shells. They were broken, and their sharp edges lacerated like knives.

Solifrax flickered, reflecting red, and gold, and purple. The shield pulsed with its own clear moonsheen. Niarkos crossed spears with Jemail, who whooped indignantly and was saved by Andrion's shout. With a shrug Niarkos turned, saw the officer he had felled struggling to rise, and whacked him with the butt of his spear into a vat. He splashed and wallowed. Purple dye fountained in rose and lavender droplets, anointing Sardian as well as Minran.

Andrion's clear voice rose above the tumult, directing the battle. The reek of the charnel house hung in a shivering cloud above building and vat. Purple slime splashed and eddied in rivulets, in currents, in waves washing the combatants down the beach into the sea. . . .

Dana's vision elongated like a candle flame in a breeze and went out. She groped after it, senses quivering open, but could feel only the remote clash of sword and shield.

Suddenly her unguarded awareness trembled to a crawling dread. Gooseflesh tightened her skin. The darkness simmered with more than just the poison of creeping dumb creatures; a relentless malice gathered itself over Minras—something beyond the power even of Eldrafel, or perhaps it had been roused by Eldrafel's power, who had set the elementals, Tenebrio and Taurmenios, to feuding—her thought frayed maddeningly into nothingness.

"And now?" called Tembujin.

"I do not know, I do not know!" The tremulous piping grew louder, joined by a flute, gaining definition as the world outside the window coagulated into day. The hour before dawn, when condemned criminals were executed. Marching steps rang in the corridor.

Dana glanced regretfully at the zamtak and its tapestry covering. The door burst open. A guard dragged her outside and threw her against Tembujin. They stared at each other a moment, black lacquered eyes and eyes cut like emeralds making a pact. The air was narcotic, in the last throes of a wasting disease. The stench of irex was overwhelmed by a stench of sorcery so strong it must have emanated from the ground itself.

The soldiers hurried their prisoners through the palace as if racing toward a finish line. Dana glimpsed the lotus pool and cringed; its lid of cinders was a scab hiding a mortal wound. Charcoal in drifts and shoals lay everywhere, crunching underfoot in bursts of shining dust. The stars were smeared like weeping eyes across a shrouded sky.

A pale figure moved on a far terrace. Dana suppressed a start. Phantom Proserfina, probably, her hands raised in urgent gesticulation. Or perhaps phantom Chrysais. But surely she was settled, once and for all.

The soldiers kicked aside the mangled bodies of snakes and centipedes. They must have lived a nightmare last night, fighting these vile creatures, unable to fight the black and malodorous air and the uneasy twitching of a land caught in an evil spell.

The stars faded. The sky was swept by an eerie opalescence. The gaudy palace decorations, abraded by the rain of cinders, were in the dawn only gray shapes. The room into which Dana and Tembujin were thrust was like a tomb, dank and dark, stirred by the tiny glints of bat eyes. . . . No, what watched them were not bats but several robed priests.

Fresh kilts, wide belts, faience necklaces and bracelets lay ready—like the ones worn by the young bull dancers in Tenebrio's moonlit temple, Dana realized. Of course. She was past surprise, past fear.

Tembujin and Dana changed into the ritual garb under the unblinking eyes of the priests, eyes that were devoid of any human emotion, humor, or hate, or even lust for the bodies displayed before them. What sleight of hand did the Khazyari use, Dana wondered with a quick sideways glance, to switch the small knife from shirt to kilt without revealing it? Probably sheer desperation.

The priests glided out. The soldiers gestured. The arena opened before them. The air gathered in it was almost too unwholesome to sustain life; as the guards shoved them onto the floor, Tembujin gasped and Dana's heart hammered. Her head seemed stuffed with yarn, her thought crawling agonizingly after the traipsing strands of Sight. Her clanking jewelry hung as heavy and cold as chains. The skin of her naked chest puckered with horror.

The great slab of the altar was decorated with . . . black flowers? No, dark red amaranth, like ancient bloodstains. Torches guttered and died along the railings. Row upon row of phosphorescent eyes, wide with anxious anticipation, gazed down upon them. Other dancers stood like wax dolls, faces set in an oddly emotionless, no doubt drug-induced, elation. Dana's tall and rounded form, Tembujin's strong shoulders and thighs, contrasted sharply with the others' slender sexless bodies.

In a box at the side sat Gard, overseen by several burly soldiers. Did he know about his mother's death? Probably. Probably he suspected its cause. His delicate features were stern beyond his years, those of an orphan who has had to learn harsh lessons in self-sufficiency. Dana grimaced with pity and dull anger when she saw that Gard bore upon his narrow chest, half concealed by a purple cloak, Andrion's necklace. The boy's shoulders were rounded, his neck oddly lengthened, his body crushed under the weight of the moon and star. In the feeble light the necklace was tarnished brass, its power stubbornly muted.

Rue sat beside Gard, as sumptuously coiffed and painted as Chrysais had once been, her eyes so bright as to be slick. Her open dress emphasized the scrawniness of her body; her breasts might have plumped somewhat under Eldrafel's ministrations, but still resembled stunted apricots. She gazed out over the arena, her face set in rancid arrogance apparently meant to imitate, but which only mocked, Chrysais's bravura pride.

Priests herded in several garlanded bulls. The animals jerked and shifted nervously, emitting plaintive bellows. Tembujin laid his hand upon his belt; there, Dana told herself, that was where he had concealed the dagger. We shall at least sell our lives dearly; no, we shall not die, burnt offerings upon a demon's altar—this is not the altar of the demon, but of the dishonored god. . . . Her perception grasped not clear image but mazy impression.

Eldrafel sauntered across the arena and posed beside the altar, naked except for his dancing costume, glowing despite the chill. "Khalingu," Tembujin spat, "if I have to watch him making love to himself again I shall surely vomit."

Dana agreed. "I should think the gods themselves would vomit."

As if a dyke were breached in the east, beyond Mount Tenebrio, waves of crimson light washed across the low ceiling of the sky. Row upon row of watching faces blushed. But the dawn could not lighten the forbidding bulk of Zind Taurmeni, or restore the bright colors to the palace facade; no wind eased the chill contagion of the air. The music grew even keener, a high-pitched, fast-paced wail which trembled in the stones of the arena. Yes, Dana wailed silently, yes, this was my vision in Cylandra's basin, only my vision was different—not fair, O gods, not fair! Her head spun, the mountain looming higher and higher, the palace slumping into slag, the sky stained with blood.

A gateway opened. Two soldiers dragged in a tall, lean figure, head drooping, face dirty. . . . Dana's heart jolted free and fell with a resounding crash into her belly; surprise and fear, as fresh as if she'd never felt them before. Andrion. They had Andrion.

Eldrafel's brows arched in amazed pleasure. Then, with his usual sublime self-absorption, he smirked and pirouetted and escorted the two soldiers and their prisoner toward the altar. One man held the shield, one the sword; their faces wore no expression beneath their close-fitting leather caps. The ubiquitous hooded priests shuffled into place behind them, their hoods thrown back to reveal their dark and eager faces.

The dancers jostled each other. Dana slumped. But wait—she shook herself free of the muck that clogged her mind and looked again at the booty the soldiers held. The shield pulsed with subtle but unmistakable motes of light. The sword hummed patiently, just at the edge of hearing. And yet Andrion seemed hardly conscious. He stumbled over the cinders and his eyes—his eyes were downcast, their expression hidden.

The bulls bellowed, milling about their attendants. With a shout, one was sent charging toward the dancers. A thunder of hooves, a vast intake of breath from the watchers; two dancers jumped, twirled, and died. The bull was upon Dana. Tembujin shouted some incomprehensible epithet. Gracelessly, she dodged—they cannot expect us to dance!—and felt the hot breath graze her neck. She could have swore that she saw, from the corner of her eye, Andrion flinch.

Eldrafel leaped over the bodies, launched himself into the air, somersaulted and landed upon his feet. Perfunctorily, it seemed, his interest elsewhere. Another acrobat lunged, slipped, and was trampled. Two seized Dana, thrusting her into the bull's path. Its crazed bellows ricocheted from the walls of the arena, driving like nails into her mind—she wrenched herself away from the cool, limp hands, stumbled and fell. The huge musty bulk of the animal whisked by her. Tembujin seized her and pulled her up. At her feet lay a young girl, red-splashed face twisted in ecstasy. Dana turned away, sickened.

Tembujin crouched, evidently trying to consider the bull no

more dangerous than one of his own obstreperous ponies. But
Eldrafel was gesturing. The bull, with many lowings and
stampings, was lured away. The dancers clustered, unnaturally
bright eyes glazed with bafflement. The guards laid their
burdens of man and weapon across the altar, so that Andrion
was splayed out, blank face toward the vermilion sky, shield
and sword arranged on either side.

Dana stood suffocating. So Eldrafel was changing the lit-
urgy; the blood of these pitiful children was not enough to
slake his thirst for power, he was impatient for Andrion's. . . .

The soldiers beside the altar stood stolidly. Tembujin lurked
behind the dancers. The tiers of faces swayed raptly. Rue
flounced forward, lips parted. Gard looked unblinkingly upward, his face ashen, lips moving as if praying. The gory
dawn drained away, leaving the sky colorlessly translucent;
the rising sun was a suppurating sore on the horizon. The
music swelled and ebbed in a fever dream. A scream swelled
like a tumor on Dana's vocal cords, just one scream that
would break open the heavens and release the wrath of the
gods upon Minras. . . .

Eldrafel danced about the altar, leaning over Andrion,
taunting him. Andrion smiled. Eldrafel's resplendent manner
frayed. His steps grew faster and faster. Andrion ignored
him, smiling serenely; waiting done, pretense done, an end at
hand.

Goaded, Eldrafel snapped and whirled, his fluid grace
clotting into clumsiness. The luster of his eyes clouded with
frustration and rage. He picked up a waiting dagger, an
obsidian blade polished to a brutal glitter.

"Tenebrio!" His smooth voice cracked. "My lord, my
father, lord of darkness! Take your sacrifice!"

Dana jerked as if slapped. But this is not Tenebrio's altar—he
has called upon the wrong god. . . . The ground shivered
beneath her feet.

Her mind careened from sight to sight. Tembujin in one
lithe movement stabbed the closest guard and threw Dana the
man's spear. Even as she caught and clasped the shaft, she
saw Andrion seize sword and shield and with a quick, taut
grin ward Eldrafel's blow. The two guards who had brought
him in turned not to him but to the waiting priests. Of course!
Insane laughter bubbled on her lips. Those two guards were
Niarkos's men, freed from the dye works; their hands were
flecked with purple, as if by a royal disease. A guard struck

at her and she lunged with the spear, impaling him. The music ceased abruptly with a piercing wail.

Dana was not cold, but blazing hot. She stood back to back with Tembujin, skin rasping not unpleasantly against skin, sensing his glee as he fought at last. She knew her face was twisted in a sick intensity, she saw not the men she fought but Andrion leaping from the altar, Solifrax biting—impeccable motion, deliberate, meticulous—a filigree of white fire igniting the miasma, burning it off. . . . Eldrafel struck again, and his dagger exploded against the brightness of the shield.

The Sardian guards defended Andrion's back. Shouts arose from a gateway—yes, of course, it all seemed so logical now—Niarkos led his remaining men directly into the clump of skittish bulls and sent them stampeding across the arena, scattering soldiers and priests as effectively as much larger force. What audacity! Dana exulted. Andrion, you idiot, to take such chances to free us!

The bellowing of bulls, the shouts of men, and Rue's shrieks of calumny swelled upward and burst against the sky. Solifrax and shield danced in an intricate pattern around Eldrafel, driving him back.

And Eldrafel's perfect features knotted into a leer of outraged pride; the last vestige of his cool manner strained and snapped. He screamed. His body twisted, erupting with tongues of black flame that sizzled and popped against sword and shield and Andrion's glowing face, that licked the altar and fragmented it. The rock, strewn with the red petals of amaranth, seemed to bleed.

The ground rumbled. The arena, flickering with swords and bodies, the sky itself spun crazily. Dana faltered. A sword skinned a bracelet from her arm. Eldrafel called upon Tenebrio and attacked again; grimly silent, Andrion parried, but could not turn the black flames and reach Eldrafel's vulnerable back.

Mother! Dana howled silently. Let us end it, for once and for all, let us end it! Her nostrils stung with sorcery, her throat was clogged with sorcery, her hair stood on end with sorcery. She fell back against Tembujin, momentarily overwhelmed. He snarled some impatient comment on her clumsiness. Mother, her mind cried, too much sorcery, like spark after spark after spark upon tinder; betrayed Taurmenios, too, has a temper to lose!

The floor of the arena cracked, a fissure zigzagging faster

than a man could run from railing to railing. The earth
heaved. Dana staggered, but then, so did everyone else. The
hysterical bulls crashed through a barrier. A wave of panic
spread through the stands.

"Gard!" Andrion shouted to Niarkos, the herald's trumpet
of his voice cutting through the confusion. "Rescue Gard!"

But even his voice was consumed in the tremendous reverberating crash that rocked the world. Every living soul in the
arena stood petrified as the sound rolled along the sky and
vanished. The ensuing hush was so absolute Dana thought the
noise had deafened her. But no; she heard her own blood
strumming her ears, and Tembujin's heartbeat and the throb-
bing chime of the shield. And she heard Eldrafel's gasping
wail of dismay. He has gone too far, she thought. We have
goaded him into going too far. And he knows it.

The top of Zind Taurmeni disappeared beneath a roiling
cloud of darkness that surged up and out across the sky, silent
billows blanking out the sunlight like a shutter slammed
across a window.

Chapter Nineteen

ANDRION WINCED, HIS senses crushed by the furious bellow of Taurmenios. The grim satisfaction of battle cracked and disintegrated into the stillness. The thrill of Solifrax and star-shield faded into a thin warble of dismay. And did I never really believe in the gods? he asked himself lamely.

Eldrafel uttered only one cry of distress. Then his lips drew back in a snarl and his eyes roiled as if with ash. A man would be frightened, Andrion thought between the waves of his own amazement, but this demon's spawn is angry that neither god nor man will meekly bow to him.

The multitude gathered in the arena stood like figures in a stone frieze, petrified in attitudes of anxiety and alarm, the battle between sacrifice and celebrant no longer important.

The cloud swirled into mighty wings. The wings flapped. A sulfurous wind howled across Orocastria and flattened its inhabitants like reeds. The wind scorched Andrion's mouth and lungs; even as he gasped, he was swept into a sprawling tangle with one of his own legionaries. Dana and Tembujin dropped, rolled, crouched in wheezing bundles amid the ash.

The wings fell. Cinders and hot pebbles like drops of fire hammered across the stones of the palace and pelted into the arena.

The first to gather his wits and run was Eldrafel. He skimmed through the infernal avalanche, shoving more than one of his own followers aside, and vanished into a gateway. Thwarted, Andrion shouted to himself as he leaped up, but not yet, by the short feathers of the god, defeated!

Several people were struck by plummeting stones and collapsed before they could rise. Soldiers threw down their weapons and scrambled for shelter. People screamed, struggled, fell, and were trampled in the stands. No time now to hunt Eldrafel.

"Gard!" cried Andrion. He thought he saw the boy's white, terror-stricken face carried away. "Harus, protect him!" He coughed, his mouth and throat scored with ash and with the foul breath of the mountain.

The air seethed with a tangible darkness. Eyes slitted, Andrion shouted, "Sardis! Sardis, to me!" He lifted Solifrax as a beacon, but it was only an attenuated strand of light in the murk. He lifted the shield as a roof, and pebbles struck it in peal after muted peal.

Andrion led the Sardians in a stumbling rush across the arena, over a shattered barrier, into a gallery beneath the first terrace of the palace. There they huddled in an alcove so dark Andrion could see little more than the various eyes glistening in the weapons' luminescence. The proper number of eyes, he decided after a quick count, including the malachite shards that were Dana's and the jet beads that were Tembujin's. Thank the gods of someplace other than Minras for that.

The ululating wails of the people of Orocastria echoed down the gallery, punctuated by the rhythms of running feet and the clattering of pebbles and cinders. Innocent dupes or corrupt accomplices, Andrion thought, how could they know that the forces they aided Eldrafel to raise could not be controlled? Something was poking him, like a stitch in his side—he shook himself. "Niarkos!"

A flash of teeth. "My lord!"

"Admiral, take your sailors, make your way to the harbor and ready a ship for us. Anything will do."

"Yes, my lord. My pleasure." With a few brusque orders Niarkos organized his five sailors and plunged out into the gallery. "Take pieces of that barricade for shields," he shouted.

Andrion allowed himself a quick grin; the great sea lion was so angered by his humiliation in the dye works that he would single-handedly stop Taurmenios's gaping mouth with a boulder, if his emperor asked him to.

The star-shield jerked abruptly, almost dislocating Andrion's shoulder. It emitted a few motes of silver and was answered by the sword. Shields, yes, he told himself.

Tembujin, with unusual discretion, conducted the two remaining soldiers into the gallery. They stood blinking into the murk, working their way through the expletives of Sardis, the Empire, and Khazyaristan. Wisps of ash eddied around them and banked against the walls.

The rattle and clump from the alcove was surely Dana's

jewelry, falling to the ground. Perhaps the dry, gray rain began to slow, or the shield and sword grew brighter, or Dana's eyes flared with a light of their own; Andrion could see her smudged face, lips parted eagerly, jaw jutting, as she tore the ritual jewelry from her body and cast it down. He cleared the scum and the emotion from his throat. He slipped the shield from his arm and held it; compelling, the surface tingling to his touch and its voice a constant murmur in his ear, bearing itself proudly rather than letting him carry it.

He set his teeth and gave it back. How patient Dana had become, not to have snatched it from him long since.

She grasped the great disk as closely to her as a child and inspected it. Jangling doubtfully, it inspected her in return; recognizing her, it trilled a greeting. She slipped it onto her arm with a moan of gratification.

Andrion's outstretched arm seemed appallingly naked. His mouth quirked in annoyance, his brows in amusement. He tightened his grip on the hilt of Solifrax and slapped it against his thigh.

"Do not ever do that to me again," Dana said.

"Take the shield?"

"No, no! Lie there so meekly under the demon's knife!" With a toss of her head she threw back her hair, its blond waves like fluted drapery.

"I knew I could not disguise myself as a priest again. How else to get close to Eldrafel? But only his back is vulnerable."

"He would not scruple to stab you in the back. Or Gard."

Testily, Andrion replied, "I know that. I long ago abandoned any thoughts of honorable combat with him." Solifrax carved a glimmering swath through the gloom. Yes, the holy effluvia was settling, leaving the air misted with dust and hysteria.

Dana weighed the spear in her hand. "Where is Sumitra?"

"Jemail rowed her over to Al Sitar, the little island between harbor and sea. We shall pick her up on our way home."

"Home," Dana murmured. And then, hard and brisk, "All is not well at home."

"I know that too."

Her hand clasped his arm; look at me, I would spare myself nothing. "Do you know that Eldrafel stole your necklace and gave it to Gard?"

"Yes." Her hand seemed delicate, the dirt on it an anomaly, but its grip was impossibly firm. "No harm done, thanks for once to the caprice of the gods who ordered this game so subtly and so strictly."

She nodded assent, distracted. "And now—I believe Gard is in the throne room now, where we first met Chrysais. Years ago, was it not?"

"Ah!" he exclaimed. "Thank you. Let us go get him."

"You go get him. I must rescue something else."

"Please?"

Dana explained, "Sumitra's zamtak was left in her cell, wrapped by that scrap of tapestry I asked her to make to warn Nikander. I must save them. A matter of honor, you see."

I could say too much, Andrion thought, and there is too much I can never say; words, delightful and foolish. He took off his grimy cloak and with an apologetic smile wrapped it around her torso, more for his sensibilities than for hers. He stretched awkwardly around sword and shield and met her lips in a kiss that was gritty, slightly acrid, and as inspiring as a paean.

"At the harbor," Dana whispered, strangled on dust and contradiction. She was a clear gleam driving back the shadows. She was gone.

The air was growing cold again, riming Andrion's damp lips. Dana had not said thank you for his care of the shield. But then, why should she?

Tembujin, he discovered, had also shed his cursed jewelry. Andrion led him and the two legionaries up to and through the palace. It hardly seemed the same place, the garish designs scoured away, the columns cracked and toppled, and he was hard put to find the correct passage. They slid across the terraces in drifts of charcoal and stumbled over an occasional body so shrouded in ash as to seem only a desiccated husk. Indoors the thick twilight deepened to lightlessness, stirred by dust motes that danced tauntingly in the glow of Solifrax. The earth itself thrummed, and the massive stones creaked like wicker.

Andrion's shoulders grew tighter and tighter; something watched him. Many things watched him, he decided, including Tembujin, who took this expedition away from the harbor with ill grace and a continuous profane commentary. The two soldiers' eyes were wide with caution, but they seemed relatively nerveless; not for nothing had Andrion had Miklos, back in Sardis, pick the steadiest of his command.

Suddenly the dark, close passage evaporated into nothingness. They stood in what might have been a cavern, ceiling and walls suggested by a tentative luminescence, air eddying with foul breaths. The throne room, yes; Andrion lifted Solifrax and it flared, a stark white light defining like a lightning stroke the faded, peeling frescoes, the dizzying tiles damped by dust, the basin that Chrysais had stirred cracked and empty except for a coating of slime.

And someone sat on the winged throne. Death, Andrion asked himself, surveying his domain? Almost; it was Eldrafel who leaned back negligently, legs crossed, arms splayed, fingers dangling. He was not even dirty. His face and body shone with the sickly pallor of the mushrooms in Tenebrio's cave, each separate hair and lash edged with phosphorescence, each jewel winking green, blue, red, like spider's eyes. When he saw Andrion his remote, misty gaze coalesced into resentment.

Andrion shivered as if engulfed by a clammy cloak. Eldrafel, the inhuman beauty of metal and stone, except for the tiny unholy flame stirring in his eyes. . . . He shook himself. It was so silent that faint cries echoed eerily from outside. "The pleas of your own people," Andrion said, "that you have damned."

"Leader of souls," crooned Eldrafel. "Shadow made flesh."

Andrion would have thought the man insane, except that he had never been convinced of his rationality. "Where is Gard?" he demanded.

Eldrafel nodded. Andrion spun about. The dense black shadow of the throne did not repeat the shape of wings but was warped into the form of a gargoyle. There, in the darkness, Rue stood holding Chrysais's jewel chest. She eyed Andrion with a maniacal smirk. Gods, does she assume Eldrafel caused this convulsion as proof of his power? If her brother is half the fanatic she is . . . His thought stuttered. Gard sat in a dismal crumple, his wrist caught in her talon of a hand. The necklace brightened feebly and then dulled again, just long enough to illuminate the child's eyes glazed with fear and horror, his small features hideously withered.

"Gard!" Andrion called, aching to reassure the boy, but he stared fixedly into nothingness. Solifrax flared again, shattering the darkness. The necklace sparked, but Gard did not react.

Eldrafel stood, posing in an attitude of exaltation. His

voice boomed through the chamber, shriller than the hum in the ground, but it, too, set the stones to trembling. "Pay homage to the living god come from the sea, bearing news of the unfortunate death of Andrion Bellasteros, King of Sardis, Emperor. Pay homage, as the legions will, to me!"

Andrion's gut twisted cruelly. Indeed, Rowan had been stirring his pot for months now, and it was high time for Eldrafel to go and see what had floated to the top. His comment to the perversely exultant face was short, ugly, and to the point; his mind flashed as bright as the sword, enraged. He leaped forward. Tembujin and the Sardians closed behind him, spears raised, feet scrabbling in the dust. Eldrafel gestured, quick and sharp, and liquid blackness splashed from his hands. Andrion's left arm was naked; he warded the infernal blow with the flat of Solifrax, and the sword froze in his hand, burning his palm.

"You would still use sorcery, even now?" he shouted. "You have used too much, demon, and it wanes!"

Eldrafel laughed. Blackness lanced again from his hands, upward, to spatter in a crackling crescendo against balconies and ceiling.

Andrion had just enough wit to recoil, spinning with the others back into the hallway. The throne room rocked, the walls rattled, and with a roar the roof caved in. The Sardians crouched, hiding their heads from the crashing plaster and brick, suffocating in the roiling dust.

Gard! Andrion plunged through, over, around the rubble back into the room, slipping and sliding uncontrollably; he fell in a miniature avalanche to the foot of the throne and was almost crushed by the precipitous arrival of his soldiers. Tembujin leaped catlike over them all and landed on his feet.

The throne lay on its side, splintered into knife-sharp shards. Eldrafel, Rue, and Gard were gone. Tembujin probed through the rubble. Then, with a grimace of disgust, he turned to Andrion. "So, Eldrafel moves on to bigger and better realms."

Bigger and better realms indeed! Andrion set the hilt of Solifrax against his forehead. The sword warmed itself and tingled against his dirt- and sweat-caked skin. Every time I think we reach an end, he shouted silently, the end slides from our grasp! Too much to hope that Eldrafel would perish tidily at the hands of the gods—no, they have to leave a poor fool like me to tie up the loose threads.

He lashed out in frustration, Solifrax chiming. Let him

believe he has killed me. Let him believe that Tenebrio is still strong. In the end—and we will come to an end—his own pride must bring him low. Andrion's flesh thrilled one more moment to the receding resonance of the necklace; then it was gone. Gard, another god's pawn. Again he sliced the air.

The legionaries shied, but Tembujin stood his ground. His face beneath its coating of dust was acute, deliberate, sardonic. "We shall find the boy when we find Eldrafel, back on the mainland."

"I know that!" Andrion snapped. Tembujin shrugged. The Khazyari, damn him, knew just when to goad and just when to shut up. Andrion set his teeth so tightly his jaw writhed. He led his men out the nearest door and was promptly lost in the tangled gloom of the labyrinth.

They plodded through nightmare, through endless shadowed corridors, searching for the unattainable, Gard, or light, or the outer door. The sword in Andrion's hand hummed very faintly with the resonance of the shield, now close, now fading; he could not follow it through this maze of rooms, and porticoes, and passages. Then, not surprisingly perhaps, he saw a hint of a shape before him; Proserfina, gesturing. They went the way she indicated, and came a few moments later onto a devastated terrace.

Tembujin said under his breath, "What did you see?"

"A ghost."

"Mmm. The gods are much too intimate with Minras to suit my taste."

"An unhealthy intimacy," Andrion agreed. But then, he had encountered his own tutelary deity here; nothing, nothing was easy.

Dana loped across a lower terrace, cradling a bundle in her arm. Her spear was tipped with fresh crimson. Of course, she would kill for a possession of Sumitra's. Andrion laughed and groaned simultaneously, swallowed dust and coughed. Solifrax spat an inquisitive spray of sparks. Dana vanished into an alley, either unaware of or not taking the time to acknowledge Andrion's scrutiny.

The air had cleared somewhat; the sun was a white-hot disk stamped upon a sky like gray canvas. City and harbor were defined by a thin glaucous light, each ruined building, each ship a distinct silvered image. A trireme cleft the ash-matted water toward the harbor entrance, oars rising and falling rhythmically. The idols, stained a mottled green, shifted un-

easily at its approach. Andrion squinted through watering
eyes. Yes, there was the purple-clad, gold-crowned shape like
a work of art adorning the foredeck. No, not even the wrath
of the gods themselves could get rid of the man; he had more
lives than a snow leopard of the Pathay! Andrion spat into the
dust, but still his mouth tasted like a garbage midden.

He glanced behind him, at the mountain. Had the rock rent
itself open? It was hard to tell, for the entire slope was
obscured by a flowing black mass. No, it was not black, but
fissured with red, and seemed to be oozing downward in
wave after torpid wave as if the mountain itself melted.
Andrion frowned, not knowing what was happening, far from
sure he wanted to know. Perhaps the god was purging his
bowels, ridding himself of the disease that was Eldrafel.
Wisps of blue smoke coiled like phantasms over mountain
and city and crossed the face of the sun, cutting it into
glowing segments.

Andrion turned again to the harbor and stood transfixed. I
am hallucinating, he told himself firmly. One of his soldiers
emitted a cheer. Tembujin grounded his spear with a surprised, "By Khalingu's teeth! Look at that!"

Around the point of land where Niarkos's ship had met
destruction glided a Sardian galley. "Why, Harus," Andrion
breathed. "Thank you!"

The trireme faltered, its oars leaving whorls in the turgid
water. Then it steadied and plunged between the colossi so
quickly the winged bulls seemed for a moment to totter on
their pedestals. The wicked ram on the prow of the behemoth
aimed directly at the galley. Andrion gestured wildly, rowing
invisible oars, turning imaginary rudders.

Specks of seamen furled the galley's sail. Oars flailed. The
galley turned. The trireme's oars, blurred with motion, churned
the water. The huge ship brushed by the smaller and left it
wallowing in its wake.

"Not big enough game for you, Eldrafel?" said Tembujin
derisively.

Andrion's hand was clutching Solifrax as if he would squeeze
the hilt in two. Quelling a brief giddiness, he said in what he
hoped was a calm voice, "I must chide Miklos for leaving
Rhodope sooner than I ordered."

"Certainly," said Tembujin. "You do that."

The galley hovered with commendable caution outside the
harbor entrance. Andrion hurried his men toward the nearest

stair. The oozing red-laced blackness nudged into a vineyard.
Each vine spurted with flame, fell, and was consumed by the
heavy tide. Gods! Andrion exclaimed to himself, it is some
kind of liquid fire! And its path was directly toward the
harbor mouth, as if drawn by the colossi of the spited god. Of
the spiteful god. Did Taurmenios know what he did, prefer-
ring suicide to Eldrafel's contempt? Or had he been driven
berserk, striking blindly, unaware?

Zind Taurmeni belched, spraying the city with cinders and
a particularly noxious breath. Andrion's eyes burned and he
choked. Several figures toiling across a far terrace dropped in
their tracks. The Sardians sprinted from the poisonous envi-
rons of the palace downward into the city.

They picked their way through streets clogged with rubble
and with staggering people, some purposefully carrying bundles toward the docks, some huddling with stricken eyes,
incapable of movement. Bodies, crushed by falling masonry,
or apparently suffocated by dust and foul air, lay abandoned
in the gutters. Fires muttered in several buildings.

A shrieking mob thronged the jetties, fighting to get onto
the docked ships. The one knot of efficiency was Niarkos and
his men, bending a fresh, new sail onto the rigging of a tidy
little merchant tub. A Rexian purple sail, Andrion saw, gleaming in variations from lavender to violet to maroon despite the
rain of soot. He skidded to a halt by the gangplank. "What?"

Niarkos gave a mighty heave on a line and the spar shivered and rose. "We worked our fingers to nubs on that sail,"
he said from the corner of his mouth. "It was to go on His
Elegance's trireme, but he must have decided not to wait for
it. It was lying here abandoned, my lord, and I thought it a
shame to waste all our effort."

"Carry on," Andrion said with a nod. So Eldrafel had
been planning to make quite an entrance onto the stage of the
Empire, ostentatious to the point of self-parody. That was not
surprising.

Dana emerged from the ship's cabin, wiping dust from the
shield. When she saw Andrion she leaped lightly across to the
jetty. "These people will riot soon," she said, "and start
shoving one another into the sea. They have no one to lead
them." Even as she spoke, Andrion glimpsed one of the
constables who had arrested Niarkos running madly along the
dockside, eyes rolling, throwing aside an old woman.

The viscous stony flood touched the far edge of the town.

With a crackling sigh, several houses burst into flame and were moments later obliterated. Explosions echoed from farther away across the island, and banners of ash surged upward to swallow the sun. The ground rumbled and the air whimpered. The tumult along the docks approached panic.

Andrion turned to Dana, Tembujin, and the legionaries, seized upon those passing faces that were the most coherent, and shouted orders. Slowly the human tide began to eddy around the clear lights of sword and shield, and the mob sorted itself into various ships.

Several ships cast off, their gunwales lined with pale faces, and more than one cleared the gauntlet of the colossi. Andrion at last sheathed Solifrax and climbed a few rungs up the mast toward the furled purple sail. He peered through the grainy twilight toward the harbor mouth. The Sardian galley coasted close to Al Sitar, waiting for the lead ships of the flotilla to approach. A rowboat skimmed the crusty swells, its wake leaving a pleat all the way to Al Sitar itself.

Thank the gods! Andrion's face split into a grin as the boat came alongside the galley. He watched so intently as many hands lifted Sumitra aboard and Jemail scrambled up behind her, that he was shocked to feel the rough wood against his chest and realize he was still here at the jetty. She was safe, and the child within her.

Andrion laid his cheek against the mast and let his mind spin free. He saw Sumitra convincing Jemail to row her out to the strange ship by threatening to row herself and leave him marooned. He saw a cloaked and helmeted Miklos bow before Sumitra and listen intently as she gesticulated. He saw Jemail tapping his spear upon the deck, no doubt eyeing with deepest suspicion the legionaries who eyed him.

With a determined sigh Andrion roused himself. Dana, Niarkos, and Tembujin were oddly foreshortened figures upon the docks. The molten rock had devoured almost all the city; where had once been porticoes, avenues, and brightly-painted facades, were now smoking cinders. Only the great piers of rock around which the palace had lain like drifted confetti emerged above the destruction, charred sentinels half obscured by creeping tendrils of smoke. A stony tributary flowed relentlessly into the arena even as Andrion watched, and filled it for the last time with blackness and fire. Poetic justice, perhaps, but he could not help but think that in this battle of primeval powers, both sides lost. The gods must be as foolish as men. But if so, why were they gods?

The leading edge of the torpid avalanche reached the sea, just at the jetty anchoring the nearest colossus. The rock hiccupped with blue, red, and yellow flames, brighter in the gathering gloom than any painted building. Dark, probing tongues touched the water. With a tremendous hiss a cloud of steam boiled up, laying a scintillant pall over the devastated face of the city. Andrion squinted; as the avalanche overwhelmed the jetty, the closest statue reared, hooves beating the air, horns tossing, wings flapping, and plunged into the melted rock. Lurid flame leaped up and swept it away.

One ship rode the bow wave of the avalanche to safety; another veered so closely under its fiery brow that its sail smoked. Other ships hastily turned back. The second colossus danced on its pedestal and then chose immolation like its mate, Taurmenios sacrificing himself to himself.

The liquid rock oozed across the harbor mouth and closed it with a great ridge of steaming slag.

Andrion stared blankly for a moment, his lips shaping silent epithets. So you test me again, and again. He shook his head, trying to jog his exhausted mind. And it produced, oddly, an image of Gard sitting on a bench by the lotus pool. Andrion winced, but followed the thought; Gard used to hunt in the marshes at the shallow end of the harbor. . . .

He slithered down the mast more quickly than he had intended, his muscles creaking with protest, his flesh impaled by splinters. "Niarkos!"

The group on the dock, staring in rapt horror at the avalanche, started at his clarion call. The sea lion lumbered about. "My lord?"

"How is the tide?"

At least Niarkos did not look at him as Jemail often had, doubting his sanity. "Flooding, my lord. Almost at the full."

"Another small favor then," Andrion responded. The glint in Dana's eye told him that she was unspooling his thought faster than he would speak it, but everyone else was now staring raptly at him. "The marshes," he called. "These merchant ships are round-bottomed, of shallow enough draft to be pulled across the marshes to the sea."

It was evidence, he thought, of the fear and desperation of the trapped people that they did not argue with him. Within moments the ships remaining at quayside had cast off and lurched through water that crunched against their bows toward the shallow, reedy area between the mainland and the far end of Al Sitar. The Sardian galley followed along the other side of the island; the ships that had already escaped set sail and disappeared into the murk.

"By all the gods," grumbled Niarkos to Andrion, "I had wanted to bring a trireme home to Sardis. But they were too big to pull across the shallows."

"We shall see one of them again," Andrion replied bitterly. Damn Eldrafel, to make him so eager to kill.

With a chunk the ship grounded against a mud bank. A few birds exploded with accusing squawks from the reeds, but most of them had fled to more congenial nesting grounds.

Niarkos swore without discrimination at his own men and at the Minran sailors who had materialized at Andrion's call. Within moments they attached ropes to the ships. Men and women alike ranged themselves like beasts of burden along the cables. They pulled, slipped and fell into the gray mud, rose and staggered on. Andrion and Dana and Tembujin pulled with the rest, groaning with effort and gasping from the foul odor released from the swamp as it was churned by many feet.

Dana began some epithet about evil smells, but did not have enough breath to finish. Tembujin went white beneath his bronzed skin and screwed his eyes with effort. Andrion's shoulders quivered. The reeds slapped him across the face; rotten vegetation buckled beneath his feet. Someone fell into a scummed pothole and had to be dragged out.

Suddenly another shoulder pressed against his and he turned, dazed, to see Miklos, stripped to his chiton, pulling beside him. "Greeting, my lord," the centurion said, as calmly as if he encountered Andrion in a Sardian avenue.

Andrion mumbled some courtesy and threw his weight again against the ropes. Other Sardians burst through the muck and joined the Minrans. Andrion could barely see the mast of the galley slowly rising and falling like a beacon before him. The marsh itself heaved. Slime splashed up his legs. A cloud of gnats spun with unerring aim into his eyes, nose, and mouth. Perhaps, he thought, the streaming sweat would wash them away.

Several small explosions echoed from Zind Taurmeni. Every ship lunged forward at once, jerked with terrified strength.

The round bottoms left huge gouges behind them, scars quickly scabbed by bubbling mud and gas.

Reeds, and gnats, and the deadening weight; Andrion was delirious with pain. It took several moments for him to note that he was not squelching in the slick mud of the marsh but was splashing in water. He peered between his lashes. His eyes uncrossed and focused upon the galley; it seemed to drift in midair as gray waves rocked it against the gray sky. Sumitra hung onto the railing, straining toward him so intently that for a moment he felt her strength soothing the burning in his arms and back, her breath blowing the fresh scent of jasmine into his laboring lungs.

He sputtered, seized sanity, and shouted, rather strangled but with spirit nonetheless, "We have reached the sea! One more effort!" And with one more effort the small ships were manhandled onto the beach, where the rising tide floated them.

Andrion crawled over the gunwale of the galley at Sumitra's side and clasped her, the spindle around which the world reeled. An apparition appeared before him; a human body plastered with mud and dirt, sweat and soot, topped by two obsidian eyes. Oh, it was Tembujin. *I must be that filthy too.* Each of his teeth wore its own coat of algae, but Sumi's kiss did not falter.

Dana leaned against the rail. She was unrecognizable except for her glassy green eyes and the disk of the shield on her back, which managed a dull but brave gleam despite its splatters of muck. Jemail hovered to the side, covered with more than a little mud himself. Niarkos bellowed from the rigging of the merchanter, organizing the flotilla. The purple sail unfurled in a splendid cascade of color, flapped and bellied. Yes, there was a wind, tentative, stained with sulfur and rot and the ghastly stench of the burning city, but a wind nonetheless.

Andrion ached as if he had been beaten. His tongue was as cracked and dry as a burned branch. His mind spun crazily about an abyss of exhaustion. He forced himself to stand upright; *no, I cannot collapse into blissful oblivion, not yet.* He laid an arm across Sumitra's shoulders, more to support himself than to reassure her. Something, he thought, had for hours now been poking his side like a thorn. He fumbled behind his belt and produced Chrysais's sardonyx amulet,

carved not in Eldrafel's image but in that of Tenebrio. Blear-
ily he stared at it.

Dana stared, too, catching what breath she had. "It
changed," she said. "Perhaps it carries some last mote of
Tenebrio's wasted power."

The amulet leered. With a curse Andrion thrust it back.

The flotilla passed Al Sitar. The harbor mouth was gone,
Orocastria was gone. A grimy cloud swirled upward, closing
the sky with a silent curtain of grit; florid light danced along
its underside like the illusory flames Eldrafel had summoned
from the pit on Tenebrio. Chrysais's funeral rites, Andrion
thought. She has taken her realm and many of her subjects
with her into the grave.

Miklos was offering him a cup of water. Clear Rhodopean
water, somewhat stale from its cask, but sparkling fresh in
Andrion's mouth. He swished the liquid around his teeth,
swallowed, found his voice. "Centurion, your orders were to
wait a month before coming after me."

Miklos cocked his head to the side like an owl. "It has
been a month, my lord. We left Sardis under a full moon, and
I left Rhodope under the next full moon."

Laughter crackled in Andiron's chest. "I meant a month
after I left Rhodope, Miklos. Under the quarter waning moon."
He eyed his officer with mock severity.

"Ah, well, my lord—I fear I misunderstood. But after the
message came from Queen Chrysais . . ."

"What message?" demanded Andrion, his humor vanish-
ing with a snap. Tembujin stopped squeezing the mud from
his tail of hair and stepped closer.

"A Minran merchant brought it to me on Rhodope. That
you and your party had been lost, shipwrecked on your
arrival. The Queen said she was concerned, my lord, about
your sword, which had been found on the beach. . . ."

Andrion's scowl stopped Miklos's words in his throat.
Solifrax hissed beneath its coating of dirt and mud. "No
wonder you came immediately. Thank you, Miklos."

The centurion bowed gravely.

"What did you do with the message?" asked Dana, eyes
wide with alarm.

"I forwarded it to Governor-General Patros in Sardis, my
lady."

"The hell you did!" she exclaimed.

Miklos returned, with emphasis, "Such was my duty, my lady."

Dana stamped the deck in fierce despair. Andrion made an impatient, placatory gesture, trying to think. So Patros, and by corollary Ilanit, thought they were dead. Of course Eldrafel would send such a message on ahead, laying the foundation for his own arrival with Gard, the heir. What is surprising, Andrion told himself sourly, is that I never realized that that was what he had done. What, by all the gods, by any god at all, will I find when I return?

"A merciful blindness," Sumitra murmured. "We had quite enough to occupy ourselves without worrying over the anguish of our friends and relatives at home."

Andrion glanced from Dana's stricken face to Tembujin's contorted features. Slowly each relaxed into a weary nod. Sumi, as usual, was right.

The ships rounded Minras's southern shore, sliding through a sea that heaved as slowly and thickly as a nauseous stomach. Only now did Andrion realize the full extent of Taurmenios's anger; the entire island was a charred hulk. Ash, smoke, and soot stretched in monstrous plumes all the way to the horizon.

The ships approached the bulge of Mount Tenebrio on the east. Andrion saw that the mountain was rent by a chasm, the one across the floor of the evil temple grossly swollen and spewing black fumes like clouds of bats. It might be early afternoon in Sardis, in Sabazel, but here it was eternal dusk.

Sardis and Sabazel. Something sparked in a crevice of Andrion's mind, and he seized eagerly upon it. "That message is for the best," he announced. "What better way to give Eldrafel the lie than to appear at his back, just as he claims the Empire for Gard?"

Dana vented a grim laugh. "Indeed, I shall appear at his back."

"I beg your pardon, my lord?" asked Miklos, not knowing those names.

Andrion dreaded explanations. Chrysais, he thought, had us lulled into complacency; a master touch, to send that message about Gath's death. Who would suspect a helpless widow of plotting the overthrow of an emperor? Andrion's breath exploded in a growling sigh. As helpless as an adder. "And have you had messages from Sardis in return?"

Miklos frowned. "No, my lord, I fear not."

Andrion inhaled to swear. Sumitra gasped and pointed back toward Minras.

Blackness boiled with dizzying speed into the sky. Lightning coruscated in the turbulence, flickering in tortured branches between sea and land. Flickering and forming into sketches, winged bulls, a gargoyle, chariots . . .

Andrion shot a look at Dana. She did not flinch. "Of course," she murmured, her voice thin and taut, "the fiery chariots that have haunted me—they are not Sardian, they warn of Sardis's destruction!"

"How could that cloud threaten Sardis?" asked Miklos.

But Andrion was chilled to the bone; this time Dana was not misled. The chariots seethed in spectral shapes, horses and drivers clearly defined, and then swept away. The cloud parted, coalesced, parted again.

An immense detonation rolled across the sea, swelling, swelling, until the sky itself reverberated with it and Andrion's head was shattered with its pressure. A shrieking wind took every ship aback, flinging every human body like spilled cargo onto the deck.

In a roiling cloud of black fire Minras disappeared. The sea shuddered and dashed itself into whitecaps. A blast of steam cleft the dark cloud with white. From the purple-sailed merchanter came a wail of dismay. Niarkos? Andrion asked himself, struggling to the rail. The sturdy sea lion, bleating like a calf?

The horizon beneath the cloud gathered itself into a mountain of water. A mountain that came rushing forward, spume like fangs upon its face. And Andrion realized what Niarkos shouted. A tidal wave. A tidal wave that would indeed destroy Sardis.

Chapter Twenty

DANA WAS NOT quite sure what a tidal wave was. But the tone in Niarkos's voice, and the sudden pallor of Andrion's lips, stirred her mind.

She saw a wall of water bearing down upon the delta of the Sar and inundating it, uprooting trees, tossing galleys about like twigs, sweeping away the port of Pirestia and throwing the remains like projectiles at the walls of Sardis. It flooded the precious irrigation wells and canals with seawater and reduced the rich farmlands to a salt marsh.

She shivered; no, such a wave would not necessarily destroy the city itself. But it could wring out its guts and leave it poor and feeble, even more susceptible to the vile blandishments of Rowan and Eldrafel; the priest-king would no doubt turn even unanticipated disaster to his own purposes.

The ocean buckled, the wave mounting higher and higher, Andrion's height, twice, thrice. Dana looked up into murky blue-green depths. The galley heeled over and stayed almost on its side for an excruciatingly long moment; Andrion held Sumitra tightly against the mast; Tembujin, Dana, and Miklos scrabbled for the rail and clung like monkeys. Here there is no shore to struggle toward, Dana thought, only the bottomless sea to devour us all. Cold droplets lashed her face and drummed across the deck. A sailor slipped and with a wail disappeared into the sea.

Just below the crest of the wave the galley wallowed upright and hung suspended, falling and yet not falling as the surge of water fell eternally forward beneath it. Divine grace, Dana's mind stammered. Do not question it. The other ships bobbed like bits of seaweed on a swell. On a swell before it encounters the shore and becomes a breaker. But no shore lay

east of Minras until the rocky shoals a day's journey from
Rhodope.

Wind howled against Dana's ears. A clean, cold, salt wind
scoured her lungs. Wind! she exulted. But this gale was not
Ashtar's breath but the rush of their movement as the flotilla
was carried eastward with breathtaking swiftness. And that,
Dana realized, that dark beetling blotch on the horizon was
Eldrafel's trireme riding the same wave. Damn the man, or
demon, or whatever he was! We escaped, and yet he goes
before us like a shadow cast by the setting sun!

Water burbled and seethed beneath the bow of the galley.
Wood and rope labored, groaning, but not one human voice
uttered a sound. The purple sail flapped thunderously and
ripped from top to bottom once, twice, until it became streaming purple pennons. Purple pennons waving above Bellasteros's
gold pavilion, above Andrion's gold pavilion; Dana's thought
shrieked like the tortured air. Her white-knuckled hands kneaded
the railing in a paroxysm of terror and elation mingled. The
shield sang a fierce paean to wind and water, and to the
profound silence beyond. Shock, she told herself, squeezing
oddly detached runnels of reason from her mind; her consciousness was sustained like the ships by a thread of time
that spun out and out and out until reality faded into eternity.

The wave swept on. The sky lightened, becoming an elusive silver rose. The curtain across the sun thinned into gauze
and then vanished. The great red disk touched the horizon and
saluted it with a splash of scarlet. Scarlet pennons. Scarlet
and purple. It was evening. Dana gasped for breath and
woke.

The remote shape of the trireme vanished into gathering
darkness. Someone shouted, intruding words into the rush of
air and wave. The sea ahead of the wave was sucked back
toward it; just breaking the surface was a line of rocky shoals
like ruined stone walls. Rhodope? Dana asked herself. That
was the word the voice shouted. The name of Rhodope. The
wave had carried them half a month's journey in one day.
Carried like lice in the robes of the gods.

Awareness darkened Andrion's dazed eyes. Sumitra stirred.
Tembujin muttered something about horses and camels. Miklos
twitched beside him, but Jemail continued to clutch a hatch
cover as if married to it.

Something prickled in Dana's mind, down her neck and
along her shoulder blades. The shield emitted a quizzical

chime. This wave might not destroy Sardis, but it would annihilate Rhodope, Sardis's ally. The flotilla might be swept around the island, or it might be dashed into splinters of wood and bone against Rhodope's shore.

Dana's thought wrenched with the birth pang of a desperate certainty. She lurched from the rail and seized not Andrion's arm but his belt. There, the sardonyx amulet. She held it up, gold and white glinting with its own fell light. The tiny twisted face seemed to laugh.

"Ah!" Andrion croaked, his voice soggy but his mind plunging after hers. "The last mote of dying Tenebrio's power, to appease the last wrath of dead Taurmenios!"

He secured Sumi's hands on the mast. Solifrax flared from its sheath, steaming in the sea spray. The shield yanked Dana's arm upward. She threw the amulet against the embossed star, and the star snapped in its own rain of silver droplets. Andrion's wrist flexed, and Solifrax speared the miniature gargoyle through its stony heart and crushed it against the light of the shield.

It emitted a piercing alien scream and wriggled between blade and shield. An icy wind pealed down from the east, dashing against the towering wave and its accompanying gale. The water was struck into foam. The wave faltered, shivering into fissures, embankments, towers of liquid. The ships tossed and spun crazily, and Dana and Andrion fell together toward the rail.

The gargoyle's cry trailed into nothingness. The wind intensified. The ocean heaved, convulsed, and began ponderously to spin. Dana's damp, gritty hair whipped across her face and she shook it away. Whirlpool, her thought shrilled. A whirlpool large enough to swallow the entire fleet, sides glassy gleaming blue-green eyes watching, waiting. . . . Her thought cracked like lightning. So did Solifrax. As one, she and Andrion threw the shard of sardonyx into the maw of the sea.

And were flung back in a tangled pile against the mast as the ship turned upside down. No, Dana thought, peering out from water-prismed lashes, no, we only took a breaking wave. She was drenched, chilled to the bone, her body only tatters of flesh about her will. But the huge wave was gone, and the sea, while dancing in torment, no longer cowered before the wrath of the god.

The wind from the east purled through the rigging, carrying

the elusive odor of anemone. "Thank you," Dana wheezed, "thank you, Mother."

The shield burbled and fell silent. Andrion sheathed Solifrax with a sigh and hugged Sumitra and Dana both.

I shall laugh, Dana thought dazedly. I shall cry. I shall howl hysterically. But she was drained, and could only cling shamefacedly to Andrion, resting her face against his sepia-stubbled cheek. His body quivered next to hers. Sumitra's lustrous gaze lay softly upon her. Does she hate me for loving him? But she is incapable of hatred. And Sabazel does not demand that I hate her.

A shadow swelled along the western rim of the sea, night rising from the grave of Minras, not from the east. For a moment a rainbow arched overhead, cruelly indifferent. Then it winked out. Shadow consumed the sky. The disheveled flotilla struggled on toward Rhodope.

A crescent moon, the evening star a sparkle at its tip, followed the sun down a lurid western sky. Sumitra considered them and what they symbolized; sword and shield, Sardis and Sabazel, Andrion's necklace. She glanced at him through her lashes.

No messages had waited on Rhodope. Even after two day's rest and food, after a shave and a haircut and several baths, his cheekbones were as harsh as cut stone, his expression so tight that deep lines bracketed his mouth and eyes. His eyes in the crimson twilight smoldered.

"No," Dana said wearily in answer to his question, "we only caused the destruction of Minras because we would not bow our necks meekly to Eldrafel's blade. It was he who unleashed the wrath of Taurmenios, as he meant to unleash Tenebrio."

"He underestimated the power of Taurmenios," reflected Andrion, "and overestimated the power of Tenebrio."

"Who overstayed his welcome on Minras, I daresay." Tembujin slapped lacquer on the bow presented to him by the governor of Rhodope, his face concealed by his fringe of hair, his gestures as taut as his bowstring.

Did the generations of gods pass as did the generations of men? Sumitra asked herself. But to that she had no answer. A breeze, the last remnant of the mighty wind that had laid the wave, wafted over the shore.

"That amulet," Andrion said. "It did have some power in

it. But it could not have been too much a part of Eldrafel's plot, or he would never have abandoned it."

"Khalingu's tongue!" Tembujin muttered. "The entire island is destroyed, and still Eldrafel is not dead!"

Dana wiped the shield in her lap; carrying it, she had refused a bow and taken a sword instead. "The amulet did not enspell Chrysais, Andrion, if that is what you think."

"She bought her choices," Sumitra said, "and paid for them."

Andrion shook his head sadly. With a sigh Dana, too, gazed up at the heavenly necklace, her face shimmering with its implacable beauty and with the rippling clouds of the Sight. "Gard thinks he caused the destruction by his desperate prayer for intervention in the arena."

Sumitra grimaced with pity. The child was force fed maturity; she pleaded that he would have a strong enough stomach to survive. Andrion's crisp profile softened. He reached from his chair, captured Sumi's hand, kissed it. The baby in her belly tried a slow somersault, and despite the solemnity of the moment, she smiled.

"Gard lives then?" Andrion asked Dana.

"The wave cut half a month from our return trip," Dana replied, "but it did the same for Eldrafel, and Gard and Rue with him. He will be on the mainland before us, Andrion."

"Eldrafel has to take the Empire now," said Sumitra quietly, "or he will have no realm at all."

"If his father Tenebrio was the source of his power," offered Tembujin, "then surely his power has been greatly dissipated with Tenebrio's death."

Sumitra said, "He used his power as he used everything, extravagantly; has he not used it up?"

"I hope so." Andrion's fingertips drummed on the sheath of Solifrax, raising small whorls of light. Red evening faded into a night dusted with silver, servants moved along the porch of the governor's mansion lighting lamps, and Ashtar spread her stars across the sky. Even here the stars were slightly smeared, tentative, and the sea breeze was tainted with ash and decay.

The zamtak, still wrapped by its piece of tapestry, lay beside Sumitra's chair. Despite the delirium of their arrival on Rhodope, she had remembered to thank Dana for saving it. But grave Dana had shrugged gratitude away. Sumitra picked up the instrument, slipped off the covering, began to tune it.

The tiny trills and plinks formed a minor melody, repeating the note of the breeze. Below the prominence where the mansion stood, the sea intoned a harmony to the music.

Just music. No purpose but to express a moment of peace before the struggle began again. Miklos and Niarkos, aided by a bemused Jemail, were even now preparing the Sardian legion stationed here to return home. As they settled the Minran refugees here. Only a few refugees, a tithe of the population of the once prosperous island. Sumitra essayed a brief jig but her fingers slipped on the strings, producing an uncomfortable twang. A plaintive ballad, yes, that would do. Solifrax sighed like embers settling. The shield ran with faint, distracted rivulets of light. Like Dana's eyes, the silken sheen of moon and star not quite smoothing the troubled soul beneath.

Sumi's hand stroked the zamtak, calmly, calmly—the Empire is Andrion's, and Andrion's it will remain—the gods test him, they goad him, but he has never betrayed them, and they will not abandon him. . . .

Dana's face twisted, not in pain but in labor. "What do you see?" Andrion asked quietly. Tembujin laid down his bow and bent forward to listen.

Her voice floated on the music, a melodic parody of the evil words she repeated. "Sabazel must be the home of witches; true women are too foolish to rule a kingdom. And they must consort with demons. Why else would they seal their borders so tightly, if not to hide evil secrets?"

"Many men have been received there graciously," Andrion snorted, "although they want only to amuse themselves; in their shame they are likely to believe such lies, are they not?"

"No men, no children," snapped Dana. "I would wish to receive no men at all." But the shield spattered wry light motes, as did Dana's eye.

Just music? Sumitra asked herself. Her fingers thrilled on the strings, drawing Dana's voice to continue, drawn to Dana's continuing voice.

"The spells of Sabazel are devious indeed. The conqueror Bellasteros himself was subverted. Lord Andrion his son was tainted by its wiles. But they are free now, safe in the wings of Harus, who shall protect them in the hereafter from the poisons of the demoness Ashtar."

Andrion growled some epithet.

"By the wiles of the Sabazians the barbarian Khazyari

were offered peace, and given the land good men bled to defend. Lord Andrion, rest his merciful and honorable soul, was blinded by the witches, and did not see his own sister Sarasvati corrupted; he did not realize what blasphemy he uttered when he wished to make her half-breed child his heir. But he is free now, protected by the wings of Harus from the poisons of Ashtar.''

Tembujin's face hardened. The litany of hate went ineluctably on. ''Sardis and the Empire have suffered drought and pestilence because the kings who rule them have been ill as well. But soon there shall be a new king, Andrion's true nephew, innocent of the guiles of Sabazel, fresh and unspoiled. And with him he will bring a new god. The living god, from the purple depths of the sea. He shall scour the land clean and restore it to health; we must prepare ourselves for his coming.''

''How can anyone believe such tripe?'' Tembujin snarled. ''Even if that fat little hypocrite had dosed everyone in the Empire with some evil herb. . . .''

''I think Rowan has long since supplanted Bonifacio,'' Andrion scowled. ''He would need to dose only a few magistrates and priests. The people were already ailing, and their king in his uncertainty abandoned them.''

Sumitra sent a spray of melody over him, soothing him. ''You had to leave the Empire, my lord, so that you can now return.''

He offered her a taut smile, the sinew in his jaw snapping.

''Hail Rowan, the right hand of Tenebrio. He shall lead us to celebrate the coming of the god—we shall reclaim the diadem, the power of the emperor, that was so vilely stolen by the demon-women—we shall avenge their corruption of Governor-General Patros, who was enspelled by their queen to give his only legitimate daughter, Valeria, to a Khazyari. We shall root them from our midst, slay them all in the name of Harus, throw down the walls of their sorcerous citadel and sow their fields with salt.'' Dana gasped at her own words, and choked on the horror of it. ''Two legions,'' she whispered, ''gather on the borders of Sabazel.''

Sumitra's hand fell with a tooth-wrenching discordance from the strings. Her mind spun between disbelief and fearful certainty. Why should I be loyal to Sabazel? she asked herself. And she answered, Sabazel has never hurt me. Sabazel gave me Andrion.

"Waste Sabazel in the name of Harus?" exclaimed Andrion. "If they do such a thing, they will be irrevocably committed to evil!" His hand slapped Solifrax against his thigh, emitting circles of light and sound, a martial drumbeat beneath Dana's voice.

Dana crouched over the shield in her lap, her face drained of color by its pale, stubborn glow. Tembujin rose to his feet with an oath, strung his bow, twanged the string. The note quavered down the wind, and the zamtak chimed in reply.

Dana leaped up with a cry, as if stabbed in the back. The shield pulsed with pinwheels of light, but her eyes went glazed and flat. "Patros!" she called. her voice spun out and snapped. "Patros," she moaned, sinking again into her chair.

Andrion reached for her. "What, what is it?"

"Now," she choked. "Right now, as we sit here, now." She closed her eyes, turning away from Andrion's hand. "He sits quietly with Kleothera and Declan in his tent, eating a thin soup—he will eat nothing that Kleothera has not prepared with her own hand, and they will give him little. Gods, how he has aged, torn by his loyalties—he came with the army to try and stop it, to speak reason to the commanders, but too many of them look through him and do not hear." A tear sparked on her cheek.

"He wrote to Ilanit, warning her, and sent the message by a legionary—the ranks, Andrion, the ranks are confused and wary but not yet corrupt—Rowan sniffed the man out, caught him and read the message. He comes, like Rue, bloated with zeal and righteousness, and Bonifacio behind him puffed and pitiful—but I cannot pity him.

"No! They accuse Patros of treason, of collusion with Sabazel—father, deny it—no, he will not, he denounces Rowan. My brave, my foolish father!" She gulped and steadied. "They drag him from the tent. Kleothera rises, indignant, queenly, Declan in her arms. Bonifacio whispers to Rowan, that the babe was born in Sabazel to—to Andrion's whore; Rowan smiles and pulls a dagger from his robes!" Dana leaped up, raising the shield, screaming in mortal anguish, "No, not my child! No!"

Sumitra's heart clenched, squeezing the breath from her body. In one smooth bound Andrion was at Dana's side, Solifrax a gleaming arc across the glowing surface of the shield. The star burst in brilliance. A wind stirred the stars in

the sky so that they chimed. Servants peered astonished from
the doorways of the mansion.

Dana swayed and Tembujin caught her, easing her back
into her chair. "The lamp," she wheezed. "The hanging
lamp in the tent. A gust of wind has dashed it onto the desk,
and the maps, the papers are flaming—pure white-hot flame
licking Rowan's robe. He retreats. Voices, and running feet
from outside, and Bonifacio burrowing into the canvas. Run,
Kleothera, run!"

For a moment the silence was so deep that the susurration
of the sea reverberated across the terrace and shattered against
the wall of the palace. The cresset guttered into pennons of fire.

"Valeria," Dana said. Tembujin started. "Valeria looks
from her own tent, clutching her children to her skirts. She
sees Kleothera, Declan clasped screaming to her breast, racing through the camp. No one knows what has happened. No
one stops her."

Solifrax guttered like the torches and faded. With a mourn-
ful tremor the shield quieted. "Kerith," cried Dana. "Kerith
and a patrol are lurking outside the camp. They take Kleothera
and the babe, they rush into the darkness with them." She
swayed, as if herself clinging to a saddle. "They will be safe
behind the Horn Gates. For now."

"No sentries?" Andrion demanded, in a voice that had
made many a soldier cower. "No patrols?"

"And Valeria?" prompted Tembujin. "And my children?"

Dana's brow was clammy white, her eyes glossed with
tears. "Centurions mutter among themselves, disturbed. Patros,
loyal Patros—they cannot believe him treasonous. They cannot believe his daughter Valeria treasonous, and her children,
though half-breeds, are only children." Even her lips went
white. "Forgive me," she murmured to Tembujin's metallic
face. "I repeat what I hear. And I hear, I see . . ." Slowly
her seared face relaxed. "Astra, my lovely Astra, will soon
peer at baby Declan and ask why in the name of the goddess
has he been returned!"

The sea muttered uneasily below them and the wind set the
stars to dancing. Sumitra looked from face to face, seeking
reassurance, but saw none. In the faint light of the shield
Dana's cheeks were streaked with drying tears; "I acknowledge my father," she whispered to herself, "I acknowledge
my sons; forgive me." Tembujin's mouth was crimped so
tight his lips were hidden, and his tail of hair rippled like a

war banner in the wind. Andrion tested the edge of Solifrax against his thumb and smiled a grim, humorless smile.

The child moved again below Sumi's heart, and she set her hand on the mound of her belly. There, there was the comfort. "The wind turned back the wave from Sardis," she said quietly. "Irony, that Ashtar should save Sardis when Sardis so threatens Sabazel."

"It is not Sardis that threatens," said Andrion. "It is Eldrafel and Rowan. They use Sabazel to conquer Sardis, and through it the Empire."

Tembujin muttered an outraged, "Half-breeds!"

The zamtak trilled faintly. Sumi glanced down at it. The tapestry was crumpled beneath its edge. She picked up the cloth and smoothed it out. "Look!" she exclaimed. "The pattern has changed!"

Three faces bent over her shoulder, green eyes, brown eyes, black eyes. Yes, the image was subtly different. Nikander's stitched face looked out of the picture; in the uncertain light the image seemed to nod the proconsul's calm and stoic assurance. Behind him fluttered scarlet pennons. Beside him his legion welcomed a squad of Khazyari cavalry from Iksandarun. Every face was turned toward a faint lavender peak crowned by a crescent moon with a star at its tip; Cylandra, calling Andrion home.

"Tomorrow," Andrion said, "we shall not sail so far east as Sardis. We shall sail directly to the coast at Bellastria, my father's old camp, where he first met my mother. Eldrafel has arrived too soon upon the scene; Sabazel has not been conquered, cannot be laid before him as a prize, will not serve to bind the army to him." And with a dry laugh he added, "Tenebrio never was fed his proper sacrifice, was he? No wonder he failed, as his son—"

A rush of wings interrupted him. As one they turned. There, on the edge of the rooftop against the sky, sat a falcon, preening its feathers unconcernedly. But its eye sparked more brightly than the stars.

Andrion saluted. "As his son Eldrafel will fail."

At dawn the legion left the shore and the town of Bellastria and climbed the escarpment that defined the tangled river bottom of the Jorniyeh. At dusk it camped on the flank of the high plains sacred to Ashtar. Scouts rode on, into the glare of the sunset, threading the fissures of land that lay like a grassy drape below Sabazel.

Andrion stood on a rocky prominence, on granite, not the tremulous black rock of Minras. "You are sure?" he asked Dana.

She allowed him one quick green gleam of amused disdain.

Andrion's ears still rang with the shouts of the people of Bellastria. Where Eldrafel, he had quickly learned, had landed the day before, and from whence he had plunged like a rapist toward Sabazel and the climax of his lust for power.

In Bellastria Andrion had seized a moment's grace and presented Niarkos with Eldrafel's abandoned trireme. During his tour of inspection the sea lion had been as voluble as a delighted child, while Jemail's lugubrious face had nodded attendance, his own reward still theoretical.

Andrion set his hand upon the humming hilt of Solifrax. His gut was hollow, seething with molten rock, hot and heavy. He told himself for the hundredth time, Eldrafel in his bravado comes too soon. The legions are not yet corrupt. They have not yet fought Sabazel. They will not obey if ordered to fight their brother legions.

Or would they? Andrion slapped Solifrax against his thigh. It shot fiery streaks through his body. If Eldrafel, in his sublime self-confidence, had acquired a habit of underestimating, Andrion, ruminating on his doubts, had not.

The wind stirred with the faint flavor of musk and smoke. The Sardian legions lapped like a noisome tide at the very gates of Sabazel's city, despoiling the fields and the flocks and the wind itself. Incredibly, they still posted no sentries; whatever Eldrafel was, he was no military leader. Even though he believed the rightful emperor to have perished on Minras, Patros to be safely leashed, the legions sufficiently rotted— gods! My finely honed legions, blunted!

Solifrax, hot against his flesh, was as sharp as a razor. As was his patience. "He is coming?" he asked.

"Yes." Dana stared into the twilight, her eyes glittering like beacons warning intruders away from the stony borders of Sabazel. Her features were drawn thin, her flesh so gnawed from within it stretched transparent over her bones and revealed the spirit beneath. On her arm the shield pulsed with an insistent music, exchanging resonances with the wind. Solifrax murmured restively in its sheath.

Andrion glanced over his shoulder, toward the east and the

oval nacreous moon that watched, aloof and unstained, while
the caldron of the western horizon bubbled with purple, mauve,
scarlet, Rexian dye swirled with blood.

"Soon?" he asked again.

"Soon!" Dana snapped.

Tomorrow would rise the full moon of mid-winter. The day
of birth, Andrion thought, the day of battle. I shall be twenty-
six tomorrow. When my father was twenty-six, he had not yet
met my mother.

Had Rowan hinted to the legions that Andrion, that
Bellasteros, were sons of Sabazel, and therefore to Sardian
eyes bastards undeserving of the diadem? If Chrysais had
known the truth, then so did Eldrafel.

But Eldrafel found it easier to claim Andrion dead than to
discredit him; if anyone had earned the diadem, Andrion had,
and the legions knew it. He would gamble on that, as he
would gamble on Eldrafel's strength having been sapped by
the unexpected devastation of Minras, as he would gamble on
his arriving too early, before decay had quite eaten away
loyalty. . . . His thought came full circle and chewed its tail.

"There!" exclaimed Dana.

Solifrax skreeled. Andrion started forward. Hoofbeats rang
down the wind. Across the waves of golden grass floated a
black spot that swiftly became a galloping black horse.
Andrion's heart leaped. "Ventalidar!" he shouted. "Here I
am, boy; come to me!"

Dana said, "They led him out caparisoned with your armor, your helmet, brought from Sardis for the purpose. They
said he was to be a sacrifice to your memory, and a plea for
victory." She chuckled. "Rowan tried to ride him, you see,
and was thrown onto his face before them all."

"Good for you!" Andrion shouted to the horse. The beast
was indeed god-ridden, like his master; his escape was an
omen. Andrion grinned. Ventalidar thundered up the slope
and reared, prancing and whinnying as if to say, so there you
are. About time you returned.

Andrion caught the trailing reins and patted the stallion's
damp, pungent shoulder. One fetlock was splashed with rust;
he had struck someone down in his break for freedom. Too
much to hope that it had been Rowan himself. Ventalidar's
eye glinted in subtle equine amusement.

A spray of winter lilies, waxy white with the faint smell of
rot, hung from the armor piled on the saddle. Andrion ripped

the flowers away; hellebore, were they not? The dancing hooves mangled them into the grass.

Dana drew her sword and cut the ropes holding the armor. Yes, it was indeed Andrion's own, polished into mirrors that reflected the rippling black plume of the helmet. Andrion held up his black cloak; it billowed in the wind. A very small storm cloud indeed, compared to the angry fumes of Taurmenios. It would, however, serve.

The strands at last knit themselves into a pattern. My pattern, Andrion thought, not Eldrafel's. But the cost of that pattern had yet to be tallied; so much depended on whether the perverted legions would fight their own brothers. Surprise, a sudden reappearance as if shot from some celestial bow. . . . With confidence damping but not extinguishing his dread, he turned and led Ventalidar, Dana at his side, into the light of the rising moon.

Chapter Twenty-One

A DRY-STONE WALL snaked along the crest of the hill, the slate as skewed as the slopes of Zind Taurmeni. Behind the miniature battlement crouched Andrion and a score of legionaries, secretly eyeing the city of Sabazel.

He blinked, dazzled by the supernal clarity of the morning. His eyes seemed as sharp as a falcon's, carving precise, lapidary images of plain, city, mountain from the light. Cylandra was an ethereal sketch in silver, a pale contrast to the opulence of Rexian purple; the plains were an unadorned brown, the stone city gray. The sky was the achingly deep sapphire of Ashtar's gaze. The austere, implacable beauty of Sabazel, he thought, its magicks subtle and eternal.

The uncanny light filled his veins with liquid fire. The cold, pure wind rang his mind like a great bell with peals of confidence, and anger, and a certain salty humor.

The camp before the Horn Gate had been half concealed by a blue haze of smoke like a nuance of sorcery. Now, as Andrion watched, the quickening breeze teased the haze into oblivion. In the encampment stripped so distressingly naked trumpets brayed; centurions rode desultorily up and down straggling lines of men between tents huddled in haphazard clumps. The falcon standard of Harus drooped upon its perch before the stained cloth-of-gold pavilion. Miklos or Nikander or Patros would have had more than one officer's rank for allowing such a pathetic mockery of a Sardian camp. But Eldrafel thrived upon mockery.

There he was, a cap of gold atop a makeshift dais. Legionaries passed in review before him, their feet rising and falling as raggedly as those of a huge centipede. Andrion snarled, "God's beak, I have seen Tembujin's children march more smartly than that!"

Dana's face glowered like the shield. "He profanes Ashtar's

258

midwinter rites,'' she hissed, ''leading armed men to the Horn Gate.''

''He profanes everything he touches.''

On the dais beside Eldrafel stood two brown-robed priests. One made exaggerated flourishes and declaimed, ''Witness the living god come from the sea!'' Eldrafel bowed graciously. A half-hearted mutter of acclamation and a tentative clash of weapons warbled upon the wind. The other priest—Bonifacio, no doubt—was as squat and still as a lump of dung.

Beside the dais a cloaked woman, her jewels tiny winking eyes in the sun, stood with a boy. Gard, Andrion called silently. Gard, wake up, the end is near! A ripple of fire at his throat, and the child stirred fitfully. Rue's hands on his arms coiled like tentacles. Andrion winced. ''And Patros?'' he asked Dana.

''Tried and condemned, and spared only long enough to watch the victory.'' Her voice spattered against a reef of furious indignation.

A row of glints like bright coins were spears held ready above the Horn Gate. Twin points of copper were Sarasvati holding an insistent Astra up to see. And that gleaming helmet? Dana emitted a long exhalation, part sigh, part sob. ''My mother,'' she said. ''She has been healing ever since we—ever since the shield was recovered. She is weak, but would crawl, if necessary, to be here at this moment.''

Ilanit would, at that. ''Do they think to come out and fight a pitched battle?''

''Only men commit such foolish bravado. Better to sit out a siege.''

''But the sheer weight of the legions . . .'' Andrion saw the city burning, Danica's garden bare blackened sticks, survivors and their children hiding like goats among the crags of Cylandra. Eldrafel be damned, he carried destruction like a plague. Lord of shadows indeed.

The scene before Andrion seemed as static and stilted as a theatrical tableau. The sun blasted the substance from every figure, making each shadow only a delicate gauzy shape. Was this how the gods viewed the actions of men, joy and anguish alike only decorations upon the remote crystalline scrim of the world? Then I shall be no god, he swore, but a man, and suffer the indignities of living.

With a grim smile he backed down the slope. A mirage

shimmered on the far horizon, a long wavering line pricked by light. Nikander, as was his custom, arrived exactly when he was needed. Andrion dispatched a legionary with instructions; Nikander would need no explanations.

The waiting soldiers eyed Andrion, something of his numinous if severe glow reflected in their faces. And Miklos watched him, and Tembujin, and those men assigned to guard Sumitra. She had refused to be left behind in Bellastria, saying resolutely, "You shall win, so what worry do I have?"

"What if I lose?" he had asked, although he knew he would not.

With her own wry humor she had responded, "I would soon have no worries then either."

Sumi glowed, too, her flesh polished mahogany, her hair spun black silk, her eyes fathomless depths of certainty. How rounded her belly had become; the swirl of her gown framed that lovely bulge. "My lord," she called, "a gift for your victory." Several heralds came forward bearing banners made from the remains of the purple sail. Bellasteros had marched under purple pennons; Sumitra's perception was . . . moving.

"My thanks, my lady." Andrion cleared his throat, saluted her, turned to his officers and in a few terse words gave his orders. He climbed the hill again.

Another lackadaisical ovation echoed from that Sardian camp. This one remained silent. The soldiers, ranked in wave after ordered wave, hidden behind the ruined wall, were centered upon Andrion, Dana, Tembujin, Miklos.

Eldrafel was showing Gard like a prize animal. His sickly sweet voice wafted upward, its accent playing for effect, not for meaning, like an intoned spell. "Queen Mother Chrysais pined away after the death of her husband—boy legal heir, grandson of Bellasteros, child of the gods."

Tembujin snorted in disgust. The wind snapped like a whip.

"Gods who vouchsafe loyalty, honor, love." Andrion gagged on that voice saying those words. "Minras is more loyal to Sardis and Empire than some Sardians themselves."

Rowan strode from dais to pavilion. From its darkened interior emerged a gaunt, white-haired man, his arms folded around and tied to a wooden yoke laid across his shoulders. He was clothed in rags, and the weight of the yoke forced his back to bend, but still he stood with a quiet dignity, blinking dark disdainful eyes at Rowan as if the priest were a worm unworthy of notice.

Rowan flounced away, discomfited by that cool scrutiny. "Patros," breathed Dana. The faces above the gate quailed, and an infant's sudden wail was quickly muffled. Soldiers stood, eyes averted in shame, more like an honor guard than warders around the stern form of the governor-general.

Other soldiers trundled a cage made of sticks, like one for a hunting dog. But in this cage were children. Three dark heads clustered protectively about a fourth, the smallest; four sets of sharp, black eyes gazed with bewildered truculence upon their tormentors. A woman clung to the cage's side. Her unveiled face turned accusingly on the guard who tried to dislodge her grasp, and with an awkward bow he desisted.

Andrion's distant tableau shattered into thousands of tearing shards. Dana gasped. Tembujin remained deathly still, but from his throat came a sound like the rumble of Zind Taurmeni just before its eruption. Andrion seized the Khazyari's arm just as his body wrenched upward, just as his mouth opened to shriek an epithet, and pulled him down again. "Not yet."

"My children!" Tembujin's hoarse whisper boiled from his lips. "He has my children in a cage!"

"I can see that."

"The plot was against me at the beginning, last summer in Iksandarun; has the plot come circling back to me then? Was it all against me?"

"Do you doubt me?" Andrion demanded. "In only a few moments their ordeal will be over, I promise you."

Tembujin's eyes raked Andrion's face. No pretension, Andrion assured him silently. No conspiracy. A rash promise, yes, but . . . His heart thrummed, firing motes of power through his senses, and Solifrax strained in his hand.

Dana laid her face upon the light-roiled surface of the shield and muttered something about the fragility of borders.

Eldrafel's voice was nasal, choked by his own gelid bile. "Governor-General Patros so corrupt . . . sell own daughter to Khazyari. Sabazians admit Khazyari to sickening rites . . . collusion . . . conspiracy . . ."

Bonifacio's withered face stirred with interest. His skin seemed too big for his body, as if his vital organs had been mummified while he lived. "My father would have had him flayed for his treachery," snarled Tembujin.

"He looks as if he has already been flayed," Andrion returned. "Is it his conscience that has eaten him alive?"

Well-rehearsed, Rowan slapped Patros and jerked Valeria away from the cage, throwing her into the dust. Tembujin tensed, his shoulder shivering against Andrion's. "Wait," he repeated to himself, "wait, wait."

Patros, unperturbed, turned his back on Rowan; he narrowly missed the priest's face with the swinging end of the yoke. He tried to bend and help Valeria. The children remained silent. Strong blood, Andrion thought. Born, like me, to play this everlasting game.

Bonifacio squirmed, his hatred for the Khazyari not enough to sustain him now. "Ah," murmured Andrion, "do you feel my eye upon you?"

A mumble of dismay coursed through the legions and died away. Several soldiers moved toward Rowan, hesitated. Gard frowned at the caged children. Ethan, ever his father's son, tried a jaunty wave at the strange boy. The wind grew stronger, as cold as if emanating from an ice cave atop Cylandra.

Eldrafel stood in purple kilt, purple cloak, and turquoise, lapis, jade necklaces, the chill of the wind nothing to the cold void in his soul. "Unfortunate end of Andrion," came his incessant voice. "Drawn by Sabazian and Khazyari plot away from duty . . . unfortunate end, end of dynasty. Revenge . . ."

Rowan made a rude gesture toward the gates of Sabazel and was greeted by equally rude catcalls. Valeria regained her feet and returned to the side of the cage like a needle to a lodestone. Although she was the blood mother of only two of the children inside, she strained through the bars to embrace them all.

As Chryse, Andrion thought suddenly, had embraced Sarasvati and him both; a shame Chrysais had left her side too early to have inherited more than a mockery of her feminity.

Eldrafel assumed a grandiose pose and declaimed, "Andrion Bellasteros—we shall never see his like again!"

"Perfect!" Andrion exclaimed. "My thanks!" He leaped up. His cry was as bold and sweet as a trumpet, "Greeting, my people!" He snatched the reins of Ventalidar from a groom and threw himself into the saddle.

Eldrafel froze, so stiff that his limbs seemed to be in danger of cracking from his body. Rowan and Rue, with identical starts, spun about. Bonifacio stood staring. Gard flushed with relief; Patros and Valeria staggered with joy.

The falcon standard looked up with a flutter of wings. From the battlements of Sabazel came suspicious mutters. Every face in the assembled ranks turned, wave after wave like the swiftly unfolding petals of a flower, toward Andrion.

Deliberately he pulled the reins. Ventalidar reared, hooves scything the air. Deliberately he drew Solifrax and thrust it upward in salute. The sword gathered the sunlight, flashed blindingly, chased even the wisps of shadows into nothingness.

Ventalidar bounded down the hill. A halo surrounded horse and rider; black plume rippled, black cloak snapped, bronze armor and black coat shone. Each prancing hoofbeat reverberated like a clash of cymbals in the wind. The purple pennons streamed on the hilltop, beside row after precise row of soldiers. Sumitra and her guard crept forward to the crest of the hill, and at her insistent gestures, down its near side.

Dana mounted and stood in her stirrups, shield raised. The embossed star swirled and then burst in a light equal to Solifrax's. Screams of joy echoed from the walls of Sabazel, as did a thundering roll of javelin butts against stone. Tembujin glanced at his family, eyes and mouth slitted, spat an oath and leaped onto the nearest horse. He sprinted toward Nikander's advancing troops.

Some of the legionaries shambled to attention. Others stood with their mouths open, struggling toward understanding.

Eldrafel assumed his usual insolent posture. But, Andrion realized with a thrill, he was indeed weakened; his complexion was not golden but sallow, his eyes were shadowed by faint purple bruises. "Shall I never be rid of you?" he asked tepidly.

"No," Andrion responded. "You wanted my interest; now choke on it."

Rowan stood at one stirrup, Rue at the other, four liquid eyes scummed with ambition raised to him. "An impostor," cried Rowan.

"The real emperor died on Minras," Rue shrieked.

"Andrion's stallion would not bear an impostor," shouted Dana, her clear voice riding the wind. "Solifrax would not shine for anyone but him."

The soldiers shifted. So did Eldrafel's smooth features. "The true emperor would not stop his legions from defeating his enemies."

"I would stop them from committing any more folly than they already have." Andrion gestured, using Solifrax as a dramatic prop so he would not have to use it as a weapon. "If the Sabazians had brought pestilence upon the land, would they not have spared themselves? But Sabazel, too, is ill, with the disease spread by this fiend who names himself a god. He sacrificed his own land to his greed for power, and now he would sacrifice ours."

The legions were listening. Eldrafel stood hands on hips in overblown indulgence. Andrion had to respect the man for facing the last tatters of his plot so unflinchingly. But then, his pride would not admit that it was the end. If he had been content with Minras, if he had not been hounded by his own divinities into overreaching . . . Andrion shook himself. It was too late for pity.

A distant grumble of hooves and marching feet echoed like thunder down the wind. Andrion lowered the sword. Every eye lowered with it, to fix upon Andrion's face. "Follow this hideous perversion of a man and defeat Sabazel. Then he will blame our ills upon the Khazyari. After the legions squander themselves defeating the Khazyari, who will remain to defend Sardis and Empire?"

The ranks muttered. "The diadem," said Eldrafel, sarcastically dulcet, "was stolen by the Sabazians. How can they mean no ill when they hold that sacred relic?"

Andrion smiled, with such relish that Eldrafel stepped back a pace. "Sabazel keeps the diadem safe from dirty, grasping hands. They will give it to him who deserves to wear it." He turned to Gard.

The boy's clear gray eyes were as bright as a burnished blade, and as merciless. "For a few more months," Andrion told him quietly, "you are my heir. Go to the gates of the city and bring me the diadem."

Eldrafel maintained his attitude of elaborate indifference. Rue and Rowan hissed like twin adders. Dana urged her horse forward, shoving them aside; she scooped Gard onto the saddle and covered him with the shield. The necklace of the moon and star twanged like a bowstring. The shield chimed. With a derisive toss of her head at Eldrafel, Dana cantered to the Horn Gate, the boy sitting tensely upright before her.

Rowan shouted, "Of course Andrion would claim the support of Sabazel. He is one of their bastards, not the son of Bellasteros at all!"

"So," Andrion said between his teeth, "you play that game. And I grow so very tired of that game." He summoned a herald. Decisively, defiantly, he told the man what to proclaim.

Sumitra's eyes sparked. Miklos suppressed an ironic smile. The herald, with appropriate flourishes of his trumpet, called, "Be it known that Danica, queen of Sabazel, bore Bellasteros the conqueror, King of Sardis, Emperor, a son. And that son is named Andrion, beloved of the gods, favored by Harus of Sardis and Ashtar of Sabazel with the power to preserve both lands and the Empire as well!"

"My fealty to Andrion Bellasteros, Emperor!" called Patros.

"And mine!" Miklos shouted.

Scarlet pennons glanced around the shoulder of the hill. Nikander and his aides advanced as calmly as if on parade. "And mine," said the pronconsul's dour voice, the words dropping like stones down a well.

"Thank you," Andrion returned, with as courtly a bow as possible on horseback. Ventalidar stamped his approval. The subverted soldiers realized they were bracketed by two other legions; their ranks contracted. It was hardly the moment to dispute Andrion's birth.

The Horn Gate opened a crack, admitted Dana, and a moment later released not only her but an honor guard, led by Kerith armored to the brows and Sarasvati clad in simple shirt and trousers, bearing the radiance of gold in her hand.

Andrion saw Eldrafel's hands flex in frustration, grit seeping under his pearly carapace. Rowan summoned several Minran soldiers from behind the dais. Sumitra played a trill of notes upon her zamtak, or perhaps the wind trilled in Andrion's ears, or perhaps it was only his own blood pounding, throwing his thoughts forward like waves breaking upon a shore.

The mob of soldiers muttered, each soldier, each officer groping through his individual nightmare. Faces turned from Andrion to the advancing party of Sabazians to the legions around them, harrowed by understanding.

"My army will fight yours," purred Eldrafel, for Andrion's ear alone. "Whoever wins is in the right."

"You have no army," Andrion returned loudly, so that all might hear. "These legions are mine. I shall not amuse you by wasting my own people against each other." His voice lilted on the low notes of the zamtak, certainty played by Sumi's demure steel hand. "My father outlawed ordeal by combat the day I was born. But if that is what will defeat you, then I myself shall fight you hand to hand. And he who is in the right shall win!''

Bonifacio's face convulsed as though he were an imbecile trying to spell his own name. Rue darted a malicious glance from Andrion to Dana to Sumitra, a cornered animal wondering where to strike first. Her eye caught her brother's, and as one they licked their lips.

"And you will use your pretty toy sword against an unarmed man?" scoffed Eldrafel. "What then will you prove to your army?"

"That you are far from unarmed," Andrion replied. He dismounted and leaped lightly onto the dais. Solifrax, upraised in threat, sang. His body sang, luminous with power and passion.

But Eldrafel, a cold, sterile husk, did not move. "You will not strike first," he crooned. "O man of honor, you will not strike first."

Andrion's mind was a prism, it seemed, at one moment coalesced into brilliant awareness, at the next spinning into individual reflections. He was drunk, and yet he had never been more lucid.

He saw Bonifacio scuttle off the dais and be caught short by a thicket of Sabazian javelins. "Shall we go pig-sticking?" asked Kerith.

Dana replied, "Not quite yet." She drew her sword.

Gard's solemn mien did not change. The boy's eyes were genuine, Andrion thought, and Eldrafel's counterfeit. Sarasvati's hair flamed in the sunlight, like the red highlights in his own hair, like Gard's smooth chestnut crown, like the purple and scarlet pennons ranged about the disheveled camp.

Rowan hissed. The Minrans drew their swords and sprinted toward the cage. Valeria flattened herself against its side. Patros stumbled toward her. "Tembujin!" Andrion shouted from the side of his mouth.

But the earth already vibrated to a roll of hoofbeats and a fierce war whoop. Khazyari cavalry burst from behind Nikander's legion. Tembujin leaned low, bow singing. The leader of the Minrans spun and fell, an arrow protruding from his chest; the others quailed. Small voices chorused, "Father! Father!"

Tembujin, another arrow already nocked, grinned maliciously at Rowan. "Come! Come and fight honestly, face to face!"

The priest retreated into the ranks of soldiers. Nikander gestured and several of his troops ran forward to release the prisoners. Valeria sagged into the milling children. Patros, grimacing as he moved his cramped muscles, handed them all into the pavilion. Tembujin and his men sat frowning, bows ready, watching Andrion.

Andrion knew that they watched, knew the lines of each face that watched him as if he himself had sketched them with light upon matter. And yet he saw only Eldrafel, face frostily impassive, a mist muting his icy glitter. Andrion blinked. Sorcery—Solifrax burned, and Eldrafel's shadow rippled away from him. Rippled, changed, and reformed. . . . Andrion braced himself.

Eldrafel struck. A blaze of darkness broke against the blade of Solifrax. Andrion leaped aside, stung as if with a spray of ice needles. Just needles, not deadly bolts. A shout echoed from the legion, buffeting his back. Another dark flood, another spatter of light and shadow. The pain was invigorating; now they see, he thought. Now they see what he is.

But his sight grew thicker and thicker as the reek of sorcery encompassed him. Even as he knew the sun shone brilliantly, his eyes were clotted with smoke and ash into a murk like a Minran dusk. Solifrax was a wisp of luminescence, as puny an artifact as it had been during the last cataclysm of Taurmenios.

Eldrafel stepped, turned, stepped again, dancing with the shadows he created. Andrion parried, each movement refined to the sparest gesture, squinting through the gloom. The tension between them wove an intricate pattern of rushing shadow, of spilling light, twining, snapping, and coiling again.

Nikander mounted Patros on his own horse even as neither eye strayed from the combatants. Sumitra stood entranced, her zamtak clutched to her breast, while her escort muttered and Rue circled behind her. Rowan threaded his way through the legions, whispering lies so subtle they seemed to appear spontaneously from the sorcery-tainted air. Dana and Kerith, Sarasvati and Gard dismounted and ranged the edge of the dais.

Tembujin's frown deepened until every line in his face curved downward. He urged his horse through the unresisting soldiers.

The wind whined. Andrion heard it, felt its icy blast stirring eddies in the stench, could not respond to it. The prisms of light in his mind reflected distorted images of the faces around him, faces elongated into sneers like those on the face of Tenebrio. . . . The prisms shattered, and each emitted a cloud of darkness.

I am strong, gods, gods, no sorcery can baffle me! Solifrax flamed, and the shadows guttered, discomfited. Eldrafel snarled, his teeth gleaming between his lips. Neck, Andrion thought, spinning to the side. Neck and leg. Eldrafel spun too. His clothing, as darkly purple as a thunderhead, swirled around him, spreading smoke upon the air.

An infant shrieked, far far away upon the walls, the note piercing the haze gathering upon Andrion's thought. His mind ignited. He saw Eldrafel, and himself dancing to Eldrafel's lead. He saw Rue circling behind Sumitra, her hand reaching inside her gown. He saw Dana start violently at the baby's cry. He realized Tembujin was calling to him, urgently, right at his side, "Andrion! Do you see darkness? There are only ashes in his hand, cinders and wrack, feeble illusion!"

Rowan rushed toward Andrion's back, dagger upraised, Minrans and a few corrupt legionaries at his back. Sarasvati swept Gard aside. The star-shield leaped up and rang like a huge gong. Dana's sword struck, and Kerith's javelin with it, in perfect synchrony. With a hideous garbled cry Rowan fell. His armband sizzled into cinders; Rue snatched hers off with a wail of pain. The Sabazian guard struck down those men, Minran and a handful of Sardians, who threatened them. The watching legionaries opened an arena around them but did not raise their own weapons.

Andrion threw back his head, grinning fiercely. No shadows. Rowan impaled on sword and javelin like a fly upon pins, eyes glazed in death. His own friends, his people, steadfast. He lunged and Eldrafel pirouetted.

The demon's face warped; his hand leaked darkness, but Andrion did not try to parry it. Stung, he laughed. The smoke and shadow thinned. "You grow weak," he said. "You have gone too far, tried too much, asked more than that corpse your father had to give."

Rue jerked a dagger from her gown and fell upon Sumitra. The escort started. Sumi instinctively struck back. With a clangor of tearing strings the zamtak struck Rue on the shoulder. Bone and wood both fractured; the erstwhile serving woman fell to the ground with a cry and was surrounded by swords. Sumitra shot one quick appalled but gratified look at Rue—her nemesis, felled at last—before turning back to Andrion, the zamtak only an irrelevant bundle of wood and wire in her hands.

Tembujin nocked an arrow. Dana leaped onto the dais, shield raised. Andrion lunged again. Eldrafel spun from one to another to another. His features melted and ran, their perfection distorted into a grotesque parody of themselves. Shadows dribbled from his fingertips.

With a snarl he turned his back. Not surrender, never surrender—lofty contempt for the gnats that annoyed him in this world. . . . Simultaneously Tembujin fired and Dana struck, scoring both legs. Eldrafel shrieked. His face twisted even further, becoming unrecognizable. Slowly, slowly, the only moving object in the great silent throng, he staggered, fell to his knees, and bowed before Andrion.

Andrion's breath wheezed between his lips. His heart racketed in his chest. Now! He raised Solifrax and with all the force of his body brought it down onto the slender nape beneath the golden curls.

A shock nearly jerked the sword from his hand, his arm from his body. The nape was vulnerable, yes, and gaped with a gory wound. But the demon's head twisted suddenly around to face upward. The mouth opened in a reverberating shriek, split, peeled away. Like a huge chrysalis tearing open, Eldrafel's body emitted a monstrous shadow that swelled up and up and up, blotting out the sun, stilling the wind with a fell scream.

The shadow shaped itself into a gargoyle, bat's wings flapping, nose meeting chin in an evil leer, eyes distant shards of ice. A taloned hand grabbed at Andrion.

Andrion wrenched his wits into coherence. Solifrax fountained fire and thrust back the grasping hand. Dana stepped to his side, the shield a caldron of light. Tembujin stood calmly drawing back his bowstring and saying, "Only a little dark cloud—strike again, Andrion, and kill him!"

The shadow, Andrion saw through slitted eyes, was a spectral gray, tenuous, not like the dense smokes of self-immolated Taurmenios. The sun glancing through the cloud rained coruscating sparks upon the terrified faces of the multitude.

With a cry of his own, the name of a god, most likely, Andrion touched the sword to the shield. Lightning blasted every shape around him into nothingness. Only the shadow

remained, transfixed by light, face amazed and dismayed. . . .
A wind howled down from Cylandra, and the dark form
shredded into nothing.

At last, Andrion told himself. At long bloody last. The
faces, the pennons, the Horn Gate, the distant mountains,
wavered and solidified around him. At his feet lay a perfectly
formed human body, blond hair ruffled by the wind, gray
eyes transparent with bafflement. Andrion stared, expecting it
to putrefy before his eyes. But it remained as still and lifeless
as the marble statue it had most resembled in life.

His ears roared. No, it was the people around him calling
his name in a glorious litany, "Andrion Bellasteros, Andrion
Bellasteros!" Even an overtone of women's voices unashamedly acknowledged his title.

Dana lowered the shield. The lines in her face eased.
Sarasvati and Gard stepped onto the dais. Andrion's loyal
sister lifted the helmet from his head, letting the wind kiss his
hair; she placed the diadem upon his brow and his nephew
pressed the necklace of the moon and star into his hand. "My
thanks," he croaked. He cleared his throat, shouted, "My
thanks!" to all his people who, as weary of games as he was,
welcomed him home.

Deafening cheers, led by Patros and Nikander. A few
legionaries struck out or tried to run, but most submitted with
haggard faces to their colleagues. Thanks be, thought Andrion,
that they choose to pay in tears, not blood.

Miklos raised the falcon standard. "The emperor himself is
the god from the sea!" he exclaimed. Pandemonium. Dana's
mouth crimped, nonplussed and amused.

Very clever, Andrion thought. Someone stood beside him,
took the necklace, fastened it about his throat. Ah, Sumitra.
He was going to tremble, chilled to the marrow. But he
clasped her to his side with his free arm, and she steadied
him. The diadem tingled, and the necklace sparked, and
Solifrax hummed some satisfied tune of its own until he
seemed to stand in a swarm of bees. The blade of the sword
was unsullied, a clear crystalline crescent like a new moon.
With a sigh he sheathed it.

Kerith's features were links of chain mail. "You know the
law," she said to Andrion. "Remove these men from my
borders!"

"Kerith," Andrion returned amiably, "shut up."

Her eyes snapped, but she desisted when Dana tucked her

arm beneath her own and the light of the shield bathed her
face. "With your permission, my lord," said Dana, "we will
keep Rue with us, in Sabazel. Justice?"

"Justice," nodded Andrion. The serving woman, supported
by two Sabazians each a head taller than she, wriggled with
the slimy disgruntlement of a grub plucked from underneath
its rock and thrust into sunlight.

Bonifacio crawled to Andrion's feet. "My apologies," said
Andrion to Tembujin's dark features. "I underestimated this
creature's spite, and overestimated his virtue."

"A serpent," the priest burbled, "I nourished a serpent in
my bosom; surely the emperor in his godlike anger will see fit
to kill me mercifully. . . ."

His flaccid face brought bile into Andrion's throat. "No,"
he said, "you chose corruption, you may choose a place of
exile in which to rot. Get out." Bonifacio scrabbled at
Andrion's greaves, blubbering, until soldiers carried him away.

"I accept your apology," said Tembujin, with a half salute
that came very close to being an obscene gesture. But he
grinned as he did it.

The wind keened, the pennons bellying like sails before it.
Surely there was no scent of lotus in that clean air? Andrion
inhaled. No, there was not. It was a pure blast; the gods only
knew he needed to be purified. The voices of the multitude
were a tidal wave foaming through his mind. Above him a
falcon skimmed the vault of the sky.

Eldrafel's body lay at his feet, aloofly, incongruously beautiful. He looked closer. A maggot crawled from between the
parted lips.

He turned away and ordered, "Burn it."

Chapter Twenty-Two

ANDRION HAD EXPECTED the smoke of the pyre to be thick, black, and foul. But it was only a colorless strand, coiling up into the twilight like supplicating hands, emitting no odor at all.

"He was not truly human flesh," said Tembujin.

Andrion's consciousness was bloated by too many disparate images, too many emotions. His mind flapped painfully from thought to thought; his body was askew, borne sideways by the sheathed weight of Solifrax. He replied, "No, something of him was human flesh. See?"

Gard sat stiffly on the edge of the dais, suffering his newfound aunt, Sarasvati, to stroke his hair, which was almost the color of her own. All Bellasteros's children had red hair, Andrion told himself, a legacy of that stranger in Sabazel. Of the god, his will made flesh indeed.

Gard had watched impassively as the shell that had been his father was consumed by fire. As he had watched his entire world consumed by fire and wind and wave. It might take years before it would hurt. Until then, Andrion would hurt for him.

Tembujin said quietly, "I shall take Gard to live with me. Horses and camels to ride, and children to play with—he will heal."

"Gods," Andrion said, part epithet, part prayer. The diadem branded his brow, the necklace was a band of flame about his throat. The sun bled across the horizon, draining the sky to a clear turquoise luminescence against which every rock, every tree, stood in sharp outline. "Come," he said, and led Tembujin toward the pavilion.

The scene inside was not a divine tableau; the torches flickered and smoked and the arms were tarnished bronze.

The people who looked up at his entrance, summoning smiles to their exhausted faces, were human beings. He loved their every imperfection.

Valeria ran into Tembujin's arms; he hid his face in her hair, so that Andrion could not see the expression on it. They stood like an island amid their children, who tugged at Tembujin's breeches demanding, "What did you bring us? What did you bring us?"

Andrion smiled; their ordeal had been despite, not because of, their parents. Perhaps their impishness could in time scour those grim lines from Gard's face.

Nikander greeted Andrion with a bow. "My centurions and I thought we were mad, to be so drawn toward Sabazel. But my scouts revealed the truth soon enough. My apologies, lord, for not realizing you called." Andrion shrugged away the apology and thanked the gods for laconic Nikander. He collapsed into his own armchair, not caring if Eldrafel had sat there. It had never been his.

"Please, sit," Andrion told Patros, who dropped gratefully back into his own chair. Kleothera stood on one side, Declan's little face gurgling above her shoulder; Ilanit seated herself on the other. Patros and Ilanit were similarly gaunt and white-haired; Kleothera seemed a turtledove beside two ibis. So this was the Queen of Sabazel, her attitude seemed to say. So what if she has been my husband's lover these twenty-five years or more. Is she not a mother, and a grandmother to boot? Declan slobbered into a toothless grin as Ilanit, her grave humor undefiled, winked at him.

Sumitra seated herself at Andrion's side, regarding the ruined zamtak on her lap with an expression so mingled of wistfulness and relief that Andrion said quickly, "We shall find you another."

"Not like this," she returned. "But its purpose has been served." She set it aside, laid her sleek head against Andrion's arm, laid her hand on her stomach. "And I shall have other matters to occupy my time."

A centurion bellowed outside, and another farther away. The measured tread of a work crew approached and faded. Surely, Andrion thought, his distended head was illuminated like a lamp, his thoughts revealed for inspection by everyone before him. But then, he had nothing to conceal. Bring on the petitioners, the secretaries, the accounts. Such concerns would be as intoxicating as new wine.

Miklos stood holding the falcon standard, well content. "Have you ever had a yen for the priesthood?" Andrion asked him.

"My lord?"

"Well, I suppose there is some acolyte, from Farsahn, perhaps, who will be found to be loyal. Perhaps you would prefer a generalship."

"My lord!" Miklos grinned. "I am hardly of mature enough years."

"But surely of mature enough initiative," said Nikander.

Something odd tickled Andrion's chest. He realized it was laughter. He let it bubble from his lips.

The doorway opened. A sentry snapped smartly to attention. Dana and Kerith entered and strolled to the dais. Equal tenacity of spirit, Andrion thought, but thankfully somewhat mellowed at the moment. "Sabazel was once at the rim of the world," said Dana without preamble or honorific. "I am perturbed to find it now a Sardian parade ground."

"We shall move tomorrow, I promise."

"While sparing a few men for the winter rites?"

Andrion, to his intense discomfiture, flushed as red as the sunset. "I shall ask for volunteers," he said. And silently to Dana's bleak but somehow amused green eyes, not now, love. Forgive me.

She allowed him a wan smile. That was not what I asked, love. After Minras, I am not quite ready to recognize the demands of the body.

"May I offer you birthday greetings, my lord?" said Patros, filling an awkward silence. "And may I ask a favor?"

"Thank you," Andrion replied. "Yes, of course."

"May I have your permission to retire? You and your father have led me a merry life; have I not earned some rest?"

"Certainly," grinned Andrion. "With my compliments."

Some time later he left the voices in the pavilion—which were compelling by familiarity, not magic—to escort the Sabazians to the edge of the camp. The bonfires lit for the benefit of the work crews cast a faint blush across the indigo sky. Several soldiers watched his colloquy with the women, curious but not critical. Had he ever really feared their knowing his birth? That game was over.

The full moon, a serene white circle nestled in a silver corona, hung unstained a handsbreadth above the horizon.

The eastern face of Cylandra was spangled with its light. The shadows were so innocent as to be banal. "Would we bless the light if we had no darkness?" Dana asked.

"We hide in shadows when the sun glares too brightly," Andrion replied. "Thank Ashtar on my behalf. I shall come again soon to celebrate the rites, I promise."

He kissed Kerith's cool cheek. He embraced his sister Ilanit and his cousin Dana. He laid his hand on the simmering surface of the shield, evoking a chime. He stood, armored by diadem and necklace and sword, as the women crossed the empty ground toward the Horn gate and the torches, like distant stars, beside it.

A small shape, a child, rushed to meet them. The moonsheen picked red from her hair. Astra. Andrion lingered to see Dana sweep up their daughter, the heir to Sabazel, before he turned to his own borders and went inside.

Sumitra laid the skeins of yarn on the handiest flat surface, the top of her distended stomach, and considered them. Lustrous purple, and crimson for the sun—yes, just right. She threaded her needle with the chosen strand. The rejected skeins bounced to a thrust from underneath. She soothed the restive baby with a pat; not much longer, little one, not much longer.

From the opposite side of the tapestry Valeria laughed. "You look like an overripe melon," she said. "Surely I was never that big." Her needle flashed, pulling taut a silver strand that defined the rim of the star-shield.

"Oh yes you were." Laboriously, Sumi shifted in her chair, leaning sideways to reach the tapestry. One stitch, two; the smooth yarn between her fingers, the swoop and tug of the needle, the slow revelation of the image—a purple cloak draping the shoulders of an auburn-haired man—was deliciously mesmerizing.

The living man sat at his desk nearby. "I think Sumi has been waiting until you arrived," he told Sarasvati with a teasing smile. "All is well in Sabazel?"

"The first buds were just breaking when I left," she replied. "For such a cold, dark winter, I do believe spring has come early."

"Yes," said Andrion. His eye sought and found Sumitra's rotund form, and rested there as if admiring a work of art.

Another stitch, and another. She glanced up at him, and

around the room. Each familiar face, each ordinary object had an aura that fell upon her eye like a benison. She contemplated the play of lamplight upon texture—creamy stone, dark wood, and pale linen drapery—rich in substance, not in decoration. Rich in nuance, as different voices blended in ever-changing, ever-similar harmonies, and a cool jasmine-tinted breeze caressed her skin.

The children there, one red head bent beside the black ones over a game, small faces intelligently intent—a pattern to savor, indeed. . . . She realized the thread dangled slack from her fingers, and she smiled at herself. Her mind moved with the somnolence of her body, constantly pausing to appreciate the smallest things.

"Well," said Sarasvati, so quietly that Tembujin looked up from the dagger he honed, ears pricked, "I do have one bit of grim news. Rue miscarried of a—a monster; she cried that Queen Chrysais had cursed her, that the woman's ghost haunted her. At last we found her beneath a precipice on Cylandra, dead. I did not know if Sumi wanted the ruby stud, so I brought it."

For a moment the room was so silent Sumitra could hear the tread of the sentries outside. And yet those measured steps were more vivid than the memory of Rue's face, with or without the ruby. The tiny hole in Sumi's nostril had closed; it had been only affectation, after all. "Sell it," she said quietly, "and hold a feast for the people when the child is born."

Perhaps Valeria had no more memory of Rowan's face; she nodded, cut her thread, tied it. The shield sparked in Dana's hand, and her green yarn eyes gazed with their own truculent honesty upon the world outside Sabazel.

"So Rue killed herself," Andrion said. "I hope she took with her the last of Eldrafel's poison."

"Hey!" protested Ethan. "You moved my piece!"

"I did not," Gard retorted. "I was ahead!"

"You were not," chimed in both Zefric and Kem. The little girl watched, thumb plugging her mouth, eyes wide.

With one sharp gesture Gard upset the board. "Then I shall not play!" he shouted as the playing pieces skittered across the floor.

"Gard," said Andrion sternly. Tembujin's black eyes flashed. "Gard!" The miscreant wilted, and with lip outthrust began to rearrange the game.

Gard, King of Minras, no land, no patrimony. Sumitra's gaze intersected Andrion's. She shook her head slightly; some poison might never be cleansed. The boy had been dragged so abruptly into maturity that he had stretch marks on his soul.

He stood at her elbow, the startlingly perceptive gray eyes inspecting her sketch of Zind Taurmeni. "It was much larger than that," he stated. And, generously, "But I suppose you can only suggest it." His thick Minran accent had already taken on a Khazyari burr. He began to sort Sumitra's yarn.

"Gard?" Ethan called. "Are you playing?"

"Not now. Later."

With a sigh Andrion turned back to his desk. "I just had this letter from Patros. They have retired to a small holding outside the walls. If he can keep Declan out of his ink pot, he plans to write his memoirs."

"I cannot wait to read them," said Sarasvati.

The broad double doors opened and a secretary looked in. "My lord," he called. "Captain Jemail to see you."

"That was a speedy journey," said Andrion. "Send him in."

The hawk-nosed Minran's plumage was exceptionally fine, Sumitra thought, cloak and breeches and turban of the finest silk, and a dagger at his side encrusted with semi-precious jewels. "The caravan proved profitable, I take it," Andrion greeted him.

Jemail pulled a purse from behind his sash and laid it with a flourish upon the desk. "Your investment, my lord. I hurried back to return it with interest."

"That was a gift, Captain."

Jemail drew himself up. "I wish no debts, my lord."

"Indeed." Andrion's eyes crinkled, but he kept a straight face.

"And," said Jemail, snapping his fingers, "a gift for your lady."

Sumitra laid down her needle. Yes, Jemail had taken his caravan to the Mohan, but what—A plump, dark-eyed woman glided in the door, knelt, handed Jemail a wrapped package.

'My wife," said the Minran offhandedly as he opened the cloth. "Bought her in Ferangipur." He held up a new zamtak, the wood polished to a mirrorlike sheen and embossed with silver stars. "For you, lady."

By levering herself on the tapestry frame Sumitra managed to flounder to her feet. She took the instrument and ran her fingers over the strings. Out of tune, of course, and—well, pleasant but mundane. Thank the gods for that. "I appreciate your thoughtfulness, Captain," she said.

Jemail bowed punctiliously. His wife glanced up, her eyes not at all shy, but as firmly quiet as Sumi's. Andrion leaned back in his chair and laughed.

The bedchamber was thronged with shadows. Odd, Sumitra mused, I would have thought I would be frightened of the dark. But here, her body snugged in the curve of Andrion's, nothing was frightening.

"The new zamtak has no power in it?" he asked, his lips on her ear.

"No."

"And that pleases you?"

"Yes."

He laughed quietly. "The power is in the wielder, not the instrument. It is choice, not chance, to wield." He surrendered his doubts, she realized, as he had surrendered his irascible heroism, to domesticity.

Solifrax lay on its table at the side of the room, crowned with the diadem, quiescent. Perhaps it was the necklace that sighed to Sumi's touch, perhaps Andrion. Haunted by the echo of unredeemed lust, they made love only in long resonant silences, in embraces as still as a spring evening. Someday, Sumi thought, we shall again touch flesh to flesh, and risk again the complications of the body. Someday. And she, too, laughed. Adults as squeamish as children, experience a curse to overcome.

Andrion kissed her. "What?"

"I waited for you to rescue me, and I waited to escape, and I waited to be rescued again. This waiting now, love, is a blessing." She twitched her robe aside and laid his hand on the taut flesh of her belly. The child stretched, testing the world from the safety of the womb.

The night lamp flickered, and the shadows twirled slowly across the ceiling. Dancing, Sumi said to herself. Stitching light irrevocably to darkness, a simple pattern beyond the complex game of the gods. Just as the sword was a simple crescent, and the diadem a simple circle, and the zamtak's simple melodies could mend the raveled edges of the soul. . . . She smiled. The heart would make its own choices, seek its own level, without fear.

She dozed. Her abdomen tightened and then loosened, as it had so often recently. It tightened again. And it twisted, harder and harder, wringing the sleep from her body.

"Oh!" she said, in a breath of anguish and delight.

Andrion was instantly alert. "Yes?"

The lamplight blurred before her eyes. After a time her belly twisted once more, so consuming her consciousness that she was only vaguely aware that Andrion was at the door calling for Sarasvati and Valeria.

Dana rested her elbows upon the cold, hard rim of the bronze basin. Bemusedly she contemplated the images shifting within the depths of the water, faces caught in the purest illuminated crystal. Her mind stirred, embroidering the images with voices, with scents, with the fresh dawn breeze that dissolved the mist. Jasmine, yes; she smelled jasmine.

Sumitra lay in the great bed, eyes dark not with pain but with determined effort. Valeria dripped wine between her lips. Sarasvati probed gently and announced, "The baby is lying correctly, Sumitra. Big, strong child—twice as large as Andrion was at birth, I daresay."

Sumi, a gravid goddess, smiled serenely. Surely she, too, was touched by the gods, to heal, like Andrion, not to destroy, like . . . Dana would not let the names form even in her thought.

She saw Andrion pacing up and down the passageway, his hand knotted on the hilt of Solifrax. Helpless, his thought echoed, I am helpless, I did this to her and I cannot help her. The diadem tilted rakishly over his brow, just as he had slapped it on in the middle of the night. As he had worn it when dawn blossomed up the sky and playfully chased a new moon before it, when morning brightened toward noon.

Dana laid her chin upon her arms. The shapes were more lucid than any she had seen since—since midwinter's moon. During the spring she had had only an occasional twinge of empathy or intuition, not the blasting Sight that had both harrowed and served her during the long struggle on Minras and had at last, apparently, burned itself out. "Thank you," she whispered. Her breath rippled the surface of the water and the images danced. "I want to see this, Mother; but Mother, if you take the Sight from me forever, I will not complain."

Heresy? Perhaps. But Ilanit was slowly passing the rule of Sabazel on to her daughter, and Astra asked to lift the star-shield onto her own arm; as the seasons pass, so pass the generations of women.

Andrion released Solifrax, glancing down at the sword as if shocked to see it by his side. And what good will you do now? he asked it. He swept aside clustering attendants and burst into the bedchamber. "Women's work, my lord," a man protested. Andrion growled and slammed the door in his face.

Dana shook her head with a rueful smile. Was it so wrong, then, to love him? She had lain more than once in Kerith's arms, reassured by the tenderness of her touch and the long silences resonant with words unsaid, and had horrified herself by imagining Andrion's arms and his male body urgent against hers. Was Sabazel not enough, the presence of men only brief thunderstorms disturbing the equanamity of this blessedly mundane life?

Andrion sat beside Sumitra. As if it had been waiting for his arrival, an expulsive thrust jerked her upright. He held her, a strong arm behind her shoulders, his face wrenched with equal effort. She lay back, gasping, and their eyes exchanged a message that made Dana's heart ache, not with jealousy but with—a certain regret. She closed her eyes for a moment, and pressed her hands to her flat, echoing belly. Astra, Zefric, Declan—I need not wish for more, ever.

Sumitra rose, wrung again and again, while Valeria and Sarasvati murmured encouragement; her sweat-sheened face was both serious and rather surprised. Andrion was so pale as to be slightly green. But he set his mouth and held her upright, gently supported her, raised her again.

Noon in Sabazel, noon in Iksandarun, and the radiant sun painted brief rims of shadow around the bronze basin, around the walls of the palace and city. Sumitra cried out, not in agony but in triumph. Sarasvati exclaimed in delight and lifted the plump, wet, mottled-pale baby upward.

It was, of course, a boy. His sturdy limbs thrashed, disoriented, and his little mouth opened in a perfect O of indignation. He screamed so loudly the room rang with the cry; I am! I am! Cheers resounded from outside the room. Sumi scooped the clinging tendrils of her hair from her face and laughed a laugh tempered with tears.

Valeria laid the baby on a soft blanket. Sarasvati waited until the pulsing cord went slack, tied it off and cut it.

Andrion watched, his cheek against Sumi's hair, the rich dark depths of his eyes swirling damply.

The baby snuffled and quieted. Valeria handed him to his mother. Sumitra carefully touched the round cheeks and smoothed the sparse hair with its hint of auburn. The baby's eyes opened. They were a lush indigo, promising the brown depths of his father's gaze; they focused with cross-eyed intensity upon the gleaming diadem.

"Marcos," said Andrion, voice thick. "Marcos. Not because I would make of you a warrior, my son, but because I would wish for you the name of the man my father. And if you come in time to the surname Bellasteros, then I would have it only an honorific."

Little Marcos boggled at his father, mouth working, fist waving purposefully. He hiccuped. Valeria turned his face toward Sumitra's breast; he rooted a moment, and then attached himself so firmly that Sumi gasped with pleasure.

Dana gasped, and her own breasts tingled. For a moment Andrion looked directly at her, sensing her presence like a quicksilver shape upon the sunlight. They shared one soft smile of perfect understanding.

His image thinned and dissipated. Dana watched sun motes spiral up, up through the water, coming from some infinite depth, conveying light but no message.

She lay her forehead against the now warm metal. Tears welled within her throat; what purpose, to deny them? They glided silently across her cheekbones to drop in tiny prisms into the basin.

A touch on her shoulder. Astra said, "Are you sad, Mother?"

Dana folded the child in her arms. "No, I am not sad." The patterns of life and death were as poignantly round as the shield; never quite finding contentment, they circled back on themselves, and so reconciled the contradictions of the mind and of the flesh.

Astra's dark eyes glinted. She nodded toward the basin. "You were watching the emperor. He would not be my father, would he?"

Dana stared at the child, brows quirked. So she, too, had the Sight. Not surprising. Not surprising at all. "You are not supposed to know your father," she teased.

Astra shrugged, shook her head, and reached out to stir the water in the basin, setting the sun particles to dancing.

The heart, Dana thought, makes its own choices, fearlessly.

• • •

Andrion settled the diadem on his head, his breastplate on his chest, Solifrax at his side. Every metal surface gleamed as mirror bright as the sun-burnished sky. Spring flowers tumbled in drunken profusion from the gardens atop the palace, and chimes rang in the fretwork surrounding them. Perhaps it was the wind that chimed in his ears; it did not matter. A lark caroled above the walls of Iksandarun. The army and the people waited. The gods kept their own counsel, mute, consigned to their places in the deep echoes of the mind, and no longer, thankfully, stirring the brilliant pool that was the world.

Sumitra opened the bundle she held to display Marcos's puckered face to Gard. Gard said, "Such a mite, to be the heir of the Empire."

"Yes," said Andrion. "Nevertheless, he is."

"And he may have it," said Gard, with an emphasis that could only come from one who had seen monarchs devoured by power.

Andrion shared a glance with Sumitra. The boy's eyes were filled with light in which no shadow stirred. But in his veins flowed the blood of a god and the blood of a demon, just how uneasily mingled time would tell.

"May I go now?" Gard asked, blissfully unaware of adult analysis. His booted feet were already carrying him backward across the flagstones. "Ethan has a new pony, and he said we could play pulkashi."

"Go on," Andrion said with a smile, and the boy turned, almost colliding with Tembujin.

The Khan laughed and sent him on his way with a playful swat. "Are you ready?" he asked Andrion. He settled his bow on one shoulder, his long hair on the other.

"Yes." Andrion lifted Marcos from Sumitra's arms. A centurion called an honor guard to attention. The palace gates opened. A multitude of voices roared as Andrion stepped out, Tembujin and his lion plaque on one hand, the falcon standard on the other.

With becoming gravity a priest signaled the massed army and people to silence. "The blessing of almighty Harus upon this child," he called. "May his spread wings protect this heir to the Empire."

And vouchsafe him the power to preserve, Andrion thought. You may even, my lord grandfather, bequeath him your nose.

"In the name of the god!" called the priest, his magnanimous gesture including all gods.

Ah, Dana, Andrion thought. Very carefully he held the tiny form of Marcos up to the populace. The baby clenched his eyes, screwed up his face, shrieked. The glittering falcon standard seemed to shriek in reply, and the people cheered approval.

Andrion lowered the child and tucked him into the crook of his arm. Here, feeling more secure, Marcos quieted. His eyes, bright little gems, gazed out wonderingly at the width of the world.

The legions shouted again, saluting with a clash of swords against armor. Andrion drew and lifted Solifrax in reply.

Marcos's eyes fixed unblinkingly upon the gleam of the sword. "Not yet," Andrion murmured to him. "Not yet."

Tembujin bowed in fealty. The purple and scarlet pennons rippled in the wind, circling. Circles within circles, Andrion thought; the generations are born, know sorrow and joy, and pass away. He sheathed the sword and turned back to the gateway, to where Sumitra waited, to where his life and hers and the child's lay in an infinite pattern before them. The wind sang, And I shall be with you wherever you go.

Yes, Dana, he smiled. Like twin sigils over Iksandarun shone the sun in splendor, and the waxing moon's sardonic smile.